THE WICKED INSTEAD

BY VIVIEN WEAVER

Hard Limits Press

First edition trade paperback published 2012.

Copyright © by Vivien Weaver.

All rights reserved. Except as permitted under the U.S. Copyright Act of 1976, no part of this book may be reproduced, distributed, or transmitted in any form or by any means, or stored in a database or retrieval system, without the prior written permission of the publisher.

This is a work of fiction. Names, characters, places, and incidents are either the product of the author's imagination or are use fictitiously, and any resemblance to actual persons, living or dead, business establishments, events, or locales is entirely coincidental.

Contact information
Hard Limits Press, LLC
2201 SW Holden St Apt A101
Seattle, WA 98106

ISBN: 978-0-615-61806-7

Cover art and design by Sarah Viehmann
Editor: Tiger Gray
Copyeditor: Jessica Belk

www.hardlimitspress.com

The righteous man is rescued from trouble, and it comes on the wicked instead.

> *—Proverbs 11.8*

When I heard that all the world was questing,
    I look'd for a palmer's staff and found,
    By a reed-fringed pond, a fork'd hazel-wand
On a twisted tree, in a bann'd waste-ground;
But I knew not then what the sounding strings
    Of the sea-harps say at the end of things.

> *—"At the End of Things", Arthur Edward Waite*

For Tiger.

TABLE OF CONTENTS

Chapter 1	1
Chapter 2	12
Chapter 3	23
Chapter 4	38
Chapter 5	53
Chapter 6	62
Chapter 7	76
Chapter 8	94
Chapter 9	115
Chapter 10	134
Chapter 11	144
Chapter 12	162
Chapter 13	180
Chapter 14	195
Chapter 15	214
Chapter 16	230
Chapter 17	251
Chapter 18	265
Chapter 19	277
Chapter 20	301
Chapter 21	312
Chapter 22	323

CHAPTER ONE

"Get your hand off."

Lindsay tried to move his hand from Cary's wheelchair, but he wasn't fast enough and Cary swatted him anyway. Lindsay shifted his weight from one foot to another, glancing at the closed hatch of the Explorer. There was no one on the dark road or the empty parking lot behind them to see what was inside, but Lindsay still felt like everybody could tell. Maybe God could tell.

"We done this before," Lindsay said.

"Yeah," Cary agreed.

An engine buzzed somewhere down the road. They both turned.

An Econoline van pulled into the lot, its tires popping on the gravel. Lindsay met his brother's eyes. He didn't say, *Are you ready?* He knew Cary would answer: Guess we better be.

Three figures got out, two from the cab and one from the sliding door. Lindsay stood at Cary's back, squinting into the headlights at them. He couldn't make out faces, but he studied their outlines to make sure none of them reached for a weapon. Lindsay let the silence stretch while Cary stared, forcing the trio to speak first.

"Let's see them." It was a woman's voice. She didn't sound foreign, but he couldn't tell if she was a local or not, either. She and the two other figures—Lindsay guessed they were male—stopped several feet away. Lindsay was a little surprised to see the woman, but judging by the way they looked at each other and then back at him, they were even more surprised by Cary, fully framed by the headlights. Cary wore a wide grin, probably because he'd won the stand-off. His eyes were the color of maple leaves in late spring—Delaney green, their father called it—and glittered in the harsh light. Those eyes could charm everybody from the checkout girl at Wal-Mart to the grouchy secretary at the doctor's office. He was pretty and he knew it. "Why, sure." Lindsay opened the back hatch of the SUV. Cary moved forward and Lindsay let him run the show.

Cary pulled a hard case into his lap and opened it. "The Saiga 12. Russian, designed from the AK-47, but a little more low-profile for your average personal security and sporting customer." He sounded like a salesman. Lindsay didn't think the others realized Cary was making fun of them. "It's made to be semi-automatic, but you might could get a few more shots out of it if you treated it nice." Cary handed the gun to Lindsay. "I wouldn't recommend taking a test shot in this neighborhood, but I bet you'll like it."

"You know how to use those?" one of the men asked. Lindsay saw Cary's sharp smile flash. He held out a hand and Lindsay passed over the rifle. Cary caught it, spun it to his shoulder. He held it just as steady as he'd learned when they were kids. "Bet I could figure it out."

"Enough," the woman said in a tone that reminded Lindsay of their great-aunt when she was annoyed. "Do you mind if I inspect them first?"

"Okay." Lindsay figured that was part of the deal, but maybe she didn't do this all the time either. He stood back from the Explorer with Cary, who had surrendered the rifle to the woman. The men inspected and loaded the weapons. Lindsay tried not to shift from foot to foot while he waited. He wondered what time it was and then wondered why it mattered. Another set of headlights appeared, but the vehicle turned onto a side street before it got too close.

The men got back in the van. The one who had spoken to Cary returned with a hard-sided briefcase, spy movie style, and handed it to Lindsay. Inside were stacks of small bills, wrapped with paper bands.

"It weighs thirty-six ounces."

Lindsay ignored him, not about to take his word for it. He emptied the case, stacking the cash on the digital scale in the back of the Explorer. The reading showed they'd brought enough.

By the time Lindsay looked up from the scale, the man had disappeared, and Cary wore a smirk. He must have won the staring contest. He always won.

"You do good work," the woman said. "You have a workshop somewhere?"

Lindsay barely resisted looking at his brother, tension crawling into his shoulders. They'd never said they were the ones who modified the weapons. Was she ATF, trying to dig deeper and get them to give themselves away?

But Cary was on it. "We just sell 'em. We ain't responsible for any modifications that may or may not be made on them that may or may not be legal."

Lindsay couldn't be sure, but he thought he saw the woman smile. "I guess you won't give us the name of your guy, then."

"Don't know what you're talking about," Cary said.

"We'll just have to continue doing business with you, then."

"That a bad thing?" Cary shot back. Lindsay sighed, hoping he wasn't going to have to break apart a verbal dog fight. But now he was sure the woman was smiling.

"You're wound a little tight, aren't you?" She turned to Lindsay. "I don't envy you."

Cary laughed. Lindsay said nothing.

* * *

"Something's going on with her," Cary said on the way home. Lindsay was glad he'd mentioned it; he'd been thinking the same thing since they left.

"Don't know what, though."

"Nah." Cary's voice was casual, but he rubbed his lower lip with his thumb, a sure sign he was thinking about it. "I'm hungry."

"Wendy's?"

"It's past midnight. They're closed. McDonald's, I guess."

McDonald's was the only place open besides Wal-Mart, and there was a line at the drive-thru. Now that they didn't have an audience, Cary fidgeted while they waited. He turned on the radio, turned it off, drummed his fingers on his thigh. For somebody who could be so still sometimes, he could be annoying as hell.

"Quit," Lindsay said. "What's wrong with you, you cain't sit still?"

Cary leaned over and started pushing buttons on the console. Lindsay crossed his arms, deciding to ignore him; he usually stop if Lindsay didn't rise to the bait. Cary turned the radio up until it hurt Lindsay's ears. Lindsay winced and reached over to turn the radio off. "*Quit!*"

Cary smirked at him and sat back in his seat. "We got another client yet?"

"Not yet," Lindsay said, relieved Cary had stopped teasing. "Wade said he wanted us to do the first meeting with the next one, though." He made a face. He hated the business part of the gun selling.

"Guess he wants us to work hard for that twenty-five percent, huh? Lazy bastard," Cary snorted.

"He gets us clients," Lindsay said. "What else are we gonna do? Ain't like we know nobody in that business."

"We could figure it out."

Before Lindsay could answer, the cell phone in his pocket vibrated. A second later, Lady Gaga's "Alejandro" came blaring from it. He scrambled to pluck it from his front pocket, but his fingers kept slipping. Cary howled with laughter once he figured out what the song was.

"Jesus Christ, that's the queerest thing I ever heard."

"Shut the hell up," Lindsay growled. "Amy must'a done that."

Cary slumped over the dashboard, gasping for breath as the song continued. "B-but who downloaded it?"

"She did!" The phone came free, but it slipped from his fingers and clattered to the floorboard. "Dang it, Cary!"

"I didn't do that, butterfingers." Mercifully, the ringtone stopped. Before Cary could gloat too long, his own phone rang. It was another song Lindsay had heard at Amy's apartment. He recognized the whiny voice as Miley Cyrus.

"What the hell?" Cary yelped, fumbling in his own pocket.

Lindsay could barely see the road from the tears of laughter in his eyes. Cary cursed at him again and answered the phone.

"Hey, babe. No, I'm still up. We're just driving. Maybe getting something to eat. You just get home?" Cary's girlfriend, Jessie, worked the closing shift at Applebee's with Amy. "Yeah, okay. You want something? McDonald's. Okay. See you in a little bit." He hung up.

"Third time this week," Lindsay said. "You picking out rings yet?"

"Shut up."

"You never usually spend that much time with her."

"Her place is a pain to get around. Her roommate's a slob."

"It ain't like you ever have to leave bed while you're there," Lindsay said, earning one of Cary's dagger-eyed looks that reminded him of their father.

"It ain't like that between us."

Lindsay stayed silent. Cary's paralysis didn't mean he couldn't have sex, but he'd kept that part of his life mostly to himself these five years.

"She seems like a nice girl," Lindsay offered.

"Will you take me over there or should I have her pick me up?"

Lindsay sighed, knowing he'd get nothing but the prickly side of Cary for the rest of the night. "I'll take you."

* * *

A knot of unease sat in Lindsay's chest as he pulled away from Jessie's rented house, all the way on the north side of town. He thought it might be because Cary was still irritable; he hated leaving things on a bad note with his brother, even though Cary would probably be over it by the time he got back from Jessie's.

He'd nearly forgotten about his missed call from Amy until he spotted the blinking light on his cell phone near his left foot. He managed to retrieve it at a stoplight.

"I've got a bottle of Beam and a case of diet. At least call back, okay?"

That tone in her voice always sent a stab of guilt through him. He called back. "I'll stop by for a little, but I gotta pick Cary up in the morning from Jessie's place, so I cain't get trashed."

"He can't take the bus? There's a stop right by Jessie's house."

"He's got a doctor appointment."

"The bus runs right by St. John's, too."

Amy was starting to sound annoyed. She was pretty understanding about his position as Cary's caretaker, but thought he went overboard sometimes. "I'll call him."

Her voice sounded instantly happy. "Good."

"When did you change his ringtone?"

She laughed. "When you came by work yesterday. Jessie helped, but don't tell Cary. Did he hear yours when I called?"

"Yeah." Lindsay's face warmed. "Forgot to change it. His was worse, though."

"Yeah, I know." She giggled before she hung up.

* * *

Cary woke when the first rays of sun snuck into Jessie's bedroom window. He lay there for a while trying to remember his dream, which left him feeling funny. But, no, he'd been feeling weird since last night.

They'd only done a couple of gun deals, but this one was different. His memory of the scene was colored like special effects in a movie. The headlights had split into a rainbow, and the clients were outlined in different colors: the woman in fuzzy blue, both the men in yellow.

He felt like he had in the hospital, on so many drugs he hallucinated and saw colors around everybody. What the hell was wrong with him?

He drew in a deep breath and concentrated on where he was now. This was real; Jessie was real and solid. But even her presence beside him didn't do much to comfort him.

He liked Jessie just fine, but he had to be on guard around her, the same way he did with most people. It wasn't anything personal; she'd been really good to him. She'd moved her bedroom downstairs into a much smaller room so they could sleep in the same bed—more than he'd asked—and tried to make sure her roommate didn't leave too much crap all over the floor. She never complained about having to pick him up or having to deal with the realities of his paralysis. She never pushed him for sex.

She was *too* accommodating.

He decided he wasn't getting back to sleep and sat up to move into his chair. Jessie was still soundly asleep, and her roommate would be, too. He considered waiting around for Jessie to get up and take him home, or calling Lindsay. In the end, he decided he needed a little time by himself.

6:37. He had a little while to kill before the bus came; it would have just left the station a few minutes ago. Jessie's bathroom wasn't accessible, but he managed to squeeze in. He was as quiet as he could be, changing his leg bag and splashing his face with water. He grabbed his pill bottles before going out to the kitchen.

He and Lindsay had been raised to be neat, and the state of Jessie's kitchen always made him cringe. He took a clean glass from the dishwasher, where they usually stayed until the sink was too full of dirty ones, and poured orange juice.

He nearly dropped the carton of juice when a figure passed on the other side of the peninsula. He paused. Nothing. The figure crept into the edge of his peripheral vision again, but the refrigerator door blocked his view. He swung the door shut and twisted around, ready to get on to Jessie's roommate for trying to scare him.

Nothing.

The hair on his arms and neck prickled. He knew he had seen something. Jessie didn't have pets, and the sun wasn't in the right spot to cast a shadow. Cary's heart beat faster, and his body buzzed with adrenaline—not the kind he remembered from hunting, when he'd spotted a buck and knew exactly what to do next, but the crazy fight-or-flight energy he'd sometimes felt when he'd been cooped up too long at home, the kind that had often driven him and Lindsay into town to make mischief.

But there was no mischief to be made before seven on a Saturday morning, and nothing to be done about his restlessness. He took his pills and drank his orange juice in the dining room, where he could see the kitchen, the hall, and the living room. He set his glass in the sink with the rest of the dirty dishes and glanced around the kitchen again. This was stupid. He was being stupid.

But he still hadn't calmed down.

Jessie didn't wake as he dressed in the bedroom and left a note on her laptop telling her where he'd gone. It was almost seven when he left the house.

The air had turned from chill to spring-warm over the course of the last weekend, and plants had burst into life. As a boy, he'd spent endless hours just watching that happen, seeing the grass turn from brown to emerald green, watching the trees turn white and pink and purple with flowers, seeing the morning dew make everything look like it was made of jewels. This kind of morning seemed to have been touched by God's own hand, and it made Cary -feel better. He stopped under a blooming red bud tree against someone's back fence to wait for the bus.

As he settled in to wait, something moved at the corner of his vision. He tried to ignore it, but the adrenaline surged back into his system. The three from the night before wouldn't hesitate to come after them if they thought they'd gotten a bad deal, or if they just didn't feel like paying. He watched it out of the corner of his eye, his body shaking with tension. A shadow bobbed a few yards away, low to the ground, then disappeared. What the hell. It wasn't a person, or at least it didn't look like a human shadow. A trick of the light? He couldn't shake the wariness and was glad he'd forgotten to take his handgun out of the chair holster last night.

This early in the morning he was the only rider. Sometimes he chatted with the driver, but this driver played the local NPR station too loudly to talk. As they got closer to the depot, more people boarded, and Cary tensed every time the bus ground to a halt. What was wrong with him? The crowd was the same as always. He didn't *get* jumpy, especially not because he thought he saw shadows.

His cell phone vibrated. Lindsay. Somehow, Lindsay always knew when he felt funny.

U ok

Yeah why

Nothin i guess

On my way home

Want me 2 pick u up

Ill be fine

Got ur key

Yes mother

Lindsay didn't answer, which meant he'd irritated his brother until Lindsay had stopped talking. Good.

Fifteen or twenty other people milled around the depot platform when Cary arrived. The bus home wouldn't arrive for another half hour, so rather than wait around the platform, he decided go to the bakery catty-corner from the depot. It often had cinnamon rolls ready early in the mornings.

He turned the corner and stopped dead across the street from the depot parking lot. In his peripheral vision, he could see a fuzzy black shape, a little smaller than an average-sized man. He turned his head. Only a few cars in the parking lot.

When he faced forward again, the shadow drifted into his vision. Was this what they called tunnel vision? Was he having a stroke or something?

Metal pressed against the back of his neck. "What were you looking at?" a woman's voice asked.

Two thoughts passed through his head in quick succession: one, he should have been paying better attention, dammit, and two, the woman had a brass pair, pulling a gun in broad daylight.

"I was just trying to figure that out." His heart raced with the same fight-or-flight adrenaline he'd felt in Jessie's place, though he was keenly aware he was in no position to do either. The gun digging into the back of his neck discouraged turning his head, too, but now a blue haze mixed with the shadows.

"Keep moving. We're going to the parking garage."

He recognized her voice now: the woman from last night.

Too much to hope the rent-a-cops at the depot would notice what was going on. Cary ground his teeth. Five years ago he'd have been a match for anyone, gun or no, but he hadn't exactly brushed up on cripple grappling skills. He moved down the sidewalk toward the parking deck at the end of the street. She let him go under his own power, probably to keep his hands occupied on the wheels.

The parking deck had security cameras but he didn't know if they were monitored real-time. He doubted it; Springfield was the kind of city that figured the presence of security cameras was enough in most cases. He couldn't get his cell phone from his pocket without her noticing, either.

So he had to let himself get kidnapped. How the hell had *this* happened?

The woman made him roll straight into the elevator and face the wall. He could see his reflection in the glass, but he couldn't see any more than her feet and the blue haze. She was good. He had to admit that, but he wondered what it mattered if he saw her. He'd already seen her once, and she had to know he'd recognize her voice.

The elevator door opened on the third floor. "Back out," she told him. The gun wasn't pressed against him now, but he had no doubt it was still pointed at him. He backed out of the elevator and turned toward the exit, but she moved quicker and he saw neither hide nor hair of her. As he wheeled into the dim parking garage, he half-expected to see that damn shadow. Nothing.

Nothing, except a Midwest Security car pulling around the corner. Relief swept through him as the car pulled to a stop in front of him.

"Get in the back," the woman said from behind his right shoulder.

Oh, hell no.

Cary wrenched the chair around, hoping to catch the woman off-guard and grab her, but he turned too quick. His chair tipped, and as if in slow motion, he felt himself falling. He had good reflexes and threw an arm out in hopes of catching himself, but his balance was already too far gone. His hand skidded on the rough cement and he collapsed into a heap.

He froze when he hit the ground. All of a sudden he was back in the woods, breathing wet leaves and dirt, unable to move his lower body. He forced away the memory and took stock as quickly as his jumbled mind would let him. He could see the security vehicle to his left, past the overturned chair. Other cars, parked along the corridors. No one else.

The woman. The gun. Where was she?

He heard movement near the car, then a door opening. He could get at his gun, maybe, but he lay on his right arm, and his legs were tangled with the chair. But maybe. He threw his weight to his left, just to shift himself a little. He faced the ceiling halfway, but his shoulder was still twisted underneath him. Maybe if he shifted just a little more—

A male face, middle-aged, swam into view. Something stabbed his neck and he saw no more.

Chapter Two

Chapter Two | 13

Lindsay had drunk way too much the night before to be awake so early but his nerves had returned, driving him up off the couch where he'd slept. He still felt halfway drunk when he groped for his cell phone to text Cary. When Cary snapped at him, he realized he was clucking like a broody hen. He decided to drop it for the sake of keeping the peace.

The living room was too bright to consider going back to sleep, but he was still too drunk to drive home. He tried to remember when he'd last looked at the clock before passing out, but decided he didn't really want to know how much sleep he didn't get.

Cary would be on his way to St. John's by now, or maybe waiting for the bus at the depot. His appointments usually lasted a couple of hours, so he'd be done by ten, probably. Lindsay figured he'd go pick Cary up, as sort of an apology for ditching him that morning.

He decided to text Cary to tell him he'd meet him after the appointment, and received no response. He wasn't sure what to make of that; Cary was obsessed with his phone and always responded.

Just stop it, Lindsay told himself, disgusted.

He made coffee. His hangover hadn't kicked in yet, so he tried to hold it off with some B-12 Amy kept on the counter for times like this. The morning traffic report on the local classic rock station said there were already three wrecks in the usual places: somewhere on I-44, somewhere on Sunshine, and Kansas Expressway and Walnut Lawn. He'd never get over the number of traffic accidents here. In Arkansas, some old boy might take a curve too quick and wrap himself around a tree or try to out-run a train at a crossing, but that only happened every once in a while. Here, people seemed out to kill each other.

Lady Gaga started singing from Lindsay's phone and he scrambled to answer it, his face warming. He was too distracted by his embarrassment to notice what the caller ID said.

"You up?" Uncle Wade.

"Yeah."

"Just rolling outta bed with your girlfriend?"

Lindsay wasn't sure how to take that. Before he could say anything, though, Wade continued,

"Come on outside. You owe me some money."

Outside? Lindsay peeked through the gap in the bed sheets covering the front window. No vehicles he recognized. When he looked through the peephole in the front door, though, a familiar gangly figure lurked in the breezeway.

"Come on out, boy," Wade said.

Lindsay hung up and padded down the hall to Amy's room. Her door was mostly closed, the fan on. He didn't hear any movement. Lindsay switched off the coffee maker before it got too far into its cycle and went for the front door.

Lindsay wasn't sure whether Wade was younger or older than Dad; all he knew was that they'd been born within a couple years of each other. He and Dad didn't look much alike. Wade was skinny, had blond hair instead of brown, and while he still had green eyes, they looked more like murky lake water than maple leaves. His face always had a pinched look like a cat that was wary of being kicked.

"How'd you find me?" Lindsay closed the front door as quietly as he could and stood in front of it so Wade couldn't step past him and go inside.

"You ain't that hard to find." Wade looked him up and down. "I know where you go."

The words sat heavy in Lindsay's stomach. "I got the money in my vehicle." At least he could get Wade away from the apartment. Wade shrugged in that who-gives-a-fuck way he had and ambled toward the parking lot.

"It go okay last night?"

"Like you care," Lindsay said.

"You turn them poison teeth on somebody else, boy. I done all this as a favor to y'all. I didn't have to."

Lindsay knew he was right. He decided not to say anything else. He opened the back door of the Explorer and reached for the hard-sided briefcase under the back seat.

"You take your cut?" Wade asked. He stood directly behind Lindsay, crowding him.

"Not yet."

"Well, do it then."

Lindsay gritted his teeth. Wade always had a way of making it sound like he was doing Lindsay a favor and was impatient about it, even though Lindsay and

Cary had done all the work, had taken all the risk. While Wade blocked the view of anyone who happened to wander through the parking lot, he opened the back hatch and weighed out twenty-five percent of the money from the briefcase. Just a few more minutes and he could get Wade out of his hair.

"What's crawled up your ass this morning?" Wade watched the scale over Lindsay's shoulder like he was afraid he'd get ripped off twenty dollars. Lindsay decided to ignore the question.

"What time on Friday?"

Wade cuffed him on the back of the head. Unlike Dad, who could get people scurrying around with just his voice, Wade had often smacked Lindsay to get his attention. He'd rarely dared to hit Cary. "You better start showing some gratitude, Lindsay Jedidiah. You act like you're entitled to this work. If it wasn't for me, where would you be?"

Lindsay turned to stare at him, too baffled by the question to bother hitting back. He had no idea what to say to that.

After only a second, Wade dropped his gaze. He could never meet anyone's eyes for long, even Lindsay's. "I'm looking after you," he grunted.

"We're looking after ourselves." Lindsay shoved the briefcase at him. "What time on Friday?"

"Eleven. Lot six." Wade turned and walked toward the other end of the building without a goodbye.

That was fine with Lindsay. He retreated to the apartment. He didn't know how Wade managed to confuse him so badly. He could at least hate Dad for everything he'd done, but he couldn't get Wade.

Well, at least that was over for now. Amy would be hungry when she woke up. Lindsay started the coffee maker again and fried some eggs in spite of his flip-flopping stomach.

When the eggs were almost done, Amy shuffled out of her bedroom, squinting. "Can't decide if I'm starving or about to puke."

"You should eat. B12's right here." Lindsay put two eggs and two pieces of toast on a plate and set it on the counter, along with a cup of coffee.

"Thanks." Amy curled up in the recliner in the darkest corner of the room with her food. Lindsay sat on the couch across from her. "You and Cary have a fight or something?" She must have seen the look on his face, because she added,

"You were pissy when you came over last night and now you look like somebody kicked your puppy. Stands to reason you're stressed over Cary. You're like an old married couple."

Lindsay shrugged. He decided he needed ketchup for his eggs and got up. "I said something about Jessie last night and aggravated him."

"What did you say?"

Just when he thought he'd brushed off his nerves, they were back full-force. "I guess it was what I said about him and Jessie. I told him he wouldn't have to get out of bed if he stayed with her. I was just teasing but he got pissed."

"About what?"

"They ain't. Y'know."

"No way. They still haven't had sex?"

Lindsay found the ketchup and returned to the couch. He dumped too much on his eggs, but he didn't care. "He don't have sex with every girl he meets. So what?"

"Yeah, but they didn't *just* meet, and they're not like us. They're actually dating."

He stabbed his eggs with his fork, and they both winced at the screech of metal on ceramic. "That's their business. I'm sorry I brought it up."

He didn't have to look up to know she was scowling at him. She was pretty good at it, but her glare wasn't as withering as Cary's. "I guess you're right," she said. "She hasn't said anything about it, so maybe it doesn't bother her. You have to work tonight?"

"Got the next three days off. Was thinking about going to the lake."

"Too bad I have to work," she sighed. He nodded, though he was glad she'd be busy. The last thing he needed was to have to keep her distracted while they talked to their client. Wade's visit was a close enough call. "Is Travis coming?" she asked.

Lindsay's face grew hot before he could stop it, and he barely managed to keep himself from squirming. When she'd figured him out, she'd almost immediately figured out his feelings for Travis. She was a lot like Cary and would never let it go, damn it. "Doubt it."

She smirked. "And here I figured you hadn't called me because you'd finally gotten over yourself and asked him out."

"*Amy.*"

She lifted her hands. "Okay, okay. I'm going back to bed." Thank God she at least stopped teasing when he asked her to. She shuffled back down the hallway.

By the time Lindsay had washed his breakfast dishes, he figured he was sober enough to drive. He stopped at home to shower and change clothes before he drove to St. John's to meet Cary.

Ten o'clock came and went. He went to the physical therapy wing and greeted Lorraine, the nurse at the reception desk.

"I haven't seen Cary today, honey. The computer says he was a no-show for his appointment this morning."

His anxiety spiked, this time straight up into fear. Much as Cary hated hospitals, he never missed a doctor's appointment, if for no other reason than they'd be charged a fee for missing. He murmured a hasty "thanks" to Lorraine and went back to the car, texting as he walked.

Were r u

He waited in the truck, drumming his fingers on the steering wheel. No response for fifteen, then twenty minutes. He had just picked up the phone when it rang. Annoyance flashed, then relief, then his nerves returned stronger than ever when he saw Jessie's name on caller ID.

"He with you?" he said by way of greeting.

"He left before I got up this morning. He's not answering his phone."

"I know." Lindsay thought of the clients from last night. Cary had clearly pissed off one of the guys. But pissed off enough to do something? He didn't know. Damn it, they were never meant to get into the gun business. They'd listened to Wade too much, they both had. They'd been trained to fight with weapons, not sell them.

"You think he's okay?" Jessie asked, the concern in her voice echoing Lindsay's.

"Yeah," he lied. "Maybe his battery went dead. He's probably on his way home. I'm headed that way."

"Well, have him call me."

"Uh huh." Lindsay hung up and tried to think. His cell phone rang again, this time with the text message tone. Cary. Thank God.

All the text contained was an address on West Walnut Lawn. Lindsay read it again, irritated. What the hell did that mean? Did he expect to be picked up? Why would he be all the way on that side of town? Jackass.

Suppose....

Suppose what? There was no reason to think anything had gone wrong.

Well, there was only one way to find out. Maybe he wasn't cut out for arms dealing, if it made him this tense even when he wasn't working. Cary would probably laugh if he ever found out.

He tried to distract himself by figuring out why Walnut Lawn rang a bell. As he passed through a commercial area with shops and restaurants and a Wal-Mart, he remembered the traffic report from that morning and the accident at Walnut Lawn and Kansas Expressway.

The address turned out to be within shouting distance of that same intersection, in an apartment complex nicer than anything he'd ever lived in. He circled the lot a couple of times before he texted Cary.

Dont see u

Apt 308. West end.

The text didn't seem much like Cary. Lindsay told himself he was being paranoid, but he couldn't shake the feeling. He found a space at the west end of the parking lot and found the right building at the far corner.

Then he realized 308 was on the second floor. There was no elevator.

* * *

Cary woke up on a carpeted floor, tangled in a fleece blanket and soaked in sweat. He'd been asleep—unconscious—on a futon, and he'd managed to slide off of it in his sleep. He was still dressed except for his gun, his cell, and his shoes, and his chair was within arm's reach, and his nerves were on fire all the way down his spine.

The hell?

As he disentangled himself and sat up, he looked around for Lindsay. No sign of him in the room. It wasn't that big a space, about the size of his bedroom at home. The only furniture was the futon and a cheap corner desk with a laptop on it. He had seen the furniture and probably the electronics in Wal-Mart. No decorations on the walls.

The big window, which was uncovered and open, had a seat. Judging by the light, it was late afternoon or early evening. He didn't hear anyone else moving around, so maybe he was alone. He reached into the pouch on the back of his wheelchair. All his pill bottles were there, thank goodness.

He dry-swallowed a couple of Vicodin, but he didn't want to sit and wait for it to kick in. Pulling himself into his chair, even after he tied his feet together, was a bitch. His legs had a habit of going whichever way they wanted if he didn't tie them, and his stiff muscles didn't want to cooperate. When he finally made it into the chair, fresh sweat poured down his face. The sunlight heated the room to a million degrees. He wiped his forehead and moved so he could at least catch the faint breeze. He could see the branches of a flowering pear outside the window. Which meant he wasn't on the first floor.

Nice.

His cell phone and gun were nowhere to be found. He left the room and checked the master suite immediately to his left: empty except for a couple more twin beds and another TV. No Lindsay. There was a bathroom across the hall. He could get his wheelchair through the door without squeezing. In the bathroom, he found a new urine bag within easy reach. Great service, for kidnappers. He peeled his shirt off and draped it over the edge of the tub.

The hallway led to the living room, which had a vaulted ceiling and a fan circulating the cool evening air. The room was empty except for a scratched-up card table and several very familiar hard cases. Son of a bitch.

The sudden wail of sirens and the flicker of blue-and-red lights brought him to the glass balcony doors. From his vantage, he couldn't see what had happened, but he could see a lot of lights.

The front door opened.

"There's a tree in the way." The woman's voice again. He spun around—more carefully this time—and looked at her. She was a little taller than average, stocky and athletic, dark hair and gray eyes. He didn't recognize her, but he did recognize the halo of blue shimmering around her.

"You go out and blow somebody up?" he asked.

She laughed. "Would you be offended if I did? You're the one who sold us guns. But no. That place takes care of itself." She walked toward the hallway without explaining her last statement. "You can see better from the room you were just in."

Cary narrowed his eyes, but he couldn't not see what was going. He followed.

She knelt in the window seat with her back to him. He wondered if the screen in the open window would hold if he shoved her hard enough.

"You can sit up here. Want help?" She patted the space next to her. He ignored her and pulled the chair up beside the seat. He'd been too distracted to look beyond the tree before. Now, he noticed a road with a grass median outside, beyond a drainage field maybe three hundred yards across. Police, firemen and EMTs clustered around a dark-colored SUV, or what was left of it, pancaked against a giant tree on this side of the road. Cary wondered if the crash had woken him up.

Lindsay. He was sure that was the back end of an Explorer.

As if she'd taken the thought from his head, the woman said, "It's not Lindsay. Looks like your vehicle, though, doesn't it?"

Cary was so relieved he didn't snap back right away, although he wondered how she even knew that wasn't Lindsay's car. "That supposed to be a threat?"

She raised her eyebrows at him. "No. Any idea where he might be?"

She didn't know where Lindsay was? What kind of spying and kidnapping operation was she running? But then, Lindsay was always the more level-headed one. He'd be too smart to get caught like this. "Looking for me, I'd guess."

She pushed away from the seat and went over to the laptop. "Yeah, well, I made it easy on him, but apparently he got suspicious and wouldn't come." She reached up into a cubbyhole above the desk and pulled out his cell phone.

Fuck you, he thought.

"You might want to call him and let him know you're okay." She said it like she was reminding him.

"Am I? Maybe you should tell me what the hell's going on," Cary snapped.

"I will, once you're both in one place."

"So I'm a hostage."

Her 'no shit' look reminded him of someone, but he couldn't think who. "If you want to think of it like that. However you slice it, I need to talk to both of you. We'll get him here eventually. It'd just be easier and safer for everybody if he came here under his own power, like he should have this morning. This is a residential neighborhood, after all. We can't be tearing the place up."

"Fuck you and your residential neighborhood. We'll take you out, bitch." Even as he made the threat, Cary knew it was unlikely and kind of stupid. She couldn't have carried him up the stairs by herself, and he doubted she'd deal with Lindsay by herself, either. The two guys from last night and the guy who had drugged him were probably around somewhere. Maybe—probably—trying to hunt Lindsay down.

She put one hand on her hip. "Are you done?"

He drew in a breath through his nose, trying to control his temper. "If this is about guns—"

"It's not. It's nothing you can imagine, so can we *please* cut the bullshit and get Lindsay here?" She looked like she wanted to smack him. He gave her a look that let her know he'd smack right back.

"You got to give me *some*thing, little girl," he said, trying to mimic Lindsay's patented reasonable tone. "If all I got to go on is I'm a hostage, my brother's gonna take exception. I ain't the only one who knows how to use a gun."

He saw her think about that and wondered if she had any guns stashed nearby. She couldn't be carrying beneath her t-shirt and jeans. What kind of kidnapper was she, anyway?

"Listen," she said. "We need you to do something for us."

"Who's *we*?"

"Me and the people I work for." She glared at him as if he'd stepped out of line for asking that question. "It's something only you could do. The last thing we want or need is for one of you to get hurt just because you're stubborn."

Cary couldn't help it; he laughed. "Yeah, I bet. Look, if you wanted us to do work for you, you're sure as hell going about it all wrong. I ain't inclined to do a damn thing just on principle. All you had to do was ask, instead of putting a gun to my head."

Her irritated look turned to smugness. "It wasn't a real gun."

Cary felt a hot flush of anger and humiliation. She'd herded him like a dumb, lame cow with something that wasn't even a *gun*? "You're losing whatever chance you got to make me kindly disposed toward you. You can push me and drag me and carry me wherever you want, but just because I'm a cripple don't mean I'm a pushover. You can't make me do nothing. I don't give a damn *what* it is."

Something flashed in her eyes, something he'd seen in the mirror more than once: desperation. She moved faster than he'd have reckoned, and when she faced him again, she held a pistol, a real one, pointed at his face. Apparently she did have one stashed nearby.

"So help me God," she said, her voice ragged, "If you don't get him in here...."

"You ain't been taught right." Cary heard the words come out of his mouth before he realized they were going to. Adrenaline surged through him, but he felt no fear. 'Look at how your hand's shaking. If you yank that trigger the way it looks like you're going to, you're liable to miss my head."

To her credit, she took his advice. Before he could move away, she shoved the gun against the back of his neck again and grabbed a fist full of his hair. "You want another spinal injury?"

She wasn't going to shoot; she was probably afraid to. She might threaten, but she was too unsure of herself to do it. He hoped. He decided to wait till later to puzzle over the idea of someone who bought guns but was scared to use them. "You don't waste breath on being politically correct, do you?"

"The hell is this?"

Cary jerked his head up and was surprised to feel her release him. A second later, the gun came away from his neck. Lindsay stood in the doorway, backed by two others, staring at them.

"Emily?" Lindsay said. "That's *Emily?*"

Cary looked back and forth between them. "The hell is this?"

Chapter Three

Lindsay had spent hours planning a one-man assault on that damn apartment. It had been too long since he'd done any fighting, though, and he'd been trained to defend mostly. He knew how to wire a bomb and how to shoot somebody, but without Cary work with, he didn't know how he would launch an attack. The entire time had been agony, wondering if they'd just get rid of Cary if he didn't show up. But he remembered their father's lesson on hostages. People only took them if they wanted something, and they knew they wouldn't get it if they killed the only hostage they had. If you had more than one, sure. You could still bargain for the survivors.

That lecture was about the time Lindsay realized Lewis was crazy.

That didn't mean, though, that Lewis hadn't been right sometimes. Lindsay wracked his brain, trying to decide what the kidnappers wanted. They hadn't made any requests. The only thing he could think of was they wanted him and Cary. For something. While that meant they probably wouldn't be killed (right away), he didn't know what it *did* mean.

He had to concentrate on thinking of a way into the apartment and back out again with Cary, but he kept getting distracted worrying about how Cary was doing right now. He told himself there was no need to worry. Cary would fight like a wildcat, chair or no chair. The kidnappers didn't know what they had on their hands.

He'd been watching the apartment with a pair of high-powered hunting binoculars from the parking lot of a funeral home across Kansas Expressway. The car wreck had startled the bejesus out of him; it had sounded like someone slamming the world's biggest car door. Because he wouldn't have been able to live with himself otherwise, he'd called 911.

When the emergency vehicles arrived, they blocked his view. There was no other good place to sit and observe the apartment from the vehicle, so he had to park and lurk in the complex parking lot on foot.

Lindsay and Cary had been able to sneak around the woods unnoticed, but it was harder in an apartment complex with buildings and cars instead of trees. He spotted a black guy standing between two cars a split-second before the guy noticed him. Lindsay turned like he was headed toward one of the buildings. The guy headed in his direction and Lindsay knew his cover was blown.

"You are looking for your brother." The guy's voice seemed too low to carry so far. Lindsay couldn't make himself keep walking. He turned to look at the guy.

"What?"

The guy was short and wide, black as asphalt with a big scar across one side of his head. "Apartment 308 is to your right." He had an accent Lindsay didn't recognize. "I will take you there, if you wish. You will find he is safe."

"Who are you?" Lindsay studied the guy's silhouette, checking for weapons. No bulges in his t-shirt and jeans. If he made a move, Lindsay could pull his knife.

"My name is Sefu. Will you come, Lindsay?"

Lindsay's skin prickled and he forgot to breathe. How the hell did the guy know his name? Before he could ask, though, Sefu continued, "I am not deceiving you. Your brother is safe and sound. Please come and see."

The only thing Lindsay could think to do was go along. The guy might be tricking him, but he couldn't walk away if Cary might be inside.. All that really mattered was making sure Cary was safe. They'd figure out the rest later.

When Sefu opened the door of the apartment, Lindsay heard Cary's voice, sharp and sarcastic. Well, if he was feeling ornery, he was probably okay. Lindsay wasn't at all prepared to see him doing verbal battle at gunpoint against another familiar face.

"The hell *is* this?" he blurted.

The girl immediately released Cary and moved away. No way. He hadn't seen her properly in the shadows the night before, but now in full light, he could swear it was—

"Emily? That's *Emily*?"

Cary stared at him, then at her, then back at him. Cary had his hackles up and was doubtless wondering who to be mad at. "The hell is this?"

He was definitely okay. Lindsay kept his attention on the girl. "It's been a while." He moved forward, putting himself at Cary's left shoulder. If he couldn't draw his gun, Cary could probably get it if he needed it.

"Yeah. Look." She clicked the safety on the .38 she had been holding against Cary's neck and reached to set it on the desk. "I have a lot to explain, I know. But I needed you both in one place first."

"Y'all can stop right there." Lindsay barely felt it when Cary pulled the gun from his holster and twisted in his chair toward the two guys at the door. "Unless you want to see if I really can use this."

"No more guns, I think," Sefu said. "We are not here to talk about guns or to use them." At his gesture, he and the other guy backed up into the hallway.

"We'll get a lot more done if we just stop hissing at each other and you let me talk," Emily said. "I don't know about you, but I'm getting pretty sick of this dance."

"I'm just getting started, sweetheart." Cary swung the gun to point it at her. "This a friend of yours, Lin? You want to explain a few things after I give her a fucking spinal injury?"

"I met her while you was in the hospital. Emily," Lindsay said, "Why would you kidnap my brother?"

Emily gave a sharp sigh. "Will you put the gun down and give me ten minutes to explain?"

"Don't see why he should put the gun down," Lindsay said. "Answer the question."

"Okay. I needed you both in one place."

"You couldn't use a phone?"

"Would you have come if I asked?"

Lindsay paused. No, of course they wouldn't have.

"Ten minutes," Emily said. "It's about you and it's important."

Lindsay was about to say no, but Cary said, "Fine."

The front door opened again, and Emily moved past them out of the room. Lindsay sat down on the futon and faced Cary. "Why'd you say yes?"

"She's got something to say about us," Cary said. "Did you date that bitch or something?"

Lindsay narrowed his eyes. He knew Cary was just trying to get under his skin. "You know I didn't."

"Why didn't you tell me about her?"

"She was an LPN in the cancer ward or something. I kept running into her and we had coffee a couple times. In the hospital. Is that enough, or are you still butt-hurt?"

Cary didn't answer, but his expression turned from angry to curious on a dime. "When I woke up, they had all my stuff in the bathroom," he said, lowering his voice. "Leg bag and everything. That explains that."

"I guess. The two guys introduced themselves to me, too." He shook his head, utterly stumped. "This is...."

"Weird," Cary said.

"Yeah."

"Do you want something to eat?" Sefu poked his head in. "All we have is sandwiches, but there is plenty."

Lindsay glanced at Cary, who had apparently decided to be curious instead of mad. "We'll be out in a minute." Sefu disappeared.

Cary put his hand on Lindsay's arm. He nodded toward the window, where they could still see the flashing emergency lights. "I think it's got something to do with that. And I want to find out.

"Me too." Lindsay pushed himself up. "Where's your shirt?"

"Bathroom." Cary didn't seem in a hurry to get it. He went straight down the hall toward the kitchen.

* * *

Cary rolled into the dining area next to the kitchen, where they—whoever *they* were—had set up another card table. The black guy, who'd spoken to them in the bedroom, sat on a folding chair. The girl, Emily, was in the kitchen digging out sandwich fixings and pop.

"Diet, right?" Emily asked, looking at Cary.

"Are you trying to show off how much you know about me?"

"That's not the half of it." The voice had come from the living room—no, the balcony. A tall, middle-aged white guy came inside. He was bony and long-faced with curly black hair. The guy who'd drugged him.

"My name is Sandor. You've already met Sefu. He's from Africa." For some reason, Sefu looked amused. "And Emily, who is from the area."

Sandor looked between them as he spread Miracle Whip on a piece of wheat bread. Not a southern-raised boy; no self-respecting southerner would eat Miracle Whip on anything but white bread. "You're not going to believe a word I'm saying, so just hear me out. First, did either of you see anything, or feel weird earlier today, like you knew something was going to happen?"

Cary's stomach clenched. "What's that supposed to mean?"

Sandor's shrewd look drew Cary's eyes toward Lindsay's face. Lindsay's jaw was tight, nostrils flared, and he stared hard at Sandor.

"Thought so," Sandor said. "Well, you're not going crazy, though you might have felt that way. You just knew we were coming."

"It's a good thing you didn't know how to identify the prescience," Sefu said cheerfully. "We would have had a much harder time getting you here."

Damn right, Cary thought. He opened his mouth to ask a question, but Sandor beat him to it.

"If you're going to ask who we are, that's a little more complicated. Since I doubt you're long on patience, I'll keep it as short as I can. We all have different roles, but all deal with one thing: the World Tree. More specifically, mapping, studying and preserving the World Tree. We informally call ourselves the Arborists, for obvious reasons."

Sandor took a bite of his sandwich and washed it down with a gulp of iced tea. "Ever had a physics class?"

Cary shook his head.

"Well, the basic principle is that no energy is ever created or destroyed. It all just goes somewhere else. Now, here's where I bring Star Wars in. That energy flows through all living things. Like the Force." Cary had no idea what Sandor was talking about, but he didn't want to show just how ignorant he was. Sandor gave an unexpected grin as Emily rolled her eyes. "She hates that comparison. Anyway, like everything in nature, energy runs in patterns. Incredibly complex patterns, like a spider's web or a snowflake or a tree. Get it?"

Cary wondered if this was really happening, or if he was still lying in the parking garage with a head injury and hallucinating the whole thing. He wasn't sure which was better. But then he looked around at them sitting around the table: Lindsay beside him, Sandor at the head of the table, everyone watching while Sandor talked. How many times had he seen this growing up, eating supper while Dad told them how the world worked? Dad had always said the world was going to Hell and they all needed to be ready to fight the forces of evil to prevent it. They would fight his way to Heaven in God's name. Cary had always believed Dad, and sometimes he still did. He decided to see where this was going.

"I guess," Cary said.

Sandor nodded. "The World Tree is a pattern like that. Its energy makes up all the forces in the world. Weather, earthquakes, kinetic energy, life. The force that through the green fuse drives the flower. Know that one?" Without waiting for an answer, he continued. "Dylan Thomas. Anyway, everything is held together by this interlocking system. We call it the World Tree because human beings need to name things. If you look at mythology, one of the things almost every culture has in common is this idea that the world is supported by something. Yggdrasil, Ashvastha, *axis mundi*. Seen that movie *Avatar*? Well, James Cameron wasn't far off."

"Are you a philosophy professor or something?" Cary asked.

Sandor's eyebrows went up. "Why?"

"You remind me of one of my teachers at OTC. He gets going and talks a blue streak about whatever comes into his head."

"I'll take that as a compliment." Sandor took another bite of sandwich. Cary realized he was hungry and reached for the white bread and the Miracle Whip.

"What does this have to do with us?" Cary asked.

"Well, I'm not done yet. Bear with me. So, earlier I said the World Tree contains energy that dictates all the forces in the world. The only word that adequately describes this other force is magic."

Lindsay shifted in his chair and rubbed the back of his neck. "Magic? You're telling us we oughta believe in magic."

"You believed in God, didn't you?" Emily broke in, looking at Lindsay. "I remember you telling me about how hard you prayed over Cary when he had MRSA. How is this any different?"

Lindsay gave her a wounded look. Cary bared his teeth at Emily in his defense, but she held up her hand and glared at him. "I'm talking to Lindsay."

Cary wanted to rip into the bitch, but Lindsay turned his big, worried eyes on Cary, silently begging him not to. Lindsay never wanted him to make a fuss.

"Sentient beings have the capacity to access and manipulate magic," Sandor continued as if nothing had happened. "Call it the collective unconscious if you want. We can make it conscious, and we can use it to do different things."

"What things?" Lindsay asked.

"Hold on, I'm getting there."

Sefu had gotten up and returned from the kitchen with a six-pack of PBR. Cary almost liked him at that moment. Sandor opened one and took a long drink before he continued.

"In Hungarian mythology, they say everybody has two souls. Anima and animus, if you want to get Jungian again, though really, they aren't necessarily gendered, just different forms of the self." He didn't seem to notice or care that he'd lost Cary past the mention of two souls. "The first soul we know exists with the body. The second one exists somewhere in the aether. Where doesn't matter. The point is, it's this second soul that can tap into and manipulate magic. Humans have varying abilities to communicate with these souls and so they have varying abilities to use magic."

"How do you know all this stuff? Can you prove it?" Lindsay asked.

"Well, yes," Sandor said, "But not in a scientific way. Like I said before, magic is being studied. It's just that you can't be hindered by the limitations of science to do it. You have to accept that it is in order to look at it. Sort of like religious faith." He looked between Cary and Lindsay. "Which you understand, right?"

Cary felt Lindsay's eyes on him and turned to meet them. *Could this be real?* Cary wondered. Lindsay looked like he wanted to argue but he was too polite to do it in front of company.

"Now I can get to what this has to do with you," Sandor said. "We—and by we I mean the people in this room—have been waiting for you guys for a long time."

"We have something to do with magic," Cary said.

"Maybe everything." Emily said quietly.

"There were once two brothers who went on to father the Huns and the Magyars, who eventually became the Hungarians," Sandor said. "There are just as many legends about brothers in mythology as there are about trees. I'm not saying you're going to go on to father any nations, but we believe you're going to be pretty significant to us and the World Tree."

Cary barely managed to swallow his beer before he burst into laughter. "The hell are you talking about? Some kinda prophecy?"

"Something like it," Sandor said.

* * *

Lindsay managed to catch Cary's eye and touched a hand to his mouth, the signal they'd always had when one of them had something to say when they were alone. Cary set his beer down and touched his left temple, letting Lindsay know he understood.

"Okay," Lindsay said. "So what're we supposed to do?"

Emily stood up and went into the kitchen to fuss around. Cary used to do the same thing. It always drove Lindsay crazy, the way he could never stop moving. "There's something wrong with the tree. It's like a living thing—it is a living thing. When a tree gets sick, it starts dying, rotting from the inside out. Sometimes it loses branches, or it even falls." She pointed through the kitchen pass-through, toward the road and the accident. "The World Tree has the same thing going on, just different symptoms. There's a minor branch running down that stretch of Kansas."

"It causes car wrecks?" Cary asked.

"It's corruption of the energy. It can cause different things: natural disasters, car wrecks, freak accidents, even hauntings," Emily said. "And that's just in this realm. There's a big branch that runs along I-44 that's affected heavily. There are places like this all over all the worlds. We can't really figure out what's going on."

"Most of us, we are not strong enough to deal with the fundamental flow of energy of the Tree. We can only do small things, or deal with the aftermath," Sefu said. He nodded to Emily. "Some of us are healers like Emily. We try to direct medical cases of people hurt by energy corruption to them. Some of us study the Tree and its history in hopes of finding an answer. This is what Sandor does."

"What are we supposed to do, then?" Cary said.

"We think you're táltosk." Sandor's dark eyes brightened. "Fairly rare táltosk, really."

"Tal-tosh?" Lindsay echoed. "What are they?"

"You," Sandor said. "The question is, what are *you*. And I can't explain that."

"Well, try," Lindsay said.

"He's serious," Emily said, as if Sandor needed to be defended. "We know next to nothing about the real táltosk, and what we know, we can't explain."

"Why cain't you?" Lindsay asked.

"For one, they aren't exactly forthcoming about what they can and can't do. None of us except Sandor has ever seen a real one. Two, magic is an incredibly personal experience. Like emotions. Can you describe with words how you feel watching the sun set or when you lose someone you love? I can tell you I help people heal, but I can't tell you how I do it. You either know or you just don't get it."

"I'm not doing diddly if I don't know what I'm getting into," Lindsay said. He rested his elbows on the table, trying to imitate Cary's hard stare. "You think we're important. You want us here. So you should try to explain."

"Well, fine." Sandor rubbed his cheek until it was red. "Táltosk serve several functions. They guard the World Tree, primarily. They keep the balance of magical forces against interference from the activity of sentient beings. Get it?"

"No," Lindsay said.

Sandor sighed.

"The human body regulates itself if it's normal and healthy," Emily said. "But if it's sick or injured, or if there are environmental factors that constantly affect it, then it needs help. Everyone affects the Tree's energy whether they know it or not. The táltosk help balance what people do to the Tree so it doesn't get out of whack."

"That's what's happening to it right now?" Cary asked.

"Exactly," Sandor said. "Now you get it. Partly."

Cary fell silent, his eyes shining. Lindsay could guess what he was thinking: that Dad was right, that they were meant to be glorious warriors of God and save the world from the forces of the devil. But the stories didn't match up. Did they?

"The guns," Lindsay said, eying the hard cases stacked in the living room. "What about them?"

"Some of us are warriors, like me," Sefu said. "Human violence is another side effect. We try to stop it. Unfortunately, this sometimes means we must use violence, too. I believe you understand this, yes? You were raised this way."

A deep unease crawled into Lindsay's bones, and this had nothing to do with anticipation of anything. How long had they been shadowing him and Cary? How much did they know?

"You know that, huh?" Cary pinned that wickedly intense stare on Sefu, eyes bright with fury. Out of the corner of his eye, Lindsay could have sworn he saw

Sandor flinch ever so slightly, but Sefu just tilted his head.

"We know a few things."

"Like what?" Cary gripped the edge of the table. "You don't know nothing."

"We do, actually," Sandor said.

Lindsay's heart fluttered into his throat. He put his hand on Cary's shoulder. "Cary."

"You *what?*" Cary pushed his chair back from the table and turned it toward Sandor.

"Well, that's what I do. I record the Tree's history." Sandor's eyes were wide, though it was hard to tell whether he was surprised, scared or both.

"You better fucking explain what you mean," Cary growled.

"My family is sort of an archive of information," Sandor said. "We're called recorsas. We observe and we learn as much as we can, and then we pass the knowledge down to our heirs. I was born knowing everything that's been collected by my family since…I don't know, probably before Christ. My daughter knows everything I knew at the point she was created, plus everything I've told her and everything she's learned herself since then. We're more or less a living record of the World Tree. Like tree rings."

Lindsay forced himself to speak. "What d'you *know* about us, exactly?"

"We know where you were raised and by who," Emily said, eyeballing Sandor, who just looked confused. "We know you're important."

"You ain't telling the whole truth," Cary said. "I swear to God I'll kill you with my bare hands if you don't start talking."

Sefu stood up behind Sandor, and all of a sudden Lindsay's skin erupted into gooseflesh. He didn't see any weapons on Sefu but knew the situation was about to get way out of hand. Sefu was within grabbing distance of Cary.

"Cary Judah Delaney, stand down."

Their father had always used their full names when they were really in trouble. For a second, Cary looked at Lindsay like he was about to throw a punch. Lindsay whispered,

"Please."

Cary gave in after a long, long moment. Lindsay felt his shoulder relax a little.

"Please allow us to explain," Sefu said. He was the only one who still looked calm. He sat back down next to Sandor.

"I *could* remember anything the Tree remembers," Sandor said, "But I'd have to think about it."

Lindsay wondered if that was supposed to make them feel better.

"What d'you want from us, then?" Cary demanded.

"We want you to save the World Tree," Emily said.

"How?"

"It's being corrupted. We don't know how or what's responsible for it. All we've been doing is treating the symptoms rather than getting to the root of the cause. That's what we need you for," Sandor said.

Lindsay clenched his teeth. He wanted nothing to do with any of this. He wanted to go back home and go back to their lives, which were messed up enough without all this. "What've you got to give us? Why should we do this?"

"You don't want to be part of something that matters?" Emily said. "You're happy working construction and selling guns to pay the bills?"

Happier than I was being a servant of God, Lindsay thought.

"You oughta give us something, if you're asking for our help," Cary said. Thank goodness he wasn't raring to jump into this.

"Well, if you're looking for something mundane, I have people in a lot of places. City officials, lawyers." Emily gestured to the gun cases in the living room. "Police."

Lindsay gritted his teeth. "Are you blackmailing us?"

"No, I'm saying I can make sure your gun operation stays under the radar. In fact, I can see that you get a deal with us. Sefu says you make good weapons, so we can work something out."

Lindsay paused. What *if* they didn't have to work for Wade? They could finally be free of him.

But no. They'd just be trading in one boss for another.

"Something else," Emily said. "We have your táltos horses."

Cary leaned forward, his eyes lighting up. Damn it. "What horses?"

"Every táltos has one," Sandor said. "They're made to serve the táltosk as magical helpers. We went to a lot of trouble to find yours."

Magical horses. *Great*, Lindsay thought. *Now I'll never be able to drag him away from this craziness.* "Can we think about it?" he asked before Cary could say anything else.

"What the hell is there to think about?" Cary hissed in Lindsay's ear.

"That is fair," Sefu said. "We have rented the apartment across the hall as well. You will stay there tonight, and we will go early in the morning."

"Okay." Lindsay got up and looked back at Cary. "C'mon, Care." *Please.*

Cary's mouth tightened, but he said, "See you in the morning" and turned toward the door.

He followed Cary across the hall to apartment 304; the others stayed behind. "Jesus lord, Cary Judah," he said as soon as the door shut. "Why the hell would you say we might do this? They been spying on us for God knows how long."

"There's something really going on here," Cary said. "I mean, it sorta makes sense, don't it?"

Lindsay had forgotten, until that moment, that Cary had once been the biggest believer in their father's preaching. "No, it don't make no goddamn sense!"

"What don't make sense?"

"You still believe in God and the devil and all that?"

Cary sat back in his chair, his jaw tight and eyes sharp. "What are you talking about?"

"You think the devil made you get hurt? You think God was supposed to save you and give you your legs back?"

Cary's breath hitched. Lindsay had to turn away from the spasm of hurt that flickered across his brother's face, but he forced himself to continue.

"I was there, Care. Everybody prayed at home. I prayed in the hospital the whole time you had that infection. But no matter how hard we prayed, you didn't get no better. That's because it wasn't no devil that made you sick. It was a bullet and an infection. God didn't save you. The doctors did."

"So what? You think all of it's bullshit? You sure sounded like you was buying it back there. I wanna see what they're gonna show us. Besides, Wade's screwing us, taking seventy-five damn percent. We could make our own money and not have to worry."

"How d'you know they'd pay us more than we're getting now? How d'you know they wouldn't screw us too?"

"You'd rather work for a cheat and a bastard like Wade?"

No, he didn't. Wade had barely mentioned Lewis in the year and a half since he'd tracked them down, but Lindsay had always known Lewis was probably behind the gun selling. When Wade had offered to let them in on the business, though, they'd had no other choice. They'd needed the money to keep the house. Lindsay had agreed without asking Cary first. Cary had been pissed at the idea of doing anything for Wade, but he'd caved when Lindsay mentioned that the money would free Cary to go to school. It was his fault they were being screwed. "I ain't saying that either. Look, Care." Lindsay sucked in a breath. "Why ain't we in business for ourselves? We do all the work anyway."

That stopped Cary short. "Yeah. We do."

Lindsay kept talking, hoping to God he'd see reason. "We could call that guy we sold to in November. He said he might want more and that was a big batch. Maybe he knows people too."

"Yeah," Cary said again. "We could do that. Let's do that."

Thank God, Lindsay thought.

"What about this táltos horse thing?" Cary said. "You think it's something like the World Tree, not real horses?"

Damn it.

"I don't wanna know," Lindsay said. "Let's just go home."

"Why? You don't wanna find out what they are? They're supposed to be for us, right?"

"No, I don't wanna find out what they are." Lindsay folded his arms, trying to push down the tears of frustration that welled up. "I wanna go back home and do our own business."

"You wanna know what they are as bad as I do," Cary said. "Lin, we're special. We're supposed to do something big. I at least wanna see these horses."

Something big. Lindsay heard Lewis's voice saying that squeezed his eyes shut, trying to will it away. He wasn't right. He *wasn't*. They were just normal people, not warriors of God, not anything.

"What is it?" Cary asked. He didn't respond.

"Lin, tell me. I hate it when something's bothering you and you won't tell me."

The pleading tone in Cary's voice melted Lindsay's aggravation. He rubbed his face with both hands.

"The last time I went home, while you was in the hospital, Dad was there. He actually talked to me." Lindsay had been floored when Lewis approached him. Lewis had always made it clear he was never man enough. Whatever notion of a man had existed in Lewis's head, only Cary fit it. Lindsay and Andy had never counted. Andy had died and Lindsay might as well have been dead to Lewis. Lindsay had often thought that, even then, Lewis had known about him somehow. Maybe he'd sensed it.

"He was drunk," Lindsay said. Another surprise; Lewis was the soberest man he'd ever met. "He said when you got hurt, it broke his heart."

Cary's eyes flickered, then his face hardened and he turned away. He'd never admitted how badly it had hurt him that Lewis had never spoken to them after the accident. Cary had been the special one, Lewis's favorite. Lindsay wondered sometimes what that was like. He never had Lewis in the first place. Nothing to lose there.

"He said he'd always expected big things from us," Lindsay continued. "You and me, that's what he said. Us." Lindsay's chest squeezed, remembering that. It was the first time Lewis had ever said he expected Lindsay to *do* anything. "And you getting hurt ruined that."

Cary turned back to him. "Like what Sandor said. Us together."

Lindsay gritted his teeth, hating the idea that Lewis had been right about anything. "Yeah."

"Lin, let's just see these horses. See what this is about. We don't gotta do nothing if we don't want to."

He wasn't going to get out of this. He slumped back in his seat. "Okay, Care."

Chapter Four

Cary felt like he'd barely closed his eyes when Emily knocked on the door the next morning. The five of them left in Lindsay's Explorer. Emily directed Lindsay north on Highway 13, through the city and past little towns that reminded Cary of where they'd grown up in Arkansas. Smoke rose from hay fields where farmers were clear-burning a winter's worth of growth to start new planting.

They turned off just past a Good Samaritan Boys Ranch and bumped down a dirt road for a good half hour. It reminded Cary of home more and more. A knot formed in his chest.

The smoke grew thicker as they drove. Soon they spotted blackened fields ringed with wisps of red flame. Sandor opened the window, letting in a wave of smoke that made Cary's eyes water.

"Close the window," Emily said.

"I like the smell." Sandor leaned up between the front seats to speak to look at Cary and Lindsay. "From what we know about the horses, they like fire too."

Cary and Lindsay exchanged a look, wondering what kind of horses would linger anywhere near a fire.

"Stop here," Sefu said. "I will find Jerome."

The Explorer rolled to a halt and Sefu slid out of the back seat. He walked straight into the smoke and disappeared.

Cary squinted through the smoke and heat waves, toward the trees past the burn line. He saw nothing when he glanced back, but all three of the others were staring out the windows. He watched for movement. Still nothing.

"Keep going," Emily said. "There's an old barn up ahead on the left. You can pull up next to it."

Cary's throat was raw and he could barely keep his eyes open by the time they'd reached the broken-down barn a quarter mile up the road. They were past the burned fields, at least. Emily and Lindsay got out. Cary wished he could, too.

"Go look if you want," he told Lindsay.

Lindsay shook his head. "I reckon I can wait a little longer."

Grateful for his brother's support, Cary sat back in his seat.

"Jerome—that's the groom—says they're about half-tame," Sandor said. He'd opened the door to watch, blocking Cary's view. "They're drawn to humans, but they're shy unless they know you and trust you. And people say they don't trust anyone but their riders." He cleared his throat. "I hope you have some experience with unbroken horses. We haven't yet seen if they'll accept another rider after theirs dies."

"Some," Cary said wryly, ignoring the chill at Sandor's last words. They'd both grown up on the back of a horse and had broken plenty, but he'd only ridden as part of occupational therapy after he'd been hurt. "So they *are* horses."

"More or less," Sandor said. "They're magical constructs. To be honest, I'm not that familiar with them except on a theoretical level. Nobody really is, except the táltosk."

"You want us to ride these things you don't know nothing about," Lindsay said.

"Well, yes," Sandor said. "Every full táltos has a horse."

Lindsay turned to stare at Cary as if to say, *You don't really want to do this, do you?* Cary shrugged. "Every táltos has to have a horse."

"Cary."

"C'mon. Let's just see 'em. Cain't hurt to see 'em." Cary sensed he was on shaky ground. If Lindsay was feeling really ornery, he'd leave this place with Cary no matter what Cary said. But he knew Lindsay had to be just as curious as he was.

Lindsay just snorted.

More waiting. Cary checked his cell; there were several missed calls from Jessie, but he didn't have any signal out here.

"Shit. Jessie was supposed to pick me up for class this morning."

"I forgot to call and tell her you were okay, too," Lindsay said. "She's probably ready to raise hell by now."

"Your girlfriend?" Emily asked. When he nodded, she passed him her phone. "I've got a couple bars. We don't need her filing a missing persons report or something."

The phone was one of those stupidly complicated touch-screen things, and he mis-typed Jessie's number a few times before he got it right. Jessie answered before the first ring had finished. She must have had her phone right next to her.

"Hey, it's me," he said, trying to sound neither too weird nor too casual, knowing she'd be upset. "I'm fine. Just lost my phone yesterday. Lin said he's sorry he didn't call you back."

"Well, thank God."

He felt bad for worrying her, but couldn't help wondering if she *had* called the police. "Where are you? I was just at your house."

"We decided to go't the lake a little early with some friends from back home," Cary lied. With three or four lakes within driving distance, she'd never guess which one. He'd taken a gamble, though; he didn't often miss class just to go out and have fun.

"The lake?"

"Yeah. Just needed a break." That was true enough. "Sorry I didn't call sooner. Just now got cell reception."

"Listen. We need to talk—"

"I'm on my friend's cell. We'll talk when we get back. I'll call you. Tell Amy too. 'Bye." He hung up and handed the phone back to Emily.

"That was cold," she said.

"What do you care?" The second-to-last thing he needed was Jessie giving him something else to stress over. The last thing he needed was another woman getting on to him about it.

"You don't think she'll figure out something's up?" Emily scowled right back at him. "If I was your girlfriend, first I'd smack you and then I'd figure out what you were really up to."

"You must have your boyfriend whipped," Cary said. "Poor guy."

"Didn't you just agree not to make this harder than it needs to be?" Sandor broke in.

"It wasn't all his fault," Lindsay said. Cary gave him a grateful glance. He always took Cary's side when he argued with someone else

They waited a good half hour after that, watching the morning sun begin to burn away the dew on the grass and watching the smoke rise to make the air hazy. The breeze shifted, bringing the smoke toward them. Cary and Lindsay tied bandanas over their mouths and noses, and Emily and Sandor pulled up their shirt collars to cover the lower half of their faces.

Cary spotted two people through the haze. One of the figures was Sefu, and the other one was a lighter-skinned black guy who looked like he wanted to be a rapper, with baggy clothes, a thick gold chain necklace and a fancy ball cap. They walked with a firm grip on what looked like tow chains. The chains themselves were taut, attached to something he couldn't see yet. Cary burned with curiosity and willed them to walk faster.

Then something changed. Between one breath and the next, a thick veil of smoke flowed past.

And then he saw them.

He heard indrawn breaths all around him, which made him realize he had been holding his own. Behind Sefu and the other guy were two tall horses of no breed he recognized. Their manes and tails were fine-spun gold, and their bodies would have been perfect white if not for the gray smudges along their legs and their muzzles. A green shimmer surrounded around them, and even from this distance, their eyes shone bright with intelligence—and anger.

Of course, Sandor had to ruin it by talking.

"Our only guarantee of finding a horse is to capture the ones formerly used by táltosk. It seems like only táltosk and people like Jerome, who we call grooms, can even identify them. We don't really know how they're bred, if they're a different species or if there are different breeds of them. Obviously, it's a big secret—"

"Hush," Cary told him. He didn't need anyone to tell him there was something incredible about these two animals. He couldn't have put it into words, like Emily said. There was just something different in the way they were shaped, in the way they moved, in the way they looked at him.

They didn't fight the leads, but they looked ready to kill anyone who stepped too close. Cary had seen horses like that before: ears back, teeth bared, their entire bodies quivering with rage and the urge to fight as they faced down a rattlesnake, or a coyote who threatened a foal.

And he and Lindsay were supposed to ride these animals.

"Found 'em browsing through the burned fields looking for embers," the lighter-skinned guy said when they were close enough to speak without raising his voice. Cary thought he was the other guy from the gun deal.

"Embers?"

"They really eat them?" Sandor said.

Jerome just gestured to the mare's gray muzzle. Cary realized the smudges weren't markings. They were streaks from walking around in the ash.

"You might as well come and get 'em," Jerome said.

"I ain't getting near no horse while she's in a temper like that," Lindsay said. He wasn't one to be shy with horses, even wild ones, but these two were something so *different* that Cary couldn't blame him for his hesitation.

"It won't get no better." Jerome shrugged. "I ain't gonna be the one who runs after 'em next time they break out the paddock, either."

Cary saw Lindsay consider it. He recognized the expression: protective, calculating the danger to Cary more than himself. Sometimes Cary tolerated it, knowing Lindsay meant well and that he'd never stop anyway. But the longer Cary watched the horses, the more restless he felt.

Cary studied the stallion Sefu held. The horse snorted and pawed the grass. Though he still looked furious, he didn't attack. He could have killed Sefu with a single kick while the man stood there with his back turned; he looked like he wanted to, but some invisible force stopped him.

"Why ain't she trying to trample you?" Lindsay nodded toward the mare, who stared intently at the back of Jerome's neck. The look on her face almost made Cary want to laugh.

"These leads got magic in them calms the horse," Jerome said. "A little."

"Your presence does much as well," Sefu said. "They fought us most of the way here. Fortunately , they are weakened in power without táltosk to ride them."

"Grooms tend táltos horses when they're bound to táltosk. That's how his magic is focused," Sandor said. "He can control them if he—never mind, you aren't listening."

Cary wasn't, not really. He wondered why he suddenly felt cold. It took him a moment to realize the stallion's dark, intelligent gaze had settled on him.

* * *

"Lin."

Lindsay started when Cary's hand came down on his arm and winced when Cary's fingers dug in, clutching in a way he rarely did. Lindsay turned toward the horses.

The look in the stallion's eyes gave him chills. They held so much intent, so much *knowledge*, as if he were a person. A person he should be wary of. Cary's hand trembled on his arm. He suddenly remembered Cary laying in the hospital bed, Cary's hand gripping his so tightly he had bruises for days afterward.

He had to remember to breathe. "You okay?" he asked softly.

He realized he'd moved instinctively to put himself between the horse and Cary when Cary made a frustrated sound and leaned around him to keep looking. "I wanna see him up close."

"Cary." A jolt of alarm shot through Lindsay. "Look at him. He ain't even half-tame. He's—"

"You cain't tame something like that." Cary met his eyes, and far from the utter terror and hopelessness Lindsay had seen the last time he'd been like this, Cary's face glowed. "Bring me to him."

Lindsay tightened his jaw. "I couldn't get you away fast enough if he decided to act out."

"Jerome's been keeping them in a paddock," Emily broke in. She raised her voice to speak to Jerome. "Can we bring them to the paddock?"

"Who's we?" Jerome said dryly. "Fine. It's just behind the barn."

Jerome and Sefu circled the barn with the horses, and Sandor and Emily followed. Cary lifted his eyebrows at Lindsay.

He sighed. "God dammit to hell."

"Watch your mouth," Cary said. Lindsay wanted to smack him for being smug. He drove the Explorer around the barn and parked it near the paddock.

"If they had this all along, would've been a good idea to maybe put the horses in it," Cary said as Lindsay reassembled his chair.

"Jerome did," Emily said. "We charged the fences with magic, but eventually that runs out. With the horses, it runs out a lot quicker sometimes and they escape. We haven't figured out why yet."

What they called the paddock looked different than any Lindsay had ever seen, made from ten-foot walls of kudzu vines. It looked more like an ivy-grown wall in front of some old rich guy's mansion than anything made for horses. Lindsay expected to hear normal horse sounds like stamping and snorting, but all he heard was birds and the kudzu shifting in the breeze.

"Gate's around back," Jerome called. "Come on, now."

Lindsay pushed Cary's chair through a few yards of thick grass. Sure enough, the grass had been cleared away to the reddish Missouri dirt near the gate. Inside, metal gleamed on all sides of the paddock. A lower fence of metal mesh split the area in half. The mare stood behind it, watching the scene intently.

Lindsay opened the gate just enough for them to get through and pressed a hand to Cary's shoulder, telling him without words, *Right behind you.*

Cary pushed himself forward toward the horse.

"Let me hold the lead," Lindsay told Sefu. Sefu looked relieved to hand it over, and for now, Lindsay gave the stallion a little slack. The horse lowered his head and turned his ears toward Cary. Lindsay wondered what made the green sheen in his fur.

Cary stopped a respectful distance away and put his hands, palm up, on his thighs. He sat still and quiet. If anyone had ever doubted his ability to be patient, they had never seen him with a horse. Lindsay knew this routine and he let Cary do what he needed to do. Everyone else watched Cary, too, except for the mare, whose eyes were focused on the stallion. She looked a little doubtful about the situation.

The stallion's head turned, and one eye met Cary's. Cary stared back. Lindsay's sweating hands tightened on the chain.

"Let go of the lead, Lin," Cary said, his voice barely above a whisper.

"Uh. That ain't a good idea," Jerome said, eyeing the stallion.

"The hell I will," Lindsay said.

"Just do it. Come on, look at him. He ain't gonna do nothing." Cary flicked him a warning glance, his don't-protect-me look. Lindsay reminded himself that Cary knew what he was doing, chair or no chair. Still, the mental image of this damn horse going wild, his hooves crashing into Cary's skull, made him want to resist on principle.

"You're like a goddamn mother hen, Lindsay." Cary kept his voice low and gentle for the benefit of the horse, but his expression and the use of Lindsay's full name was hardly gentle. "I'll put *you* in a chair if you don't drop that lead."

Lindsay let go.

The horse dropped his head, and the loop of chain around his neck slid down.

With a couple of shakes, it fell off.

Cary smiled a little. "You're smart, ain't you? Sandor, this guy got a name?"

"Probably," Sandor said from behind the gate. Lindsay could see he and Emily had managed to push aside the curtain of kudzu and were watching them through the metal mesh.

"You cain't tell me or you're being a smartass?" Cary asked.

"Ask him yourself," Jerome said.

To his credit, Cary didn't even hesitate. Under the circumstances, maybe the suggestion wasn't that odd. "What's your name, fella?"

Then Lindsay could have sworn he heard the stallion speak.

* * *

Cary stared. Clear as day, he'd heard a voice. Everyone was still looking at him expectantly, except for Lindsay, who looked like a fish he'd just pulled into the boat. The horse was still watching him, too, looking him dead in the face.

"Szablocs," the voice said again. "Do you understand?"

The words were slow, as if he had to grope for each one. But surely to God it wasn't the *horse* who had spoken. Cary looked at Jerome, standing near the fence that separated the two halves of the paddock. He had to be throwing his voice, or something.

"I understood the last part," he said, watching Jerome's mouth as he waited for a response.

The horse's head darted out in a flash and grabbed the sleeve of his T-shirt, tugging it. Cary yelped in surprise and found his view blocked immediately by Lindsay's ass.

"You move," the voice said. "I am speaking to him."

It had to be the horse. The tug and the voice were part of the same message. The horse could have taken a chunk out of his arm, but he hadn't even used teeth. Cary glanced down at the smudge of ashes on his sleeve. Ember-eating, talking horses.

"It's okay," he said, giving Lindsay's flank a push. "Get your ass outta my face. He didn't mean no harm."

Lindsay narrowed his eyes. Cary knew not to aggravate him too much. His tolerance for these shenanigans was nearing an end. It wasn't beyond Lindsay to drag him out of here if he thought Cary's recklessness had gone too far. But for now, he moved out of the way.

"Look," Cary told the horse. "My brother's liable to grab my chair and pull me outta here if you do something like that again, and as you can see, ain't much I can do about that. So have some manners and we'll be dandy."

The horse's ears flicked. Cary supposed that meant the animal understood. He felt only a little ridiculous for having a conversation with a horse.

"I'm Cary," he continued. "I couldn't even begin to say your name, so we'll have to think of something to call you. This is Lindsay. He don't mean no harm either, but he's my big brother and—"

"He is not mine."

The more the horse spoke, the weirder it was. His mouth didn't move at all, but Cary heard the words.

"If you're trying to say I'm yours, you're wrong," Cary said. "I'm nobody's."

The horse snorted and tossed his head. He turned his body away from Cary, who pushed himself backward as quickly as he could to avoid flying hooves. But nothing happened. The horse just leaned up and tore off a mouthful of kudzu vine, ignoring them.

"Uh," Cary said.

"You pissed him off," Jerome drawled.

"You think?" Cary folded his arms, glaring at the horse. "What's your deal?"

The stallion said nothing. Jerome snorted.

"What'd I say?" Cary demanded.

"You refused him," Jerome said. "Rejected him. What d'you think you said?"

"*Rejected* him? I just said I don't belong to nobody. Lord God above, that damn horse is just like a woman." Cary turned and moved toward the gate.

"Asshole," Emily said.

* * *

Lindsay watched Cary storm off, struggling to keep a straight face, though he wasn't sure what expression would appear if he let it. The stallion still had his back to everyone, and for the first time, he looked like a regular horse.

"Maybe I oughta try and talk to her," Lindsay said, nodding to the mare. So far, she hadn't followed the stallion's example.

Jerome stepped aside from the inner gate. Lindsay moved closer to the mare, slowly, and spoke softly to her.

"You mighta heard, I'm Lindsay. What's your name?"

"Menyerth." She stayed a few feet from the fence, but she looked him in the eye, and Lindsay understood what had made Cary shake so hard. She seemed to see into him, *through* him, with the kind of wisdom and smarts most people didn't have.

When Lindsay and Cary were kids, they would have foot races through the woods, running at breakneck speed up hills and then half-jumping, half-sliding down the other side. Cary was sneakier and so he won most of the time, except when they ran to the ten-foot bluff that bordered a shallow creek. Cary, for all his daring, was afraid of heights. He would still jump, but he always hesitated. Lindsay knew he would win because he just *jumped*. That feeling when he first knew he was falling and there was nothing to catch himself on, like the only thing he could do was surrender to it, was a lot like this.

The part of his mind that was always aware of Cary's position made him hear the wheels crunching in the dirt. Cary gave Lindsay's belt loop a tug, something he'd done since they were kids. It grounded him a little, and he stepped inside the other half of the paddock. Cary followed, but stayed at the gate.

Unlike the stallion, she watched him with curiosity rather than suspicion. Her long ears, more like a deer's than a horse's, cupped toward him. Her body was a little tense, but he didn't think she saw him as a threat. She just didn't know *how* to see him. The feeling was mutual.

"I ain't ever done this before, and I don't wanna say or do the wrong thing," Lindsay said, having learned a lesson from Cary. "It's nice to meet you." He didn't try to pronounce the name she'd given him, afraid he'd offend her by mispronouncing it. He just decided to treat her more like a person than a horse. She seemed that way anyway.

No response, not that he'd really expected one. He didn't guess she'd had a good impression of people so far, dragged away from her browsing on a chain and locked in a paddock with strangers talking at her. He kept moving forward by inches, and she kept holding her ground.

She was the most beautiful thing he'd ever seen. Where she wasn't smudged with ash, her hair was pure white—not white hair white, like ivory, but the color of white paper or new snow. Unlike a regular horse's hair, hers didn't shine in the light, making her outline a little fuzzy. Her mane and tail had probably never been trimmed, but the hair looked finer and softer than any real horse's. Her eyes were pitch black and shining. He couldn't tell which way she was looking, they were that dark. The same intensity and knowledge shone in them as he'd seen in the stallion, and he got the feeling she knew a whole lot more than he ever would. As he moved to stand beside her, he realized the greenish cast came from her green skin. She was tall, a good 16 hands.

He glanced over and saw Cary watching, and beyond him, the stallion peeked too. They wore the same curious expression, and it made Lindsay smile.

"Can I touch you?" he asked the mare. In response, she pressed her muzzle into his hand. He felt a little shock, like finally getting to hold the hand of someone he really liked on a date. The same warm-jittery feeling came over him, and he couldn't stop grinning.

The stallion snorted and turned his head back again as if to say, "If you think I'm going to do *that*, screw you."

The mare pulled away then, and Lindsay could have sworn he saw an apology in her expression.

* * *

Cary had tried to get the stallion to speak or even to acknowledge him the rest of the morning and into the afternoon, but the horse wasn't having any of it. The mare followed his lead and wouldn't speak to Lindsay, either. Jerome had no explanation; he just said that horses, like people, had their own reasons for doing things. Cary knew that, but these horses didn't react to anything a normal horse would.

Cary couldn't understand why the stallion had gotten pissed off. He said so to Lindsay while they went grocery shopping in Wal-Mart.

"He's just like you, fool," Lindsay said as he marked laundry soap off the list. "If somebody insults you, d'you just let it go?"

"How the hell did I insult him? So I told him I don't belong to him. That's the damn truth. I sure don't belong to no horse." Cary had to stop for a mother and four little kids who were taking up most of the aisle. The kids stopped acting out and stared at him. Cary liked kids, so he spared them a wink and a wave.

Their oblivious mother didn't look up.

"Excuse me, ma'am."

She glanced over at him, and he looked pointedly at the space between her cart and the aisle, about six inches too narrow to let his chair through. She just turned back to the chips.

Screw that. He shoved the cart backward so he could get through and caught up with Lindsay at the end of the aisle. By agreement, Lindsay had finally stopped playing bodyguard for every public situation, though these situations happened more often than they ought to, in Cary's opinion. "I hate this place," he muttered.

"Maybe he wanted you to just say you accepted him," Lindsay said.

"He ain't no person. He's a damn horse."

"Well, that's what I did with Men— Mer— whatever her name is. I thought of her like a person."

Cary thought about that while they loaded up on chicken noodle soup. Lindsay was always better at the emotional stuff, and he was usually right. "Well. I'll get him to talk. I wanna know where this is all going."

"But maybe if we find out, there's no way to get out of it," Lindsay said.

"This is important," Cary said. He followed Lindsay down another aisle while Lindsay frowned at the shopping list. "Ain't nothing we need here. This is all the organic shit."

Lindsay stopped and turned to face him, folding his arms in that way that reminded Cary of their great aunt Betty. "More important than paying bills? In case you noticed, we got a lot of them. On top of that, I got work and you got school and you said we could start business for ourselves. We cain't just go off riding or whatever just 'cause we feel like it. That stuff is important."

Jesus, Lindsay could guilt trip just like Aunt Betty, too. "I never said we wasn't gonna start business for ourselves. We can still do it. But this *is* important. You said Dad thought we was supposed to do something big, and now we can."

"I'm sorry I ever told you about that."

"Why? You don't believe it now? What's been up your ass about Dad?"

Lindsay's shoulders sagged and he looked down at the floor. He looked a lot shorter than 6'2" and held himself like he hurt somewhere inside. Cary remembered him standing like that when Dad yelled at him and felt like shit for making him do it. "Never mind, Care. I don't wanna talk about it." He turned away and pushed the cart down the aisle.

Cary ignored the people glancing their way and followed Lindsay, his throat tight. "Lin."

"What."

"Let's grab some beer and go on back home. We'll come back when it ain't so busy."

After a pause Lindsay mumbled, "Okay."

* * *

Cary couldn't get Lindsay to say anything as they packed up the Explorer. The entrance to their trailer park was right next to Wal-Mart. One end of the park was separated from Glenstone, one of the busiest roads in the city, by a narrow grass median and a wooden fence. They'd been lucky enough to buy a trailer on a lot at the opposite end, where it was quieter. It wasn't much, but they'd been brought up to despise the idea of paying to live in someone else's house.

While Cary had been in inpatient rehab in St. Louis Lindsay had been down here during the week, working and modifying the trailer to make it accessible, driving the three hours each way to St. Louis on the weekends. It was more than Cary could have ever brought himself to ask for, but Lindsay had simply told him to shut up and accept it. Cary had, but he'd refused to remain a charity case. He'd gone to work at TeleTech, in shouting distance of home, until he had enough money to go back to school.

Of course, school hadn't happened until they'd started selling guns.

Finally, after they'd gotten the groceries in the house, Cary couldn't stand the silence anymore. "I'll keep going to school and we'll call that guy we sold to in November. But when we got time, let's see where this goes, okay? I wanna go talk to them horses without anybody else around."

Lindsay shoved his hands in his pockets and sighed. "I dunno, Care."

"Don't tell me you ain't curious. You wanna ride that mare."

Lindsay looked down at his feet again and blushed.

"See? I knew you did. Never thought I'd see you blush for a girl horse."

"Lord, Cary Judah," Lindsay said. He slugged Cary's shoulder and Cary knew he was forgiven.

By the time they finished unpacking, a storm was brewing, thunderclouds gathering tall on the horizon to the southwest. At five o'clock exactly, the golden hour for spring storms, they heard the tornado sirens. No rain fell yet, but the sky looked ugly.

Lindsay went outside to make sure everything was ready in the storm shelter in the yard, but they didn't listen to the weather guy's advice for everyone in a mobile home to seek shelter elsewhere. They'd lived in the country long enough to take their own counsel on the weather. They watched the storm on KY3 news instead. As tornadoes and funnel clouds were spotted along the I-44 corridor west of Springfield, Cary couldn't help but think of Emily saying there was a branch of the World Tree underneath it.

When Cary went to bed, he dreamed. He and Lindsay were running—in the logic of dreams, he paused to try to remember the last time he'd had a running dream—from something they couldn't see, stumbling and falling and dragging each other along while voices shouted at them from all around.

The horses, Cary thought. *Where are the horses*? If only they could find the horses, they could get where they needed to go.

Trees were crashing down around them, landing in their path, barely missing them. Cary clung to his brother's arm and kept running, but then, a shadow of something much larger appeared at their feet, something that kept growing bigger, threatening to overtake them. He could see the horses up ahead, but could they get there in time?

"Hey."

Cary felt himself snort as he woke up. The room was still dark, and he found himself tangled in the covers again. Lindsay stood at the door, tousled and sleep-eyed.

"You okay?"

"Yeah. Just a dream. Was stupid."

"I had one too. You think it's…Sefu called it pres-something. Maybe something's gonna happen."

"Maybe it was just a dream, too." In no mood for conversation, Cary rearranged the covers and flopped back against his pillow after turning it to the cool side. Lindsay shrugged and disappeared from the doorway.

Just before Cary fell asleep, he could swear he saw a darker shadow pass down the hallway.

CHAPTER FIVE

There were storms overnight, and sirens twice more before dawn, but no tornadoes touched down inside the Springfield city limits. Lindsay and Cary were up early again and out the door by seven, armed with apples in hopes of bribing the horses if nothing else worked.

"Do magic horses even like apples?" Lindsay wondered.

"All horses like apples," Cary said, tucking half of his apple into each thigh pocket of his cargo shorts. Lindsay did the same, hoping Cary was right.

Leaves and branches littered the streets, like evidence of a violent crime scene on one of those cop shows. The stoplight at Walnut Lawn and Kansas Expressway was out, and a utility crew blocked one of the southbound lanes to work on it. They passed the apartment complex where Emily and the others were staying; Lindsay thought he saw a gutter hanging down from the side of the building, torn off by the wind.

Lindsay couldn't think of Emily as their sister. Cary was his brother—they'd spent their entire lives together, knew each other better than anyone, squabbled and smacked each other around and made each other laugh and took care of each other always—but Emily was a stranger. A potentially dangerous stranger.

Did she know she was their sister? Lindsay wondered. Had she known all along? She knew so much about them already, how could she not? She hadn't told them anything, either. If she'd just told them instead of grabbing Cary like she did, they'd have gone right along. There'd have been no need for all that. He just didn't get it.

The Explorer struggled in the mud once they left the highway, and Lindsay winced, begging it to keep going. He half-expected to find the paddock gone and the horses hidden from them when they finally arrived, but it still sat next to the rundown old barn. The barn and the parts of the wooden fence that still stood around it had suffered in the storm. Lindsay didn't recall seeing any kind of shelter in the paddock and wondered how the horses had fared. If they were anything like the ones he'd grown up with, they'd have gone crazy with fear.

"Don't see Jerome," Cary said, leaning out the passenger's side window. "Didn't Sandor say he stayed with the horses?"

"Yeah." Lindsay parked near the barn and got out, peering around. He circled the barn. No Jerome. There was no sign of any people inside the barn, either, though was a cot, a camp stove and a plastic bin in one corner. Lindsay couldn't guess how long Jerome had been gone and wondered if he'd left to get supplies or something; there were other tire tracks around the back of the barn.

"He ain't here," Lindsay said when he came back to the car.

"Good. We can talk to 'em in peace," Cary said. "Go check make sure they didn't escape."

The horses were still in the paddock. Though the rain had washed away the ashes, their legs were covered in mud, and they looked less than pleased to be standing in it. He pressed his lips together, annoyed at Jerome for not bringing them into the barn the night before, then at himself for not figuring the mud would be too deep for Cary's chair.

He had the horses' attention, though the stallion looked like he was trying not to show it. "Listen," he said. "My brother's chair won't make it in here, and I doubt you want to stand here in the mud anyway. We need to talk to y'all. If I open this gate, can we find a better place to do it?"

He guessed—hoped—they were uncomfortable enough to agree. After a long moment, the stallion tossed his head, which Lindsay guessed meant he agreed. Lindsay waded through the mud to open the inner gate, and the mare stepped out.

"Jerome ought to've provided for y'all," he said, glancing around the paddock. "No food, no water, no shelter."

"He did not come back," the mare said.

"Some groom." Lindsay left the paddock, patting his right thigh in a gesture he would use to signal his horse back home to follow. He caught himself and wondered if they'd be offended by it, but they walked right behind him.

Cary waited in the Explorer. "They been in there all night?"

"She said Jerome didn't come yesterday to tend them."

"That'll never do. We got something to put water in?"

The horses were already wandering away. Lindsay shrugged. "Maybe they know where they're going."

"Or maybe they're about to ditch us," Cary said. He slapped the door of the Explorer. "Come on, brother."

Lindsay followed the horses in the SUV; luckily, they headed in the direction of the burnt fields instead of the meadows beyond the barn. They stopped a few yards past the burn line and just waited, staring at him with intelligent, expectant eyes.

The ground here was firm enough for Cary's chair if Lindsay pushed hard enough, though too soft for Cary to push himself. Lindsay didn't like the idea that Cary couldn't get away quickly from the temperamental stallion. Lindsay stopped him several feet from the horses, and Cary and the stallion seemed to take stock of one another.

"He wants you to accept him," Lindsay reminded him.

"I know." Cary tilted his head toward the stallion. "Look," he said after a few seconds. "We got off on the wrong foot. I didn't mean no offense. I don't know how I feel about belonging to nobody, but…I accept you."

The stallion stood stock-still. He met Cary's eyes and stared into them the same way Jerome had. The staring contest went on for a long, long time. Lindsay fidgeted, and the mare shifted her weight. Neither Cary nor the stallion moved. Finally, the stallion flinched first. He tossed his head and shook himself, spraying sheets of water in every direction. Lindsay had never seen so much water come off a horse.

Cary got soaked. He sputtered at first, wiping his face, then grinned. "You got nerve." He held out one hand, palm up. The stallion ignored Cary's hand and his nose went straight for the apple in his pocket. Cary yelped in surprise, and Lindsay thought he might fall out laughing, half in relief and half because Cary had finally run across a horse who matched him.

* * *

The stallion had relaxed a little after Cary had surrendered half the apple, but Cary was no fool and kept the other half back. "If you're good and don't trample me or nothing, I'll give you the other half. Okay?"

The stallion snorted. Cary grinned at Lindsay. "See? All horses like apples."

After that, he'd finally gotten Lindsay off his back so he could be alone with the stallion. Now Lindsay and the mare wandered around the field together, Lindsay talking a blue streak. The stallion hung around Cary, staring, but at least he didn't turn his back.

Cary stared right back, palms sweating. "Listen. You gonna trample me if I get in the floor right now?"

The stallion snorted. Cary watched him for another minute, but the horse didn't move a muscle. Cary drew in a deep breath and lowered himself to the ground. As hard as it was to get back in his chair, this was a really stupid thing to do. But he'd done dumber things. Probably.

He stretched out in the grass like he used to do as a kid, not caring that the ground was still wet underneath. The stallion stood nearby, studying him. At first, Cary wondered if the horse was criticizing him somehow, but he decided to think of it like being observed by a doctor. He knew that feeling well.

Cary burned with questions, but on principle he made the stallion speak first. Cary sensed the horse was just as curious. In spite of his nerves at first, Cary had nearly dozed off when he heard that eerie voice again.

"Your legs."

He opened his eyes to find the stallion sniffing around his knees. For the first time in a while, he felt a little self-conscious about how skinny they were. He'd lost a lot of muscle tone in the hospital and hadn't gained much back in rehab. "What about 'em?"

"They have injury."

Cary pushed himself onto his elbows. "It's my spine's got the injury, so my legs don't work."

"Why?"

Cary twisted his mouth around the bitter taste that welled up. "Good question. Maybe I'll try to answer it someday."

The stallion gave him a searching look. "You have injury."

Cary knew, somehow, that he wasn't talking about his spine anymore. "Everyone does."

"Why does your brother not heal you?"

A laugh escaped Cary's throat, though he didn't think the question was funny at all. "It ain't that easy. I'm sure he would if he could, and I'd heal him too. But we ain't no healers."

"You are táltosk."

Cary jerked. If Sefu and Sandor calling them that was a shock, it was nothing compared to this. His skin tingled and buzzed like he'd stuck his finger in a light socket, and for a stupid, panicked second, he forgot to breathe. The shock left him feeling lightheaded and shaky, forcing him to lay back down. "I don't even know what that means. I know it's got something to do with magic, but I dunno what *that* is, really. So I'm lost."

The horse was studying him again, and this time, Cary squirmed, sensing the creature saw deeper than anyone had ever seen before. Maybe things he didn't even know were there.

"Better if you don't know," the stallion said.

"What's *that* supposed to mean?"

"If you think you know, you won't know."

Cary rolled his eyes. "You sound like a damn fortune cookie. You ain't big on explaining things, are you? Well, guess what. I'm an ignorant redneck and you'll have to do some explaining so I can understand."

The stallion stamped so hard Cary felt the vibration under his head, but he made no other threatening gestures. "Humans and words. It is not words. I cannot explain it to you. I cannot use words this way."

"You been using words just fine so far. Listen." Cary pulled out the other half of the apple, more than willing to bribe. "You gotta understand something. Humans use words. That's how we understand things. So if you want me to understand, sometimes you got to explain it."

"I don't want you to know," the horse said, his eyes on the apple.

"I think you're lying," Cary said. "Only people who're good with words can really lie well and you ain't good with words. You coulda gone off somewhere or whatever you wanted to do. I reckon you coulda killed all of us if you put your mind to it. Sefu had his back turned and here I am, laying here. I cain't get up and run away, but here you stay and you ain't done nothing to me. That's how *I* see it. I'm damn tired of being told nobody can explain this to me, so I'm asking you to try."

For a minute, the stallion wore that same irate look he'd had when Sefu held the chain lead, and his long ears went flat against his head. Cary forced himself to stay calm, wondering if he'd gone a step too far.

The stallion snorted and tossed his head. "Words are not always enough. Sometimes they stop you. If you cannot think without words, you are no use. You must feel and see only. You understand?"

Without warning, Cary's mind jumped back to when he was thirteen, and Dad had reckoned him old enough to start the "real" part of his preparation to become a warrior of God. Part of that was learning survival skills for the apocalypse, which would surely come within their lifetimes, to weed out the wicked and the weak. Mankind would be left to fend for itself, and only the ones who proved themselves worthy would make it to Heaven.

So on his thirteenth birthday, he was driven twenty miles from home with a blindfold on and told to find his way back through the March woods. All he'd had was a squirrel gun, a basic hiker's survival kit, without a compass, and a couple of plastic trash bags to keep dry with.

It took him four days to get home. Near the end, he was so tired, dehydrated and starving, he literally couldn't think; all he could do was walk and feel, like some wild animal. Fortunately, he'd stumbled into woods he knew and eventually recognized the family's property.

Eleven years later, he'd found himself lying face-down in the dirt not far from where he'd been dropped off. He'd done nothing but breathe and feel pain for God knew how long while Dad ran to get Lindsay and Wade. He'd stopped himself thinking then, couldn't bring himself to wonder why he couldn't move his lower half. He'd kept up that habit in those long months in the hospital.

"Yeah. I get it." He cleared his throat. "Well, look. Sometimes I'll try to see things that way and sometimes you try to talk. Deal?" He held out the other half of the apple as bait, figuring it had worked last time.

The stallion took it. The voice was clear even while he crunched the apple, which Cary guessed meant that however he talked, it didn't involve his mouth. "Maybe you will understand. Maybe not. You think too much."

"Thanks." Cary sat up. "We cain't keep y'all here. I reckon y'all want a better place to stay than that paddock, and some real food. Do y'all even eat?"

"I need nothing. Only no ropes, and no fences." The stallion looked toward the paddock.

"I know what you mean." Cary reached for the latex PT resistance band he kept knotted to his chair and tied his ankles together, then hefted himself up into the chair. To his surprise, he felt the stallion's nose under his ass, helping him up. "Thanks." He settled in the chair, then whistled for Lindsay, on the other side of the field with the mare. "Well, we got a friend out Willard way who's got a farm. You may not like fences, but I guess you noticed I cain't get around here too well. If I'm gonna ride you, we'll have to make some adjustments."

The stallion eyed him. He didn't have to use words to say, *You think you're going to* ride *me?*

Cary laughed. "That's right, fella. It's gonna happen."

* * *

Lindsay didn't know how long he'd spent with the mare, just talking. He never talked that much with anybody except Cary, and then only sometimes. He didn't exactly say anything—he just talked, and the mare listened better than anyone he'd ever met.

By the end of their one-sided discussion, she had a name. It had happened by accident; he'd said, "Listen, Sis...."

So he called her Sister. He'd never had Cary's way of flashing a smile at women and getting them to listen. Ever since he was little, most girls had made him uncomfortable. But maybe because she wasn't a human person, he could talk to Sister. He'd talked to his horse back home, too; horses didn't judge people.

"What d'you think of that?" He nodded to Cary and the stallion, still wary of each other but at least face-to-face now instead of face-to-rump. "Is he like that with everybody, or did Cary rub him the wrong way? He does that. Either you like him right off or he pisses you right off."

"Szabolcs favored his rider," Sister said.

He nodded, understanding. "So nothing personal, then." He grinned. "That would piss Cary off. He always wants to make people feel something about him. What about your rider? Man or woman?"

"My rider is female." She glanced at him. "Until you ride me, and then my rider will be male."

"I think maybe there's more to riding than just getting on your back," Lindsay said. "Wish I knew what it was. That's the thing. I don't know if I *should*."

"Why?"

"It ain't just about the magic," Lindsay said. "Maybe if it was, it'd be different. But there're people, and they always make things complicated. You know?"

"I know," she said.

"I mean, Sandor and them are telling us one thing—not much, really. They're keeping back more than they're saying. And then there's everybody saying we're special. I don't know who to believe. Are we special?"

"Yes," Sister said.

"Really?"

"Do you trust me?"

Lindsay blinked in surprise at the question. She hadn't seemed like she had lied so far—maybe horses couldn't lie.

"Maybe. Probably."

"Then ride, and you will know what you are."

Lindsay walked beside her without speaking for a while. Maybe they didn't have to work with Emily to have the horses. They could do it in secret, just like they'd come here, and find out what this was all about.

He realized then that he was willing to give up on just going home and living their normal lives to have Sister. He'd never wanted anything more. "I hope this isn't a bad idea."

Sister said nothing.

When Cary whistled from across the meadow, Lindsay headed down the slope toward him.

"Can he ride?" Sister eyed Cary, and Lindsay was glad Cary couldn't see the doubt in her eyes.

"He rode while he was doing therapy. I reckon he'll figure out how to ride that stallion, too. That's one thing you got to learn about him. You tell him he cain't do something and he'll do it just to prove you wrong. He's been that way since he was little."

Whatever had gone on between them, Cary and the stallion seemed to have come to some sort of truce, though Lindsay didn't sense the easy familiarity he felt between him and Sister, like they'd already known each other for a long time. But then, for all he was good at faking it, Cary didn't feel that for many people.

"I reckon we'll be out as soon as we can," Cary was saying. "In the meantime, don't tell Jerome and them we came here. And don't let them move you somewhere else."

"You'll be okay out here?" Lindsay asked Sister.

"We need nothing," she said. "But come soon."

"You're ready to ride that mare, ain't you?" Cary said as Lindsay pushed him through the grass to the vehicle. "I knew it."

"Don't rub it in, okay?"

Cary wore a smug grin as he pulled himself into the passenger's seat. "We should call Trav and move the horses to his place. He's got room and I can ride there."

"You cain't ride that horse straight off. He needs to get broke first. You've only ridden at the therapy center since the accident, with a gaited horse who's been trained," Lindsay said. "You forget you got thirty-three vertebrae and you only broke one?"

"One and a half. Don't you start mothering me. And that horse ain't no animal who's gotta be trained." Cary reached over to turn on the radio. Lindsay shut it off; he couldn't think with music playing.

"That's the problem. He's got as big an attitude as you do. What if he gets it into his head to hurt you?"

"He weighs a thousand pounds. I reckon it don't matter if I could run a marathon. He'd find a way anyway." When Cary's voice took on that fake reasonable tone, he had made up his damned bullheaded mind and wouldn't be swayed. He turned the radio back on.

"Dang it, Cary, that ain't funny Shut that off. I cain't think."

Cary slapped his hand away from the radio. "Keep your eyes on the road and both hands on the wheel, dipshit. You got a cripple on board."

"This is *my* car." Lindsay smacked the back of Cary's head. Cary punched him in the thigh, and he was glad he had cruise control on. It was only fair game to hit back, though not as hard as he once would. "I don't want you riding that horse until he's been broke."

"Sure, whatever."

"You like making things aggravating on purpose."

"If you're just now figuring that out, you're dumber'n I reckoned." Cary gave up trading punches now that they were back into traffic. "I'll be okay, Lin. The horse has attitude, but not as much as I got."

"Lord, I hope you're right."

CHAPTER SIX

It turned out Lindsay didn't have to call the guy they'd sold to before. He called them the next day and asked to meet them on Friday, mentioning nothing about Wade. Lindsay started to feel a little better. They could do this. He could get to know Sister and finally be away from Wade.

They left early Friday morning for the long drive to the meeting place on Bull Shoals Lake near Diamond City, Arkansas. Cary frowned his way through English homework on the way, and Lindsay let him pick the music: always Led Zeppelin while he studied.

It was only Friday morning and most of the crowds wouldn't have arrived at the campground yet. The arrangements they'd made with the client directed them to a campsite out of view of the main campground. It wasn't made to be wheelchair accessible, but the ground was fairly level and the grass was kept cut short. Under the guise of setting up their site, they unpacked coolers, charcoal, wood and a tent from the Explorer. Cary started on the fire while Lindsay put down a tarp for the tent.

They'd barely had time to fake a campsite before an old, rusted F250 that had once been white pulled away from the road toward their site. Wade's vehicle.

"What the hell?" Cary said. "How'd he know about this job?"

Lindsay put aside his mallet and stood. Damn, he'd been too excited to have an independent job to make sure Wade didn't know about it. Now he was going to show up and ruin it.

Both cab doors opened at the same time, and Lindsay tensed. Wade had someone with him.

The man who came around the truck from the passenger's side was tall, though shorter than Lindsay and Cary. He had the same short haircut, though what hair remained was mostly grayish yellow. He had the Delaney green eyes, though they were sunken into his face now.

Dad looked old.

Lindsay locked eyes with him first, and he knew he must be staring like a fool. He felt nothing—not anger, or sadness, or even surprise. His heart felt blank.

Then Dad set eyes on Cary and all that changed.

Cary sat taut as a bowstring, his hands on his wheels. He was deathly pale, his mouth tight. He met Dad's eyes as he always had, but Lindsay could practically see the pain radiating from him. Dad took a half-step toward him, and Lindsay lunged forward.

"If you come a step closer to him, I swear to God—"

"Easy, boy." Wade put a hand on Lindsay's shoulder. "Don't go swearing anything you'll regret."

At this very moment, Lindsay doubted he would regret anything. He turned on Wade, tempted to spit in his face. "Why the fuck did you bring him here?"

Wade shrugged. "The man wanted to see his sons. I'm his brother, and as it happened, I could help him out. Man's got a right to see his children, don't he?"

Lindsay gritted his teeth. "He gave up that right. You take him away now and let us do our business."

"This is your business, son," Wade said. "Who d'you think booked this appointment? That fella you talked to is a friend of mine."

Lindsay's stomach plummeted.

"As for the other, that's what you say," Wade continued, "What about your brother?"

Cary hadn't moved. He stared straight ahead, and he shook visibly. Once upon a time, a look like that was a signal for everyone to clear out unless they wanted to be on the receiving end of a temper explosion—except around Dad, whose presence forbade that kind of outburst. Now, Lindsay wasn't so sure that control would hold.

Though he wasn't nearly calm enough himself to try and get Cary calmed down, he moved closer. He removed the gun from the holster on Cary's chair, glad Cary didn't resist, and set it on the concrete picnic table beside his own. That was as far as his peacekeeping efforts extended, but at least Wade and Dad got the hint and followed suit.

"I'd thought to see you walking around by now, Cary," Dad said.

He knew better than anyone how to cut into Cary. Lindsay watched all the fight drain from Cary's body, but the pain and fury remained in his brother's eyes.

"It ain't happening."

"I prayed about it," Dad said. "Did you pray about it?"

"You don't even *know*," Lindsay snarled.

"Same old big brother Lin," Dad said, managing to be dismissive and insulting in a single sentence. "Maybe if you didn't baby him, he'd—"

"*Stop!*" Lindsay shouted. "Just stop."

Dad started and stared at him. Out of the corner of his eye, Lindsay saw Cary and Wade staring, too. Lindsay had never raised his voice against Dad before, but he just couldn't stand hearing the poison pouring from his mouth.

"Now, Lewis," Wade said. "We didn't come here for that. Not today."

Dad gave Wade the look Cary had inherited, the shut-the-fuck-up look. Wade drew back and dropped his eyes. When Dad turned that look on him, Lindsay refused to do the same. He managed, just barely.

"Dad," Cary said.

Dad sighed as if glaring took all the energy right out of him. "All right, son. Can I sit down? My knees are awful bad today."

Even after five years, it wasn't in Cary to refuse a direct request from Dad. Lindsay noticed for the first time how stiffly Dad moved and how relieved he looked to sit. Wade leaned against the pole of the awning over the picnic table, and Cary parked himself at the opposite end. Lindsay sat beside his brother.

"Now, you're probably wondering why I came to see you boys." He still called them *boys*. "Or maybe you could care less."

"You been running Wade all this time, I know you have," Lindsay said. "How come you ain't come to see us for a year?"

Lewis ignored him. "There's some things you got to hear."

Lindsay couldn't think of a single thing he wanted to hear from this man. He glanced at Cary. Cary was still stony-faced, and his hands gripped his knees so hard his knuckles were white, but he was listening.

"Well." Dad cleared his throat. "I got cancer of the pancreas. Stage four, they call it. Terminal."

All the breath left Lindsay's lungs; he forgot how to breathe, and spots danced in front of his eyes for a second. The numbness began to creep back in right after.

"How'd you know?" Cary asked.

"I went to the doctor."

Cary's face twisted in confusion. "Doctor?"

Lindsay clenched his fists, cold anger twisting his gut. Dad had never let anyone go to the doctor when they were growing up, not for a snake bite or a broken leg or a fucking paraplegic injury. Lindsay had dragged Cary out of that house *himself*. Before he could say anything, though, Dad said,

"Finally. They said I could try chemotherapy, but I reckon it's God's will, if He wants to call me back."

"Good," Lindsay spat. Let him go to his God, the bastard.

"Lin." The hurt in Cary's voice stopped Lindsay short before he could tell Dad exactly what he thought. Lindsay gritted his teeth. Cary *always* took Dad's side, would never let Lindsay speak ill of him.

But then, Cary could never see Dad the way he could.

They sat in silence for a while. All Lindsay could hear was the distant engines of boats on the lake, the breeze in the trees, and Cary's quick, shallow breaths. He tried to hold back the words on his tongue, but they stung him like bees until he let them out. "Why would you bother to tell us now? We figured you'd wrote us off for dead anyway. What d'you *want*?"

Dad fixed him with a hard look, but this time, Lindsay didn't back down. He'd been caught off-guard before by Dad's presence, but it was years too late for the man to scare him anymore. He hoped.

"Fine," Dad said. "You want to know, I'll tell you. Now, you boys know my views on Heaven. I done my best to make myself worthy of it, but I been praying, and I realized there's one thing I ain't done. That's to finish preparing my boys for it. I wanted to make sure you kept up with my teaching. That's why I tested you with the gun making. I need you to be worthy of taking up my mantle."

"The hell does that even mean?" Lindsay demanded. "All you done is—"

"All I done is the best I could. I trained you to fight the forces of evil, and I thought I taught you well enough how to spot them. But I left off before I was done, and this time I couldn't protect you from the creatures of darkness. I'm here to warn you against them."

Lindsay's skin crawled as it always did when Dad talked about evil. He had a way of making it sound like the scariest ghost story, at once terrifying and thrilling; Lindsay had often wondered if Dad didn't enjoy preaching on evil just a little bit.

"I know all about it," Dad said. "Word gets around. Don't let your heathen sister fill your head with all that about saving the world with magic, boys. Only God can decree whether to save the world or destroy it. Be worthy of God. Don't give in to Satan."

Cary caught on first. "*Sister?*"

Dad nodded. "When your mother left, she was carrying. I found out some years ago she had a girl, Emily. I tried to find them, but I never could until it was too late to have any hope for her. She was raised bad and now she works for the forces of evil. I've always told you that evil often comes in a nice-looking package. Satan knows how to trick a man, and he's working through her and all them with her. You'll go straight to hell if you follow them."

Lindsay watched Cary's face while Dad spoke, watched his expression turn to that same old expression of desperate confusion, wanting to believe but not sure he could. Lindsay had steeled himself against this, but Cary had always been the one to hold out that fragile hope of having *something* in his father to believe in.

Lindsay couldn't stand it another minute.

"Enough!" he snapped. "You come in here claiming you want to see us after five years, but you're all about fire and brimstone and the damn forces of evil again. That's all you ever care about—not us. Go back where you came from. We don't want to hear no more."

For a minute Dad looked like he had in the old days, like he was about to slap the sass out of him, but then his shoulders slumped and he looked old again. "I did come to see you, but it don't look like you want to see me. I reckon I've said my piece and I should leave you boys to think about it. When you're ready to talk, Wade can get you in touch with me."

He let out a pained groan as he stood and straightened to look down at them, wearing an expression Lindsay had never seen on him before. "I always thought you could do something great stand at God's right hand as His warriors. I'll pray you come to your senses and forsake the evil that tempts you so I can rest easy in Heaven. Be worthy, boys. Make me proud." He turned then and walked back to the truck. Wade straightened, too, but Lindsay caught him before he could leave.

"That was a dirty trick, Wade."

Wade shook off his hand. "Wasn't no trick. If you've got a brain in your head still, you'll listen. Your dad's made mistakes, but he's trying to help you now."

"He ain't helped nobody," Lindsay said.

He watched them drive away and felt fear creep in to make his heart race, as if his body had just realized he'd been in their presence. He swallowed and sucked in a deep breath, trying to just keep thinking straight.

Lindsay had braced himself for this day, for Dad to try to walk back into their lives again and take them over. Lindsay had always known it might happen, but he figured if Cary was in school, he might not want to fall back to their old lives under Dad's thumb. As time went by he'd started to relax. Maybe Dad didn't want them anymore. That was fine with Lindsay, though he could never tell Cary that.

He should never have agreed to work for Wade. He'd known better. They could have figured out something to do. Anything to avoid seeing that *look* on Cary's face.

When he turned back, Cary hadn't moved. He was bent over, his elbows on his knees and his hands on his head. For the first time since he was in the hospital, Lindsay saw tears on Cary's face. Lindsay's chest contracted so hard his own eyes watered.

"Jesus, Care." He sat down and pulled his brother's head against his shoulder. "Oh, Jesus."

* * *

For a bitter moment, Cary hated Lindsay for the way he just accepted Dad's disappointment and wanted to ask him why he didn't seem to give a damn. But Lindsay had been dealing with this for a long time. Dad had always been disappointed in him. Lindsay was too good to say, *Now you know how I feel*, but Cary felt ashamed of his self-pity anyway and shut up his crying.

They had planned to spend the rest of the day at the lake, but neither was in the mood after that. Lindsay insisted on packing up the vehicle by himself. Cary felt too tired to do anything but sit in the car anyway.

He didn't know who to believe or what to say about their conversation with Dad. Nothing about what Emily and the rest had said felt *wrong*, either in his heart or in his mind. Didn't it match what Dad always told him, that they *were* important? But maybe they were important, and the devil wanted them for himself.

Could the horses be from the devil, too? That stallion sure had attitude enough, but Cary felt like he and the horse had a lot in common. They could be hard, they could be assholes, but they weren't *bad*. Cary understood the horse. He had never understood Dad.

But some part of him wondered why Dad would come to see them after five years of ignoring them if he wasn't really worried. And he wasn't always wrong.

Make me proud, he'd said.

That had hurt.

You're not proud? He'd wanted to say it. *I pulled myself together again and got a job and I'm going to school to make something out of my crippled self that's better than I would have ever been, and you're not already proud? How much does it take? Why did you stay away all these years?*

But he'd had no voice to speak, and Dad had turned away again, thinking only that they *hadn't* done something.

"Care?"

Cary turned to look at Lindsay. "What?"

"I shoulda checked to make sure Wade didn't have nothing to do with that meeting."

Cary shrugged. He didn't have the energy to be mad at Lindsay. "Dad was the one who's really behind it. And you know how sneaky he is."

Lindsay took his shirt off and stuffed it in the washing machine. He flopped on the couch. "We might as well take the job with Emily."

"Dad just said she's no good. Why the hell would we do that?"

Lindsay sat back on his heels like Cary had hit him. "So you believe him."

Cary shook his head. "I ain't saying I do or I don't."

"You do. You always do."

"I do not. I don't *know*, Lindsay, so shut the fuck up about it."

Lindsay looked away. Cary instantly felt like shit, watching Lindsay's face twist like that. He knew Dad always made Lindsay feel bad. He knew he'd had it better when it came to Dad's favor. It was no wonder Lindsay had his hackles up still.

"I'm just saying. We shouldn't swallow everything they say."

"What about the horses?" Lindsay turned that anxious, hurt look on him. He could barely stand looking at it. "Should we believe them? What do they got to lie about?"

"Shit, Lin." Cary dug the heels of his hands into his eyes.

"You don't wanna go see 'em again? Talk to 'em?"

Creatures of darkness, Dad had said. Cary just couldn't see it. But Dad had always known more about good and evil than they did. He had no idea what to say.

"I wanna go," Lindsay said.

More silence. Rain battered the roof and Lindsay got up to make sure the usual spots in the ceiling weren't leaking too badly. Cary switched the channel but couldn't find anything worth watching. By the time he ended up back at KY3, Lindsay came back in and flopped on his couch.

"I really don't know if I believe him, Lin. I'm telling the truth."

"I believe you," Lindsay said in a small, tight voice.

Cary was at a loss for how to comfort him, didn't even know what was going on in his head. He sighed. "Well, I reckon it won't hurt to see what they're about."

Lindsay nodded. After a while, he said, "Care? Remember when we did these?" He poked the C-shaped brand below his collar bone. They'd been stupid drunk and playing with cigarette lighters. Lindsay had convinced him it would be a good idea to brand each other with their first initials. At the time it had just been something to do.

"Sure," Cary said, touching the L on his own chest.

"That's what matters, huh?"

He smiled at Lindsay's shy tone. Lindsay had a way of figuring out what he was thinking even when he tried to hide it. He knew what Lindsay meant: that the two of them still had each other, and they were still proud of each other. "Yeah, Lin. You're right."

His mind wandered back to Emily—their *sister*—after a while. He considered mentioning her, but Lindsay looked like he was thinking and Cary didn't interrupt. As they sat watching the weather guy comment on funnel clouds being spotted for the third time that week, Lindsay finally got around to talking.

"You think Mama's still around?"

By 'around' Cary knew he meant 'alive.' He tried to picture their mother's face, but the image was hazy; he'd only been five when she'd left. "I dunno. But...." He trailed off. Lindsay had always been closer to their mother and more sensitive about her.

"But what?"

Cary made his voice as gentle as he could. "But if Emily found us and she didn't come along to meet us...." It might mean she was dead.

Lindsay didn't meet his eyes. He was quiet for a while before he said, "Emily looks like her. When you were doing your homework earlier, I went through that box of stuff Michelle sent with me last time I went home. I found Mama's high school yearbook."

"Let me see," Cary said.

Lindsay got up and returned from the back bedroom, where they stored equipment and worked on weapons, and returned with a leather-bound yearbook from 1978, the year before their older brother Andy was born. Their parents had gotten married two weeks after Mama's high school graduation.

The page was marked with a piece of yellowed ribbon. It took Cary a moment to find the photo. Fifth row down, second to the right. Mary Sullivan. She definitely had Emily's face, except for the mouth.

Lightning flashed outside just before rain started pelting the roof. According to KY3, the storm was following the I-44 corridor exactly, as it usually did, attacking it with a vengeance. Cary shuddered and set the yearbook aside.

"Why shouldn't we just keep in business for ourselves, Lin? We still got people we can sell to."

Lindsay picked up the yearbook and cradled it in his hands for a second before he set it back in the box. "We don't got no people who ain't Wade's people. Wade will find out about it."

"What's he gonna do?" Cary said. Wade wasn't like Dad; he was a bastard, but he was weak.

"He'll tell Dad, that's what he'd do." Lindsay got up with the box and disappeared into the back bedroom again. When he came back, he curled up on the couch. "Dad would put a stop to it." You don't think he's been behind all this the whole time?"

Cary tried not to wince. He couldn't believe he hadn't thought of that. The accident had ruined Dad's dreams for him. That was why Dad hadn't come to see them all these years, because he couldn't be a warrior of God anymore. Not as a cripple. But now Dad was dying, and they had magic, and he wanted them to be warriors again.

Be worthy. Make me proud.

The damn Miley Cyrus song started playing from the coffee table. He picked up the phone. Jessie.

"Hey. Just calling to see if you guys were okay. It's stormy here again and I didn't know what lake you were at."

"We saw it was gonna get bad, so we headed on home," Cary said, holding back a sigh. She had the worst timing. "I was gonna call you as soon as it cleared up. "You doing okay?"

"Yeah. Thanks for asking." Something in her voice made him wince. "We were in the basement till the sirens stopped."

He had the uneasy sense he was sitting on quicksand that was about to give way beneath him, and he scrambled to correct the situation. "You said you wanted to talk. Want me to come over?"

"That's okay. Maybe tomorrow. Glad you're okay. I'll call you."

"Okay." As they hung up, Cary noticed she didn't say, *You call me.*

"Care," Lindsay said. Cary looked up. "You told her you lost your cell."

Cary looked down at the phone in his hand. "Shit."

* * *

Lindsay couldn't think about anything else but Lewis and Cary the next day. He took Cary to a tutoring session at the college and then just drove around town without knowing where he was really going. He thought about going to see Amy, but he didn't like bothering her with family stuff. She had both her parents and her siblings. They were normal.

While he sat in the McDonald's drive thru, he stared at his phone. He could call Travis. Travis had known him since those first days in the hospital, since he was totally alone and clueless and crazy because nobody would let him into Cary's quarantine room. Travis had done everything for him, given him a place to stay and gotten him a bank account and a vehicle and a job. And Travis never judged.

So as soon as he had his food, he parked in the McDonald's parking lot and dialed.

"Hey, stranger," Travis said. His voice gave Lindsay a warm feeling in his stomach.

"Hey. Sorry I ain't called in so long. How's it going?"

"Well, I know y'all got a lot going on." From anyone else that would sound put out, but Travis was nothing but genuine. "Edy was in the hospital for a while. She's doing better but she's in assisted living now."

"Lord, Trav." Guilt twisted down Lindsay's spine for even thinking of calling Travis to complain about *his* problems. Both Travis's parents and now his sister were so sick they had to be in a nursing home. At least Lindsay still had Cary at home. "She with your parents?"

"Yeah, at least they're all together. I go to see them whenever I can."

"Well, tell 'em I said hi. I'll go by and visit sometime." Lindsay stared at the unwrapped burger in his lap. He couldn't bring himself to eat it, so he took a drink of Dr. Pepper.

"They'd like that." Travis paused. "So what's up? You sound all wound up." When Lindsay hesitated he said, "I don't mind hearing your problems, Lindsay. I know that's why you called."

Lindsay felt so bad he almost couldn't speak, but he didn't just want to hang up either. "Just a lot of weird stuff going on."

"Like what?"

"My father come back."

Travis was quiet for a minute. He didn't know everything about Lewis, but he knew some and Lindsay figured he'd probably guessed more. "He still there?"

"No. Dunno where he is. He just ambushed us and preached on evil and left again." Lindsay fiddled with a french fry and tried to eat it, but the salt dried his mouth out even more.

"Then why'd he come in the first place?"

"Long story." Lindsay wasn't about to drag Travis into all this magic stuff. Travis was normal. He wouldn't believe it and didn't need to be bothered with it.

"A'ight. So how're you and Cary holding up?"

"Cary still falls for his crap, Trav." Lindsay had to catch his breath against the anger that rushed into him. "He was doing so good since he got outta the hospital and now it's like Dad's poison is in him again. He thinks Dad cares about him and he's listening to all that shit again. It's gonna hurt him."

"Have you told him all that?"

"He won't *listen* to me. He knows I hate Dad and he thinks that's fine for me but he's got some duty to him because Dad's dying."

"Dying? You didn't mention that."

"Of cancer."

Travis paused. "Jesus, I'm sorry, Lindsay."

"For what?" Lindsay asked, ready to snap at him for being sorry Dad was dying. Lindsay sure wasn't sorry.

"For everything."

Lindsay's eyes blurred with tears and his throat stung. He didn't want to cry in public, for Christ's sake, but Travis's gentle tone almost unraveled him.

"Why don't y'all come up for a couple days?"

"Yeah, okay," Lindsay said, remembering Cary's suggestion that they hide the horses on Travis's farm. "Hey, mind us bringing a couple horses?"

"Horses? When did y'all get horses?"

"It's, uh. It's a long story. We kinda found 'em."

"Well, sure. I got some space in the barn." Travis sounded a little confused. "You'll have to tell me that story when y'all get here."

"Yeah, okay."

When he hung up, he wondered what the hell he was going to tell Travis.

Chapter Seven

On the way home from Cary's class, Lindsay mentioned Travis's offer to put them up. Cary was glad they'd have a place to keep the horses, but he couldn't stop thinking about Dad and Mama and Emily, all scattered around and not talking to each other. That wasn't what family was. He wondered how they'd gotten this way.

Before they'd even reached the truck in the carport, a silver Civic, several years old, pulled in behind it.

Oh, hell. He gestured for Lindsay to pull his chair out. Without a word, Lindsay retreated into the house. Jessie waited for him in the driveway.

"I wanted to talk to you in person," she said.

"Sure, honey," Cary said. "What about?"

"Why did you lie to me about not having your cell phone?"

"What?" Cary blinked.

Jessie folded her arms. She looked upset rather than pissed, which he hated. He'd rather she was pissed at him, but she had never once gotten mad. "What were you doing when you said you lost your phone?"

"What the hell would I be doing?" Cary clutched his wheels, trying to wrestle his temper down. She didn't deserve that. "I'm sorry. What's going on? What's got you upset?"

"I wish I knew!" It was almost a shout. Cary blinked again; she really was upset. "You've been sneaking around and lying to me for months now, and a couple days ago you go missing and nobody bothered to let me know if you were even okay. What am I supposed to think?"

"I have no idea." The words were out of Cary's mouth before he could stop them. She looked a little surprised and tilted her head at him. He thought rapidly as he spoke. "I been treating you bad, and I know it. There's been some family stuff going on, and, well, I didn't want to worry you about it. It's complicated." He took a deep breath. The story was true enough. He figured it sounded fairly convincing.

"Family stuff." She looked doubtful. "You've been sneaking around because of family stuff? What's so bad?"

"I told you about my family—"

"Barely." Her doubt turned to hurt. "Look, whatever's going on, I really don't like all this secrecy. I don't know whether to believe you or not. I just get this bad feeling there's something shady going on."

Guilt crawled in the pit of Cary's belly, but impatience, too. He didn't have *time* to deal with this, but he'd never intended to be hurtful to her. "How can I make this better?"

"You can stop lying to me, for one thing. What really happened with your cell phone?"

"I forgot to call," Cary said, figuring he could be truthful about that. "It's been a crazy couple days. I'm sorry. I feel awful about it."

She tilted her head and the tense line of her shoulders relaxed a little. She looked like she was considering believing him. "Are you going to tell me what's going on?"

"I really don't want to get you involved. I done said that."

"Is it dangerous?"

"I don't know." The truth.

She sighed and looked away. Tears glittered in her eyes, and he felt like the world's biggest asshole. Jesus. He'd never meant to make her cry. "I don't know if I can do this."

He pushed himself forward, but wasn't sure if he should touch her or not. "Jess."

"You're such an idiot sometimes." She wiped the tears away with the heel of her hand. "I care about you. But I don't know anything about you, Cary. You never tell me anything."

Of all the things he'd heard in the past three days, this confounded him the most. "If I could tell you what's going on, babe, I would."

"Why can't you?" She didn't wait for an answer. "Look, if you're trying to think of an excuse, don't bother. I'm getting tired of hearing them. You obviously don't trust me enough to tell me, and I guess I have to accept that." She took a deep breath. "I'll let you get back to whatever you were doing."

He watched her walk back toward her car, struggling to think of something to say. "So what now?"

"I don't know." She ducked into the car and shut the door.

* * *

Cary looked a little bewildered when he came inside. Lindsay lifted his eyebrows, silently questioning, but Cary just went into his bedroom and shut the door. Lindsay gave him a few minutes before he followed.

Cary was playing Zeppelin. That was usually a cue that he was studying and wanted to be left alone. Something told Lindsay he wasn't studying this time, though. He walked in on "Black Dog" and found Cary stretched out on the bed, staring at the ceiling. He'd turned on his laptop and opened a textbook, but they lay abandoned on the bedside table.

"I heard people see black dogs when they think they're gonna die," he said in an offhand kind of way. "I never did. But I guess that ain't much harder to believe than all this, is it?"

Lindsay closed the door and sat on the bed beside him. "What's really got you? And don't bullshit me."

Cary looked like he might get aggravated for a minute, but his frown smoothed a little. "I think Jessie broke up with me."

Lindsay wouldn't have thought that girl would have the spine. "You think?"

"Yeah. I dunno." Cary pinched the bridge of his nose. "She thought something shady was going on, so I put her off. She got all upset and told me I'm too secretive."

Lindsay sat back and tried to keep a straight face. "You hear what you're saying, right?"

"Was I supposed to tell her the truth?"

Lindsay shrugged. "Probably not. But you cain't blame her for getting upset. Girls don't like when they think you're keeping secrets and they don't know why. It don't matter the real reason."

"You know that, huh?"

Lindsay smacked the side of Cary's head. "Don't be an asshole. Yeah, I knew that."

"So what'm I supposed to do?" For someone who'd dated more people than Lindsay had ever thought about dating, Cary was often completely clueless about women.

"She wants to feel like she can trust you, and you can trust her."

"Come on. I cain't, with all this."

Lindsay just gave him a look.

"So I should lie."

Lindsay stretched out beside him. "I'm saying, tell her what she needs to hear. You like her, I know you do."

"Yeah."

"So try acting like it."

Cary turned his head to give Lindsay that open, thoughtful look Lindsay knew he never gave anyone else. "It's you who got the brains."

Lindsay felt his mouth twist. "Nah. I'm just the wussy queer who understands girls."

"Lindsay Jedidiah." Cary moved faster than he'd reckoned, and he got a face full of down pillow. "Stop that talk and take a damned compliment."

"I'll take you out," Lindsay said. He picked up the other pillow and they walloped each other until they were both laughing again.

* * *

Cary was glad to leave Springfield for Travis's house. He liked the Travis. Lindsay had met him while Cary was in the hospital—Travis's sister had cerebral palsy and had been in the ICU in the same wing as Cary. He'd been the one to get Lindsay and later Cary set up with jobs and bank accounts. He'd also helped them get the car and even the house. And he'd done it out of the goodness of his heart, completely ignoring their protests against charity. They owed him a lot. He'd been the one to get Cary to try therapeutic riding, too, saying it had done his sister good. He was a big, rough redneck with pretty eyes, and Cary strongly suspected Lindsay had a crush on him. Since you just didn't ask about things like that, he had no idea if Travis was even that way.

Travis's house sat on a slope overlooking several hundred acres of cow pasture. Once upon a time, the pastures were at capacity, but there were no cows visible in the fields nearest the house. The place was almost as remote as the paddock had been, though the roads were a little better. The house itself was way too big for one person, inherited from Travis's parents, who were both in a nursing home, and was fully accessible to accommodate Travis's sister. It was just the kind of place Lindsay and Cary wanted for themselves.

The drive to work and school was a lot longer from Willard, but they were nearer the horses. Once they'd gotten settled and could leave without being rude, they drove a little ways north on Highway 13 to the paddock. Cary was glad the ground had finally begun to dry out. He wanted to sit with the stallion again and talk. See whether he was a creature of darkness like Dad said.

When the Explorer circled a stand of trees, Cary couldn't see the paddock where it was before. There was still a muddy circle where the horses had trodden, but there was no fence, no kudzu. No horses.

Lindsay stopped the vehicle and circled the barn while Cary twisted in his seat and looked around, trying to figure out how the hell somebody would have gotten a huge paddock out of the area without at least a heavy-duty vehicle. He only saw one other set of tire tracks and they looked too small. Maybe they did it with magic, but he had no idea how the hell somebody would do that.

Lindsay came out of the barn. "Jerome's stuff is still there. It don't look no different from when I was there last."

"Fuck." Cary looked around again. "You see any hoof prints?"

Lindsay shook his head. "Grass is too long except for the mud over there." He drew in a breath like he was going to say something else, but he didn't.

"What?" Cary prompted.

"What if Dad took 'em?"

Cary's chest tightened. "What the fuck? Why would he do that?"

"He don't want us to do none of this, Care. He wants us to get away from 'em."

"But Dad don't got magic. He couldn't a' tore down a fence without a vehicle and there ain't tire tracks big enough. He didn't do this."

"Then who did?"

"Emily and them."

"Why would they? They brought us to the horses in the first place."

"To make us do whatever they want. Get in the car. We're gonna go have a talk with this bitch."

Lindsay looked doubtful, but Cary didn't care as long as he drove. He told Lindsay to head toward the hospital. Emily ought to be working.

The problem was, St. John's was a big hospital with several buildings and they didn't know which one she worked in. Lindsay said they shouldn't just go around asking, that it would be creepy, but Cary was bound to find her. Lindsay just sighed and said she'd worked in the cancer building when he met her; maybe she was still there.

The woman at the main desk had never heard of Emily. "Sorry, honey. I've been working here ten years and I've never seen any girl who looks like that. Are you sure she worked in oncology?"

"Maybe I got it wrong," Cary said. "Could you maybe find out for me? I got her cell phone and I don't wanna leave it in lost and found. Y'know?" He held up his own cell. She studied him and he made himself look angelic. After a minute, she turned toward the phone on the desk.

"I'll call the switchboard."

"Thanks." Cary gave her his best smile.

Lindsay stared at him as the nurse picked up the phone. "What?" Cary mouthed. Lindsay just shook his head.

"Okay," the nurse said when she hung up. "She works in the main building in ICU. You know where that is?"

Cary's teeth clenched. "Yeah."

"It's a secure ward, though, so you'll have to talk to security at the door."

"Thanks, ma'am. You been a big help and real sweet." Cary smiled again and went back toward the vehicle.

"Care?" Lindsay eyed him as he pulled himself into the passenger's seat.

"This is different," Cary said firmly. "I'm okay this time."

"Yeah." Still Lindsay looked pale when he got in.

"What was you giving me that look for?" Cary asked in an attempt to change the subject.

"Huh?"

"While we was waiting."

"How d'you do that to people? Tell 'em stories like that and get 'em to do what you want?"

Cary shrugged. "Just gotta make 'em think it's a good idea, I reckon. Even if it's just for a minute."

Lindsay just frowned.

They had to enter through the emergency room on the north side of the main building. Lindsay shook visibly and Cary didn't feel too great himself. He didn't remember being brought here from the Harrison hospital after the accident, but he remembered the smell and the way things sounded in the tiled halls.

They made it as far as a waiting room on the second floor before a security guard stopped them. "Are y'all here to see somebody? There aren't any regular visiting hours in this ward."

"We're actually here to see Emily. She's a nurse," Cary said, putting on the face he used to make men think he was friendly. The guard's eyes narrowed ever so slightly.

"She's busy right now. I can have her come out if she has a minute, but y'all will have to wait downstairs in the ER waiting room. What's your names? I'll let her know who's visiting."

Before Cary could decide how to answer, Lindsay said, "Cary and Lindsay. Could you tell her it's important?"

The security guard looked back and forth between them. His eyes settled on Cary. "Were you in here a while back?"

"Yeah." No sense denying that.

"Gimme a minute." The guard left through a set of doors, sliding his ID card to open them. Lindsay darted forward and caught the door before it shut. He held it almost closed for a few seconds, his ear pressed close to the crack, then beckoned Cary forward.

The ward was empty of staff; the guard had already disappeared. A green glow, the same color Cary had noticed surrounding the horses, hovered near the floor.

"What the hell are you doing here?" Emily appeared from a side hall. Her hair was messy and she looked like she hadn't slept in days, but the blue haze around her was brighter than ever.

"We come to talk to you," Cary said, squinting against the mix of colors. "The horses are missing."

Emily gave them a narrow-eyed stare for a minute, then turned back down the hall. "Come with me."

She stopped at the desk and spoke to another nurse, who looked almost as tired as she did. "Where's Mustafa?"

"In with Brian, I think." The nurse looked up at them with none of the gentle niceness Cary's nurses always showed him. "Who are they?"

Emily just said, "They're fine." She gestured them to come with her. "I'll take you to one of the empty rooms first." She walked down the hall and opened a sliding glass door to another room.

Cary wheeled into the room. It was just like any intensive care room he'd seen—exactly like the one he'd spent months in—but it felt foreign. Maybe it was because he was entering it under his own power. Last time, it had been on a stretcher. Rather than glimmers of color, he kept catching glimpses of shadows here and there.

"It feels weird in here," Lindsay said.

"There was an incident last night," Emily said. "Jerome is dead."

A shiver ran down Cary's back and he turned to face her. "How?"

"He was shot. Someone brought him in. He was found on the side of the road." She folded her arms, eyes hard and jaw tight. Suspicious.

"Listen, we didn't have nothing to do with it," Cary said.

"I know that. He wasn't dead when he was brought in. He was killed in the hospital, along with four other patients."

Lindsay made a quiet noise of surprise. "How'd that happen?"

"We're trying to find out." Emily pushed both hands through her hair. She yanked her ponytail holder out and tugged her hair back again. "And now the horses are gone?"

"Yeah." Cary's stomach sank. Unless Emily was a really good actress, she didn't have anything to do with the horses' disappearance. If she didn't take them, who did?

"Well, shit." Emily sank to sit on the edge of the bed. "You shouldn't have come, you know. You're a security risk. It's not safe here."

Cary snorted. "Thanks for the warning."

"Security risk?" Lindsay asked. "Why?"

"Because someone infiltrated our security already to do this. They could come after you. Also." Emily jerked her chin at Cary. "How the hell was I supposed to know you'd come here?" She shook her head. "Fuck. Stay here. I need to figure out what to do with you." She left the room.

"Let's get outta here," Cary said.

"Wait a minute." Lindsay stood with his head tilted. Rather than looking nervous and upset, he wore a thousand-yard stare, like a dog who heard something in the distance. "You don't feel something weird?"

"This place is fucking creepy on a normal day," Cary said. "What are you talking about?"

"Feels like there's something here, or there was. Like something that could reach out and touch you."

"What are you smoking?" Cary stared at him.

"You ain't seen no shadows?"

Cary paused. "Well, yeah." The longer he looked, in fact, the thicker the shadows got. But he didn't need to see the room; he knew exactly what it looked like. The bed sat in the middle, linens folded at the foot, the TV mounted in the corner near the ceiling. Around and behind the bed were the various monitors and plugs that tethered the patient to the wall. When he'd been here he'd felt like a robot being powered through an AC adapter. The green glow was still there, but dimmer and murkier where the shadows touched. They were thickest around the bed.

"Huh." He rubbed his lip. "Let's go look at the other rooms."

Lindsay turned to him and nodded, maybe understanding Cary's purpose. His eyes lit up with the same curiosity Cary felt. "I'll go left, you go right."

The hall was as quiet as a hospital ever got. Emily was nowhere in sight, and the only other visible nurse sat at the desk bent over paperwork. She didn't look up.

As soon as he started moving, shadows danced around him. He noticed they got thicker near certain rooms. Empty rooms. They were almost solid, hovering to either side of him, when he opened one of the sliding glass doors. Immediately his ears filled with static, like from an old radio. His sinuses prickled, like he'd snorted pop. When he put his hands on his wheels, his fingers stung from a thousand tiny sparks.

"S'cuse me," someone said behind him. He nearly jumped out of his skin and had to back out of the doorway to turn around. He recognized the janitor's face. "You aren't supposed to be here without permission—hey, Cary, isn't it?"

"Yeah. Hey, George." Cary put on a smile. "Haven't seen you in a while. Thought you were over in the PT wing."

"Got transferred." George's bushy eyebrows knitted. "You visiting, or...?"

"Well, sorta." Cary decided to take a risk and gestured into the room. "Looking into some things."

"Oh." George's eyebrows shot up, but he seemed ready to back down all of a sudden. "Didn't know. Sorry."

"No big deal. Hey, listen, was you here last night?"

"For a while, yeah."

Cary leaned forward a little, his elbows on his knees as if sharing a secret. He'd found people were more likely to keep quiet about things they thought they heard in confidence, even if they weren't actually secrets. "You notice anything?"

George shook his head. "Nah, man, nothing. I wasn't on when all that went down, anyway. I went home before. It happened late."

"Do you know who was on? Are they here now?"

"Probably not till later. That's Carlos." George frowned. "I heard they're questioning everybody who was on that day. Tell them I didn't see a thing. I sure as hell didn't do anything. I'm not. You know, that way."

"I believe you," Cary said.

"Maybe this doesn't mean anything, but I kept getting shocked last night. You know, like static."

Cary bit the inside of his cheek, trying not to let his thoughts show on his face. "Anything else?"

"Nope. Sorry, man. I wasn't much help."

Cary shook his head. "I think you did help. Thanks. Cover my back, huh? My brother's on the other side."

"Yeah. Sure."

Cary didn't trust anyone but Lindsay to really have his back, but he knew George would at least tell him if someone was coming. People did that kind of thing if you asked them to. His skin prickled as he went into the room and shut the door. For a few minutes, he just sat, looking and listening. For what, he didn't know, but maybe there was…something.

When the bed covers rustled, he was sure he was going to have a heart attack.

"Emily?" Jerome's voice.

Jesus *fucking* Christ.

His heart hammered in his throat so hard it felt like it was going to choke him, Cary just sat there for a minute. He couldn't remember the last time he'd been frozen with fear like this, but everything in him screamed at him *not* to move forward. He could hear the machines, the regular beep of the heart monitor and the other beeps that sounded like alarm clocks and microwave timers, but the sounds were muted, like he was still on the other side of the door.

But the privacy curtain was open, and the bed was unoccupied, linens stacked nearly at the foot. All of the monitors were unplugged.

"Emily?" the voice asked again.

A recording. It had to be. Someone's sick idea of a joke. Annoyance overcame Cary's fear. Was everyone just messing with their heads? He rolled toward the bed, listening for the source of the sounds. They were realistic; the heart monitor beeping seemed to come from the monitor itself, and the rustling came from the bed. Either his mind was tricking him, or maybe there were two hidden speakers.

He reached toward the bed and felt something grab his hand.

The world turned pitch black; even the street lights and the lights from the hall vanished. Then a web of green light flared to life. It traveled outward from what looked like a pool directly beneath them, crackling with potential energy. He could *see* people too, human figures in varying shades of color. Most of them were pastel; they looked a little like someone had hung Christmas lights on skeletons and animated them. A few had deeper, richer colors. Two were sky-blue: one looked male, and the other female. He knew the female figure was Emily.

One figure stood out from the rest. It was directly across from him, a brilliant, blazing silver-green. Wisps like locks of long hair cascaded from it, bleeding into the web of light. The figure outshone anyone else Cary could see. He saw its head turn toward him as if pulled by a string, and he didn't need to see the details of a face to know it was Lindsay. He heard himself laugh aloud, and the phantom touch on his arm suddenly disappeared, startling him back to reality as if someone had punched him in the face.

The lights from the hall were impossibly bright and the room blazing hot. His stomach turned so violently he had to bolt for the bathroom and barely made it to the toilet in time to puke. Once he started, he couldn't stop, his body wracked with dry heaves. Sweat poured down his neck and back, and the cool air made him shiver in spite of the feverish feeling in his face.

"Cary?" Emily's voice sounded hollow coming from the empty room. He didn't reply, too busy gagging still, and didn't protest when she came into the bathroom. Thankfully she didn't turn on the light. "Well, I see you figured out how to see magic. Have a good trip?"

"Trip where?" he managed.

"Well, nowhere. I mean like acid trip. That's what it feels like, anyway."

The outer door slid open again; Cary knew Lindsay's footsteps. "You okay? What was that?"

Cary just shrugged. He'd stopped dry heaving, at least, but it felt like he had a million-degree fever, and his insides felt like they had been hacked up and scraped out like a pumpkin. He pulled off his shirt and stuck it under the faucet. When it was drenched with cold water, he draped it over his head.

"Answer me," Lindsay said. "Are you okay?"

"I will be," he said, the nearest thing to a confession of how miserable he felt.

"In other words, no," Emily said. "I can help."

Cary shook his head. The last thing he needed was her laying hands on him. "Just let me have some aspirin."

"Don't be a stubborn douchebag. I'm a healer. It's what I do." Cary said nothing, just filled the paper cup beside the sink with water. It tasted like liquid metal. He almost puked again.

"Look," Emily said, "You wanted me to be straight with you. I'm being straight now. If all you do is take aspirin, you'll feel like shit for a week and you won't be any use to anyone. If you let me help you, you'll feel better inside of fifteen minutes."

Lindsay sighed and murmured, "Just let her, Care."

Cary found himself considering it. "Say it."

"Say what?" Emily asked.

"*Admit* it. Don't act like you don't know what I'm talking about."

"You are *such* an asshole." She shifted her weight from foot to foot, then said, "Fine. I'm your sister. Your full sister."

"No, you ain't. My father sired you and my mother gave birth to you. That's my brother." Cary jerked a finger at Lindsay.

"Point taken." Did she sound a little hurt? How did he always manage to do that? He shouldn't feel guilty about it, but he did.

"Okay, well, do what you're gonna do."

"Wow, thanks, I needed your permission to do anything." She turned and left the bathroom.

* * *

Lindsay thought Emily was just as proud and prickly as Cary could be even though she'd been raised away from Dad. Where Dad or Cary would have started walking out the door and just kept on going, expecting to be followed, she stopped and folded her arms. "Are you coming?"

Cary went out into the room. Lindsay saw him glance toward the bed. Maybe remembering his own long stay in this hospital? Lindsay wondered again what had happened; his skin stung like he had a bad sunburn.

"We'll find a clean room. There's too much interference in here," Emily said. "What did you do?"

"Don't got a clue," Cary said. Lindsay suspected that wasn't entirely true and decided to ask about it later.

"What d'you mean, too much interference?" Lindsay asked.

"Too much magical activity of one kind in a certain space can interfere with another kind. Sandor would tell you it's all the same, but that's not how human minds perceive it or deal with it. It's like saying gravity and electricity are the same." She led them down the hall, bypassing several empty rooms. Each of them gave Lindsay that too-warm feeling, but it wasn't as bad as the room they'd left. They passed a short brown guy with designs shaved into the sides of his head. The guy stopped to stare at them.

"What went on in 217? I felt something." He had an accent Lindsay couldn't identify, like someone on TV.

"Good question," Emily said, her voice flat. "This is Mustafa. He's one of us."

"And this is who?"

"I'm Cary, and this is Lindsay," Cary said, staring up at Mustafa as if he hadn't just been puking his guts out. Mustafa gave Emily a questioning look, but she shook her head as if signaling him to be silent.

"I'm taking them to a clean room. I'll talk to you later."

Lindsay tried to catch Cary's eye as they moved down the hall, but Cary looked straight ahead. Emily opened the door of another room and Lindsay could feel the difference between this one and the one before. Even the air was easier to breathe. She reclined the bed, spread a sheet over it and lowered it. "Lay on your stomach."

"Why?" Cary demanded. Lindsay winced. Ever since the accident, Cary had refused to lie on his stomach if he could help it.

"Because your spine is the origin of all your nerve endings, which you know, and I need access to it."

"I can sit up," Cary said. "I ain't laying down."

Emily gave Lindsay a 'deal with him' look, one Lindsay was used to. A lot of people seemed to think Lindsay would get him to do what they wanted.

"Let him sit," Lindsay said. "You can get at his spine that way."

Thankfully, Emily just nodded, and Cary transferred to the bed. He sat stiff, his lips tight. Lindsay moved closer for moral support, sitting in one of the all-too-familiar waiting chairs.

Emily studied his spine, her gaze lingering on the long surgery scar at the small of his back as Lindsay's had done many times before. "If this had anything to do with energy corruption, someone might be able to heal it."

Cary fell silent for a long, long time. Lindsay's pulse quickened at the idea of having his tall, athletic brother back again, walking. "Well, it ain't, so there's no use in talking about 'if,'" Cary said. "It ain't such a tragedy as everyone thinks, anyway."

"Well. All this is going to be even harder for you."

"So what? I'll live."

Lindsay wondered how things could be just that simple to Cary. Emily just shrugged and put her hands on either side of his spine. She didn't comment when he jerked in either surprise or protest. Her hands pressed firmly into his back, like a massage, and Lindsay became aware of a cool current, like air conditioning leaking from under a closed door. It spread up from the floor and through her hands, traveling into Cary. For a long time she just stood like that. Lindsay watched Cary, but he had fallen still, barely breathing. Lindsay shuddered; it reminded him too much of watching Cary in the hospital, silent and unresponsive.

Finally, Lindsay felt a jolt of energy, like somebody had closed an electrical circuit. The energy lasted all of a couple seconds, and then she stepped away.

"That's it?" Cary asked.

"Your body and your connection with magic conduct energy a lot more readily than a regular person, plus we're over a node."

"Node?"

"A place where several Tree branches cross. It's like a well of magic." Emily gestured toward the floor.

So that was what Lindsay had felt when they walked onto the floor. "I feel it," he said.

Emily nodded and stepped away from Cary. "That's all you need." The cell phone clipped to her waistband buzzed, and she picked it up. "Which is good, because I've got an emergency downstairs. Try to stay out of the way up here. I'll be back when I can." She jogged out of the room.

"Feel better?" Lindsay asked.

"Don't feel like puking no more." Cary shrugged.

"What happened?"

Cary's eyes flickered; Lindsay couldn't remember the last time he'd looked so disturbed. "I think I saw Jerome's ghost."

Lindsay felt a chill. "Ghost?"

"I wish I was bullshitting you." Cary tugged his T-shirt back on. "I went into the room and I heard his voice. I thought it was a recording, but I felt something touch me." He shuddered. "It made me see…magic, I guess. Like with the horses."

Lindsay nodded. "I felt something. Musta been you, but it was too quick, so I didn't get to think about it. What'd you see?"

"People. Everybody in the building, seemed like. They all had light, but some had more than others, and different colors too. You…" He grinned suddenly. "You looked like a goddamned angel, brother. Righteous fire and all."

Lindsay blinked, feeling his face heat unexpectedly. Only Cary would describe something holy with profanity. "I wouldn't go that far. I ain't no angel."

"No? All you was missing was the wings. It was awesome."

"So, what, the ghost was trying to tell you something?" Lindsay tried to change the subject.

"I guess. Dunno what, though. Wonder if I could see the magic again. Without the ghost."

"You'll make yourself puke," Lindsay said, though he was curious, too, to find out what it—whatever it was—would be like for him.

"Well, we was called in to do something. Let's try and do it. Sandor and Emily said you gotta believe something before you see it, right? So let's just look for it."

Lindsay started to tell him he wasn't making any sense, but when he thought about it, it *did* make sense. He watched Cary's eyes focus into the middle distance and stayed still and quiet to let him concentrate. As he waited, he let his mind search for that togetherness he'd felt for those few seconds, while Cary was seeing magic. To his surprise, it wasn't hard to find; he felt it not far away, like a vibration down a metal pipe. It grew stronger and stronger until his palms itched. It *felt* familiar.

Cary. Of course. He still sat there, frowning in concentration. He used to try to play Travis's guitar, though he never agreed to be taught. He often tried this finger placement and that, never quite getting the chords right. Lindsay knew Cary would rather figure this out for himself, just like a guitar chord, but the wrong notes made his teeth ache. He reached out and touched Cary's shoulder.

The room went black and vertigo overcame him; he was vaguely aware of sitting down hard on the tile floor, but he still clung to Cary. He saw figures, lit up like Cary had described. He felt them, too, all buzzing in his mind. But there was a sense beyond sight and sensation, a nameless *knowing* he'd only caught glimpses of before. Taking over his view in all senses, loud, bright and fully present, was Cary, blazing like a charcoal fire, almost too bright to look at.

"Holy shit," Cary murmured. "I can *feel* them, too."

Lindsay understood then that they were sharing. Together, they made something stronger than the sum of its parts. "I can see them."

The blue figures began to turn their heads. The one nearest them walked toward them, and beyond it, Lindsay spotted something odd. Something dark and slimy, like oily mud.

Then Mustafa opened the door. "You've got to be kidding me."

If Lindsay hadn't already been sitting, he'd have fallen flat on his ass. The room brightened, and the light pierced his eyeballs like needles. What came next felt like a kick in the head.

"What the hell?" Another voice asked from the door, then, Lindsay hard a collective indrawn breath.

"The princes."

Lindsay couldn't make it to the toilet before he puked.

Chapter Eight

Though Cary felt pretty rotten all over again, he didn't feel as miserable as Lindsay looked. Lindsay had taken over the hospital bed and lay with his eyes squeezed tight shut even after a shot of painkiller, which had made him puke again.

"Well, thanks," Mustafa said. "You wrecked our last clean room with your flashy magic trick. Now where the hell are we going to put a patient if we get one before the cleaners get here?" Cary could only guess what he meant by 'cleaners,' but at this very moment he didn't give a damn about any of that.

Most of the nurses had gone back to their work after ogling and gossiping among themselves about 'princes.' Not wanting to reveal how ignorant they were, Cary kept himself from asking the obvious question.

"You must be idiots or really new at this," Mustafa had said once everyone else had left. "That's twice now you've shown your power without bothering about where."

"Did you think we was showing out? We was trying to figure out what's going on."

Mustafa hooked a thumb at Lindsay. "Judging by the way your brother looks, you were trying to kill a fly with a shotgun. I'll give you the benefit of the doubt and guess you're new at this and you didn't really mean to draw attention to yourselves. You can't do that. You're putting everyone in danger."

"We're new at this," Lindsay said, his voice slurred with pain and opiates. Out of consideration for his condition, Cary didn't smack him for the bald-faced admission.

"Great." Mustafa rolled his eyes. "So we have a couple of heavy duty magic wielding princes who have no clue what they're doing. How long have you been with us?"

By 'us,' Cary assumed he meant Emily and her goonies. "We ain't with nobody. We met Emily a week ago."

"Merciful God." Mustafa rocked back on his heels. "She didn't tell me *that*. Well, that's excellent. Now we all get to deal with you." Mustafa sighed. His cell phone beeped. "Shit," he muttered when he looked at it. With one last glare in their direction, he left the room.

"Let's get outta here," Lindsay said, struggling to sit up.

"Lin, you cain't drive like that."

"I'll get Amy to come pick us up. I don't feel like staying here no more and getting jerked around."

Even if he didn't want to deal with Lindsay's pushy fag hag right now, Cary was more than happy to leave. "Need a wheelchair?"

"Funny. No, I'll be fine."

Cary backed up to give him room to haul himself out of bed, and grabbed his arm when he started to waver. "You're a mess, brother."

"Just get me outta this place."

"Push me." Cary turned himself toward the door, and they made their slow way back to the front desk. They were in view of the red Exit sign when two hospital security guys came marching in. Cary recognized one of them as the guy who'd met them outside. He stopped in the middle of the hallway, eyebrows lifted in surprise at seeing them.

"Nobody in our out," he said.

"What's going on?" the nurse at the desk asked.

"High-security patient coming in."

"We don't have any clean rooms!"

"The cleaners are on their way up," the other security guy said. His eyes fixed on Cary and Lindsay. "Better go back to your room, boys."

"Shit," Lindsay whispered.

* * *

Since there was nothing else to do, Lindsay returned to the hospital bed and accepted another round of painkiller. He fought to pay attention while Cary harassed anyone who passed by for information, but eventually, his mind gave up and fell into a stupor, worse than he'd ever had while drinking.

Voices woke him, he didn't know how long later. One of them he knew belonged to Cary, but it took him a while to figure out who the other person was. One of their cousins? No, nobody from home. Emily. He tried to summon the concentration to speak, but it took all his will to even understand what they were saying.

"Looks like you're stuck here for a while. I told you to lay low. If they didn't know who you were—"

"You never said that, just like you never told us who they think we are, so don't play that game. How's us being here going to help anything, anyway?"

"It's a matter of security, to them. You're high-profile, so—"

"So they'll keep three high-profile targets in one public place. *That's* smart."

"Look. I don't make the decisions."

"Who does?"

"The *goji*. Guardians. They're like the security team. Sefu's one of them. I'm trying to contact him, but he's not answering his cell."

"Y' know, if you'd told us a lot of this crap last week, we'd be in better shape."

"We were going to tell you. It's not my fault all this happened at once. No one could have predicted it."

Lindsay managed to open his eyes, though it was harder than he would have reckoned. Cary turned toward him. "Good morning, sunshine. How you feeling?"

He tried to decide. His head still felt like it was being crushed by a semi-truck, and his body was too heavy to move, but the drugs had blunted most of the sensations—blunted everything, really. "Dunno."

Cary looked amused. "Better that way sometimes. Listen, she says we cain't leave."

"I heard. Why?"

Cary gestured to Emily as if to say, *You take this*.

She shot him a look. "Sandor's daughter is here. She was my emergency. She was attacked. She's being healed right now. We…don't know where Sandor is."

Lindsay blinked. Even in his fuzzy state, he could put two and two together. "He went missing like Jerome?"

She licked her lips. "We don't know. We're just trying to protect Bella. We had to hook her up to a heart monitor and oxygen but we switched the whole floor over to backup power and we've got someone monitoring the node. It's the best we can do right now."

Another member of their little group attacked and maybe dead; there was no coincidence there. Lindsay struggled to get his mind to work, but it felt like walking through waist-high water.

"It's got to be the same people who killed Jerome," Cary said. "But why would they want Sandor?"

"He's a recorsa—the living memory of the Tree. Remember? But he's supposed to be untouchable, neutral. Not part of or subject to any conflict. The knowledge his bloodline passes down is for everyone," Emily said

"Neutral, huh? I guess that's why he's been sneaking around with y'all," Cary said.

"Yes. The key word there is *sneaking*. Sandor believed sometimes the recorsas had to do something with his knowledge. It's against the rules, but he felt like he had to do something."

"Do what?"

Emily's eyes flickered; she looked unsure. It was not an expression that belonged on her face, any more than it belonged on Cary's. "I don't know. At least, I'm not sure. He wants you to make a difference with the Tree, but I'm not sure what he was after."

"Don't that beat all," Cary said dryly. "Well, this sucks."

Emily looked at him as if trying to decide whether he was up to something, but he gave her a straight-faced look of innocence, and she didn't know him well enough to catch on. "I'll find you a place to sleep while we wait for the *goji* to clear the area. Stay here this time."

"Yeah, right," Cary said once she'd left and closed the door. "I'm gonna go talk to this girl. You okay to walk a couple doors down?"

Lindsay tried. Though his limbs were heavy and slow to obey him, he didn't feel as dizzy as before when he sat up or turned to put his feet on the floor. "I reckon."

Cary turned to let Lindsay steady himself on his shoulder again, and they went down the hall. Lindsay felt reckless and bold, more like Cary than himself. It was probably the drugs, but it was better than being worried like usual.

"We need to talk to her," Cary said when they found the right room. It wasn't hard to figure out, with two guards posted outside. Lindsay's skin prickled all over as they drew near. One of the guards, the only one wearing a rent-a-cop uniform, studied them. Lindsay noticed his eyes went automatically to the places you could conceal a gun: armpit, waistband, thigh, ankle. But, like so many others, he only gave Lindsay a hard look, glancing over Cary as if not being able to use his legs meant he wasn't that much of a threat. Lindsay fought hard to keep from smiling.

"Sorry," the guard said. "No visitors."

"We ain't here to visit. We're here to talk to her." Cary wasn't bothering with his usual friendly charm, which meant he was either too impatient or he thought he could get something done by sheer force of will. "We're trying to figure all this out, so it's best if you let us in."

"Nobody comes in our out except for the nurses assigned to her. And you aren't nurses."

"Listen, you ain't helping nobody by keeping us from talking to her," Lindsay said. He was a little steadier on his feet now. He straightened a little, trying to present himself more like somebody who knew what he was doing and less like a drunk. He thought he'd figured out where Cary was going with this.

"So you say. Listen, I don't have clearance to let anybody but the doctor and the nurses in here. I can't help you out."

"Maybe you heard who we are," Lindsay said. "We're the princes."

The silent guard looked back and forth between them, then the guards exchanged glances. The one in the rent-a-cop uniform narrowed his eyes at Cary. "Bullshit."

"You don't think I can be a cripple and a prince?" Cary pushed himself forward a couple inches, making Lindsay, who was still leaning against the wheelchair handles, stumble. He pushed himself upright and tried to put on a ferocious glare.

"We never heard anything about a prince in a wheelchair," the rent-a-cop guard said.

A sudden flush of heat made sweat break out on Lindsay's forehead, and he felt that familiar vibration of Cary's magic again. "Well, now you heard," Cary growled. He leaned toward the guards, looking like a wildcat fixing to claw their faces off, and magic rolled off him in a wave. Lindsay pinched his shoulder hard, remembering Mustafa and Emily's warnings about showing their power. The heat and the vibration tapered off.

"Sorry," the plain-clothes guard said, wide-eyed. They both stepped aside. Lindsay looked up and down the hall, expecting Emily or Mustafa or both to come running toward them, but nobody came.

"Go, Lin," Cary whispered. Lindsay pushed him into the room, trying ignore the voice in his head that told him they had just done something else foolish. The privacy curtain was pulled back to conceal the main room, but they could hear the monitors beyond. Lindsay saw Cary's shoulders tighten.

Nobody looked good in a hospital, but Sandor's daughter was pretty in a weird kind of way. She had inherited her father's curly black hair, though his sharp features softened a little in her face. There was nothing about her that attracted Lindsay, but he could see where she might be attractive to other men, under different circumstances.

She saw them before the nurse did. Her dark eyes widened. "It's you."

Lindsay wondered if that was good surprise or bad surprise. "Ma'am, my name is Lindsay—"

"I know." She addressed the nurse, who hovered near the door like she was about to call for help. "I'll be okay."

"I was told—"

"Ma'am," Cary said. The nurse's eyes lingered on him; he flashed her the smile Lindsay had seen win over so many women. "I remember you. You was my nurse when I was in ICU. 2005. I'm Cary. Marilyn, right?"

The nurse nodded once and looked at the girl in the bed. "Ten minutes."

"No rush," the girl said.

The nurse left, but not before she gave Cary a smile. "You look good."

"I know."

Often, Lindsay wished he had whatever made women just smile at Cary like that, no matter what he said.

"You're very charming," the girl said.

"Working on you?" Cary asked.

"Not really." Her somber face didn't change. Cary looked disappointed. The girl looked at Lindsay. "Sandor said you were the quiet brother."

"I guess," Lindsay said. There were IVs and monitors on both of her hands so he didn't bother to shake hands, just nodded. "We come to help. Well, we come to figure out what's going on, anyway."

"I'm Bella Jaborsky. I'm a recorsa. Do you know what that is?" Her voice was low for a girl's but nice to listen to.

"We sorta know," Lindsay said.

"Well." Bella grimaced as she tried to change position and reached for the morphine button. "What do you want to know?"

"Let's start with what happened to you." The room began to spin and Lindsay looked around for a chair. The waiting chair had never felt so comfortable.

"I could ask the same thing about you," Bella said, giving him a doubtful look. "I must have missed that."

"What's that mean?" Cary asked.

"One thing at a time. The nurse will be coming back in soon. I was attacked by an Underworld creature. I didn't get a good look at it, but I think it was some kind of demon. It looked like a dog. I'd have to think about it to put a name on it. Before you ask, I don't know why they'd want me, or if they were out to kill me or kidnap me or what. They shouldn't have even come near me. Recorsas serve the Underworld, too." She winced again and paused for breath. "I guess that's where we start."

"We," Cary said.

"Sandor said you make things harder than they need to be. I'm not in the mood to spar with you right now, prince. You came to help, right? So will you help?"

Cary gave her one of his sharp looks. Lindsay braced himself for another sniping match like he and Emily always got into. Instead, Cary gave her his reckless grin. "Yeah, we'll help. If you answer our questions."

Bella's mouth twisted. "Fine."

"Our horses are missing. You know where they are?"

Bella blinked a couple of times. "Horses."

"Yeah. Y'know, big animals with four legs and—"

"I know what they are. I remembered them." She closed her eyes and grimaced. Thinking about it looked tiring; Lindsay could sympathize. "Call them."

"Call them?" Cary said. "Like, call their names?"

"It doesn't have to be that. Just…" She waved her hand. "Call them."

Before either of them could ask what that meant, the sliding glass door opened and Emily came around the curtain. She beckoned them over.

"I have a window of about four minutes to get you two out of here, and by the way, thanks so much for letting everyone know who the hell you are. Don't argue, just go with Mustafa."

"Wait, we finally—" Cary began.

"Goddammit, just get out of here. Trust me, if you don't, you'll be here against your will for days."

Lindsay and Cary exchanged a look. They would lose a chance to get their questions answered, but Lindsay felt like he was going to fall over and he wasn't going to let Cary do all the fighting.

"Fine," he said. Cary gave him a betrayed look, but he said, "Got to, Care."

"Thank God." Emily waved them out into the hall where Mustafa, the brown nurse, waited. He looked Lindsay up and down, then offered his arm.

"Where's your car?"

"South lot." Lindsay had no idea how he was going to get there, but Mustafa pulled him over to a wheelchair. He didn't protest, just sank into the seat. The motion of the chair made him want to puke and he wondered how Cary could stand it.

"If you've got to throw up, you better let me know," Mustafa said.

Lindsay clamped his jaw shut and managed not to. The cool night air made him feel a little better. The parking lot was half full, but he didn't see anybody else as Mustafa pushed him out to the Explorer, Cary coming behind.

"Do you have hand controls?" Mustafa asked. Lindsay shook his head. "Then give me your keys. I'll drive you home."

"Why, so you can figure out where we live?" Cary said.

"No, so you can get home. What are you going to do, call a cab? Hurry up. We can't wait."

Lindsay felt too awful to argue. He dug in his pocket to surrender his keys and let Mustafa help him into the back seat as Cary transferred.

"What the hell went on back there?" Cary asked. "Why'd you pull us away from Bella?"

"You drew attention to yourselves, that's what. And you made more work for everyone else. If you hadn't noticed, someone is obviously coming after our people. We're trying to keep you from ending up like them."

Lindsay rolled down the window and let the breeze flow into his face. His crushing headache stuck around, but after a minute he felt a little less like puking. "How long were y'all gonna wait before y'all told us we was princes?"

"Look, nobody told me much about this either. I'd only ever heard of you. I didn't know Emily had found you."

"What's with the secrets?" Cary asked.

"She tells people what they need to know. You'll have to ask her." Mustafa's voice was bitter. Lindsay filed that information away for later. Mustafa might be working with Emily, but he didn't sound like he liked what he was doing very much.

He dozed on and off on the drive home and woke when the vehicle turned onto Travis's gravel driveway. The house was dark when they pulled up, but the flood lights came in as Mustafa turned off the engine.

"Emily will call you as soon as she can," Mustafa said. "In the meantime, stay out of trouble." He opened the passenger's side back door to pull Cary's chair out. "Lindsay, do you need help into the house?"

"Better not," Lindsay said, figuring Travis wouldn't much appreciate a brown stranger in his house. "Thanks."

Mustafa shrugged. "I'm just doing what I'm told."

"How are you getting home?"

"I'll figure it out."

By the time Lindsay heaved himself out of the car, Mustafa was halfway down the driveway, disappearing into the darkness. He'd have a long walk back to the main road.

Travis poked his head out the front door as Lindsay wobbled toward the house. "What in hell happened to you? And who's that guy? I'm probably gonna regret asking, but I figure I ought to know who's just dropping by my place."

"The guy's a nurse at St. John's," Cary said. "He's with our sister, Emily."

"Oh." Travis came down the porch ramp. "Here, lean on me."

It was a weird moment to feel Travis's arm around his waist, but Lindsay didn't have much choice; he couldn't seem to find his balance. "Thanks."

"You look like hell," Travis said. "Is there something I ought to know about, y'all? You been real busy doing something since y'all come to visit me and now some nurse drives you home."

"You may not wanna know, Trav," Cary said.

"Well, if y'all are in trouble, I reckon I do wanna know."

"It ain't like you think," Lindsay said. He felt a little steadier once he was up the ramp and into the house. He didn't want Travis to let go of him, but he didn't want it to be weird either, so he straightened. "Thanks, I'm okay."

Travis eyed him like he thought maybe Lindsay was full of shit. "If it's something I need to know, I hope y'all will decide to tell me. I'll say goodnight then."

Lindsay bit his lip, watching Travis go into the master bedroom. He hadn't meant to upset him. He looked at Cary. "Maybe we oughta tell him. We're staying with him. He oughta at least know what he's getting into."

Cary shrugged. "I reckon. He might think we're crazy, though."

"We ain't? This ain't crazy?"

"Didn't say it wasn't."

Cary went to his bedroom and Lindsay, after a moment of debate, knocked on Travis's door. Travis opened it and gestured him in. Lindsay stepped in and stood near the door. The room was mostly dark except for an old lamp on the other side of the room, and the bed was mussed.

"Damn, we woke you up. Sorry," Lindsay said.

"You didn't. I was tossing and turning," Travis said. "You okay?"

"No." Lindsay chewed his lip. "I'm sorry, Trav. We shouldn't a brought this on you. We'll tell you. I don't mean to keep secrets, but it's just…I dunno. Hard to explain."

Travis just looked at him for a minute. "Am I gonna be sorry knowing what you tell me?"

"I cain't lie. I'm sorry I know," Lindsay said.

"Well, reckon I'll find out soon enough. Maybe I oughta have a few drinks in me first, though."

"Might not be such a bad idea," Lindsay admitted.

Travis smiled a weird little smile. "Y'all two've made me drink to excess more times than I can count."

Lindsay winced. "I'm sorry."

"If I minded I wouldn't a helped y'all out," Travis said. "I like having y'all around." He paused for just a second before he added, "Especially you."

Lindsay didn't know what to say to that. Travis waved a hand. "Anyway. I better get on to bed."

"I'm glad to be here too," Lindsay said. "With you."

Travis tilted his head. "Well, good."

Lindsay left the room, wondering what had just happened.

* * *

"You tell Travis anything?" Cary asked Lindsay when he came in.

Lindsay sat down on the edge of the bed. "Just that we'd tell him what's going on soon."

Cary could see Lindsay's blush even in the dim light now that he was sitting closer. "Why d'you look funny?"

Lindsay looked away. "I don't look funny."

Cary wondered what had gone on between Lindsay and Travis, but he wasn't sure he wanted to ask. "So the girl said to call the horses."

Lindsay sat down on the edge of the bed. "Yeah. But what's that mean?"

Cary shrugged. "Well, I ain't gonna go wandering around shouting for that stallion when I cain't even say his name." Still, the more he thought about it, the more he wondered if they'd ever see the horses again. Jerome, the one who'd been taking care of them, was dead. Somebody must want them.

"Bella said it wasn't like that," Lindsay said. "What if it's like a mental thing? Like we done in the hospital? Maybe we can just see them."

Cary thought about it. "Worth a try." He closed his eyes and sat back in his chair, remembering the moment when he could see all the glowing colors. Instead of trying to see people this time, though, he pictured the horses. He tried to imagine what it would be like to ride an animal like that. He and Lindsay had grown up on horseback, but he'd only ridden as part of occupational therapy since the accident. He'd stopped four years ago when Medicare decided they wouldn't pay for it. Sometimes he thought about asking Travis to help him do it again, but it wasn't the same as it used to be, walking a gaited horse around a paddock. He wondered if he could even still handle a horse with an attitude like the stallion's....

This was going nowhere. He saw nothing, felt nothing. "I'm going to bed."

"Care."

"Go on. We'll figure it out in the morning." Cary retreated to the room Travis had offered him. It had belonged to Edy, Travis's sister, and was attached to an accessible bathroom.

He didn't know how the hell they were supposed to find the damn horses. He didn't know how he was supposed to do any of this. *I'd expected to see you walking by now*, Dad had said.

Yeah, well.

It took him a while to fall asleep. He knew he was dreaming, but somehow everything still made perfect sense. He sat in short grass, warm from the sun, in a field surrounded by thick forest on all sides. It was a sheltered place with a creek bed running down the middle that was flanked by trees and brush. Cary sat high up, like he was in a tree stand hunting, except it was afternoon and he'd rarely hunted in the afternoon. A white shape moved just below him: the stallion? No, smaller.

The shape moved into the light and a halo of rainbow colors burst around it. Cary shielded his eyes and squinted, trying to make it out. It moved like a deer. All of a sudden he could see it, a white buck moving through the grass as confident as you please. Rainbow colors danced around his antlers.

Then he was following the buck, chasing after it as it sprang through the grass. He didn't know how he was moving. Maybe he was a buck too. They were headed toward the creek bed. He couldn't see the creek or the trees surrounding it anymore. Thick smoke had gathered like a cloud around it, and the edge of the burning grass glowed orange-red. The buck didn't even hesitate and neither did Cary. His heart pounded as they slowed and he stared into the smoke.

The buck bounced away, leaving Cary alone in the field. He wasn't afraid of the fire; it felt safe, welcoming. He kept looking.

He heard hooves crunching in the burned grass. As much as he wanted to rush forward, he knew he had to let the stallion come to him. Sure enough, a moment later he stepped out of the cloud of smoke, his head held high. His coat was pristine white this time, not streaked with soot, but his eyes were still shining black.

Cary opened his eyes. His skin prickled; he knew something had just happened. It wasn't the feeling of anxious dread he'd felt the night before Emily and Sandor had grabbed him, but his stomach fluttered. He sat up just as Lindsay opened his bedroom door. Cary met his brother's eyes. He didn't say anything, just pulled himself into his chair, and they went outside.

They didn't turn on the porch light, and Travis's property was far enough from anything that Cary could see no lights from the highway or from neighbors. He could see every star and even the cloudy streak that stretched across the sky, like when he was at home.

"Care," Lindsay breathed. Cary dropped his eyes and stared into the darkness. He heard the crunch of hooves on grass, and then the horses appeared, both of them. He could see them as clearly as if it were daytime. They stopped a few yards from the porch.

"Thank God," Lindsay breathed.

"We thought you was captured," Cary said. "Where'd you go?"

"A place no one else can follow, yet," the stallion said. "You called us."

"How'd we do that?" Cary could have sworn he *had* failed when he tried to call them. But he had dreamed about the stallion, he thought. He could only remember a little.

"You wanted us. We came." The stallion said it as if it were the simplest thing in the world.

"Well, shit." Cary couldn't believe how relieved he felt; any tension he'd had was gone, and everything that had happened in the past few days seemed distant, like they couldn't quite touch him. Just for this moment.

Lindsay drew in a breath like he was going to say something.

"This feels right," he said. "Don't it?"

There was a time to think about feelings and wonder why he had them; this wasn't it. "Yeah. It does." Even more relief swept through Cary when he said the words. Lindsay's smile was as clearly visible as the horses. Cary had the urge to hug him.

They went down to the yard to greet the horses. The stallion returned Cary's grin with a snort and a head toss.

"I saw you in my dream," Cary said.

"I know." The horse sounded indifferent.

"Yeah? How do you know?"

"Because I was there."

"You were in my dream," Cary said. "How'd you get there?"

"You called me and I came. Why is that difficult?"

"Smartass," Cary said. He was too glad to see the horses to care about his attitude.

"Shit." Cary turned back to Lindsay. Lindsay rarely cursed, only when he was really pissed or really worried. "We shouldn't a done this."

Leave it to Lindsay to interrupt a good moment with worry. "Shouldn't a done what?"

"Come to Travis's." The outline of Lindsay's body was stiff and tense. Cary didn't have the heart to tease him for being worried about Travis.

"Trav's got guns." He tried to sound reassuring.

"There's got to be something else we can do," Lindsay said. "We're supposed to be able to do magic, right? Jerome made up some kind of magical frame, didn't he, Sis? Could we do something like that?"

"Yes, if your magic was strong enough."

"It isn't?"

"Not until you ride."

Cary glanced at the stallion, who stared back. "Would both of us have to do it?"

"No," Lindsay said. "Absolutely not."

"Yes," Sister said.

"Why both of us? Cain't I just do it? It's dark, and it ain't safe for Cary without everything he needs."

"This is different magic," Sister said. "Both of you, or none."

"Trav's got stuff for Edy. He's got to," Cary said. "Go ask him where he keeps it."

"Edy's got cerebral palsy. Her balance—"

"Probably ain't much better than mine. Go ask him, Lindsay, or I'll ride him bareback."

The threat seemed to work. Rather than go into the house, though, Lindsay went in search of tack, muttering, "I'd just as soon not bother him with this foolishness unless it's so he can call the paramedics. Maybe they can be here when your dumb ass gets hurt and save us all some time."

He turned with a western-style saddle that had been custom-made for Edy, deep enough to help her keep her balance, with stirrups made so her feet wouldn't fall out or slide through and get caught. It looked smaller than the seat Cary was used to, but his lower half wasn't nearly as muscular as it used to be. Lindsay found a couple of straps to keep his thighs in place.

"Quick release would be better, like they use in mountain climbing," Lindsay said doubtfully. "If he shows out…"

"He won't." Cary gave the stallion a look. "You'll behave. Won't you?"

The stallion just stared at him. Cary stared back until he looked away.

"This is ridiculous," Lindsay announced. He slung the saddle over the sawhorse nearby and went back for another. Cary didn't argue. Lindsay might be right to be concerned, at least about this. Cary fought his own nerves, telling himself it had to be done. While Lindsay saddled the horses, he went inside in search of apples. He didn't find any, but found a jar of sugar cubes Travis kept for his own horses. A little bribe never hurt.

Lindsay took two of the cubes without saying anything and fed one to Sister. The stallion accepted one after sniffing it doubtfully. After that, both horses seemed calm and satisfied. Neither of them shied from being saddled.

"How d'you want to do this?" Lindsay asked. "There's a ramp out back, but you'd be mounting in the dark."

Cary took a deep breath. He reasoned they'd better do this now, in case somebody came to find them. He looked up at the stallion. "I need you to get down so I can get on your back."

For a second, Cary thought he'd just get that go-fuck-yourself look the stallion was so good at, but then he knelt as low as he could go. Cary transferred to the saddle like he would a chair, though it took him a minute to figure out how to get his right leg over to the other side. When he was settled, the stallion stood and Lindsay came over to put his feet in the saddle and strap his thighs down with knotted rope. His balance in the seat was still pretty good, and he didn't waver when the stallion stood again.

The saddle worked well enough to keep him upright and steady, and the straps helped too. Lindsay had put a hackamore on the stallion's head and Cary found he was glad for it. He doubted he'd need to direct an intelligent horse with the reins, but he'd need all the control he could get.

"Where to?" Lindsay asked Sister. He looked like he always did, more comfortable in the saddle than on his own two feet. Cary tried not to be jealous. The mare just turned and walked out of the stable, away from the house and into the dark hills. Lindsay twisted in his saddle to watch Cary. "You stay faced forward and sitting up straight. We ain't going faster than a walk when it's this dark, you hear?"

Even in the dim light from the stables, Cary could see the anxiety etched into his brother's face. As much as it irritated him sometimes when Lindsay was such a worrywart, he just plain hated being the cause of it. "I hear you, brother. I'll stay right next to you."

Gradually, the part of his mind that worried about how he sat and if he could keep his balance began to quiet down. The stallion had an incredibly smooth gait, better by far than the quarter horses they'd grown up with, and he remained mellow as they walked down the slope toward a little creek that cut through the property.

Between one step and the next, Cary's stomach turned upside-down, and he thought he'd lose his balance, though his body told him he remained perfectly steady. The stallion paused, and all of a sudden, Cary could have sworn he saw something flicker in the grass. Then he was sure of it: a wisp of light, like glowing smoke, rose from the ground and traveled toward them.

"Whoa," Lindsay breathed. "You feel that?"

Cary felt nothing, but he could see more tendrils of light wrapping around the mare's hooves and traveling up her legs in an elegant web pattern. They turned from silvery-gray to green as they traveled up toward her heart.

They turned *green*.

Cary watched the light patterns crawl up into the stallion's neck and head.

They had the same quality as the ones he'd seen in the hospital, but these were brighter, clearer. "Magic."

"Sis, are we standing on a branch?" Lindsay asked.

"Yes," the mare replied.

Cary reached out to touch one of the threads of light—magic—on the stallion's neck. It struck his fingers like a spark and he yelped in surprise, his voice loud in the still air, but the stallion didn't react. He touched it again, prepared this time, and suddenly became aware of...

Everything.

He couldn't see it, not exactly, but he knew that the web beginning in the stallion's body was only the tiniest part, and he could see all of it, the currents fluttering in the stallion to the slow, deep current at their feet, winding its way parallel to the little creek. The magical current wasn't very wide, and Cary sensed it was only a twig, one of millions or trillions, even. But he could feel its course as it snaked through Travis's property, joining up with others nearby. Each part had its own character, its own texture.

As they stood there, Cary became aware that, in some places, the current was deep, and he could barely see it, but in others, like this spot, it was right at the surface, like a spring. There were pools like this all over the property; if he was still long enough, he was sure he could count them. Emily had called them nodes.

He remembered his biology textbook and lectures from the staff at the hospital about his nervous system. Millions of nerves, sending impulses to one another through neurons. Nerve endings were the body's connection to the world. Without them, without the right impulses, the body couldn't interact with the world the same way. He knew that better than most people. A dull phantom ache settled at the small of his back where his broken vertebrae had partially severed his lower body's connection to his brain, as if reminding him.

He wondered, suddenly, if that was what was wrong with the World Tree.

"You said we could protect the house," Lindsay whispered. "How can we do it?"

"Make the connections," Sister said.

"Connections?"

"Between these places," Cary said. "Look! Feel how the magic's close here, and in other places? It's like connecting the dots."

Lindsay twisted in his saddle, looking around them "It cain't be that easy. Can it?"

"Well, what if we made a circle around part of the property?" Cary twirled his finger. "We could hit all those spots."

"What would that do?"

Cary explained his idea about neurons. "So what if we bring the message from one place to another? Make the connection."

"That's...a pretty good idea."

"I know. So?"

"So let's try it."

They rode farther out, to the crest of the opposite hill, figuring they'd make a big circle around everything in sight of the house. Once they knew what they were looking—or feeling—for, it wasn't hard to find those spots where the magic was close. They rode side-by-side in a clockwise circle, trusting the sure-footed horses to guide them in the darkness. Each time they came to a pool, they felt for the magic, which came to them like iron filings to a magnet, and it was the most natural thing in the world to pull a thread along with them to the next pool.

The stars were as bright as Cary had ever seen them, and the sky out here was so clear he could see the sparkling cloud of an asteroid field. He couldn't remember feeling quite so oddly content in a long time, with a beautiful horse, his brother at his side and no chair in sight. He began to relax, and opened his mouth to remark on the nice night.

The stallion took that as his cue.

The only warning he gave was a sudden bunching of muscles before he shot forward. Cary was too surprised to even make a sound, and barely managed to keep his grip on the reins. He heard Lindsay shout behind him, but then he could only hear the horse's hooves beating the ground, crashing through the tall grass. Cursing, Cary gripped the saddle horn and reins, concentrating only on keeping his balance. He couldn't grip with his thighs, and could no longer tell exactly what position his legs were in except that it was awkward and painful.

The stallion seemed to be dead-set on making it difficult for him; he vaulted across the creek, nearly dislodging Cary on the landing, and kept going, impossibly fast. In the starlit darkness, Cary was hard-put to see the ground ahead to know what to prepare for. He knew that somewhere out here, there was a round livestock feeder, but he didn't know where.

Then he saw it straight ahead, dark against the pale gray of the field. The bastard horse was going to run him into it.

He cursed again and went to work untying the straps that held his thighs. An emergency dismount was tough enough for someone who could land on his feet. But if he could throw himself to the left, he could tuck and roll. And hope like hell he threw himself far enough to avoid those hooves.

Miraculously, The knots Lindsay had made in the straps came free. Cary drew in a breath to prepare himself, seeing the feeder loom up in front of them. With his legs loose, he couldn't hold on much longer anyway. He shifted his weight—

—and the stallion put on the brakes, skidding to a halt. If Cary hadn't already had his arms around the horse's neck, he'd have gone over his head. Somehow, he managed to hold on, though as soon as they were stopped, he felt his lower half sliding. He hit the ground in a heap only a second before Lindsay thundered up on Sister and nearly jumped from the saddle. He hit the ground running and was on his knees next to Cary in a heartbeat. "Oh, Jesus!"

"Lin! I'm fine. I'm okay. See?" Cary straightened his legs out. "Look. Nothing broken. My ass is bruised, that's all."

"Jesus, Cary." He felt Lindsay's hands checking him, making sure that he wasn't hurt.

He pulled Lindsay into a hug, arms around his neck. "See? I'm fine." He pressed a kiss against Lindsay's temple, doing his best to soothe the panic he could feel in Lindsay's body.

"You are," Lindsay said, his voice muffled against Cary's shoulder. "You *are*."

"Yeah." Cary pulled his head away, politely ignoring the tears wetting Lindsay's face even though his throat tightened. "But if you keep carrying on, I'm gonna have to give you shit."

"That fucking horse."

"That fucking horse." Cary craned his neck to look up at the stallion, who watched them placidly. "Are you about done?"

"Yes."

"You're crazy, but you ain't dumb cooter crazy." Laughter bubbled up from his chest then, and once it started, it wouldn't stop. He lay in the grass, laughing like a fool while Lindsay looked on, bewildered. "Come on, it's funny."

"You sure you didn't knock your head?"

"Maybe when I was a baby. Come on, Cooter. Get back down so we can finish this."

Chapter Nine

The only reason Lindsay helped Cary back onto the stallion—Cooter—was that he knew that once they started, they had to finish what they were doing. His hands shook as he tied Cary's thighs again, checking to make sure Cary hadn't broken any bones. Cary still had some sensation below the damaged vertebrae, but Lindsay wouldn't put it past his brother to deny anything was wrong.

Cooter behaved like an angel as they finished their circuit, though Lindsay swore he pranced as if he'd won a game. He wanted to punch the damn horse and Cary, too, for treating the episode like it was no big deal. A sharp reprimand from Sister reminded him he had something to do, and he concentrated on drawing the threads of magic from one node to another. Before long, though, that too was as easy as drawing rope through his hands, and his mind went back to the image of Cary sliding from the horse, Cary on the ground, again.

His heart rate had almost returned to normal when they got back to to the place they'd started. The horses drew up alongside each other, and the hazy threads of light climbed up their bodies again. He started when Cary grabbed his arm.

"Lin. No harm done, okay? Don't be holding no grudge for a prank."

Lindsay was about to reply when a half itching, half hurting sensation crawled through his nerves. It started at the tips of his toes, raising goose bumps.

The feeling traveled all the way to his scalp until he could feel every part of him in a way he'd never been able to before. He was aware of his posture, the tilt of his head, the position of his hands, even the position of his feet inside his shoes. He had once seen a show on TV that said martial artists had a perfect sense of their bodies, which made them able to do amazing things. He had been taught how to use his body, but he had never felt such a connection with it before. He saw Cary shudder and guessed the magic had reached him, too. Suddenly he knew the stallion like he knew Cary and Sister. They weren't so different, Cary and the horse: proud, mistrustful, quick-witted and fierce, but unlike Cary, the stallion wasn't impulsive. He was sly and thought things through, knowing before he began how they'd turn out. He'd known he would stop in time—he'd just wanted to give Cary a scare, maybe to test him. A prank.

Lindsay didn't like it any better, but at least he knew the horse wasn't out to kill Cary.

"I'm never gonna like it when you go balls-to-the-wall like you do," he told Cary. "You might as well get used to it."

"Someday, you might be glad I do. Come on, I think it's done."

When Cooter was closed up in the stable and Cary was back in his chair, Lindsay could breathe a little easier. They agreed to wait to shower until the morning to avoid waking Travis, and Lindsay went into one of the guest rooms. It looked like it hadn't been redecorated since Travis's parents had lived here, with floral wallpaper and an aged, white embroidered bedspread. The crystal clock on the bedside table said it was almost three o'clock. Lindsay had just stripped down and pulled back the covers when he heard a floorboard creak at the door.

"What went on out there?" Travis asked. "I heard yelling."

"Dang horse decided he wanted to test the air brakes with Cary," Lindsay said. He avoided looking at Travis, who wore only boxers and a wife beater. It was nothing he hadn't seen, but something had changed since the comment Travis had made before.

"Cary okay?"

"He's fine. Hope you don't mind us borrowing your tack. Sorry we woke you."

"I had a horse like that. She was a real sly thing. She'd wait till you got comfortable, then stop dead and drop her head so you went flying over it," Travis said, waving off the apology. "I reckon you dealt with your fair share of those growing up, too."

"Yeah. When we was both well."

"Now, I thought you knew better than to talk like that." Travis leaned against the door frame. "Cary ain't sick. He's healthy as a horse, near as I can tell. And he ain't no amateur in the saddle, neither. But here you are acting like he's liable to break any minute."

Lindsay didn't try to defend himself, knowing it was about as useless as trying to argue with Cary. "You never worry about Edy like that?"

"Well, she don't give me nearly as much reason to as that brother of yours." Travis smirked. "Look, I've had a lot longer to get used to the way things are with her, so learn from me. He knows better than you what he can and cain't do.. If he wants to push it, let him. It don't sound like he come to no harm, anyway."

"No, but. Trav, when he fell off that horse, it looked just like when we found him." There. He'd said it.

Travis sighed. He ran a hand through his hair; Lindsay noticed gray at the temples for the first time. "I do believe that messed you up more'n it ever did him. But think about this: you ain't showing him no respect—hell, you ain't showing yourself no respect—if you keep on nannying him."

"Being worried when he runs off half-cocked ain't nannying. I worried about him before he was paralyzed."

"Not like this, I'll bet, or he'da kicked your butt a long time ago," Travis said mildly. "Did he get hurt running off half-cocked?"

"No."

"Well, then."

"Trav, your sister's always had cerebral palsy. You didn't wake up one morning and all of a sudden she was disabled."

"So I don't know what you could be going through. I ain't never been up nights worrying, and I ain't never wondered which one of us is actually disabled." Travis tapped his forehead. "Nah, you're right. Nobody knows what you're going through."

"That ain't what I mean—"

"You know people are up in arms about the word *disabled* now? They like *differently abled*. That's some bull, ain't it? Almost like they're trying to tell us what they can do instead of what they cain't."

Lindsay wrung his hands. He hadn't meant to make a complete ass of himself, especially in front of Travis, but he was getting good at it. "Okay, Trav. Okay."

Cary would have asked, *Okay, what*? But Travis just shrugged. "He's your little brother and you'd rather keep him around. I get it. But you'll give yourself a heart attack if you don't let some of it go. Trust me. I been there."

"You?"

"What, did you think I was Superman?" Travis laughed. "About a year ago, I had one. Stress." He pulled the wife beater up, showing a thick vertical scar that ran up his breastbone. "They cracked my chest and everything. Edy about finished the job when she found out."

"Lord," Lindsay breathed. "I didn't even know."

"I kept it quiet." Travis shrugged again. "Just make sure you don't have one yourself. I'd hate for anyone to have to deal with Cary's reaction if you got sick or hurt." He straightened and lifted a hand. "See you in a few hours."

"Yeah." Lindsay watched him go, then turned off the light.

* * *

Cary could barely move when he woke up the next morning. From what he could see without lifting his head, he was black and blue all the way down his left side, where he'd landed. He thanked everything that he hadn't bruised his right side and he could still lift his sword. Probably. Maybe.

If he could even reach his pills. They sat on the bedside table, just out of easy reach. He stretched, but he could just barely touch them. He tried to wriggle a little closer, but he couldn't even make a move without pain shooting through every muscle down to the bone.

"Lin," he called. "Lindsay!"

Travis opened the bedroom door. "Good Lord above. That horse didn't kick you, did he?"

"No. Just bruise easy." God, even turning his head to look at Travis hurt. "Where's Lin?"

"Making breakfast." Travis eyed him. "You want some water for them pills?"

"Yeah. Thanks."

Travis came back a minute later and set the water glass down, then started opening pill bottles. "How much?"

"Couple Tramadol and a couple Darvocet. One of everything else."

Travis nodded and counted out the pills. "Gonna help you sit up so you can take 'em. Don't argue, okay?"

Cary didn't argue. At least Travis helped him without giving him that awful sad-eyed, hurt look Lindsay was so good at, like he'd hurt Lindsay by getting hurt. He held his breath while Travis pulled him upright and stacked pillows behind him, but when he sat back against them, the pain drove the breath from him in a rush.

"You gonna let me check you over?" Travis asked. "You coulda broken a rib or something."

"I didn't break no rib." Cary took the pills as Travis handed them over and finished the glass of water. "Thanks."

"Sure." Travis stood. "I'll try to keep Lindsay from fussing too much, but you gotta be a little easy on him. He was real worried about you last night."

"I gotta do this. He'll just have to get over it." He'd do it just as soon as the pills kicked in, and maybe after he'd slept a little longer.

"What if he got knocked around like you did?"

Travis had a quiet, simple way of making a point that made him feel like an asshole sometimes. "Yeah, fine, I'd be fussing too," he said. "I'll be up in a little while."

"Sure. I got some of Edy's Lidoderm patches still. I'll send Lindsay in with 'em. He'll wanna bring you in food too." Travis gave him a little crooked smile. "Let him fuss a little."

Cary couldn't really complain about pain relief patches and food, so he let Lindsay take care of him for a little while. After he'd eaten, he fell asleep. He woke up once in a while to take another pill and Lindsay came in twice more to make sure he ate. He always intended to get out of bed but couldn't make himself. When he woke for good, it was morning again. He'd managed to sleep for a whole day, but at least it was a little easier to move after he'd loaded up on muscle relaxers.

He managed to get into his chair with Lindsay's help, but he couldn't even think about getting into the saddle. Instead, he spent most of the day on the back deck, practicing sword moves from his chair.

Emily called himCary early the next afternoon. "I'm sitting at the end of your driveway. How the hell did you create a circle of protection?"

"Guess we're just that special," Cary said. "What d'you want?"

"To talk about how we're going to work together."

"What makes you think we wanna work with you?"

"Maybe because you came to me about the horses. Are you going to let me in?"

"I'll think about it." Cary hung up and went to findcalled to Lindsay, who was outside in the yard with Sister. "Emily's parked on the road. Wants to come in."

Lindsay fiddled with the curry brush he was holding. "We should work with her, Care."

"We can keep working for Dad," Cary said, "What's wrong with that?'

"What the hell has Dad done for us since we left?" Lindsay's face twisted; he looked betrayed. "I cain't believe you'd rather work for somebody who hurt you so bad."

"Jesus, Lindsay, he's our *father*. What's that bitch ever done except drug me and drag me around?"

"You was all for working with them before he showed up!" Lindsay's voice broke. "Then he came in and now you just wanna do what he says. Like *always*." He sucked in a breath. "Sis, how do we let her in?"

"Use your will," Sister said.

"Dammit, Lindsay Jedidiah." Cary moved to grab Lindsay's arm, but Lindsay dodged him and walked around the house toward the driveway. The dome of magic arcing over their heads rippled, and a moment later Cary heard a car coming up the driveway. By the time Cary made it around the house, there was an opening in the perimeter of the dome, like a garage door.

Lindsay turned back. "We gotta at least talk to her. You wanna talk to Bella, right? Emily's got her."

He had to admit Lindsay was right, but he still wanted to smack him.

A dark green Malibu pulled up beside Lindsay's Explorer. "That's a hell of a piece of magic," Emily said when she got out. "How did you do it?" Her eyes settled on Cary and she added, "You look like you got mugged."

"We got the horses back," Cary said, ignoring her last remark.

"How?"

"We called them."

Emily leaned against the car, folding her arms. She didn't ask to come in and Cary didn't offer. "Well, good. One less thing. Look, if you're going to work with us, it's time we talked about some rules."

Cary hated that she just *assumed* they would play along with her, like she'd come here so they could beg for her favor. "If we decide to work with you."

"What's the problem? Listen, you might be special, but that doesn't give you license to run around doing whatever you want. What you do affects us, too. I can't spend all my time cleaning up after you. I'm trying to keep you hidden, or didn't you notice?"

"Why? I thought you said we was important and you wanted us as a symbol," Cary said.

"You saw what happened to Jerome and Bella. The same thing could happen to you if everybody knows about you. Magic users are always visible to other magic users, and the more powerful the magic, the harder it is to hide. You two are already walking around with neon signs over your heads."

Cary tensed. Dad had always taught them to lay low and not attract attention, that evil people would come after them if they did. And besides, it wasn't exactly great for a couple of gun dealers to be on people's radars.

"More reason for you to join us," Emily continued. "We can't keep a lid on your magic now that you've got the horses, but we can help keep you from getting into too much trouble."

"We'll work with you," Lindsay said. "We'll make guns for you."

Cary turned to his brother, furious. "*No*, we won't."

Lindsay's jaw tightened and he tried to glare back, but after a second he looked past Cary to Emily. "We wanna talk to Bella."

"See, it doesn't work that way. You have to work with us if you want us to give you anything," Emily said.

"You said the recorsas were for everybody," Lindsay said.

"She's under our protection."

"That's bullshit." Cary turned and pushed himself toward her. She didn't move quickly enough and his chair bumped against her knees. "We ain't playing this game. Go on home. We don't need nothing from you."

"Get off of me," Emily said, her hands balling into fists like she was going to hit him. He didn't flinch. "You're an idiot, pushing people away who can help you." She looked up at Lindsay. "You aren't going to say anything?"

"No," Lindsay said softly. "Reckon we'll take our chances."

"Get *off* of me," she said. Cary waited a few seconds just to piss her off, then backed away.

"This is ridiculous." Emily marched around the car and got in, slamming the door behind her. She barely gave Cary time to get out of the way before she whipped the car around, spraying gravel, and drove away.

"Care," Lindsay said. He was hugging himself, shoulders curled. "I wish you'd just…"

"Just what?" Cary felt bad, watching him bend in on himself like he did when somebody was mean to him. "What is it?"

"Never mind." Lindsay went back around the house.

* * *

The sun was beginning to creep into the gaps in the bedroom curtains when Lindsay's phone rang. He let it go to voice mail, too tired to answer, but whoever it was hung up and let it ring again.

"Hello." Lindsay didn't bother trying to make his voice sound pleasant.

"Your dad wants to see y'all." Wade. Lindsay felt more awake than he ought to after three hours of sleep.

"Why don't he call himself?"

"He's on the phone with your brother right now."

Lindsay cursed and threw the phone. It bounced off the opposite wall and the battery came out when it hit the floor. He didn't stop to pick it up.

"Yes, sir." Lindsay recognized that tone in Cary's voice. He sounded like an obedient dog, if a dog could talk, and he only ever sounded that way around Dad. Cary's cell flipped shut and Lindsay pushed open the bedroom door.

"He said you hung up on Wade."

"Yeah."

Cary sat up in bed and Lindsay didn't have to see in the dark to know what expression he was wearing. "I wanna go."

The air leaked out of his lungs a little. "Why, Care?"

"He's dying, that's why, for God's sake, and we ain't been to Harrison in five years. Don't you miss it?"

No, Lindsay wanted to say, *but I never did belong there like you.* "Do we even know why he wants us to come?"

"Does it matter? Lindsay Jedidiah, he's *dying*."

Lindsay closed his eyes. His jaw hurt from clenching it so hard. He wished Travis was closer, but he made it a policy to stay out of their brotherly business a long time ago after witnessing one too many knock-down drag-outs. "Last time he hurt you so bad."

"It don't matter. I can forgive him. You should too."

The thought of going back home made dread sit heavy in Lindsay's stomach, but if Cary really wanted to go, he'd go. "Okay. When does he want us?" Lewis always expected them to jump exactly when he said jump.

"Saturday at ten."

At least it was Saturday and he was off work. Not that Lewis would have cared if he wasn't.

* * *

Lindsay had griped at Cary that morning. He would always remember that.

Dad said he'd dreamed about a pure white buck, and he'd later seen it in the hills about twenty miles from home. The buck was a sign from God, he'd said, and they had to catch it to prove their worth. Like he'd ever think Lindsay was worthy of anything. Lindsay went along anyway, because what else could he do?

Lindsay hadn't been awake two minutes before Cary started whistling like it wasn't four in the morning. Cary couldn't do anything without making noise. Lindsay squinted into the lantern light to see Cary pulling on his camo overalls, the ones Dad had just bought him from Bass Pro up in Springfield.

"Shut up," Lindsay grumbled. "Why you gotta make so much noise all the time?"

"Why you gotta be such a bear in the morning?"

Lindsay snorted. "Like you're one to talk." Cary was usually liable to bite his head off for looking at him the wrong way in the morning. This hunting trip would be a good time for Cary. Lindsay would just have to listen to Dad tell him what he was doing wrong the whole time.

That was the thought he would always regret.

Cary blocked the light from the lamp for a blessed second, but it was only to lob something at him. "Cheer up."

Lindsay didn't move fast enough and a bundle of cloth hit his face. He picked it up before he realized he held the boxers Cary had been wearing the day before. "Dang it, Cary! That's nasty."

"What are you gonna do about it?" Cary knew he wouldn't do anything; that

was Lindsay, always just rolling over rather than taking Cary's bait. Sometimes he was no fun. Cary just snorted at him and caught the boxers when they flew back at him. "Hey, Lin."

"What?"

"You're gonna get that buck."

Lindsay gave him a little smile and got up to pull on his pants over the long johns he'd slept in. "Not if you get him first."

"Wanna bet on it?"

They shared a secret laugh. Dad had always preached against the sin of gambling and how it led to other, darker sins.

"Hurry up, boys." Dad's voice came from the main part of the house. He'd probably been awake for an hour already. Cary and Lindsay obeyed.

"Boots." Lindsay said.

"Over here." Cary tugged them out from under his bed. They shared the same two pairs; Cary had probably grabbed Lindsay's the last time he went outside, like he always did. He was too lazy to find his own. When Lindsay came over to grab them, Cary held them back and grinned at him. "Look how short you are."

Lindsay sighed. He was six foot two, taller than any man in the family except Cary. But Cary would never let go of the fact he was a couple inches taller. "You're wearing boots."

"So put yours on and let's see."

Lindsay tugged his boots on and stood next to Cary with his spine straight and his head up. Before Cary could gloat about it anymore, Dad appeared in the doorway.

"Well? Y'all ready?"

"Yes sir," they said together.

Wade waited in the kitchen. He handed them venison jerky to chew on the way. They pulled on coats, hats and gloves, grabbed their rifles and trouped outside to Dad's rust-red F250. Cary and Lindsay sat in the bed of the truck, trying to stay out of the wind and keep each other warm.

It was only November, but the weather had already settled into the kind of damp cold that promised a long, ugly winter. Normally during hunting season they would be worried about getting enough meat to feed the family, but Dad was dead-set on bagging the white buck first. "If we get him, boys, God will provide all we need forever." All Lindsay knew was that they would all go along with his wishes.

Lindsay's whole body was frozen by the time Dad stopped the pick-up about twenty miles from home. "Last time I seen him was north and west of here," Dad said. "About a mile and a half, down in a hollow that's bordered by a ridge on the east side. Wade, you take Lindsay. Y'all go south. We'll head north."

Lindsay and Wade nodded. Lindsay knew full well Dad intended to keep them from catching the buck if he could, but he wasn't about to invite Dad's wrath by pointing it out, either.

Cary gave Lindsay a look that said, You can get him. Lindsay tried to smile. He turned away from them before he allowed himself to think that at least he wouldn't have Dad hovering over him. Wade wasn't much better, but he only had half of Dad's overwhelming presence.

Cary felt warmer when they got moving, though the air was still damp. He'd never enjoyed the cold the way Lindsay did, so he pushed his body a little harder. He overtook Dad, but he knew Dad wouldn't mind. Dad was getting a little nearsighted and usually told him to track their prey when they hunted together, anyway.

It wasn't long before he spotted deer sign, but they had to get farther into the woods before he saw a lot of it. Every time he looked up at Dad, Dad shook his head; the sign didn't belong to the white buck. Cary had to wonder how he knew.

"You'll know, son," Dad said even though he was sure he hadn't asked the question out loud. "You'll feel the presence of God and you'll know that buck is nearby, just like I did. He's God's creature."

Cary wondered then if Dad had told Wade how to find the buck. Dad always pushed those two behind him and Cary, and they always put up with it.

After a while, Cary got impatient. He tried to focus, but he'd never been good at wandering around without knowing what he was looking for. He wondered what Lindsay was doing—probably still looking, dogged as he was when he was trying to please Dad.

But Lindsay and Wade had stopped ten minutes ago. They had reached a rise that overlooked an overgrown dry creek bed, the same bed that ran near the house. "Plenty of spots for deer to browse," Wade said. "We'll wait."

Lindsay looked at him, puzzled. Wade's lips pressed together in a flat line. "They're gonna by the ones to find that buck, Lindsay. You got to know it. We'll have work again soon enough when they do without wandering all across the damn country. We'll see if we can get us one to feed the family. Ain't nothing wrong with that."

Wade settled in one spot and waited. Lindsay didn't really think he was waiting for a deer to show up. Confused, Lindsay settled in beside him.

Cary sighed. "Dad—"

"There!" Dad said. "There, son. Don't you feel it?"

Cary paused, frowning. He felt nothing but the chill in the air and the sweat under his coveralls. But he knew he couldn't tell Dad that.

"Keep going. We're gonna find him."

The longer Lindsay sat, the more the understood why Wade had sat down. What were they looking for, anyway? Some white buck nobody else had seen. He knew as well as anybody pure white animals never lasted long in the wild. The chances of a white adult wandering around were too small to waste a day of hunting season on it. Sometimes he didn't understand Dad's visions or his preaching. Maybe God would feed them if they found the buck, but what if they didn't?

And anyway, if the buck was God's animal, why would he want them to kill it? Wouldn't He want it alive? They thought made Lindsay uneasy. Cary was convinced Dad was always on God's good side, but sometimes Lindsay wondered.

Cary did what Dad told him and kept following the trail he was on. There was something weird about it. The trail was almost too careful, as if it had been set up. Right, a deer would set up a false trail. He snorted at himself.

Then he saw it.

"Wade," Lindsay said, though he really had no idea what he wanted to say.

"We ain't gonna say nothing," Wade said. "Ain't gonna matter if they get that buck anyways."

Lindsay couldn't help but notice he said *if*.

The white buck shone in the dawn light like fresh snow against the brown winter foliage. Cary could swear he saw a flash of rainbow colors around it. The animal stood there for a second, ears perked, head turned in Cary's direction. Then it up and disappeared.

"Find it!" Dad hissed. "Where'd it go?"

For a second, Cary just stood there, the image of the buck burning into his mind.

Lindsay sighed and stared into the dry creek bed. No sign of a deer, white or not, anywhere nearby. Sure, Cary and Dad would get that buck. Why wouldn't they? They were always the types who got whatever they set out to get. He pictured Cary lifting his rifle toward the buck. The image of that thing was so clear in his mind. It stood with its head lifted, looking straight at Cary—straight at Lindsay.

"Cary!"

"Yes sir," Cary muttered. They crept forward to where he'd last seen the buck, moving as quietly as he could. It didn't take him long to spot that faint, careful trail, moving down the hill into a more heavily wooded area. Seeking shelter, like any deer. But Cary hadn't actually seen it move—it had just disappeared. How had it made a trail?

Stupid thought. He shook his head and started down the hill.

"You always gonna follow your brother?" Wade asked.

Lindsay blinked at him; he could think of nothing to say.

Wade sighed. "Sure you will. You're just like me. God help you."

That cold unease crept back into the pit of Lindsay's stomach. He said nothing.

Dad stayed at the top of the hill. Even now, the foliage was thick enough that Cary had to move slowly and carefully to avoid too much crunching and rattling. The loamy dead leaves smell rose from beneath his feet.

Shit. He'd been concentrating so hard on not making noise, he'd lost the trail.

Dad drew in a sharp breath. Cary could hear it as though Dad were standing next to him. He lifted his head and saw the buck standing bold as brass at the top of the small hill opposite them. This time, he was sure he saw a rainbow colors around its antlers.

Dad's gunshot split the air.

Wade's silence was starting to make Lindsay's skin crawl. He wanted to suggest that they find another spot to look if they wanted to bag a deer to take back as food, but Wade seemed content to sit here.

They heard a gunshot to the north a few minutes later, and Wade hauled himself to his feet. "That'll be them."

They walked back toward the truck to get the tarp and poles they'd use to carry the buck back, since Dad had insisted on carrying it back whole to preserve the skin. Wade was in no rush, loping along like usual.

They had almost made it back to the truck when they heard Dad's voice.

"Wade! Lindsay! Wade!"

Something in Dad's voice rattled him. It wasn't angry, or excited. It was... scared? Lindsay and Wade exchanged a look.

"Get the tarp and them poles! And rope! Move your asses!"

Dad came sprinting up the hill, gasping for breath. Lindsay obeyed automatically, making for the truck. Behind him, he heard Wade ask what was going on.

"He's hurt."

No need to ask who "he" was. Lindsay forced himself to run faster. He gathered up the tarp, the poles and the rope by the time Wade and Dad reached the truck. Wade took the rope and one of the poles.

"Lewis. What happened?" Wade asked.

"We was tracking the buck." That was all Dad got out before he made a sound like he was choking.

Images of flesh torn open by a buck's antlers flashed through Lindsay's mind, like somebody was showing him a grisly photo album. It had happened to other hunters, big bucks fighting back. Huge wounds gaped open, guts spilling out. Rather than Cary, he was picturing the dog he'd had growing up, who'd been killed by a nasty buck in rut.

"Lindsay." Wade shot him a look, his hand on Dad's shoulder.

Why Lindsay was expected to be the level-headed one, he didn't know.

As they hiked through the winter woods, Lindsay replayed his exchange with Cary that morning over and over, memorizing it, filling in the gaps his sleepy mind had forgotten. Cary's voice rang in his ears, teasing him, telling him he'd get that buck. Everything else was silent.

Lindsay didn't see Cary at first, or maybe his mind refused to see him. He heard Wade's, "Jesus!" But it took forever to see what he was talking about.

The blood gave him away.

There wasn't as much of it as Lindsay had pictured, just one big stain across Cary's back, soaking through his new coveralls. He lay face down in a bunch of brush; the only skin visible was the back of his neck and his hands. Just looking at him, Lindsay could tell something was wrong, really wrong. His body lay at an odd angle.

Nobody could move for what seemed like hours.

Cary made a noise. It wasn't much, just a grunt, but it was enough to unfreeze Lindsay's limbs. He stumbled the last few yards and collapsed onto his hands and knees, tossing the pipe he carried to the ground.

Cary's eyes were closed, or at least the eye he could see, and his face was a deathly blue-white. The mixed smells of piss and shit filled Lindsay's nostrils, and he felt himself begin to shake right down to his bones.

Somehow, he got his coat off and draped it over his brother's body. "Care." His voice sounded high and unsteady to his own ears. "Can you hear me? Where does it hurt?"

Cary's eye fluttered open. "I'm hurt, Lin," he whispered.

Lindsay put his hand on Cary's freezing-cold cheek. "I know. I'm here to get you out."

"Good." The eye closed again and Cary's body went slack.

A raw animal noise startled Lindsay as he scrambled to find Cary's pulse; he heard his own breathing, ragged and erratic, and realized he'd made the noise. Cary's pulse felt too fast and shallow, but it was there.

Behind him, Wade and Dad were rigging the stretcher out of a tarp, rope and pipe. Lindsay's mind struggled to think of what to do next. He couldn't panic, couldn't lose it. He had to be the level-headed one.

"Roll him," Dad said. "Do it gentle."

Lindsay moved Cary's other side and grabbed him around the middle. He'd barely lifted Cary's hip from the ground when Cary let out a low cry from deep in his chest. Lindsay cursed and let go. "What hurts, Care? What hurts?"

"Don't move me," Cary begged. "Just let me be."

Lindsay's throat tightened. "I'm sorry, brother. I got to. We got to get you to the hospital." He put his hand on Cary's hip again.

"Don't!" It was a scream, like a fiddle with a broken string. The sound froze Lindsay's bones and he couldn't force himself to do it, just knelt there. Paralyzed.

"Lindsay," Dad said behind him. "Turn him."

"It hurts him!"

"Do it!" Wade's scream this time, almost as harsh as Cary's.

Later, Lindsay would wonder why he had been forced to do it.

"I'm sorry," he choked out. "I'm sorry. I'm sorry."

As gently as he could, he turned his brother's half-limp body over—half-limp because his upper half was knotted in agony while the lower half flopped uselessly. Cary didn't scream any longer, but Lindsay wished he would instead of gasping breathless obscenities at Lindsay. All Lindsay could say was, "I'm sorry. I'm sorry."

"You curse, boy," Dad told Cary, though he hung back as Cary loaded him onto the stretcher. "You curse and fight if it helps."

"Fuck you," Cary breathed, and Lindsay choked on a hysterical laugh. He didn't think Dad heard Cary, but felt his glare on the back of his neck and knew Dad had heard him.

Eventually, Cary fell quiet; he might have passed out again, which was probably a blessing. He was the tallest one in the family and sturdy, and it was a long, cold hike. Lindsay had moments where he could almost forget he was carrying his injured brother. Almost.

Paralyzed.

Oh, God.

It took a lot longer to get back to the truck; they stopped when they absolutely had to rest. In spite of all the coats piled up on him—Dad and Wade had surrendered theirs, too—Cary was shivering so hard Lindsay could feel it through the metal pipes that made up the sides of the stretcher. Lindsay gave him sips of water because he figured it was a good idea. Neither Dad nor Wade offered any guidance. Wade bore the situation with the same grim resignation he bore everything, and Dad....

Well, truth be told, Dad looked almost as bad as Cary, pale-faced and strained. Later, when he had time to think about it, Lindsay wondered what he had been thinking about. Their brother Andy, maybe, who'd killed himself eighteen years ago, about Cary, or about himself. He wondered which mattered the most, and decided it was probably the last.

Every bone in Lindsay's body ached by the time they spotted the truck, and his knees felt ready to buckle. Cary didn't protest as they struggled to get him into the bed of the truck without jostling him too much.

The metal bed chilled Lindsay as soon as he sat down, and he couldn't imagine how much colder Cary was. He didn't dare try to move Cary again, so as Wade started up the truck, he lay on the tarp beside his brother, lending what little body heat he had left.

At first Cary didn't move a muscle; his face was twisted into a mask of pain, and twisted further as the truck bounced down to the highway. Lindsay clenched his teeth at the strangled, helpless cries that forced their way out of Cary's throat: Cary, who never let anyone know when he was in pain, betrayed by his own body.

"Jesus," Lindsay whispered. He put his arm around Cary's chest and pulled him as close as he dared to steady both of them. He grabbed one clammy hand

and held it, trying to warm at least that small part of his body.

Cary's head turned, just a little. When his eyes cracked open, they shone with wetness.

"Lin."

For a dumb moment, Lindsay just stared at him. No, this couldn't be his brother, his proud brother who always beat him when they fought because he played dirty, who was ornery enough to fling himself in front of a bull to keep it off Lindsay's back. Not this pitiful, whimpering creature, helpless as a half-dead newborn kitten. It couldn't be Cary.

But it was.

The wind that whipped Lindsay's face was colder than ever. He buried his face in Cary's shoulder and tried not to let Cary feel his sobs.

Chapter Ten

Chapter Ten | 135

Harrison hadn't changed much in the five years since Cary last saw it, but then, it had never changed much when they were growing up, either. The square seemed emptier than it had last time, and there were more new houses along Highway 7 South, but the place was mostly untouched. If anything, it seemed smaller and more desolate than he remembered, the streets too narrow and the buildings faded and worn, like people didn't care enough to keep them up. He felt like saying so, but he kept his silence, seeing Lindsay's expression. It cost Lindsay a lot to come here. Travis had offered to come with them, but Lindsay had refused. Better if he didn't have to deal with the family, but Cary had the feeling Lindsay would have felt a little better to have Travis along.

Home seemed like a longer drive from town than Cary remembered. The roads were a little better, but the dirt road that branched off the paved one looked exactly the same, steep and winding as always. Cary opened his window as they bounced along to smell the air. The recent rains kept too much dust from kicking up, and everything smelled fresh and woody.

They turned a bend to find a couple of kids playing in the road. As they drew closer, Lindsay said, "That ain't Justin and Leah, is it?"

It was. Cary remembered their youngest cousins as skinny little kids. Now they looked like puppies who hadn't grown into their paws. Leah came to Cary's window, her hands on her hips. "Uncle Lewis said we was to point you to the driveway. They changed it a while ago. You're Lindsay and Cary, ain't you?"

"You recognize us, don't you, squirt? I ain't got that old." Cary found himself smiling. She was definitely Becky's kid, sassy like her mama.

"You're a lot older than us," Leah said. Justin, a year or so younger and still shorter, pointed them toward the hidden driveway. Cary doubted he and Lindsay could find it by themselves anymore. He turned back to tell the kids to hop in, but they had already disappeared into the woods, just like he and Lindsay could do.

Once they found the track to the house, it wasn't that hard to follow. They bumped along another quarter mile till the woods opened up and the compound became visible. More reinforcements of barbed wire and scrap lumber built up the walls and, to Cary's amazement, wisps of magic interwove all of it.

"Do you...." Lindsay murmured.

"Yeah." He had no idea what that magic meant.

Wade came to open the gate; by rule, only the senior members of the family were allowed to do that. Inside, Cary couldn't see Dad immediately, but he saw the rest of the family. Aunt Betty in a crowd of chickens as always, Michelle wrangling the little kids, Kurtis lounging on the steps of his house, with Jon....

Cary's heart threatened to beat out of his chest. He swallowed and looked at Lindsay. "You ready for this?" asked, knowing neither of them were.

"Got to be."

"Praise Jesus!" Aunt Betty startled him when she appeared at the passenger's side door; she could move fast for a woman nearing 80. "Look at you boys! Get on out and give your Aunt Betty a hug."

Cary opened his mouth to reply, wondering if she remembered it wasn't that simple for him, but Lindsay whispered, "I got it." He slid out of the car and submitted to a hug from Betty while the rest of the family clustered around. Cary's mouth was bone-dry by the time Lindsay pulled his chair from the back seat.

The family fell dead silent. Only then did Cary realize none of them had seen him in the chair. The last time they had seen him, he'd just been hurt and sick.

Cary could do nothing but ignore it as he transferred to the chair, though his palm was so sweaty when he leaned on the door it almost slipped off.

"Lord God a'mighty," Betty said. "My poor boy. I'd thought...."

"Ain't so, Aunt Betty." Cary accepted her fierce hug, feeling guilty.

"Look at you all bruised up," Betty whispered. "What'd you get into?"

Cary couldn't help a little smile. She always asked him what he got into rather than what happened to him. "It ain't nothing. Ornery horse."

"What happened to you?" It was a little kid's voice; Cary didn't recognize it. He had just a second to pull himself together and come up with an answer.

"I wrestled a bear. You should see how he turned out."

The kid grinned and seemed satisfied with that answer. Michelle looked embarrassed, so Cary gathered he was one of her and Gene's brood.

"Y'all come to my place," Betty said once everyone had said their hellos, commenting on how good Lindsay and Cary looked even though, for his part, Cary knew that wasn't the truth. "Lewis has got that house so packed now."

Cary pushed himself as far as he could through the scrubby grass and muddy ground, but halfway there he got stuck and Lindsay had to push him. He felt stupid for forgetting how inaccessible this place was.

The ground wasn't the only trouble, either. Aunt Betty's house had a couple of rickety old steps leading up to it. Half the family watched as Lindsay struggled to pull Cary up backward.

The house only had one story, but wasn't much less cramped than Betty said Lewis's house was. The same knick knacks, papers and odds and ends crowded every surface, including the floor, and Betty had to move crates and boxes just so Cary could get into the living room. He hated seeing her bustling around like that, but she wouldn't let either of them help.

"I got you boys in the other room, just like when you was little," she said. "Remember that?"

"That'll be fine, Betty," Lindsay said.

Betty straightened from moving the coffee table to look at both of them. "I never thought to see you boys again. Praise God you're all right."

Cary felt like a low coward for looking away when he saw tears in her eyes. His chest ached with guilt. "I'm sorry, Aunt Betty."

"Well, now, there ain't no call for that." She put her hand on his cheek and he looked up, dutifully. "Don't think I don't understand, Cary. Now don't you fret. We'll get you right."

He didn't think he wanted to know what that meant.

"Your daddy will be back directly. Supper's ready in forty-five minutes over at Michelle's," Betty continued. "Y'all get settled in." The back door swung shut as she went next door to help cook supper.

"This ain't weird to you?" Lindsay asked. "It feels weird."

Cary nodded. 'Weird' was one word. He turned the corner, steeling himself before he pushed open the door to the back bedroom. It looked just the same: faded quilts, faded wallpaper, twin beds. A wave of nausea overcame him, looking at those quilts and that wallpaper. He'd spent three days in the bed on the right after he'd been injured, pissing and shitting himself and waiting for God to heal him.

He heard Lindsay's breath rattle in his chest and looked up. Lindsay's eyes were glazed over, and Cary knew he was remembering, too.

"Lin?"

"Huh?"

"Boys." Dad's voice startled him half to death. Damn, why was he so jumpy lately? Lindsay's face changed to that careful, thin-lipped expression as he turned.

"Good to have you home with me," Dad said. "About time, too. You glad to be back?"

"Yes sir." Cary had been able to let out some of his anger before, at the campground, but here at home, where Dad always ruled, he just couldn't. And maybe that was right. Dad still deserved their respect. "You're looking good." He looked like he'd slept more than they last saw him.

"I'm feeling good, with my boys home." Dad leveled a look at Lindsay. "You forgetting to shave, Lindsay?"

Cary remembered Travis remarking that he liked Lindsay with a little scruff. But Lindsay just said in the flat voice he used to talk to Dad, "Reckon so, sir."

"Both y'all could use a haircut, too," Dad said. "Never mind, there's time for that later. I want to talk to y'all about coming home for good. It's high time y'all did."

Cary tried not to wince. "Dad. I cain't. Not to live. None 'a these houses is accessible. Especially not the yard. It gets all muddy when it rains."

Dad leaned down and put his hands on Cary's shoulders, the way he used to, though Cary used to look up, not down. Dad stood too close and Cary's throat squeezed. "We're gonna fix you, Care. If it's the last thing I do on earth, I'm gonna make my boy well again. It was the devil that crippled you and we're gonna get it outta you. You gotta believe that." He straightened and looked at Lindsay. "We're gonna get you both fixed. And then you're gonna move home and we can all do the angel Tal's work. The whole family, together."

Cary started. Angel? "Dad—"

Dad just gave him that 'are you arguing with me?' look. All the breath left Cary and he forgot what he was going to say. Dad nodded. "Y'all get ready for dinner." He left, and Cary looked up at Lindsay.

"Care." Lindsay frowned down at him.

Cary felt a flash of irritation, and it was better than feeling like his chest was trying to cave in. "Well, what are we gonna do, leave? What would everybody think?"

Lindsay looked like he was about to say something, but he just pressed his lips together for a minute before he spoke. "You know what they're gonna do."

Cary turned his wheels toward the door. "Yeah. I know."

* * *

Lindsay helped Cary up the steps to Michelle's house, swearing to himself that if he could just find Aunt Betty alone, he'd pull her aside and tell her they were awful sorry, but they couldn't stay and they'd have to head back after dinner. He hated picturing her face when he told her, but he just couldn't let Cary stay here much longer.

He didn't get Betty alone, of course. Not even for a second.

The big hall where the family gathered to eat and pray was built off of Michelle's house, not because that family had any special status—that belonged to Lewis alone—but because the house was the only permanent building near the center of the compound. The other households lived in salvaged trailers or houses cobbled together out of whatever was available. Even the hall, which Lindsay and Cary had helped build as kids, looked rickety and unsound to Lindsay's construction worker's eye. He'd never thought that way when they'd lived here.

The tables were pushed together to create space for all twenty-something members of the family, kids included. Lindsay knew without being told that the chairs on either side of Dad were for them. No one, of course, had cleared a place for Cary's wheelchair. Before Lindsay could do it, Cary shook his head ever so slightly and transferred to the chair on Dad's right. The family members already settled watched him do it.

A few minutes later, Dad appeared. He had a hell of a sense of timing, always waiting until the minute when everyone went quiet, wondering where he was. "Let's everybody stand and say grace," he said once he was in his spot. One of the little kids whispered, loudly, to ask why Cary wasn't standing. Cary kept his eyes down, his jaw tight. Lindsay almost stayed in his chair, too, but stood when Dad gave him a look.

They all joined hands; Dad was on one side of Lindsay, Aunt Betty on the other. "Father God, we thank you for this food and for our many blessings. Thank you, Lord, for sending my boys home and seeing fit for them to redeem themselves in Your eyes. In Jesus' name we pray, amen."

Lindsay was almost certain he'd be sick if he opened his mouth, but he drew in a deep breath through his nose and managed to mouth "amen." Betty's nudge distracted him from his nausea.

"I'm okay, Betty," he whispered.

"Don't you go fibbing, Lindsay Jedidiah," she scolded him as they sat and the table erupted into talk. "You ain't all right. But we're gonna get you there."

Everyone wanted to know where Lindsay and Cary had been, what they'd been doing. Dad told the story like it was his own, and Lindsay had to admit he did a damn good job, considering he was telling it third-hand. The family seemed somewhere between fascinated and horrified by Lewis's descriptions of the city, full of sin and corruption, and the boys' lives living in the shadow of it. The way he talked, the entire world was to blame for Cary's paralysis and Lindsay's "sins with men." Lindsay wanted to crawl in a hole, and it sickened him to see something like some tiny spark of hope in Cary's eyes. Hope for what? For Dad's promised prayers to heal him?

Lindsay felt as lost as he ever had, watching Cary fall back under Dad's spell without resistance and barely any hesitation. Why the fuck had he agreed to bring Cary down here?

"Y'see, family, these boys is gonna do what I always said they was gonna do," Dad was saying, "They're gonna be real warriors of God. This evil world wants to purge itself of sin and corruption and weakness, and Cary Judah and Lindsay Jedidiah are gonna make that happen." He only ever called them by their middle names when he was yelling at them or telling them what they were going to do. "The Rapture is coming, family. Y'all know I been having dreams and visions my whole life, and it's all been leading up to this. I swore to God I would raise these boys up to be holy warriors, and here they are. Y'all, they're gonna work for an angel. And we can, too, all of us. I ain't got long left in this world…." A soft, pained moan rippled through the crowd, but Dad hushed them with a gesture. "I ain't got long left in this world. But if my death is the price I got to pay to make sure my princes stand at the right hand of the angel and lead God's army to the Rapture, then I'll pay it gladly."

Dad turned to look at Lindsay and Cary now. "Boys, I done made my peace with God. I told Him I would give my life to see y'all do this, because I know I'll see y'all soon enough in Heaven."

Lindsay was numb. He knew he should feel something, but he couldn't even guess what it was. Work for an angel. What on earth did that mean? Maybe it didn't matter; he'd heard that kind of craziness from Dad before. He could only stare at Dad until Dad stared back. "You don't doubt, do you, Lindsay?"

"No sir," he murmured. No, he didn't doubt Dad meant exactly what he said.

"Clear the tables and move 'em," Dad said. "Send the kids out. We're gonna take care of my boys."

When Dad stood and stepped away, Cary's eyes followed him. Lindsay couldn't even remember what he just ate, but he wondered if he would see it again, he felt so sick.

Lindsay had no choice but to help the men move the heavy tables, all but one, to the end of the hall despite his churning guts. The one left in the middle was for Cary, he knew. After the accident, Lindsay had hauled poor Cary onto that table three times, once every day. The entire family would pray over him, some staying near, some filing past, their hands on his chest and his forehead, for hours. Lindsay just hoped Cary had been too sick to remember it now.

But then Lindsay caught sight of his brother's face, deathly pale as he stared at the table. As awful as it was to remember Cary lying there, sweat-soaked, his face twisted and his body limp, how much worse must it be to remember lying there, defenseless?

And you're making him do this, Lindsay thought, You're all making him do it.

But was Lindsay any better, not stopping it? Could he, even? How?

"Lindsay Jedidiah." Aunt Betty's voice was soft, but it still startled Lindsay a little.

"Yes'm."

Betty's eyes, Delaney green, focused on Cary. Cary sat watching the others move the tables, his face dead.

"Lindsay," she whispered. "There ain't no making our Cary walk again, is there?"

Lindsay stared at her. No ma'am."

Betty gave him a look Lindsay would remember forever. He couldn't process it before she turned away, hobbled several steps toward Dad and fell over.

* * *

Aunt Betty was nearing eighty and the fall scared even Dad. The prayer circle turned into fussing over Aunt Betty, and that went on for the rest of the day. To Cary's astonishment, not only did Betty finally admit maybe she ought to get looked at by a doctor, Dad agreed immediately. Nothing would do but Aunt Betty's boys take her into town.

They weren't even halfway down the dirt road yet before Betty started in on them.

"Now, I know you ain't a pair of fools, so why y'all would want to come back here I got no idea. There ain't nothing for y'all here. Nothing, you hear me?"

"But Betty, everything Dad said," Cary began.

"I'm an old woman, Cary Judah, and I can tell the truth even when it's mixed up in lies. I don't think y'all can, at least not yet. Till that happens, I don't want y'all getting pulled back here where everything blinds y'all."

Cary wondered if she wasn't a little senile. "This is home. Why wouldn't we come back?"

Betty twisted in her seat to look back at him. "Ain't you heard what I said, boy? I know our Lin's a little slow to pick up the hammer sometimes, but I ain't never known you to be. Surely you didn't damage your brain, too."

This was the side of Betty Cary hadn't seen since they were teenagers, when they'd somehow managed to sneak home raging drunk. She'd waited until they were good and out, then thrown armfuls of angry chickens at them to wake them. She'd chewed them up one side and down the other until it was time to get up for training at oh-dark-thirty.

"No ma'am," Cary said.

"No ma'am what?"

"I didn't damage my brain."

"Good. Then y'all can drop me off at my friend Joyce's house and go on back to Springfield."

Lindsay glanced at her from the driver's seat. "But—"

"Y'all don't think I can handle the family? I'm getting there but I ain't senile yet. I'll tell Lewis I sent y'all back home to your city lives. You ain't ready to receive the Lord and that's the stone truth."

"He won't be happy to hear that." Cary could hear the note of caution in Lindsay's voice.

"Y'all let me worry about that."

Betty's friend lived in Harrison proper. When Lindsay came around to help her get out, she said, "I don't want to see y'all come crawling back just because it's comfortable and you know it. Serving God ain't never about being comfortable." She got out, then opened Cary's door to give him a hug and a kiss. "God bless you, Cary Judah. I don't want to see y'all come back home, you hear?"

"Yes ma'am," Cary said before he realized exactly what he was agreeing to. Never go home.

Chapter Eleven

Cary found it impossible to concentrate in class the next day. He'd gotten maybe an hour and a half of sleep, tossing and turning.

Never go home. He still didn't understand why Betty had asked that of them, but she'd always looked out for them, did kind and thoughtful things for them. She knew what was good for them.

But she'd never spoken against Dad before now, or said they shouldn't be around him.

He heard Dad's voice too. Work for an angel. He'd always said they'd stand at God's right hand someday, but something about his tone made Cary think this time he meant sooner rather than later. Cary wondered if Dad knew about magic, what Cary and Lindsay could see and feel and do. But there was that magic sparkling on the compound's wall. He wondered what that meant.

A couple of times in class, he noticed Jessie glancing toward him. That didn't help. He hadn't talked to her since she'd come to see him. He just didn't know what to say. Normally he wouldn't bother; he'd tell himself it was her problem and not worry about it. But he *liked* Jessie too much to walk away like that.

He didn't realize class was over until everyone started to get up and leave. He heard Ms. Brown calling his name; judging by her voice, it wasn't the first time she'd called him.

"Everything okay?" She asked. She was one of those teachers who noticed if you were gone or not paying attention, and he felt a little guilty for zoning out. He liked her and liked the class.

"Just had a rough week. Didn't get much sleep last night. Sorry."

She wasn't completely fooled, he could tell, but she wasn't one to push, either. "Okay. Just make sure you get notes from somebody from Thursday. I'm sure Jessie could help you out."

That was her way of asking what was going on between him and Jessie. Was it that obvious? "I'll get 'em from somebody," he said, not really in the mood to talk about it.

Jessie was waiting in the hall. She hugged her books to her chest, which made her look like a little kid. Too much to hope she was waiting for Ms. Brown and not him.

"I'm really worried about you."

Guilt churned in his stomach. He stopped several feet from her. Instead of saying something kind like he knew he should, his mouth ran away from him. "That's why you broke up with me, huh?"

She looked away, her face pinched. "God, Cary."

"Shit. I'm sorry. I'm an asshole." He'd promised himself he'd never treat her badly, and he'd been doing exactly that.

"No, I deserved it." Jessie sighed. "Maybe I don't have any right to ask, but are you okay? You look really…tired and upset."

No right to ask? What in hell gave her that idea? He heard his conscience—Lindsay's voice, always—tell him that *he* had. He swallowed and tried to come up with a neutral answer that would make her feel better but wouldn't invite more questions. "Rough week."

"Are you in trouble?"

The question startled him, though he couldn't say why. He used Ms. Brown's exit from the classroom as an excuse to hesitate. She wanted him to be more open. Okay. But about this? What could he say?

"I dunno," he admitted. "Not legal trouble. It's hard to explain."

"You haven't been home in a while."

"Been staying with Travis."

"Your life is really complicated."

A laugh escaped before he could contain it. "You got no idea."

"No, I don't. I never have." She frowned. "But I want to."

He blinked. What was she getting at? "Trust me, you don't. *I* don't want nothing to do with all this."

"But you have to deal with it. I care about you. Why can't you let me help?"

"You cain't help this, Jess." He tried to get her to meet his eyes, but she kept looking away. "This is something me and Lin gotta deal with on our own. I'm not gonna drag you into it."

"Why won't you let someone else help you and care about you?" she said. "Lindsay's not the only person in the world who can do that, Cary. He *shouldn't* be the only person responsible for that. It's not fair to him or to other people who love you."

That brought him up short. "What?"

"You are so dense sometimes. I could love you if you'd let me. Maybe I don't know what you're going through, but that's only because you never tell me. I try to help you, can't you see that? And maybe I can't solve your problems, but I can support you. You don't always have to go through things on your own."

His first reaction was to say, *I'm not alone—I've got Lin.* But maybe she was right. Was that fair? He knew how hard he was to live with. Lindsay did it and never complained, never took a break, but that didn't mean he didn't deserve one. Besides, she'd been so good to him, dealt with him the same way Lindsay did. Why couldn't he trust her like he trusted Lin?

Why was he even *considering* this? "Jess, if I told you what's going on, you'd think I done lost it. And anyway, people are getting hurt. The less you know, the better."

"The better for who? You?"

"You," Cary said. "It ain't safe for you to know."

"What if I don't care? I'm a big girl. Let me be the judge of whether I can handle it or not."

"Did you not hear what I just said? People are getting hurt. No." Cary turned down the hall away from her. He hated being harsh with her, but there was no way he could bring her into this. It was one thing with Travis, who at least knew how to take care of himself. Jessie didn't even like guns.

"Are you really afraid of me getting hurt or are you just afraid to let me in?"

"Listen, Jess, it's not you."

"Right. It's you. But I really don't get why you're punishing me for whatever's going on."

Something in him gave way. Maybe he was just tired, or maybe she had a point, or maybe he remembered what it was like being kept in the dark. He didn't want to tell her any of this craziness, but maybe he should.

He sighed. "Okay."

"I'll drive you back. Are you going to Travis's?"

Cary nodded and followed her out to her car, trying to decide what he'd tell her first. There was really no good place to start.

"We found out something," he said as they pulled out of the student parking lot. "We have a younger sister. Name's Emily."

"You *what*?" Jessie stopped at a light and turned to face him. "Holy shit. How'd you find out about her? Have you met her?"

"Dad told us. After she tracked us down. If she tries to look you up, too, she's full of shit. She and anybody with her. She ain't done nothing good for us."

"That's awful. What's she done?"

"Lied. Tried to keep us from finding out what's going on. That's sort of a theme." It *did* feel sort of good to unload, at least a little bit. Maybe he didn't have to share the craziest parts, but he didn't realize just how much the family issues were bothering him till he started talking about them. "That's part of why I ain't told you nothing. We don't know much. A lot of it don't make sense."

"Well, maybe I can help you figure it out."

Cary doubted it, but it was a nice offer. He wondered why he hadn't trusted her with at least some of this before. "Best if you ain't driving when I tell you more."

"Just how crazy and off-the-wall *is* this?" Her voice was light, but he heard a note of concern in it that warned him to be direct or stop talking.

"Not much crazier'n I usually am," he said.

"Seriously. Does this have anything to do with how you grew up?"

He hadn't told her anything about the Delaney family's compound or how they'd spent their childhood or Dad's mission to fight his way into Heaven, but Lindsay had told Amy one night while drunk, and of course Amy had told Jessie. She'd gone to Cary with her usual understanding and sympathy, and he'd carefully not told her that he thought Dad had been right about a lot of things. He'd learned a long time ago that what passed for normal in the Delaney family was anything but normal to the rest of the world.

"I really don't know. Sometimes I think it might." It was the most honest thing he'd said to her so far.

"Wow. I'm sorry. I know how hard you fought to get away from all that."

Not that hard, he thought.

"Yeah. Listen, I just wanna make sure I'm not gonna completely freak you out."

"I want to know. It would be really shitty of me to find out and then run because I asked you to tell me the truth. I'm not going anywhere."

He had to admire her bravery, but he hoped she wouldn't have cause to regret saying that. "Well. Okay."

"So tell me."

"Now?"

"Why not?"

So he told her. Almost everything. He talked about the World Tree and the people who studied it, tried to preserve it and deal with the fallout when things went wrong. He talked about what they'd discovered about magic and the fact that they were supposed to figure out what was wrong with the Tree. He told her a little about what had happened at the hospital, especially the part where the nurse had called them princes. He hadn't intended to tell her that much, but when she didn't visibly freak out, he just kept talking. He didn't mention the horses or their visit home, though he couldn't have said why.

By the time he'd finished, they were pulling into Travis's driveway. She stopped in front of the house, put the car in park and looked at him again. "Prince Cary."

He couldn't read her tone or her expression. "I guess."

"So you believe all this?"

"I seen it. Still see it, every minute. I gotta believe it."

"Well. Don't take this the wrong way, but do you think maybe the way you were brought up might make…um, well…."

"Make me more gullible?" Cary lifted his eyebrows, trying and failing to not to be irritated. "Maybe, but I see what I see, Jess. And I ain't the only one. You can believe it's true or not—"

"I was just asking. You can see why."

Cary sighed. "Look, I thought they were screwing with us at first. I cain't explain this well enough. Maybe you'd just have to see it. But it makes sense, don't it, everything about the Tree?"

"I can see how it makes sense," she said carefully.

"Forget it, if you're gonna go all social worker on me. Will you get my chair, please?"

"I don't mean to. I'm just trying to understand." Jessie got out as Travis came around the house, rifle in hand. He lowered it immediately when he saw Jessie, but she gave a little shriek and put her hands up.

"Miss Jessica," Travis said, nodding. "Sorry 'bout that. Ain't no way to greet a guest." He leaned the rifle against the house, looking sheepish.

"It's okay," Jessie said, though she sounded uncertain. When she turned away, her eyes still wide, Travis grabbed the rifle and went back around the house.

"Sorry about that," Cary says. "I reckon he's a little jumpy." He was awful at comforting anybody, especially her. She leaned against the car for a minute, then turned to give him a look.

"Does he know anything?"

"He's seen some, guessed more. Before you asked, we didn't have much choice but to come here at the time," Cary said.

"And he's okay with it?"

"I reckon. He pretty much takes things as they come."

"I guess I can't do any less." She gave him a half-smile that surprised him with its sweetness.

"Sorry I've been an asshole," he said.

She shrugged. "I've sort of gotten used to it."

Ouch.

"That ain't what I want you to have to do." He reached out to squeeze her hand. That half-smile came back.

"I appreciate that. What are you up to tonight?"

"Reckon we'll go riding. Finish up some homework. Can I get your notes from Thursday?"

"You can ride? Like, on a horse?"

Damn. He hadn't meant to give that away. "Yeah, sure. I told you I did some therapeutic riding a few years ago. Back at it."

"Cool. I'd like to see that sometime."

Warning bells went off in Cary's head. He couldn't imagine what danger

Jessie could pose to Cooter and Sister, but that felt like exposing the most private part of himself.

"But you'd rather I skipped out and quit bugging you to share," she said, apparently noticing his hesitation. "It's okay. I'll just see you in class Thursday. Or you can call me before."

What in hell did he do to deserve such an understanding, tolerant girl? "I'll call you."

"You better." She gave him a rough pat on the cheek, then leaned down to kiss him, catching him off guard. "Thank you. For sharing."

"Really?"

"Really." She straightened. "Well, have a good night."

"You got that girl wrapped around your finger," Travis said from the doorway as Jessie's car pulled down the driveway.

"I do?"

"Like you don't know." Travis picked up the rifle and turned away. "You Delaney boys are good at that."

"What's that mean?"

Travis just shook his head and went back inside.

* * *

After Cary spilled most of their story to Jessie, it was only fair that Travis should know too. He took the full explanation well, or so Lindsay thought. He blinked a couple times at the mention of magic, but took it with the same good grace he took everything.

"Explains a lot" was all he had to say. "Them horses never did seem normal. Neither did you, really." He gave a ghost of a smile and met Lindsay's eyes. Lindsay felt himself returning it, and caught Cary's curious look out of the corner of his eye.

Lindsay waited until they were alone to tell them about the visit home.

"Hell. Lindsay."

Something about Travis's face, creased with concern, made Lindsay crumble. He put his head in his hands and squeezed his eyes shut. "Trav, he's poison. Cary's still got his venom and it won't go away. Now he's talking about us working for an angel and he's got Cary eating outta his hand again."

"He's poisoning you too, y'know."

Lindsay looked up and opened his mouth to protest, to say that no, he always had it better than Cary; at least he was pushed aside and mostly ignored by Lewis. But Travis put a hand on his arm and squeezed hard.

"No, listen to me. He done just as wrong by you. I see it, Lindsay. I seen it since the first day I met you, how bad you hurt. Cary wasn't the only one who got hurt, now or then."

Lindsay looked away, forcing tears back. Travis sat back and kindly dropped the subject.

"Anyway, you don't got to worry about staying here. It's okay."

"It's not, though." Lindsay grabbed Travis' hand before he realized what he was doing. "You didn't ask to get dragged into this, but here you are anyway."

"Lindsay Delaney, I asked for it when I offered to help you out when we first met." Travis met his eyes, his gaze steady behind those pretty lashes. "I reckoned what I was getting into."

"You knew about this?" How could Travis have known? Was he one of Emily's people? Lindsay started to draw away, betrayed.

"Hey. It's okay." Travis's fingers tightened around his. "I couldn't a guessed all the magic stuff. But y'all ain't never been average." The corner of Travis's mouth tugged upward. "That's kinda what I liked about you. Didn't you know that?"

Lindsay ducked his head and flushed. "No."

"Well, it is." Travis leaned forward again. "Anyway, what Cary does is his choice. I reckon he knows what he wants to do and how."

"He wanted to make something of himself," Lindsay said.

"Well, now, and he ain't? From what y'all told me, that might be important."

"So this magic stuff's more important than real life?"

Travis shrugged. "Maybe the magic stuff is your real life now. Seems to take up an awful lot of your time."

There was something in Travis's tone that made Lindsay pause. "We ain't forgot you."

Travis made a dismissive gesture. "Did I say you did? Maybe I just want to do more to help y'all."

"More to help us? Man, you're letting us live here."

"Sure, but maybe there's something else."

Lindsay's face and neck flushed. "We don't even know what we're doing yet."

Travis shrugged and averted his eyes. "Well, y'know, if you figure it out—" He brushed his hands across his knees and rose. For a minute, Lindsay's voice stuck in his throat, but then he blurted,

"Trav."

Travis stopped.

"That wasn't...." Lindsay cleared his throat. "Wasn't a no. To...y'know."

Travis's eyes widened. "No shit?"

Lindsay couldn't help but laugh. Travis cussing was like hearing an old lady cuss. "Yeah."

"Okay then."

Lindsay was unprepared for Travis's kiss—though, he thought, that made it even nicer. They didn't touch except their lips. Lindsay wanted to grab him, but he didn't know if Travis would welcome it. As soft and as tentative as it was, though, the kiss sent little sparks through Lindsay's body, and he felt the hairs on the back of his neck rise. When Travis pulled away, Lindsay looked away, his face flushed.

"Thanks" was the only thing Lindsay could think to say.

"Sure." Travis gave him a sideways half-smile. "You should get some sleep."

Lindsay wanted to reach out to him, to pull him back, but Dad's words crept into his mind. *Sins with men.* He couldn't make himself move, couldn't even speak.

* * *

After a ten-hour work day, Lindsay was jealous that Cary could fall asleep in the car on their way back to Willard. Lindsay could barely remember sleeping at all the past few nights, and he'd only eaten because Travis made him eat. They'd already spent the profits from the gun sale to Emily on medical bills and the house payment and debt collectors and fixing a bad oil leak in the Explorer. Lindsay's part-time salary and Cary's disability check didn't go far. Being in the outside world hadn't gotten any easier in five years even with Travis's help. Lindsay didn't know how people could want so much money from them all the time.

When he rode Sister, though, all that fell away. He knew he belonged on her back, riding through the dark fields behind Travis's house with Cary at his side, where he could feel the magic dance across his skin. It was easy to forget everything else.

At Cary's suggestion, they made a circuit of the property, checking the loop of magic. Tired as he was, Lindsay let his mind drift until he was almost dozing. If he'd been paying attention, he thought later, he might have noticed something strange a little sooner.

"*Lindsay.*" Sister turned her head to look at him. The first thing that occurred to him was that she'd never used his name before.

"What?"

"*Feel.*"

Cary had stopped too, and was looking around. Cooter nearly unseated him when he began to prance, and Cary turned to face forward again. Lindsay reached out automatically to steady him, then urged Sister closer and grabbed Cary's arm.

His vision blanked for a second, but then the entire world flared into life, bright as day. He could see the rivers of summer-green magic flowing the nodes, but he could see every tiny trickle that branched out from the rivers, every tree and blade of grass and into the horses' legs. He could see the glimmers of red shifting in the trees and the brush, maybe little animals. He could feel them, too, like bugs crawling over him. Of course, he could see and feel Cary, bathed in gold. He outshone them all.

All except one.

The figure stood in the middle of one of the rivers of magic they'd tapped to make the circle, overlapping it. Lindsay's magic-sense felt the interruption like a hand stuck into the flow of water; except the water didn't keep flowing around it. The magic flowed through the figure, like a sieve. The figure itself looked like something Lindsay had seen in a book once, something from mythology, half-man and half-horse. It looked like it stood in the middle of a rainbow whirlpool, all the colors swirling around it.

It looked like an angel.

Lindsay felt Sister shifting under him, though whether she was excited or uncomfortable, he couldn't tell. He put his free hand on her neck to reassure her, gripping the reins still in case she spooked, but kept his other hand on Cary.

"You want answers," the figure said; impossible to tell whether it was male or female from its voice. Lindsay had the sense it wasn't speaking English, but he could understand it as clearly as he understood Sister. "Come with me."

Lindsay somehow managed to tear his eyes away to look at Cary. His brother was wide-eyed, eyes shining as bright a green as the magic beneath them. Lindsay knew there was no question about whether they would follow.

* * *

The horses moved forward without any encouragement, their ears pricked toward the other rider—or maybe the other horse. If Cooter or Sister were tall, that one was gigantic, eighteen hands or more. It was built like a warhorse, or what Lindsay thought a warhorse would look like. Cooter was an impressive example of a stallion, but that horse made him look skinny and juvenile. Instead of pure white, like Cooter and Sister, the horse was brushed with gray, like smoke touching its flanks and shoulders. Sister shook a little, barely enough to feel, and Lindsay wondered why.

He looked down at his hands on the reins and realized he was shaking, too. His heart raced, though his emotions felt oddly blank. Once Cary had released his arm, he as he always did, mostly blind in the darkness except for the dim glow of the magical web. He'd learned to trust Sister's night vision and his other senses, too. He could hear Cary and Cooter and feel them a couple feet to his left, could hear the owl that lived near the field and the breeze in the grass and the trees. He could smell the clean scent of hay bales nearby and Sister's weird non-smell. He could feel the weight of the clothes on his shoulders.

The longer they followed the other rider, the more he—or she?—eclipsed Lindsay's senses. Even if he couldn't see the other rider, Lindsay could *feel* his presence weighing upon him.

Lindsay's inner compass told him they were about a mile and a half northwest of the house. He twisted to see if the house lights were still in sight, but they had just come over the crest of a hill, and he saw nothing. When he felt the tingle of a node, he turned back and gasped.

The breeze had stopped, leaving heavy silence hanging in the air. Instead of the rolling cow pastures behind Travis's house, they rode down a wide cobblestone boulevard lined with trees and street lamps. The scene was bathed in twilight, the colors muted and the contrast dull.

The web of magic reappeared. He could see magic now even without touching Cary. The horses loped along a wide, deep river of magic that glowed the deepest green he'd ever seen. He could see Cary's shining form and the other rider's, too. Lindsay guessed the rider was male by the width of his shoulders. He was dressed in some kind of dark cape or something, embroidered with a silver tree. His horse–and the others, too, Lindsay realized—shone the same green as the river, almost blending in.

For a few minutes, they rode in silence, too shocked to say anything. Cary recovered first.

"Where are we?"

"The aether. Between realms," the rider said. "What do you see?"

"A street. A big wide street with cobblestones, like I seen in history books. It's empty, but there's magic everywhere. The street's over a like a river of it or something."

The figure nodded. "And you?"

"Same." Lindsay said. "The horses look different."

"You see them as they really are." The rider stopped. "We, and they, are the only things that appear as they really are in this place. Everything else you see is fabricated, because our minds required structure. Nonetheless, I think you will find this place real enough."

He sounded sort of like Sandor with the tone that said he knew a lot more than they did. The rider turned toward them, and Lindsay thought he could pick out vague facial features.

"Are you an angel?" Cary blurted.

The figured laughed. "Hardly. I am what you may become."

Lindsay had no idea what that meant. "Why'd you bring us here?"

"This is where you belong." The figure waved a hand. "Welcome, princes. Now, come with me and your many questions will be answered."

Sister started forward without prompting. Lindsay wondered if he could stop her. He looked over at Cary; he could see his brother's features clearly now, his eyes wide and his face tense with eagerness. Lindsay chewed his lip, unsure. They might be walking into a trap. Especially if Dad knew about this person ahead of time. Maybe he'd even set it up.

"Lin," Cary hissed. "C'mon."

"Care, I dunno."

"Come *on*." Cary gave him a pleading look. "This might be what we need. Somebody who can tell us things."

The pleading broke Lindsay down. All he could do was sigh and turn Sister to follow the waiting horseman.

They rode across a bridge toward a house that looked like a castle. Lindsay saw no one at first, but in the shadow of the gate as they drew closer, he spotted three people. They weren't nearly as bright as Cary or the other rider, and the light surrounding them was sort of yellow. They bowed simultaneously, and one came forward to stand at Lindsay's right.

"I will take her, prince." A male voice. He reached for the reins. Lindsay kept hold of them.

"Don't worry. They are grooms, meant to care for the horses," the other rider said. "You can follow them to their resting place if you like."

Grooms, like Jerome? Lindsay put his hand on Sister's neck, still hesitating. Sister looked back at him. "It is all right."

He didn't want to leave her, but she shifted her weight impatiently and tossed her head, urging him. He swung down from her back and handed the reins to the groom, then looked up at Cary, whose face was pinched and his hands tight on his own reins. Lindsay knew why.

"My brother—"

"I cain't dismount," Cary broke in. "Unless you got wheelchairs and a sidewalk here."

The other rider, who had already handed off his horse to the third groom, folded his arms. "I don't understand."

"I'm a paraplegic. My legs don't work. I cain't walk." Cary's voice had an edge to it that told Lindsay he was getting testy.

"I see. Your physical ability should not matter here. As I said, all of this is fabricated. You could do anything."

Lindsay's heart jumped. Cary, walking again, even if it was only in this place? But Cary wore a look that made him resemble Lewis an awful lot.

"I take that to mean you ain't got wheelchairs."

The rider shook his head. "Once we are in my place, you may create one. I will summon a litter to bring you to the manor."

"I will take him," Cooter said.

The figure looked a little amused by what Lindsay could see of his features. "Will you. Szabolcs, isn't it?"

"Cooter," Cary and the horse said simultaneously.

"Very well. I see you are not accustomed to the courtesies of rank, Prince Cary, so I will indulge you." There was an unspoken *for now* in his tone. The grooms led Sister and the other horse away, and Cooter looked as smug as Cary did when he came out of an argument victorious.

Lindsay walked beside them, glancing up at his brother. "Maybe you *could* walk," he whispered.

Cary ignored him, faced forward. He had brushed off every mention of walking again. But why? If it was a possibility, why not try it? Was he embarrassed to try in front of everyone? Maybe he would try later, if Lindsay encouraged him a little.

"You know us," Cary said. "What's your name?"

"Tal," the figure said.

Lindsay heard Cary's sharp breath beside him, but he felt numb the way he had when they'd gone home. Lewis had talked about someone named Tal. An angel. And he was *right*.

"Are you an angel?" Cary asked.

The figure's laugh sounded too sharp in the still air. "No, I am no heavenly creature."

Maybe Lewis wasn't right about everything. Maybe. But it would be a hell of a coincidence if this wasn't the same person.

"I am fortunate to have found you at last," Tal said. "I would have liked to have been the ones to introduce you to magic and to horses, but it seems you've already done a fair job of introducing yourselves. Or did you have someone to teach you?"

Lindsay thought of Sandor and Emily—not exactly teachers, but they certainly had provided an introduction. But Cary said, "We did it our own selves."

"Well, then. We will complete your training, and you will become táltosk."

"I thought we already was that," Cary said.

"Soon, you will be" was the non-answer.

Beyond the gate, the forest closed in. The path they wound through looked like the dirt roads back home, with steep banks and reddish dirt. A mix of pines, oaks, elms and maples hid the house Lindsay had seen. He'd thought it was close to the gate, not down a winding road. Then, he started to recognize things. The lightning-struck tree on the right, the spring up ahead that made one part of the room a perpetual puddle.

"Care," he said.

"You have a gift, prince Cary," Tal remarked. "Already you are creating order out of chaos. What are we seeing?"

"The road home," Cary said. "Where we used to live. But what about that—"

"The manor? We will get there soon enough. When we came through, you did not know what to expect, so you saw what I showed you, something that is familiar to me. If I wanted to, I could force you to see it again, but I was interested to see what you could do if I let you."

Cary looked down at Lindsay. Lindsay shrugged, clueless.

"I will try to explain it more later," Tal said, looking back at them. "Now, I need you to let go so I can show you how to get back to the manor."

Lindsay had no idea how to 'let go,' but when he pictured the house again, there it was, separated from them only by a rolling green field, glittering with dew.

Beside him, Cooter began to pull against the reins. Cary cursed and tried to pull him in a tight circle like he would a normal horse, but Cooter just spun and kept showing out more and more agitated. Lindsay reached to grab Cooter's hackamore, but Cary snapped, "No!" He glared down at the horse. "What the hell is your problem?"

"You won't let go," Cooter said.

"I don't even know what the hell you're talking about that. Calm down or you'll throw me, you fool."

Cooter stopped prancing, though he looked ready to shy at any little thing. "Let go."

"*How*, dammit?"

"You still see the road from before," Tal said. "You won't let me show you. Your horse can see what we see; trust him."

"Touch me," Cooter said.

Cary's hands shifted; Lindsay knew he was reluctant to let go of the reins in case Cooter decided to show out again. Though he'd probably get griped at, Lindsay grabbed the reins. The stallion glared at him, but stayed still.

Cary put one hand on the side of Cooter's neck, and after a few seconds, the tension went out of the horse. For a minute, anyway. He moved to bite and Lindsay pulled away.

"You are not good at following another's lead," Tal said. "You'll have to learn how to do that." Without another word, he led the way straight across the lawn, leaving parallel streaks in the grass where he passed. Exactly like the real world.

When they neared the top of the slope near the house, Lindsay could see parts of the rest of the property: several outbuildings of various sizes, the largest of which was a stable and a wide paddock beyond, which sloped up almost to the edge of the woods that enclosed the place.

A long, shallow set of marble steps leading up to the main doors; Lindsay worried about how Cooter would take them, but the stallion didn't hesitate, just brought Cary right up to the door.

"Now, you may create your wheelchair," Tal said. "Imagine it, picture it clearly, and one of my servants will bring it out. Or you could simply walk in," he added.

A second later, a girl in a black dress and white apron came out pushing a chair that looked identical to Cary's, down to the resistance band tied to it. She stared openly as Cooter knelt and Cary transferred to the chair; Lindsay caught Tal watching closely, too. It was a common reaction from someone who wasn't used to seeing it, but they seemed to be looking at the chair as much as Cary.

"Eventually, you will want to explore your full potential outside of your physical state," Tal said. "Don't be timid. You can't afford to be."

Lindsay had to choke back a snort at the idea of Cary being timid. He expected Cary to make a remark, but he ignored the comment and turned to Cooter.

"All right?"

"The grooms will take good care of him," Tal said.

With a *did I ask you?* look, Cary wheeled into the house.

"We need strong-minded táltosk," Tal said. "But we also need táltosk willing to listen and accept what others tell them. He does not excel at that."

"No," Lindsay agreed. Not unless Lewis told him something.

Cary stopped at the top of the stairs in the entryway. Tal stood next to him.

"There is an easy solution."

"Yep." Cary made an abrupt turn to the left, and Lindsay spotted an elevator he was sure hadn't been there before.

Chapter Twelve

Cary knew Lindsay didn't understand why he didn't just get up and walk, but he didn't feel like explaining it, now or ever. He rolled down a wide hallway with marble floors, lined with paintings and statues that looked like they belonged in a museum. The place didn't feel real at all, more like a really involved video game. He could no longer see the web of magic, but magic was still here, *in* everything.

"To your left you will find a library," Tal said behind him. "We can speak there."

The doorway was wide enough for the chair, but the door itself was heavier than he expected. He still didn't understand quite how all this was working, but he guessed the place affected him more when he was caught off guard.

The library looked like the portion of the OTC library where he liked to study while he waited for Lindsay to pick him up. Cary looked around, wondering if he'd made it look like this the same way he'd imagined the dirt road into being.

"You have a natural gift for creation, clearly," Tal said.

"What's that mean?" Cary headed for his usual spot at a table near the middle of the study area. He liked having people around him while he studied.

"Magic is largely influenced by perception. If you do not know what to expect, I can affect how you perceive something. Sometimes, with many people, I can alter their preconceptions to make them see what I want them to see." Tal gestured around the room. "Then there are people like you. But not everyone can impose his or her alternate view upon others. Only a táltos can do that."

"So, your magic don't work on everybody, but usually other people's magic don't work on you, neither," Lindsay said.

"Something like that." Tal sat across from Cary, in the place where Jessie usually sat. "You will need to learn how to see with another's eyes. That can be useful, too. If you were skilled enough, you could remake this place to look like anything you wanted. As I said, you could do anything here. That is the nature of magic: infinitely changeable. Things only exist because we want them to. They could cease to exist just as easily."

Cary frowned, trying to figure out what that meant. Lindsay looked completely lost. "If it's like that, how does it work on anybody? I mean, if you try to do something to somebody with magic and they could just change it, what's the point?"

Tal smiled. Then, almost quicker than Cary's eye could follow, he'd launched himself across the table. Cary caught the flash of metal in Tal's left hand just before he drew his gun and shot, aiming for center mass. Tal jerked back, stopped mid-leap by the impact of the .38, and tumbled to the table. Then Lindsay was there, holding a Bowie knife pressed to Tal's throat.

"Hold," Tal said, his voice tight. "Hold. I'll explain."

"I don't really care," Lindsay said. His voice was as cold as anything Cary had ever heard, and his eyes were even colder, unlike Dad's or his own hot temper. He held the knife steadily against the artery in Tal's neck. Cary felt a little shiver work its way up his spine.

"Lin," he said softly. Lindsay met his eyes with an *Are you crazy?* look, but stepped away from Tal.

"Well done, princes." Tal grimaced and sat up, holding one hand to the bullet wound in his chest. "You make quite a pair."

"I hope I killed you," Cary said flatly.

Tal smirked. "No, you don't, and you didn't. But you might have if you'd really intended to. I'll explain that later. Think for a moment, if you will, about what just happened."

"You came across the damn table at me. I reacted." Cary put the gun back in its holster but didn't buckle it.

Tal slid off the table and sat across from him again. "I came from here."

"Yeah." Cary frowned. "So?"

"Care, you drew and fired between the time he jumped and when he pulled the knife," Lindsay said.

Cary blinked. He was a quick draw, but nobody was *that* quick except in the movies. And he hadn't even realized he'd packed his gun in the chair holster until he'd grabbed it.

"I see you understand," Tal said. "You just demonstrated a few things for me. One is that you can potentially do anything, within certain boundaries, in this place."

"What boundaries?"

"You cannot completely order my place to your liking. You may create objects within it or change the appearance of rooms, as you just did, but you could not change the structure of the place."

"So we couldn't create new rooms?" Cary asked.

"You are correct. I have spent a great deal of time creating this place. The more sophisticated a structure, the more difficult it is to add to it or change it. The second thing you demonstrated is one way magic can work against a person. I did not know how you would react to my attack, and I did not know what to expect. Thus, you had the upper hand. If we tried the same thing again, I'd know what to expect, and I could divert your magic, or change it."

"How d'you know I'd even react the same?"

Tal shrugged. "You are a creature of instinct. It is hard to change an involuntary reaction. I can't be sure, of course, but it would be an acceptable risk on my part."

"You better not," Lindsay said.

"That is, if it were not for your brother." Tal smiled a little. "I wouldn't favor those odds."

Cary's head throbbed. Was that real, or could he imagine it away, too? "I shot you. You got a wound." He gestured to the bloody hole in Tal's shirt. "But it ain't affecting you? Did you just think and it went away?"

Tal shook his head. "That isn't how it works. The wound is a product of your magic. You could simply think it away, but it isn't that simple for me. I know it isn't real, and so that knowledge mitigates the effects somewhat. But it does hurt, and it could continue to affect me if I didn't know how to release the influence of your magic on me. Which brings me to my third point." He put his hand on the chest wound and grimaced again. "It is somewhat more complicated to do this to myself."

"You're doing the same thing—I mean, we seen that done before. Healing yourself," Lindsay said.

"Yes, so you have. Some call it curse-breaking, and some healing. They are in essence the same thing." Tal was silent for several seconds, then his eyes fluttered open. At some point, Cary realized, he had changed from a glowing figure to a regular guy, not much different from Cary or Lindsay except for his clothes, which looked like something from the navy guy from *The Pirates of the Caribbean*. "It depends upon who is using the magic. Some users have limited abilities; healers can see and sense magic, for example, but they can only heal a body. A táltos can do the same thing, but also much more, as you will discover."

"Like the Tree," Cary said, making the connection. "We're supposed to heal the Tree."

Tal lifted his eyebrows. "Heal the Tree? Where did you get that idea?"

Cary felt like kicking himself for his big mouth. But he wondered why this was news to another táltos. "Somebody told us."

Tal made a dismissive gesture. "Don't believe everything you hear. Many people have many different ideas about what táltosk are meant to do. Like every living thing, the Tree suffers minor ailments, but those do not add up to a plague. Some people have strange theories regarding its current state, but I can tell you that all is as it should be."

Cary's cheeks grew hot. He remembered Jessie, asking, *Does this have anything to do with how you were raised?*

And he'd sworn it didn't. They'd been gullible, believing Emily. Son of a bitch.

"So why are we special, then?" Lindsay asked.

"There was a time when táltosk were venerated. Respected, even among the little people, for their wisdom. We saved souls. Now…" Tal got up and stalked around the room. "How many even know we exist, and of them, how many would respect us for what we do? Your family are some of the few, I think."

Cary drew in a sharp breath. This was why Dad had tracked them down despite his disability, so he could prepare them for Tal's arrival. He might have been wrong about what Tal was, but surely it wasn't coincidence that Tal had showed up now.

"Some believe that you represent a new era for the táltosk," Tal went on. "I happen to agree with them. All táltosk are gifted with a certain amount of foresight, and I have every reason to believe you will do great things."

"Like what?" Lindsay asked.

Tal laughed. "I'm not an oracle. I don't know specifics. Surely you've experienced enough foresight to know that it's no more than a vague warning. Now, I believe you've been here long enough for one day. You'll spend plenty of time away from the material world soon enough; you had best adjust gradually. I'll take you back."

Cary's head buzzed with questions as they went through the house, but he wasn't sure how to ask them, or even what they were, exactly. The only one he could dredge up by the time they reached the stable was, "What's a *goji*?"

Tal glanced at him sideways, and he wondered if he'd somehow screwed up again by asking. "A creature of the underworld. Just as a tree is made up of roots, trunk and crown, the world is made of three layers. We live in Middle World. Underworld is the roots, where demons, imps and other, less sophisticated creatures live. Upper World is transcendence. Heavenly creatures live there."

"Heavenly," Lindsay said. "So, angels? God?"

"So some would say. We'll discuss that later," Tal said. They'd reached the stables, and three grooms were waiting. When Tal mounted his horse, the outline of his lower body grew fuzzy. The green glow was gone from the horse, replaced by Tal's rainbow colors. They looked like the same person.

Cooter nudged his shoulder; he was kneeling already. Cary's arms wobbled as he pulled himself into the saddle and adjusted the thigh straps while Lindsay put his feet in the stirrups.

"You'll have to think of a more efficient way to mount," Tal said. "In battle, you won't have time for Lindsay to help you. But then, you know my solution."

Cary managed to bite his tongue rather than say what he really wanted to say—after all, he was raised to respect teachers—but he was ready to punch Tal in the face if he mentioned that again. It didn't matter who the hell he was.

"What did he tell you?" Cooter asked on the way back, startling him out of his aggravation. Cooter had never actually asked Cary a question before.

"A lot. I'll tell you later," Cary murmured. Tal was riding several yards ahead and didn't seem to hear. "Who is he?"

"We told you, we don't—"

"Pay attention to what humans call themselves. Right. Fine. Who's the horse, then? You know him?"

"Emese is female. She was the first táltos horse."

"Holy shit," Cary said. "Have they always been together?"

"Yes," Sister said.

"So that makes him…."

"The first táltos," Tal called back. "That is correct."

* * *

The next morning looked like rain while Lindsay drove to work. He was glad, even if it meant losing a day's pay and wasted gas. Sure enough, around ten, a thunderstorm started up and the crew was sent home. Lindsay decided to stick around town to pick Cary up from school at three. He called Amy, but got her voicemail, so he decided to go to the trailer and pack some more clothes for a longer stay at Travis's.

He hadn't been home for ten minutes when he heard the front door open. He reached for the shotgun that hung over his bed. Cary and Jessie, maybe, or....

"Boys, it's Wade. Come on out here."

Lindsay's hand tightened on the shotgun. He sure didn't want to talk to Wade right now, especially since he *knew* Wade wasn't alone.

"If y'all want to be cowards, I can just come looking for you."

Lindsay came out with the gun. He didn't point it. Yet. "What you want?"

Even though Lewis was sitting behind Wade, he was the first thing Lindsay noticed. Cary had that kind of presence, too. "You gonna point that at me, boy?"

Maybe I ought to, don't you think, since you broke into my house and all, he thought, but he couldn't make the words come out.

"Where's your brother?" Wade asked.

"School." Lindsay turned his glare on Wade; that was easier. "What business you got that you couldn't call?"

"You got registered cellular phones, don't you?" Lewis said. "What'd I tell you about that? They can track you and listen in. What I got to say ain't for their ears."

No use asking who 'they' were. Lindsay just waited for him to get to the point.

Lewis jerked his head at Wade. "Wait in the truck."

"Lewis," Wade protested. But Lewis gave him that *look*, and of course he obeyed. Nobody ever disobeyed that look.

He turned it on Lindsay next. "Sit."

Lindsay felt his spine straighten. He clutched the gun and remained standing. This was *his* house, goddamn it.

"*Sit*, boy." The tone sent warning chills up Lindsay's back; the next step, when they were kids, was getting knocked across the room. But he wasn't a kid.

Lewis sighed. "The devil has gotten into you since you left me."

That loosened Lindsay's tongue. "*We* left *you*? You done left *us*."

All of a sudden, Lewis looked tired and old. Lindsay remembered what he'd told them last time: he was dying. The old guilt began to return. "Maybe I did," Lewis said. "Maybe I did."

He wasn't prepared for that. He realized his mouth hung open and he closed it, swallowed. "Speak your piece."

"I'd rather tell you and Cary both."

"You ain't seeing him. I swear to—"

"Don't you swear nothing you cain't answer to," Lewis said "I'll see my boy if I want to."

His *boy*. Cold rage swept through Lindsay. "Stay away from him, goddammit, or—" Belatedly, he realized what he'd said; then Lewis was on his feet, his hand raised. He was still fast, but Lindsay was faster. He pointed the gun at Lewis's chest.

"Unless you plan to shoot me, you'd best stop threatening," Lewis sad, as calm as anything. "You got murder in your eyes, but you ain't ready for it yet. Put the gun down and listen to me."

Lindsay's arms lowered as if they didn't belong to him. Lewis was right. Of course. Even if he wanted to pull the trigger—and he did—he probably couldn't. Not against Lewis. All the fight leaked out of him as it always did, and he felt that old shame grip his heart. *Coward*, he thought. *Cain't even stand up to an old man.*

But it wasn't any old man. It was Lewis.

He still didn't sit, but he leaned against the couch. He reasoned if he put up with Lewis now, he'd spare Cary having to do the same.

"You're a good boy, Lindsay," Lewis said. "You been taking care of your brother, just like I told you to when you was little. You're both good boys. You're special."

Lindsay felt himself shaking and hoped Lewis couldn't tell. Never in his life had Lewis called him special.

"Listen to what I gotta say. Y'all didn't stick around to hear it last time. You was touched by God, both of y'uns. I knew that when y'all was born. And I knew my job was to raise y'all up right so y'all could do what you needed to do. What I didn't know was what exactly that was. Until now."

This was sounding like a typical Lewis rant, but Lindsay remembered what Tal had said about Lewis.

"You're here to bring about Rapture, son."

Lindsay blinked. "What?"

"I raised y'uns to be warriors of God. Well, that's what you're meant to be. I know what y'all been doing. But you gotta stay on track. I know the devil's been courting you both, just like he tempted our lord Jesus. That sister of yours, and the others she's been working with, they'll pull you onto the wrong path. I done told you this already, but you better listen to me now. You stay away from that evil. You're too important to get lax. We cain't afford you offending God again so he punishes you."

"What are you talking about?"

"Don't play stupid, son. You ain't no fool even if you act like one sometimes. You cain't see what happened to your brother is a punishment for your sins?"

Lindsay rocked back and almost lost his balance; he felt like he'd been punched in the chest. "What...."

"You offended God, Lindsay, acting like a pervert, being a faggot. And Cary suffered for it."

"*No!*" The word exploded from Lindsay's chest. "*You did that*! You were there! That wasn't never God. That was your fault! Maybe that cancer in you is your punishment for *your* sins. Did you ever think of that?" Lindsay sucked in a breath, and when he spoke again, he made his voice quiet. Cary told him sometimes he could use words like a snake used its fangs; he drew upon that now. "You turned your back on us and I hope you rot from the inside out." Lindsay straightened. "Get out."

Lewis stared at him, and for a second Lindsay was sure he was about to get hit. He felt himself shrinking back, but he held tight to the rage that rushed through his veins like water so cold it burned. Finally, without another word, Lewis stalked out the front door. Lindsay jerked a finger at Wade, who'd come back to the front door at the sound of shouting.

"If you bring him around Cary, I'll shoot you both and gladly go to Hell for it."

"You don't know what you're doing, boy," Wade said.

"I know exactly what I'm doing." Lindsay ignored the way his heart rate jumped when Wade closed the door behind him. "Don't come near me."

The scar on Wade's upper lip twisted. "After all I done for you, you treat me this way?"

Lindsay gritted his teeth. He wouldn't let Wade pull this on him, not anymore. "Keep away from us."

Wade narrowed his eyes. "I know you been making calls. Trying to get some side work? I know."

"So what?"

"I oughta make sure you'll never get work again," Wade said. "I oughta tell people you're ATF."

"You do what you're gonna do," Lindsay said, lifting the gun. "Go away now."

Wade paused with his hand on the doorknob. "I know what you're trying to do, Lindsay. It ain't gonna work. You ain't never gonna pull him away from Lewis. That's just the way it is. If you're smart you'll just find your own way."

"Go away!"

Wade left without another word. When the door closed, Lindsay collapsed onto the couch He dug in his pocket for his cell.

"Trav, you at home? I'll be there in a little while. No, I'll let Jessie take him. I need to talk."

* * *

Twenty minutes into chemistry class, Cary started seeing shadows. They hung at the edges of his vision, just like before, and he started feeling restless, antsy. He'd pulled out of his cell before he realized it and flipped it open in his lap under the table to text Lindsay.

He'd only managed to type in a couple letters before the teacher moved to stand right next to him. He put the phone away, but after that, he couldn't concentrate. What was wrong—or what was going to be wrong?

Between classes, he went to the library, as usual. It reminded him of Tal's house and how he'd made that room look like this. A little thrill went through him to think he had that kind of power.

But it wasn't like he knew what to do with it, or with these shadows. He texted Lindsay.

U ok

He looked out the window. It was raining pretty hard; Lindsay had probably gotten out of work.

Yeah u came the response.

Weird feeling. U feel weird

been feelin weird 4 10 days anythin speshal

dunno

Nothing after that. Cary opened his chemistry book and tried to re-read what they'd gone over in class, but it didn't make any sense. He'd never been great at chemistry, but since all this started he'd fallen way behind in all his classes. Already, being a prince was a lot of work. But that was the price he had to pay. Dad had always said he had to tend to the responsibilities that were most important. Maybe school wasn't one of them.

"What are you going to school for?"

It took a moment to realize the question was directed at him, and a minute more to recognize the girl who came around the stacks to his right. Sandor's daughter, Bella. She hobbled more than she walked, like her injuries still hurt her, and her back was stiff. She eased herself into the chair across from him.

"Social work," he said. "You got sprung from the hospital quick."

"I sprang myself. It helped that no one on the shift knew exactly who I was."

Cary snorted. They weren't as good at security as they thought they were.

"So why social work?"

Cary sat back to look at her, suddenly suspicious. "What's she want?"

"Who?" If Bella was faking confusion, she was doing a damn good job of it. "If you're talking about Emily, I don't know. I hoped you did, being her brother and everything."

Cary narrowed his eyes. "So if you're not here for her, what d'you want? How'd you find me?"

"I know about you. I'm a recorsa. I want exactly what you offered when you came to see me. To find out who wants to harm me."

Cary folded his arms. He didn't like the idea that everyone was able to track them down so easily. "A lotta people want a lot from us, seems like."

She lifted her eyebrows. "That's life, especially for a táltos. Listen, it isn't hard to guess what you're thinking. I don't know if I can trust you, either, but I figure you're more or less in the same boat I am."

"And that's what?"

"In the dark about what's going on. It seems like everybody knows more than you, doesn't it?"

"I bet you know more, too," Cary said.

"Maybe. But the difference is, I'll tell you what I know."

"Why us? If you don't know if you can trust us."

"Because you can protect me."

"What makes you think that?" Cary felt bitterness well up. "Seems like everybody thinks we're the ones who need protection."

"You're the princes. You have the potential to be the most powerful táltosk anyone has seen for a long time. Why couldn't you protect me?"

The stupid part of Cary that still wanted that kind of attention from girls was plain flattered, but he remembered what Tal said, too. They could be powerful. Special. Like Dad always said. He wished Lindsay were here; he was better at seeing layers of things. But he had no reason to disbelieve her, and she did seem to need help. "They ain't gonna be happy you left the hospital."

"I don't care."

He appreciated that attitude. "You ain't worried about getting attacked again?"

"Not with you around. Even if you are handicapped, you were raised to be a fighter, right? And you carry a gun."

"Say it a little louder," he hissed. "Guns ain't allowed on campus."

Bella shrugged. "So why social work? You don't exactly seem like a hippie."

She wasn't like any girl he'd ever met. But then, she was Sandor's daughter. He decided to play along. Chemistry homework could wait. "I wanna do too much work for too little money and hang out with welfare meth addicts."

"You've got a smart answer for every personal question, don't you? I bet if I asked you how you got paralyzed, you'd say you were BASE jumping in the Grand Canyon."

"I hate heights. I was stopping a robbery. Got hit with a baseball bat. Saved a baby, though."

Bella rolled her eyes. "Right. Listen, my understanding is that civil conversation involves people sharing things. This is going to get old fast if you're too stubborn to talk to me."

"Well, if we're sharing, you gotta do to it, too. You in school? You look young enough. How old are you, anyway?"

"Eighteen."

"Jesus," Cary muttered. He'd been such a kid at that age, not ready for anything, and here she was on her own.

"And no, I'm not in school. It's hard enough to recall everything I need to without putting more fabricated knowledge into my head."

"You're just like your dad with that superior attitude," Cary snorted.

"It's fact, not a matter of superiority. Anyway, like it or not, a stratified system—"

"You keep up with that and I'm liable to strangle you instead of protect you."

"Keep up with what?"

"The lecturing." Cary glanced around. He'd been too busy arguing to realize the shadows had cleared from his vision, though his skin still crawled. Was this what was going to happen, Bella showing up?

"What is it?" she asked.

He shook his head. "Dunno."

"Did you get a precognition?" When he looked at her in surprise, she shrugged. "Educated guess. You've had them before."

Cary had only met her once, but she spoke like she just knew that was true. He hated the idea that everyone knew more about himself than he did. "Yeah. Got no idea how to tell what it's about, though."

Bella was silent for a minute, frowning. "I'd have to think about it. We have some records, but that's not my specialty."

"Sandor said he didn't know much about 'em either. I thought y'all was a record of the Tree."

"We are, but we aren't infallible," she said. He didn't ask what 'infallible' meant, not wanting to look stupid. "We have a fair number of human limitations." She made a face at the word *human* as if it tasted bad. "We can only hold a certain amount of information at one time. We can access the rest, but it takes some thought."

"So how come you'll tell us things nobody else will?" Cary asked.

She turned, eyes narrowed. She looked older than any 18-year-old ought to. But that was sort of understandable; she didn't exactly lead an 18-year-old's life, being a walking history book. He felt a little sorry for her. "Sandor is missing and I need you to help me figure out who's trying to kill me."

He might feel sorry for her, but that didn't mean he trusted her. "You ain't telling the whole truth."

"No. I still don't know how far I can trust you. Like you don't know what I'm talking about."

Cary eyed her. "Fine. What's next?"

"I'm hungry. What's to eat here?"

"Cafeteria."

She looked a little doubtful, her lips twisted. "I've heard about those places. Anything outside of here?"

"If you got a car."

She shook her head. "I took the bus. Fine, we'll go to the cafeteria."

"You gonna be a snob about it?"

"Are you going to be a jerk about it?"

Cary could have kicked himself. Whatever happened to the time when he was good with women and drew them toward him rather than running them off?

While they were in the serving line, Cary heard the text message tone from his pocket. It was Lindsay.

Can u get a ride home frm jessie

I guess. What happend?

Tell u later

That was all. Cary was beginning to think the shadows weren't warning him about Bella.

"What is it?" she asked when he put his phone away.

"Something's going on with Lin. He didn't say what."

"So your precognition extends to your brother." She sounded surprised. "Interesting."

"Why? He's my brother."

"I'm just saying, that's interesting. Not everything I say is suspect, you know."

"Sure." Cary wasn't that hungry, but he could always eat. He got some pizza and paid for Bella's meal, halfway hoping to make up for being an asshole. On their way to find a table, he spotted a bright orange backpack. The only person he knew who wore one of those was Jessie. He didn't know why, but he felt a little like he'd been caught doing something he shouldn't.

"What are you looking at?" Bella asked.

"My girlfriend's over there." He wondered if he should even say hi with Bella standing right next to him, or if that would make him an asshole too. Maybe he should wait for her to notice them.

"Well, let's get out of here, then. I really don't want to attract attention."

That solved that. He balanced his plate and bottle of pop in his lap and made his way toward the other exit.

"Hey, Cary." He'd barely made it ten feet before one of Jessie's friends called out. He stopped. Bella kept walking.

"Stop," he hissed.

"Going to the library," she muttered.

"Get back here. If I'm protecting you, you stay with me." If he had to suffer through a conversation with Jessie's friends, who'd always treated him like some weird backwoods foreign exchange student, so would Bella. She turned around and glowered.

"Hey." Jessie came over and put her hand on his shoulder. "How was chemistry?"

"Sucked." Cary waved to the two friends, Ben and Stephanie, then glanced over to make sure Bella hadn't made a break for it.

"Hi, I'm Jessie." Jessie stepped forward and stuck her hand out. Bella hesitated, but shook her hand.

"Bella."

"Nice to meet you." Jessie looked down at Cary expectantly, doubtless looking for an explanation.

"Long story. Can I talk to you later?"

"How's your semester going?" Stephanie broke in. "Haven't seen you much the last couple weeks."

"Pretty busy," he said, hoping they would take the hint. He was in no mood for small talk.

"Yeah, me too. Taking 18 hours this semester and six more this summer. When do you graduate again?"

"Dunno. Another year maybe."

"You know, I think it's really cool that you—"

Cary knew exactly where this was going: the 'I can't believe the redneck cripple is still functioning' speech. He'd heard it from both of them every time he saw them. He glanced at Jessie, then turned away. "Gotta get going."

"Cary!" Jessie's voice was sharp, but he kept going. She didn't follow, but he knew he'd hear about it later.

"Even I know that wasn't socially acceptable," Bella said when she caught up. "Why did you do that?"

"Don't have time to listen to them tell me how goddamn brave and special and inspirational I am for overcoming my obstacles. I'm not a goddamn special Happy Sunshine Cripple."

"Well, the last part is certainly true. So far I haven't seen you anything resembling happy," Bella said. "But you *are* special. Even regular people recognize that and react accordingly."

Cary slowed to let her catch up. "What's that mean?"

For the first time, he noticed she was sweating and out of breath; he remembered she had been seriously injured and felt bad. "I don't remember the full extent of it, but the short version is, people recognize magic users, even if they don't realize it. They're drawn to you. Haven't you noticed people look at you a lot? Isn't it hard to keep a low profile?"

Cary gestured to his chair. "People tend to look."

For the first time, she looked a little awkward, the typical response when he pointed out something the other person had been avoiding mentioning. "Well. Yeah. But it would happen even without that. And I bet it happens to your brother, too."

Before he could stop himself, his smart mouth ran away with him. "Sure. The first thing people notice about me is the chair. The first thing people notice about him is the fact that he's with a guy in a chair. That's the first thing *you* noticed."

"It was not."

"Don't try to deny it. Bet y'all didn't expect a cripple prince, did you?"

As they turned the corner, she cut between him and the wall and stopped right in front of him. "You use that to intimidate people, don't you? Jackass."

He lifted his eyebrows, backed up and went around her. Screw you, he thought. "I don't have to. Ain't my fault people get nervous when they see the chair."

"But you sure don't do anything to discourage that. You use it like a weapon. Any time you think somebody is about to say or do the wrong thing, you throw that word 'cripple' in their faces. Sandor was right. You do have a chip on your shoulder." For a minute, he didn't think she was going to bother catching up, but he heard her footsteps behind him again.

"So I'm a jackass," he said. "That don't really matter to me."

"It should. Don't you get it? You *affect* people, whether or not they want to be affected. When you act like a dick, people get hurt. That's the burden you have."

Cary stopped again just outside the library and studied her. The more he thought about them, the truer her words seemed. "Are you sure you're only 18?"

Bella sighed. "No. That's the burden *I* have. And to answer your question, *jackass*, none of us knew what to expect with you. Not even Sandor, whatever he said. None of us ever realized the lore was true until you were discovered five years ago by Emily."

Cary filed that information away for later. "Your dad always talked like he knew what we was supposed to do, but he wouldn't tell us."

"If he had any ideas, he didn't tell me." She looked troubled. "But if he didn't tell you, there was a reason. The recorsas are fallible." That word again. "What we find out is always subject to our interpretation. We try not to impose our own personal views on what we know. That's dangerous."

Cary stopped and dug behind him in the wheelchair pouch. It took him a minute to find the right pill bottle.

"What's that?" Bella asked.

"Vicodin. Take it after you eat or it'll make you sick." He handed her one of the pills. She stared at it like she'd never seen one before.

"It ain't gonna bite you." Cary put the bottle back in the pouch and headed for the library again. "So how can you avoid having an opinion? The only way you can see anything is through your own eyes. You cain't help but have your own thoughts."

"No, but we don't act on something because of the way we feel." She waved a hand. "The point is, if Sandor purposefully didn't tell you something, it was because he didn't want his perception to color yours. He wanted you to find out by yourselves." She gave him a sideways look. "Though I could have told him you're not somebody who just accepts what he's told."

Cary wished that were always true. "Well, if he'da told us, he woulda saved us a lot of trouble. And maybe himself, too. You plan on looking for him?"

"I don't even know what happened to him. As far as I know, his time as a recorsa is up. It happens."

"What, like an expiration date?"

"Something like that. We're supposed to look after ourselves, anyway." She sat across from him back at the library table and shoveled a piece of pizza in her mouth, then dry-swallowed the pill like a pro. "So I'm staying with you, right?"

Cary didn't know how to deal with the change in topic for a minute. He thought about it. "I reckon. I'll call Trav. We'll have to get a ride from Jess, after class."

"You mean the girlfriend you just pissed off?"

He sighed. "Yeah."

Chapter Thirteen

"So what does your dad want?" Travis asked.

Lindsay shook his head. "More fire and brimstone about how we're special and all." He didn't want to tell Travis the whole story. Travis had never known everything about how they grew up. Travis loved his parents, still had both of them. He was simple. Normal. Lindsay had never wanted to lay the burdens of his own fucked-up family on him. How would Travis look at him if he knew?

"Lindsay?"

Lindsay shook his head. "Sorry. You say something?"

"Just that you *are* special."

Lindsay flushed, wringing his hands. "But special how? We got people telling us what we gotta do, and we don't know enough to see clear one way or another. And I dunno if we oughta be working with this Tal person."

Travis disappeared into the kitchen, then came back and handed him a glass of whiskey. "Then you got to find out how you can see clear. Any ideas?"

Lindsay nodded his thanks and closed his eyes. Listening to Travis's calm voice made him realize how freaked out he was. He wasn't thinking clearly. He never could, when it involved Lewis or Cary or both. "I don't want him near Cary."

Travis moved closer until their knees pressed together. Lindsay wanted to lean against him and hug him, but again Lewis's voice floated into his mind. *Faggot.* His throat closed up and he coughed on his whiskey.

"He don't need to be near either of y'all. If he shows up here he'll find himself with a hole in his chest."

Lindsay knew that was supposed to make him feel better, but fear seized him instead and he clutched at his glass. "Trav, if he knew you was helping us, he'd hurt you. You don't know…."

"I'm a big boy," Travis said. "I dealt with the magic stuff. Reckon I can handle your old man. Let me worry about that. Anyway, is the Tal guy helping you out?"

"Dunno. Seems like he might."

"Well, maybe you oughta see what he's gotta say. Cain't hurt to learn, and you don't gotta swallow everything."

Lindsay frowned. "Maybe."

"Don't sound like you're getting much help from nowhere else."

Before Lindsay could answer, Travis's phone rang from the kitchen. He reappeared after a minute. "That was Cary. Wanted to know if I minded another guest," Travis said.

"Jessie?"

"Nah. Said it was the girl you met at the hospital."

"Bella?" Lindsay sat up. "What'd you say?"

"Well, hard to say no since apparently she ain't got no other place to go."

"It ain't like you to take in a stranger."

"Cary asked. And maybe I'm a little curious to meet one a' those folks you been talking about. Besides, I can always shoot her if she's trouble." Travis shrugged. "Before you get the chance to change the subject, you gonna tell him you talked to your dad?"

"I don't plan on it, and I'd appreciate if you didn't neither."

"Suit yourself. But he's gonna be pissed when he finds out."

"He won't if he ain't told."

Travis lifted his eyebrows. "Yeah, right."

When Jessie's car pulled up, Lindsay guessed things between her and Cary were awkward again, but she was trying to ignore it as usual. Bella got out of the back seat and Lindsay introduced her to Travis while Cary and Jessie talked in the car. Bella folded her arms across her chest and hunched her shoulders against the drizzle.

"I don't have any clothes," she said. "Or any money to pay you with. Just a credit card."

"Don't worry about it," Travis said in the warm tone he used with most women. "You're about the same size as my sister, maybe a little smaller. We'll get you fixed up till we can get you back to town for clothes."

Bella looked like she wanted to say something, but just heaved a sigh and nodded. "Can I see the horses?"

Lindsay didn't know why he hesitated; Bella was part of this magical world and, being a recorsa, probably knew more about the horses than they did. But it still felt like a really personal question. "You sure you don't wanna wait till it stops raining?"

"Fine. Okay. Then I'm going for a walk, if no one objects." Without waiting for an answer, she walked off toward the pasture.

"Hey!" Cary shouted through the passenger's side window. The spasm of confusion and hurt that crossed Jessie's face didn't escape Lindsay even though the car's rain-spattered windshield. "Where you going?" Cary called to Bella.

"For a walk," Bella called without looking back. "You want to come?"

"Kid's got an attitude," Travis said without lowering his voice. "Long as she and Cary don't set my house on fire when they butt heads, I reckon she can stay."

"You oughta see him with Emily," Lindsay said.

Jessie said something inaudible to Cary, then got out to pull his chair from the trunk. She waved to Lindsay and Travis as she got back into the car. Lindsay studied the set of Cary's shoulders as Jessie pulled back down the driveway. "You fight again?"

"No. I pissed her off. Now she's back to acting like nothing's wrong." Cary made an impatient gesture. "Women. Wade called."

Lindsay tensed. "What'd he say?"

"Dunno. Let it go to voicemail." Once they were inside, Cary checked his messages. "Says he's got work for us. I said yes."

"Dammit, Cary." It was just like Wade to go behind his back like that.

"We need money, don't we?"

Lindsay tried not to look at Travis. "Can we talk later?"

"What, you boys can talk about magic in front of me but you cain't talk business?" Travis asked. "It ain't gonna bother me none. I'll just get supper started."

Cary peeled off his wet shirt and tossed it into the laundry basket, then went into the living room to dry his chair. "Some guy from Louisiana wants to meet us. Don't know what he wants yet. Wade said he'll be up in a little while."

Lindsay pushed his hands through his hair. "Cary."

"What?"

"Why do you gotta keep doing this? Going along with Dad?"

Cary didn't look up from rubbing his chair down with a towel. "We're doing a job for money."

"You act like that's the only reason you're doing it. I know it ain't." Lindsay pressed his hands together until his knuckles were white and his arms shook. *You ain't gonna get Cary away from Lewis*, Wade had said.

"Lin." Cary's voice gentled. "Look, we'll just do this one job, okay? Then we'll do business for ourselves. If the guy likes our work maybe he'll keep working with just us. We could charge less than Wade and still make more money than we have been. Okay?"

Lindsay squeezed his eyes shut, trying not to just break down bawling. He wasn't going to win this. "Okay. But no more after this. Please."

"No more," Cary said. "I just said yes because we need the money. That's all."

Lindsay wished he could believe that. "We better work on them at home. I don't wanna get Trav tangled up in this."

Travis poked his head in. "I got a proposition."

Lindsay didn't like the sound of that. "What is it?"

"Let me in on your business."

"This ain't dealing hunting weapons, Trav," Cary said.

"You don't think I know that? I know a few things. I can learn."

"I don't doubt your skills, man, but this ain't no joke." To Lindsay's relief, Cary didn't jump at the idea, either. "If you join up, there'd be no denying you was involved if we was ever caught. I know you don't want no trouble with the law."

"Well, about that." Travis took a long drink of his beer. "I still don't want no trouble. But I got bills just like you, and you mighta noticed I ain't got as many cattle as I used to. I mighta made some purchases I cain't afford, too. I got plenty of space in that back barn ain't being used. Look, I been thinking about this for a while. You can get that look off your face, Lindsay, because I can be stubborn too."

"You're already too involved in all this," Lindsay protested, trying not to show his alarm. Travis was the one normal spot in his life. His sanctuary. They had already tainted that by telling him about the Tree and he knew too much about the family. How could they involve him in their gun trade too?

"All what? I don't see that this has anything to do with the magic stuff except for when you sold to your sister. And anyway, I believe I can judge for my own self how involved I want to be."

Lindsay couldn't believe what he was hearing. Had Travis gone crazy? "Trav—"

"If you really need justification, I'll remind you I need money too," Travis said.

Lindsay saw Cary considering it. He shook his head. "This ain't worth it, for none of us. We'll find another way—I ain't putting you in harm's way, not after what you done for us."

"He's a big boy. Let him decide," Cary said.

"Don't start," Lindsay snapped. He couldn't explain why he felt so bad about this idea, but gave Cary a look he thought he'd understand. Cary either didn't get it or ignored it.

"Do what you want to do, Trav," Cary said. "Never mind the mother hen."

Travis looked between them, his gaze lingering on Lindsay. For a minute, Lindsay thought he'd change his mind, but then he said, "Make your call. I'll help you out."

Lindsay didn't stick around to hear any more. He grabbed his hat and went outside to the back porch, shaking with anger at both of them. Why couldn't they see what an awful idea this was? Cary…maybe he didn't care. He rushed into things without thinking them through. But Travis was usually smarter than that. What on earth had come over him?

The rain had tapered to a drizzle, but it still made solid splats on the brim of his hat. The raindrops caught the light from the floodlight like diamonds, blinding him from seeing beyond the porch. Bella appeared out of nowhere.

"In case you were wondering, I asked for Cary's protection. I didn't impose myself on you just to be a pain in the ass."

He recognized her defensiveness. It was something Cary would say. "Is that how people normally treat you? Like a pain in the ass?"

She was silent. She had that dour teenager look that made him think the answer was yes. She pushed back her wet hair and cleared her throat. "Well. I said I'd answer your questions if you helped me out. So I'll answer them."

"Why don't you put on some dry clothes and get something to eat first?"

"I'm fine," she said, but she went inside anyway.

Bella's presence made things more complicated too. Whatever else she was, Bella was still a kid, and apparently, she needed them. How could they drag her into this when she had enough going on in her life?

Dammit.

* * *

Bella came back in soaked to the bone. Travis managed to get her to dry off and change clothes. He was a damn good housekeeper when he wanted to be, and he'd already set up a guest bedroom for her. She lingered in there a while; Lindsay came back before she did. Cary could tell he was still pissed, but he also knew Lindsay wouldn't say anything more about it, at least not if he could help it.

Bella came back out in a t-shirt and jeans that looked a size too big for her. She didn't quite fit the John Deere shirt. As she accepted the chicken and dumplings Travis gave her, she seemed as young as she was; young, and unsure. Cary wasn't sure what made him think unsure when what she looked was sullen and ungrateful. Maybe he remembered being the same way at that age.

After she'd eaten, she walked into the living room, turned off the TV and stood in front of it, facing them. "I guess you want to know what happened to me."

"That'd be a start," Cary said, amused at her entrance. She knew how to take charge of a room.

"Where can we go to talk?" she asked.

"Right here. Trav knows. He can hear it."

"That's a mistake," she said flatly. "Bringing mundanes into this is a mistake. He doesn't need to know my business, too."

"This mundane don't like that tone, but he can take the hint." Travis got up from his recliner. "I'll be in the bedroom."

Lindsay, the master of privacy, didn't say anything of course. Cary didn't see the point in keeping whatever she had to say from Travis. "You can trust him. Ain't like he don't already know enough to make trouble if he's gonna. Point is, he won't."

"I suppose you don't remember what I said about the influence you have on people," Bella said. "The more you let him in, the more he'll want to do for you. Even if you don't ask him to. You can't see how that could be dangerous for him?"

"We're talking about what happened to you, not asking him to move mountains for us."

Bella shot him a glare. "Are you really that dense, or are you just that self-centered? I asked you to protect me. If he hears about that, he'll want to help you. I see *you* understand." She turned her look on Lindsay, who sat with his arms folded tight across his chest. "So if you're smart, you'll keep mundanes out of this."

That included Jessie, Cary supposed. To her credit, Bella didn't state the obvious, thought her expression said enough. She sat in Travis's vacated armchair, looking like her stomach wounds still hurt, and jumped right in.

"Sandor and I usually aren't in the same place. It's like keeping the President and Vice President apart—it's just safer that way. We're supposed to be immune to any conflicts involving the Tree, but that doesn't prevent random events from happening. If my bloodline died out, the entire memory and body of knowledge surrounding the Tree would be lost. Several generations back, that almost happened. Since there are only two at any given time, we're guarded and kept safe."

"Why two?" Cary asked. "And what's the use of having all that knowledge stored in people, anyway? Why not just write it down?"

"There are always two for the sake of balance, and because two heads are better than one."

"Why just two?"

"Some recorsas have tried to create a third while the other two are still functioning. It's never worked. Nobody knows why. Anyway, that's not part of what I'm getting at. We don't write it down because writing is a crutch of memory and an imperfect way to record it. The mind isn't perfect either but it's more efficient than books. Again, off topic." She eyed Cary's beer. "Can I have one of those?"

"You ain't 21."

"Why do you care? Who's going to arrest me for drinking in a private residence?"

Cary snorted "Women ain't got no sense of humor."

Bella's dark eyes glittered. She looked like she was raring for a fight. "Go to hell, you prick."

"Jesus, I was joking. Both times. Guns down, hoss."

She blinked. "You were joking."

"Yeah. You got a case of the monthlies? If you do, I'll leave you alone. I ain't about to try no PMSing woman."

"Stop. Don't joke like that." Good God, she was wound tight. He had no idea what was wrong. Was she one of those rabid feminists?

"Fine. Didn't mean to offend." It was always this way with women: either he got them on his side immediately, or he pissed them off immediately. And eventually he pissed off the ones who liked him.

"He's got a smart mouth. You can slap it off if you want," Lindsay said.

For a second, Cary could swear Bella was going to smile. Why was his queer brother better with women than he was?

"As I was saying, the recorsas are guarded. It's mostly a formality for us, but not for the guardians," Bella said. "They're called *goji*."

Cary resisted the urge to say something. Tal had said *goji* were Underworld creatures. What did that mean, exactly?

"You're not very good at hiding what you're thinking," Bella said to Lindsay. "Where have you heard of them?"

"Emily," Cary said. "She mentioned Sefu was one. A guy we met."

Bella nodded. "Sefu guards Sandor. Or that's what he's supposed to do. In reality, he's often like Sandor's errand boy. Most *goji* stick to their purpose, which is to be guardians only, but when you start treating them like people, they act like people and they can get distracted."

"What's that mean?" Lindsay, always the one willing to get offended on someone else's behalf. "Sefu's a person."

"He's not, technically, if you're working by the definition that a person is a human. He's a sentient magical construct, like your horses. Adaptable enough to emulate a human, but that isn't necessarily a good thing when you need it for a specific purpose."

This sounded like some sci-fi movie Cary had seen while channel-surfing once. "So, if you got a bodyguard, where was he when you was attacked?"

"She was there. They killed her," Bella said flatly, and Cary felt like shit again.

"Tell us what happened, step by step," Lindsay said.

Bella sucked in a breath. "We were just getting home. We lived in Chesterfield Village, near The Palace. I'd just pulled up and I was getting out of the car. The creatures attacked me right then.

"One on me, three or four on my *goji*. They knew what they were doing, taking care of her. Now, the thing you have to realize is that both *goji* and recorsas are supposed to be untouchable—if Underworld creatures respect anything, it's the need to protect the Tree and its memory. This should never have happened."

Cary wondered if she realized she's said that already. "Do you remember anything else? Did you see where the demon things went after they attacked you?"

Bella's jaw tightened. She folded her arms across her chest and leaned back in the recliner. Cary could tell the memory bothered her more than she'd admit. She was no regular girl—she was tough. He admired that. "They dragged my *goji* off. I didn't see where. I couldn't yell. Couldn't make a sound. I was kind of half in the car, so I started honking the horn. I guess I scared the one that was attacking me, because it ran off too." She drew her knees to her chest and stared straight ahead. "I passed out not too long after that."

Cary could guess what was going through her head, everything she *hadn't* said: those long moments of listening to herself breathe, feeling pain and wetness and the awkwardness of her position, wondering if that had really just *happened* to her, trying to figure out exactly what had gone wrong. Being unable to. Unintentionally fixing in her mind, forever, the feeling of something being terribly *wrong* with her body. He wondered if she'd have scars and was glad he couldn't see his except in a mirror.

"Wait," Lindsay said. "How did anybody find you? And where was Sandor through all this?"

"I thought y'all remembered everything. Wouldn't you remember what happened to him?"

Bella's jaw tightened. "*If* something significant happened, yes. I already told Cary this. He probably lost his powers. Recorsas don't last forever. Eventually they become too human and they lose their connection with the Tree. Sandor had been acting way too human the past few years. If he decided to give up his memories, I can't keep track of him anymore. Does that satisfy you?" Without waiting for an answer, she stalked down the hall into the guest room Travis had set up for her. Cary watched her go. He couldn't quite identify how he was feeling.

"So she thinks her dad walked out on her," Lindsay said. "No wonder she's pissed."

"Yeah."

"What's going on?" Lindsay asked.

"With what?"

Lindsay's lips thinned, but he just sighed. "Never mind, Cary."

Never mind? What the hell did that mean? "You are such a damn woman sometimes."

"Yeah." Lindsay went to his own bedroom without looking back. Cary blinked, a little unnerved. He must be really pissed if he didn't stick around to bicker. But about what?

He wished he could figure *something* out, but every time he did, more mysteries came up. At least they distracted him from thinking about Dad. Dad, dying. Wanting to work with them again. Maybe it would be their last chance.

Cary shook his head and went to bed. He couldn't get his mind off Dad, or Bella.

* * *

Lindsay was outside brushing Sister when Emily called the next day. "Tell me you have Bella Jaborsky."

"Have her? She's here, yeah, but we ain't holding her hostage or nothing," Lindsay said. "She come here by herself."

"Well, good. I need to talk to her."

"Why?"

"Maybe because Sandor is still missing and she's the only recorsa," Emily said.

"So what? What do you need her for?"

Emily let out a sharp sigh. "Why are you being difficult about this?"

"Why shouldn't I be? You wanna come see somebody we're protecting." Lindsay couldn't turning Emily's own words back on her. "You wouldn't let us see her before. Why should we let you?"

Cary came in and gave him a questioning look. Lindsay mouthed "Emily."

Cary snatched the phone from his hand and flipped it shut.

"What's she want?"

"Why'd you do that?" Lindsay asked.

"'Cause you have that look on your face like she's being a bitch," Cary said. "What's she want?"

"To see Bella."

"Why?"

"She didn't say."

The phone rang again. Cary answered it with "So either you're gonna tell us why you wanna see Bella or you can fuck right off."

Lindsay leaned in. He could just hear her voice. "Let me guess, you hung up on me."

"Yeah, and I'll do it again if you don't start talking."

"Fine. I was told to check on her."

"She's fine."

"Jesus Christ, does *everything* have to be a battle with you? I was told I have to see her myself. Listen, we brought you to your horses. If it wasn't for us, you'd still be ignorant of magic and wonder what was missing in your world. And don't tell me you weren't missing anything."

Cary's lip curled and Lindsay was sure he'd hang up again, but he hesitated. "It's up to her."

"Let me talk to her, then."

Cary put the phone in his lap and wheeled out of the room. A few minutes later he came back. He didn't look happy. "Gonna meet her at six at the park near the airport."

"You have a night class tonight, don't you?"

Cary shrugged. "Reckon I done missed too many days already. Ain't no way I can pass it anyway."

Lindsay sighed. Cary had been ignoring school more and more lately. "You're gonna lose your financial aid. What if I just bring her?"

"I don't need Jessie and you on my case. I'm the one who promised to protect her and I will," Cary said in that tone that meant the more Lindsay pushed, the more he'd dig his heels in.

"Fine, whatever. Let's just give up what we worked for since we left so we can borrow more trouble," Lindsay retreated to the bedroom before Cary could say anything else.

* * *

Cary couldn't get Lindsay to tell him why he was so bitchy as they drove to the park a few miles south of Willard. Bella was withdrawn and silent too. Cary couldn't stand the silence, so he turned the radio up. No matter how loud he turned it up, Lindsay ignored it and Cary stopped trying to annoy him.

The little park wasn't accessible, but the parking lot was paved. Lindsay put Cary's chair back together and set it beside the passenger door without a word.

"The hell is wrong with you?" Cary demanded as he transferred. "Quit giving me the goddamn silent treatment."

"I want everything to be normal," Lindsay said. "Okay? I want everything to go back to normal."

"We ain't never *been* normal. How can we go back to it? Why would we want to? Dad always said—"

"Dad Dad Dad. He wasn't right about *everything*," Lindsay said. "He ain't done nothing good for us ever. He's only hurt you."

"You shut up." Cary pushed himself forward, his face hot with anger. "He done good things for us. He did a lotta good things for us."

"Like *what*?"

"He taught us to be princes."

"Oh, what, you know how to be a prince now?"

Lindsay didn't give him a chance to reply. He turned his back at the sound of an engine and walked away. Cary clenched his teeth, looking after him. "He's a fucking bitch sometimes," he muttered to Bella, who was still sitting in the back seat with the door open. Bella just shrugged.

Emily and Mustafa got out of a green Malibu several years old. Cary checked his gun in the chair holster, then motioned to Bella to stay put before he moved around the vehicle to join Lindsay. Even when he was pissed off at his brother,

Cary would watch his back.

"You don't go anywhere without your boyfriend, huh?" Cary said.

"I can think of at least ten things I'd rather be doing than talking to you, too, so let's cut the crap," Emily said. "I need to talk to Bella."

"I'm here," Bella said from the other side of the car.

"You okay?"

"I'm fine."

Emily eyed Cary and Lindsay. "Well, fine. You should hear this too, I guess." She gestured to the vehicle. "Can I at least see her or are you going to shoot me for it?"

"You can see her," Lindsay said, looking down at Cary as if to tell him not to make trouble. Cary went around the car again; Lindsay hung back behind Mustafa and Emily.

"I've got nothing but bad news," Emily said to Bella. "We've been looking for Sandor, but nobody has heard from him still. I guess you haven't had any memories of him either."

Bella folded her arms and looked down at the ground. "Not since the first night."

"Fuck," Emily whispered. Louder, she said, "Does that mean he's dead?"

"I don't know. Probably," Bella said. She didn't sound upset about it, but Cary recognized a glint of desperation in her eyes, as if she were trying hard not to think about it and what she had to do about it. Cary knew that feeling.

This time it was Mustafa's turn to say, "Fuck. You don't have any memory of what happened?"

"No."

"Leave the kid alone," Cary said. "Y'all oughta be physical therapists instead of nurses, nice as y'all ain't."

Emily put her hands on her hips and narrowed her eyes at him, her jaw set. "You're one to talk. It isn't like you're a saint. I came here to talk to Bella, anyway, so if all you're going to do is run your mouth *you* can fuck off." She turned back to Bella. "Well, I've got more bad news. We tried to send a messenger to the goji, to send you a new bodyguard. We don't know why, but they've withdrawn all contact with Middle World and they won't respond to our request."

"It's okay," Bella said.

"What? How is that okay?" Mustafa broke in.

"Cary is protecting me."

Emily's eyes swiveled back to Cary. She gave him a look he recognized: disbelief and suspicion, probably wondering how a cripple could protect anybody. "Oh really."

"Yeah, *really*," Cary said. "You wanna test it out?"

Emily threw up her hands. "Great. Well, I guess it's better than nothing. Bella, tell me if there's anything we need to know, okay? If you find out anything about the goji or your father or any incidents in the area. You have my number?"

Bella nodded. "I have it. I'll tell you."

"Good. We're counting on you."

Color drained from Bella's face. Cary knew that pressure all too well. Dad used to say that to him. *Son, I'm counting on you to be a warrior for your family.* He never knew if he'd be able to do what Dad wanted him to do, but that never mattered. He had to shoulder the responsibility. Bella was the only recorsa left, maybe; it was that way for her, too.

"Don't fuck up," Emily told Cary and Lindsay, turning back to her vehicle.

"We ain't the ones been fucking up," Lindsay said in that cold voice of his. "Maybe you oughta look at yourselves."

Cary could have sworn Emily winced before she got back in the car.

Chapter Fourteen

"Why are we letting him teach us?"

Cary wished that for once Lindsay would sound pissed instead of hurt. It would be easier to deal with his fangs than his sad eyes. "Who else is gonna teach us? Emily and them? They don't got nobody like this."

"But…."

He knew what Lindsay was going to say, that Dad had something to do with this and they shouldn't trust Tal because of it. He didn't want to hear it. He turned Cooter as Tal approached them.

"Tonight, you will cross the threshold alone. You will find your way back to my place without guidance."

Tal hooked a thumb in Cary's direction. "You, Prince Cary, may find this challenging, given your propensity for creating your own view of the world."

Cary clenched his teeth and put on his stillest expression, the way he did when Dad would try to bait them. He said nothing.

"This time, I will lead you through and show you how to cross the threshold. Next time, you will do it yourself." Tal snapped his fingers at Lindsay. "You first. Come with me."

Cary saw his brother's face darken at the finger snap. He remembered the later years with Dad, when they were grown and Dad still ordered them around. Cary saw silent resentment surface in Lindsay's eyes. But just like before, he gave in. Cary watched them walk away.

Their magical outlines, all that was visible in the darkness, wavered and rippled, then reappeared. It was like seeing them through frosted glass. The rainbow-flame figure he knew was Tal turned back and reappeared in sharp clarity only a moment later.

"Are you able to do this?" he asked.

Cary opened his mouth to snap back, but he knew Tal was just trying to rile him the way Dad did. He closed his mouth, and Cooter moved forward toward the place where the threads of magic met.

"All right, then. You can lead the way." Tal said mildly. "And you can get lost."

Cary hated the moments when he could feel his mouth about to run and he couldn't stop it. He felt it coming, knew it was about to get him in trouble, but

Dad was the only one who could ever silence him. "So show me."

Tal smirked as he came up beside Cary. "Did you treat your father with such disrespect?" As if he'd heard the thought. Something in Cary's chest clenched and burned.

"You ain't my father."

"But I am your teacher. And unlike your father, I don't have to do this. If you continue to insult me, I will stop teaching you. Do you understand?"

Cary clenched his teeth again, so hard his jaw ached. "Yeah."

"Well, then." Tal gestured ahead. "You remember the place I took you to before? Picture it. Make it. This part will be easy for you."

He had a good memory for seeing things. Tal was right; it was easy. It was a simple act of will to make the Tal's place appear around him. This time he could see it happen, like a bunch of puzzle pieces arranging themselves, and he knew he was *making* it happen. It wasn't just like creating the wheelchair or the elevator in Tal's house; then, he'd just *known* they'd be there. This was like standing behind the scenes with the special effects team: disappointing because it didn't simply happen, but cool in a different way because he knew *how* it happened.

Tal spoke beside him. Cary had forgotten he was even there. "You made the same mistake your brother did. This isn't my place. It is close, but not the same. You imagined the place, but you did not remember that it is not yours. Everyone does it the first time. Your task is to find your way back to my house.."

"Wait. This ain't the same place?"

"It is a version of it, the one you created, not mine. A shadow of the real thing."

"How do I find the right one then?"

Tal smiled. "As I said, realize you are trying to find my place, not yours. If you don't understand the difference, you won't succeed as a táltos. Now, please dismount and walk your horse."

Cary pressed his lips together. This time he knew his mouth was about to run, but he didn't try to stop it. "I don't think you get how this works."

"I beg your pardon?"

"I cain't walk."

"Yes, you can, prince. And the sooner you stop limiting yourself—"

Cary's hackles stood up. "The sooner you stop nagging about that, the sooner you can stop wasting breath. That *is* my limit. I. Cain't. Walk. Not in the real world, not in wikky-wikky-woo-world. It don't work like that. It's a fact."

"It may be true back there, but here, you have no such limitations unless you impose them on yourself. You are only crippled by your stubborn refusal to reach your potential. You have no reason not to."

"The hell you say. This is the way I *am*. I ain't walking here or nowhere. If you ain't noticed, I got four good legs under me. That's enough."

Tal's eyes narrowed. Cary stared back. He didn't care how pissed the bastard was. Tal had no right to try and *force* him to walk.

"Dismount," Tal said evenly.

"Fuck yourself." Cary turned Cooter, urging him forward even as the stallion hesitated. For a second, Cooter was so tense Cary was sure he'd buck, but he settled down before Cary had to pull him in a circle.

"I asked for respect from you. I informed you of the consequences for insulting me." Tal spoke in the same tone as before: flat, factual, without emotion. It stoked Cary's temper even more.

"Respect *me*, then. I ain't giving none if I don't get none. I'll be goddamned if I let you keep nagging me and insulting *me* like I can't do this if I cain't walk. I'll *show* you."

Tal studied him, eyebrows lifted. Finally he said, "We shall return to this."

"I'll be good goddamned if we will." He tightened his grip on the reins. "Cooter, move it."

Once again, the stallion didn't disobey a direct order, though he shook his head and tugged at the reins. They left Tal behind quickly. At first, Cary had no idea where he was going; the cobblestone street turned into the familiar dirt road at exactly the point Cary remembered. It wasn't long before Cooter came to an abrupt halt, jarring Cary in his saddle.

"He is right. If you listen to no one, you will do nothing. You will wander the aether forever and I will have to carry you. You are foolish."

"You don't get it either," Cary snapped. "I ain't gonna be something I'm not."

"Then be worthy of the title prince and not a stupid crippled pleasant."

Cary wanted to punch the back of the asshole horse's head. "Then what the hell do I do?"

"You will have to let go," Cooter warned him. "I will show you, but I can only help you if you let me."

"A'ight, well, tell me what you're doing."

"No telling. No words. Enough words. Just pay attention." Cooter set off again, taking a sharp turn off the road and down the embankment. Last year's rotting leaves made it slippery, and the smell that drifted up when they were crushed beneath Cooter's hooves made Cary nauseous. He didn't have room to dwell on that, though; he had to put every ounce of concentration into keeping his balance.

Cooter half slid, half walked down the hill with far more reckless confidence than a real horse. He didn't stop to let Cary catch his balance, not even when had to grab his mane and yank to right himself. This was a hell of a lot more difficult than riding on level ground or even the rolling hills of Travis's property. He knew his seat wasn't steady, but he couldn't adjust his weight before Cooter made another move.

Cooter stopped—Cary had no idea how he managed to stand on a steep slope like that—and looked at him. "Look forward."

At the bottom of the hill, the rolling green lawns of Tal's place spread out before them, shining with the same mist and dew. The scene was exactly the same as Cary remembered it.

But that wasn't right. Cary wasn't sure how he knew, but he knew it shouldn't look exactly the same. Weather changed from day to day; why should this look the same? Unless his mind was fooling him. Unless this was, again, his own version of Tal's place instead of the real thing.

"Oh," he said. "So how do we find the real one?"

Cooter didn't answer. He took off down the hill and Cary was again forced to concentrate on keeping his seat. When he dared look up again, in the dappled light, he caught a flash of sunlight on water below them: a creek, at the base of the slope. He knew then exactly how Cooter meant to screw with him.

"Oh, hell no, you don't."

He'd dealt with bucking and rearing and galloping horses. He and Lindsay had raced horses more times than he could count. But those were working horses, not jumpers, and he'd preferred to stay on the ground as much as they did. But Cooter apparently had no intention of staying on the ground.

Cooter hit the bottom of the hill running. Cary only had a few seconds to think. He managed to right himself, but he couldn't adjust his seat. All he could do was hold tight and hope to God the landing didn't throw him—or worse, dislodge him only halfway. He had a vivid image of his skull shattering when he tumbled off the saddle and his body being dragged along with and tripped over by the stallion.

No. Just hold on.

He felt Cooter's muscles bunch in preparation to jump, felt his front hooves leave the ground, then the back ones.

And then the world shifted.

Cary didn't feel the landing. The next thing he knew, they cantered easily across the emerald-green lawns, and Tal's presence was all around them. The afternoon sun, even the sky looked different, like Tal's mark had been cast upon it somehow. Cary couldn't pinpoint the difference, but he wouldn't forget it. He understood, and patted Cooter's neck. Damn horse wasn't even sweating.

Lindsay and Sister met them halfway to the house. Cary almost couldn't bear the look of worry on Lindsay's face. "I'm okay, Lin. Didn't fall or nothing."

The relief that replaced the worry was almost worse. "He act up?" Lindsay nodded to Cooter, who snorted and tossed his head.

"Nah," Cary lied. Lindsay looked doubtful, but before he could question any further, Tal interrupted them.

"I see you understand what I mean now. Good. I will require you to come by yourselves from now on. Come with me now."

Tal brought them out onto the wide lawn behind the house. To Cary, it felt exposed to anyone or anything who wanted to do them harm. The cheerful sun didn't soothe him much.

"If you are to use magic," Tal said, "You must know how to control it first. Summoning is the easiest part."

Cary reached for the energy he could feel below his breastbone. It was like preparing himself for a fight or for a footrace, winding his body up like a coil waiting. Golden sparks danced across his skin, and he felt hot. The energy welled up and thrashed inside him. It *wanted* to be used, and if he didn't do something with it in the next couple of seconds, it was going to find its own release.

"Be *careful*," Cooter told him. "Control it or you will lose it."

Even as Cooter spoke, Cary felt the magic slide away like a slimy fish under his fingers; his entire body tensed and his stomach heaved. It felt like being turned inside-out.

"Prince!" Tal barked. "Take hold of it. Pull it back."

Cary seized that cord of magic before it could leave him. He felt his arms reach out even though there was nothing to grab onto. But somehow it worked. He managed to get a hold on his magic, pull it back into his body and hold it in his mind. He looked at Lindsay, judging by Lindsay's wide eyes, he had felt it too.

"What was that?" Lindsay breathed.

"You are not fully bound to your magic yet. It is within you, but not part of you. You can only borrow it from the Tree. If you do not control it, you will lose it," Tal said.

"Jesus. Good to know." Cary pressed his hand to his chest and felt his heart thudding.

"As I said, summoning your magic is the easiest part. Controlling it, keeping it with you, is another. You have only borrowed your energy from the Tree; you mustn't forget that. It will reclaim its energy if you cannot master it." Tal looked straight at Cary, giving him the look. He knew the warning was especially for him, like Tal expected him to fuck up again.

"You try, Prince Lindsay," Tal said. Lindsay looked surprised, then tentative, but he closed his eyes and his face went blank for a minute. The silver-green magic was slower to appear than Cary's had been, like a sunrise. It filled Lindsay until it was so bright Cary could barely look at him, but he never once lost control of it. Cary pressed his lips together, trying not to be jealous.

"Well done." Tal nodded to Lindsay. "Remember, princes, that until you are bound to your magic, you may lose it, or it may be taken away from you. Use it carefully."

Cary wondered if that was supposed to be a threat. He felt the unsteadiness of the magic in him, ready to jump out of him at any time. He wasn't patient like Lindsay. How long until he lost his grip on it? "How can you get bound to your magic?"

"You must travel the three worlds and gain your táltos mark. That, however, is not a goal you should concern yourself with yet. One step at a time. Patience."

Cary gripped the reins and tried to take Tal's advice. It was so different from Dad, who always threw them into the deep end and let them figure things out for themselves. He could do what Tal wanted him to do. Cooter shifted beneath him as if he agreed.

Tal smirked at him. "Not to worry, young prince. You will be able to take action soon enough."

* * *

Lindsay soon forgot to be upset. During their next lessons, which lasted well into night in this place, he noticed Cary loosened up and listened to Tal more readily. Tal taught them how to fight from horseback with sabers, and Cary was as good at that as he was anything. Lindsay didn't learn as quickly, but after a while they were evenly matched. It was hard work, learning a new foreign weapon, but they had always enjoyed close-up fighting. And who didn't always want to learn how to use a sword?

Lindsay felt himself grinning when Tal called a halt; he'd just won his third bout against Cary.

"I'll git you next time, brother. And the time after that," Cary said, though he didn't seem pissed like he normally would about losing.

"You can try," Lindsay shot back.

"Well done, princes. You have natural talent for warfare," Tal said. "Next time, the lesson will be more difficult. I suggest you practice until I see you again."

"With what?" Cary asked. "It ain't like we got swords lying around."

"You have a gift for creation, Prince Cary. I'm confident you'll figure it out."

Cary did figure it out. They got up early the next morning to practice with Bella tagging along. When Lindsay walked into the tack room, two sabers hung on the wall, as real as anything. Cary really did have a gift.

Cary grinned when Lindsay came out with them. "Bet we could make tack, too."

"How'd you do it?" Lindsay asked.

"Hell if I know. I just thought, what if them swords was in the tack room?" Cary shrugged.

"You have a strong talent for manifesting your desires," supplied Bella, who had followed them out. "Be careful with that. It can backfire."

Lindsay was reminded of a story he heard once, about a genie or something like that, and it made him uneasy. Cary, of course, brushed it off, but Lindsay saw a flash of thoughtfulness cross his face.

"Can we make tack?" Cary asked.

"Of course you can."

"Huh." Cary turned and left the barn. "Hey, Lin. C'mon."

Lindsay followed, curious in spite of his uneasiness. He imagined Sister waiting for him with a saddle he'd seen in a farm supply store once. He'd admired the tooled leather, silver trim and suede seat. A showman's saddle, definitely too fancy and too expensive for the farm horses. It was the first material thing Lindsay had ever really wanted. He imagined it in white, with a sheath for his saber on the left side.

And when he rounded the corner, there Sister stood, the saddle already in place. Even the saddle blanket was snow white to match her fur. Lindsay's jaw fell open.

"Nice, brother," Cary said. "Looks like that saddle you seen in the co-up when we was little, huh?"

Lindsay flushed at the compliment. "Yeah. Yours is awful pretty, too." Of course Cooter's saddle was bolder than Sister's. It had a gold-toned suede seat and black sides studded with gold.

Cary flashed him a grin. "C'mon."

Lindsay kept an eye on his brother. As easy as it was for Cary to make things happen on the aether, he struggled with sword fighting in the real world. Any position in the saddle that wasn't facing forward threw off his balance, and without control of his lower half he spent more time righting himself than sparring. Lindsay said nothing when he repeatedly pulled or pushed himself upright, knowing Cary needed to keep going, to prove he could do it. He wasn't surprised when Cary refused a ride to school so he could keep practicing. He wasn't surprised to find Cary still at it when he got home from work, either.

"He been at it all day?" he asked Bella, who was perched on the fence watching.

"Mostly. Travis made him eat."

"He's gonna regret that later," Lindsay muttered. Sure enough, Cary couldn't even get out of bed by himself the next day. Lindsay helped him into the bathtub and tried to work out some of the knots in his muscles, but it took a full two days' rest and a whole lot of pills for Cary to be up and around again.

"Care, you cain't keep doing this. You're gonna end up doing yourself bad," Lindsay said. He tried to help Cary into his chair from the bed, but Cary pushed his hands away.

"What else am I gonna do, just give up?"

"There's only two choices? You ain't gotta rush," Lindsay said. Cary said nothing, just struggled into his chair and went out into the hall.

He didn't have a hope of keeping Cary out of the saddle. Cary's soreness and the pills made his balance worse than usual, but he wouldn't give up, moving through his exercises again and again until he couldn't stay in the saddle any longer. For the next week, all Cary did was eat, sleep and practice, not bothering with schoolwork at all.

Lindsay thought about what Travis had said. He hadn't seen Cary so determined to do anything since physical therapy, and Lindsay didn't have the heart to bring him down. Maybe this was important, too. Maybe this was really something they could do. At least, he hoped they could. He watched Cary and hoped all this wouldn't end up ruining them.

* * *

Cary sort of got used to Bella watching him practice; he'd always liked to show out a little anyway. He'd been embarrassed at first, clumsy as he felt, but she'd started volunteering pieces of advice that were actually useful. She talked like his physical therapists, using names of muscles.

"Where'd you learn all that medical talk?" he asked her, stopping for a breather. Cooter wasn't even winded, the bastard. He never seemed to get tired.

"I've been reading up on SCIs and physical therapy. I don't know where your injury is, though." She used the acronym for spinal cord injury, just like a doctor.

"Incomplete injury in T11," Cary said automatically. "Minor fracture in T10. I thought you didn't bother learning out of books."

"I never said that. I just said I didn't bother going to school. I was curious." She raised her chin in that way he had come to realize was meant to be a challenge. "I mostly found medical documents."

Cary shook his head, amused. "You're a geek, kid." But he had to admit he was flattered she'd bothered to read up on his injury. Lindsay knew it as well as he did, but no one else, not even Jessie, had waded through all of the medical gobbledegook.

"I've been called that before. If wanting to know things makes me a geek, then I guess it's true."

He was a little surprised she hadn't even looked a little pissed—every 18-year-old he'd known would have resisted being called a geek—but he'd learned she had very little ego. What a weird kid.

"I read SCI patients often have chronic pain issues. Is that why you take those medications?"

"Why else?" Cary stretched his arm, trying to decide if he ought to take another Tramadol.

"You should see a doctor before you adjust your dose."

"Thanks, Mom," Cary snorted. She said nothing.

Cary had just gone back to his workout, focusing on side parries, when something black scuttled across his peripheral vision. He brought the saber around to block it. After he got over the moment of pleasure at keeping his balance well, he realized he'd attempted to block nothing. Then the black thing crept in again, on the other side. He realized what it was then, and sat still to watch it. Was there more than one?

"What is it?" Bella asked.

"Dunno exactly. I seen it before, when something was gonna happen. Your dad called it pre-something."

"Prescience. Precognition. Foresight." Bella nodded. "Can you tell what you're seeing? Or when it's going to happen?"

"Ain't figured it out." The black shapes disappeared as quickly as they came. "Hand me my phone."

Bella slid off the fence. "You think it's something with your brother."

"No idea, but I'm gonna check."

She handed him the phone and stepped back. "You look out for each other first."

"Yeah. He's my brother. If you had one, you'd understand." Cary texted Lindsay—*u ok?*— and flipped the phone shut, looking down at her again. "What?"

She shook her head. "I didn't say anything." She wasn't a very good liar. Her feelings showed on her face sometimes, just like Lindsay.

"I'll still look out for you. I promised."

"Good. Because you're all I've got to depend on."

The matter-of-fact statement pinched something inside Cary unexpectedly and hard. For whatever reason he'd ended up being in charge of protecting a weird teenage girl who knew too much for her own good, he wanted to do it. She deserved protection, and he liked her.

"I said I'd look out for you. I didn't say I was dependable." He didn't know what made him say things like that sometimes.

"You are. Why do you think I asked you?"

Cary had to laugh. "Kid, you don't know me."

"I know the Tree's memories of you, which, considering your position, are fairly comprehensive. And I can extrapolate from that, having the capacity for abstract thought. Isn't that knowing someone?"

"The Tree's memories? It's been…watching us? For how long? How does that work?"

"Humans do make the mistake of thinking they are the only observant beings in the universe," Bella said in her snobby lecturing tone. "You've been observed since conception, as has every sentient being. It's difficult to explain unless you already know how."

Cary couldn't even comment on the logic of that statement. Everything Dad had said about growing up—*They're always watching, boys, so don't make it easy on 'em*—filled his head, and he shuddered.

"You're thinking about what your father taught you, I would guess," Bella said. "It's a shame—"

"Stop there." Cary slid the saber into the makeshift scabbard at his left hip and turned Cooter away from her.

"Sorry," Bella said. "I was just demonstrating extrapolation."

"Next time you have a thought like that, you want to keep it to yourself." Aggravated as he was, Cary did his best not to take it out on the kid. She acted like she honestly didn't know how to behave sometimes. It probably wasn't her fault—she was raised by Sandor, after all.

"So noted." Bella walked back toward her perch on the fence. No sooner had she climbed up when Cooter perked his ears, turning them toward the road. Cary recognized Jessie's car, headed toward Travis's driveway.

"Dammit. Back to the barn," he muttered. Cooter didn't need to be told twice. "Bella, go tell Trav Jessie's here and don't come running out with no gun."

He managed to dismount by the time Jessie's car pulled up to the house, and Cooter made himself scarce. He'd expected her to be pissed, but she just looked worried. That was almost worse. "Is everything okay?" she asked.

"Yeah." Lord, her expression made him feel like he'd run over some little kid's puppy. "Sorry. I've had a lot going on." Only not really, and he'd used that excuse before.

"Yeah. I was just worried something might've happened with your family, or…other stuff."

He reminded himself he'd promised to be more open with her, and hoped she wouldn't kill him for it. "Come on inside and I'll tell you. Are you skipping class?"

"I have to work tonight and I wanted to see you."

Bella met him at the front door. "Your phone's ringing. You told me you were expecting a call."

Cary glanced at the phone: Wade. Exactly what he didn't need right now. After debating a second, he flipped the phone open, said, "I'll call you later," and closed it again.

"You could have taken that if it was important," Jessie said.

"I'm with you right now. It wasn't that important." He hoped. As they moved into the living room, Travis greeted Jessie with a nod before he disappeared, and Cary said, "Jess, this is Bella."

"We met before. At school."

Oh. Right. "Nice to meet you, officially, Bella," Jessie said.

Bella looked as uncomfortable as he felt. He wracked his brain trying to figure out how he could explain the situation without having to tell the complete truth.

"Will you go check on Cooter?" Cary asked Bella. Thank goodness she got the message; she nodded and left out the back door.

"You were riding," Jessie said. "I thought I saw a horse in the field. I still want to see you ride."

"It ain't that exciting." He'd almost come to accept the idea of introducing her to Cooter, but when he'd asked, the horse would have none of it and refused to explain himself.

"That's what you've been doing?" Jessie perched on the end of the couch. He knew she meant instead of going to class.

"Part of it. We been learning how to use magic," he said.

"You and Lindsay? How do you learn?"

"Yeah." He paused. "This is gonna sound crazy to you."

"Tell me anyway."

"We went outside this world, to a different place. It's sorta between worlds. The space between the branches of the World Tree. That's what we been learning about."

"It doesn't sound crazy." He could hear the social worker carefulness in Jessie's tone. "I just don't really get it, I guess, this whole thing. But everything is okay?"

"Yeah. Mostly. We just had other stuff to worry about than school."

"I didn't see Lindsay's car. Is he at work?"

"Well, yeah. We got bills." Was she trying to accuse him or something? "I'm behind anyway. I'll go back next semester. Or when I can."

"Don't you have to stay in good standing for your financial aid?"

Cary sighed. "Don't. Please. I cain't think about school right now. I just cain't." But the more she talked about it, the worse he felt. He'd wanted to go straight through, transfer to Missouri State, and be licensed in a few years. But how the hell was he supposed to do that with all this going on?

"You could withdraw from all but one or two. Peterson would work with you. Grimes would too. Maybe the rest would give you Incompletes if you—"

"Let me deal with it my own way, Jess." He tried to keep his tone reasonable. "I know you're trying to help, but I'll figure it out."

Her face pinched with distress. "It's just, I know how important school is to you."

"This is important to me too, now. This is something I gotta do."

"Magic?"

He saw then that she didn't believe him. Not a word. She went along because she was trying to be supportive, but she was worried because she thought it was all crazy bullshit. And he had no idea how to convince her otherwise.

"Yeah" was all he could say. "Magic."

"Does she know?" Jessie looked toward the back door.

"Yeah. She's part of it. Her family…it's a long story. I'm—we're protecting her. Somebody tried to kill her."

Jessie's eyes widened. "Who?"

"We don't know yet, and it ain't something we can go to the police about it."

"So she came to you."

Cary shrugged. "Yeah. I guess—"

"*Cary!*"

He barely recognized the scream as Bella's. He pushed himself as fast as he could toward the back door, with Jessie and Travis right behind him, Travis carrying his shotgun. Bella stood frozen at the barn door facing the house, looking toward the end of the property he couldn't see. Without thinking, Cary launched his chair down the ramp and into the yard toward her, drawing his handgun.

At the edge of the property where the road curved south lurked a pack six creatures. They looked a little like hyenas, with long necks and lower hindquarters. The magic that surrounded and made them was muddy brown.

"What the hell are they?" he heard himself ask.

"They're—they were the ones that…." Bella stammered.

She didn't need to finish the sentence. Before Cary realized he had even moved, he'd shoved his gun back in its holster and extended his right hand. A shining disc flew from it. He could see heat ripple from it as it cut through the air.

The explosion when the disc hit the dome of magic surrounding the property sounded like a truck backfiring in his ear. The golden light arced across the entire dome like cracked glass, and cold pain lanced through his body. He reached for his magic, tried to grab hold of it to make sure it wouldn't leave him, but he couldn't feel it at all; he could only watch as it ricocheted off the dome, part of himself outside his body, exposed to the world. The creatures scattered, running in different directions around the perimeter. Bella screamed.

"Cary! Your magic!"

I know, Cary wanted to say, *I fucked up*. His entire body shook, and he felt himself slumping in his chair. Somehow he knew he was going to pass out, but he fought against it, trying to keep an eye on that shining cloud that moved of its own accord.

"Call it back," he heard Bella say. "You can do it. Come on, Cary, *please!*"

How? Cary wondered, but he couldn't really even form the thought fully. He just watched the magic, opened himself to it. He didn't have the will to force it.

Then he felt the magic touch him again. He fought against just grabbing it and pulling it into him, sensing it wouldn't work that way. He just let it happen, and every bit of energy he'd expended filled him again. It felt like the rush of warmth that came along with a shot of morphine. He heard a moan of relief and realized he had made the sound.

It took him a minute to figure out what had happened.

"The circle. The goddamn circle," Cary muttered. "Bella. Look! They cain't come through the circle. It's okay. See?"

She was shaking, badly, on the verge of crying and still trying to collect herself. No 18-year-old girl should be that tough. "You're right. I'm fine. I'm sorry."

"Go on inside. Have a beer. You earned it."

It was hard to tell if his stupid joke had any effect. When she turned away, Cary caught sight of Jessie on the porch and Travis halfway between them, both looking stunned.

"Well," Travis said, "too much to hope I just had a stroke."

"I reckon so," Cary said. "Hope you don't need to go nowhere for a little while. Will you call Lin and tell him everybody's fine and not to come back till I call him?"

Travis nodded and went inside. That left Jessie, looking like her world had been turned upside down.

"Are you okay?"

No, Cary wanted to say, *I almost just lost a part of myself because I acted like a fool*. But all he said was, "Sure. I'm fine."

"You were serious. About magic."

Cary nodded.

"I'm sorry. I…"

"Babe, I'd'a thought I was full of shit too." He rolled back up onto the porch. "You oughta stay for a while. Tell work you got car trouble."

She grabbed his hand, the one that had thrown magic, and squeezed it. "That was incredible. And brave."

Cary wanted to be flattered, but his mind wouldn't let him. "Ain't no bravery. We was safe anyway. It was stupid, is what it was."

When the horses reported that the coast was clear, less than an hour later, Jessie headed off to work. Cary had no idea how she was feeling, or even how *he* was feeling.

Bella's bedroom door was shut, but he went in anyway. She sat on the bed, stone-faced.

"You gonna be okay?" Cary asked.

He ought to have known better than to ask. "I don't know. I couldn't tell if they were the same ones who tried to kill me. They were too far away. I…." She drew in a shaky breath. "Panicked. I shouldn't have."

"Why not?"

She just shook her head again and turned her face down. He could tell by her breath she was crying.

"You don't gotta be brave every single minute." He pushed the chair forward until his knees were against the bed. "Them things scared the hell outta me."

"But you didn't panic."

"I been trained my whole life to fight, so that's what I did, but I sure as hell did panic. You saw it."

The next thing he knew, he found her arms around his neck. He returned the hug. One arm fit almost all the way around her skinny ribcage. "I remember what happened to him. To Sandor."

"How long you been sitting on that one?" What the hell, she'd kept this from him for *months*.

"Since I got out of the hospital. I should have told you, but I just...couldn't look at it."

The upset leaked out of Cary like air from a balloon. He *still* didn't want to think about what happened to him. How could he blame her? He sighed. He wanted to comfort her like he'd comfort Jessie, but he didn't know how to feel about the impulse. "Hey. Look at me. We're gonna figure out what happened, okay?"

"Well, I *know* what happened." Bella spoke in that gruff tone he somehow recognized as her cover-up for being scared.

"I'll tell you now."

"Okay, then." Cary was off-balance reaching onto the bed, so he disentangled from her long enough to join her. As if she realized what she'd done, she wrapped her arms around herself this time. He saw her drawing in on herself, saw her eyes begin to glaze over, and he'd be damned if he let her fall into the pit of a flashback the way he sometimes still did, the way Lindsay sometimes did even if he tried to hide it.

"Two men. Their faces aren't clear, as if maybe I need something to jog my memory. Maybe if I saw them again. I don't know. I can hear their voices but not really what they're saying. I think they either hit him in the head or drugged him because his vision is fuzzy. Woozy."

"Men. Humans?"

"Yes." She stared straight ahead; Cary could tell she was trying not to be bothered by the memory. He reached out and ruffled her hair.

"We'll figure it out, kid. If we got to, Lin and me will go around knocking heads."

"That's not really appropriate behavior, is it?"

He scoffed. "Not in polite society, maybe, but I don't see no polite folks around here."

All of a sudden, her chest hitched in hard sobs and she pressed her face against his shoulder, tears wetting his shirt. All he could do was put an arm around her shoulders and let her lean against him.

"Go ahead and cry. I'll just sit here and watch out for you like I said I would," he told her. Eventually she crept closer until her head was on his shoulder, and there it stayed until she stopped crying and fell asleep.

Chapter Fifteen

Lindsay called Cary on the drive home and made him tell what had happened. By then, Cary had recovered enough to be smug about it, describing the magic-throwing in detail.

"Cary Judah, you almost lost your magic," Lindsay said, trying and failing to keep the tremor from his voice. "What was you *thinking*?" He folded his arms. "You probably wasn't."

"I did what I had to do," Cary said; Lindsay could hear the prickly side of him rising to the occasion. "What was I supposed to do, *not* protect them?"

"You had your gun!"

"Which might or might not a' done nothing."

"The protections were still there. You mighta lost it for nothing."

"But I didn't, mother hen."

Lindsay dropped it. He just had to hope Cary would realize how dangerous his actions had been. But then, it was Cary—maybe he didn't even care.

The house and the property were quiet when he pulled up, and Sister waited for him at the edge of the driveway when he got out of the car.

"Everything okay?" he asked.

"All is well. I knew you would worry."

"Thanks." He patted her muzzle. "I reckon we should check the circle anyways. Safe for me to have supper first?"

"Yes."

Travis was alone in the kitchen when Lindsay when inside. He gave Lindsay a quick sideways smile. "Pork chops okay?"

"Sounds good." Lindsay sat down to pull off his boots. "Where's everybody? I guess Jessie didn't stay."

"Nah, she had to work, I guess. Cary's in with Bella."

"Cary almost lost his damn magic," Lindsay blurted before he could stop himself.

Travis looked up from a plate of bread crumbs. "He what?"

"What he did. He coulda lost his magic. Tal said so."

Travis was quiet for a few seconds before he said, "Wanna come help?"

Grateful to have something to do, Lindsay washed his hands and helped Travis bread the pork chops. He watched Travis out of the corner of his eye, waiting for him to say something, but he didn't.

"You're too nice to tell me I'm being dumb."

"I think you know better'n that." Travis set the first pork chop into a cast-iron skillet. The hot oil sizzled. "But I think you know what you're really worried about. Cary getting disabled again."

A protest sat on the tip of his tongue, but after a second he knew Travis was right. If Cary lost his magic, he'd lose the thing that made him feel able again, or at least as able as he could be. Lindsay couldn't stand to see that happen. He asked, "You think I'm being a mother hen?"

"No. I think you're being a good brother." Travis turned to face him. "Listen, Lindsay. I done told you Cary's a big boy and he can take care of himself, but that don't mean you ain't allowed to worry about him being foolish. God knows he's too good at that."

Lindsay frowned. "So I'm right to worry?"

"I ain't saying you're right or you're wrong. Just that you're allowed. Just thank God nothing bad happened and hope he gets some sense from it."

Lindsay knew Travis was right, but the answer wasn't exactly comforting. He set the last pork chop on a plate next to Travis and washed his hands again. "Sorry."

"What for? Telling me what you're thinking? Ain't I been trying to get you to do that for years?" Travis glanced toward the living room, then leaned in and brushed his lips against Lindsay's cheek. "You don't gotta apologize. You got plenty to worry about."

"Yeah, but...." Here he was talking about his own troubles and he hadn't even asked how Travis was dealing with it. "I bet you and Jessie was freaked out."

Travis shrugged. "I ain't gonna lie and say I wasn't. I cain't speak for Jessica, but Bella was more freaked out, I reckon."

Lindsay lifted his eyebrows. "You got a problem with Jessie?"

"Why?"

"You only call people by their real names if they got a nickname if you don't like 'em."

"I don't got no problem with her on a personal level. I just don't appreciate nobody showing up unannounced like they don't got no manners, girlfriend or no."

"She don't mean no harm. Cary'll talk to her." Lindsay didn't think that was the whole issue, but didn't press the matter. He sliced potatoes and fried them in the other cast-iron pan while Travis tended the pork chops.

It was still light out when Lindsay and Cary set out to check the perimeter circle. They drew it all over again, strengthening it with every connection made, and looked for signs of the creatures: tracks, scat, hair, anything. There was nothing except a thin film of magic in a few spots. Cary said it was brown; to Lindsay, it felt like greasy spring mud.

"You musta seen 'em," Cary said to Cooter at one point. "You know what they was?"

"I know," Cooter replied. "But I can't tell you a name."

"You don't have a helpful bone in your body, do you?"

"I am not made of bones."

"I think them two live to argue," Lindsay said to Sister. "Care, why don't we just ask Tal?"

Cary frowned. "Yeah. Well, if he ever shows up, we can ask."

Tal did show up, or, rather, one of his messengers did. They had decided to squeeze in some saber practice before it got dark and they'd just started their first bout when Lindsay spotted a figure out of the corner of his eye. He stopped Cary and turned to face it, expecting to see a hyena-like shadow, but it was more like a human—just barely, as if it wasn't held together tight enough, and it was beginning to dissolve into the air. It stood directly over a node on the west side of the property.

"Is that another Underworld critter?"

"No. It comes from Tal," Cooter said. "Look closer."

Studying the figure, Lindsay realized Cooter was right. Some indefinable quality gave the impression that it somehow belonged to him, like he'd written his name on it in invisible ink.

"Better tell Bella and Trav we're going," Cary said.

"Reckon they'll be safe?"

"They will be safe in your circle, as they have been," Sister said. Lindsay dismounted and jogged back to the house to tell the others.

The figure grew more distinct as they neared the node. Lindsay recognized it as a girl they'd seen before at Tal's place. She still wore an old-fashioned dress that looked like a maid's outfit, and her eyes were downcast.

"My master asks that you follow me carefully, princes. I will take you to meet him." Without waiting, she turned to walk away, her form fading past the threshold of this world. Lindsay hurried to follow her.

When they stepped onto the aether, the girl was fully-formed and as solid as any other person. Lindsay's sight was drawn to the back of her neck, just below her hairline. The mark there was an indescribable kaleidoscope of shifting jewel-tone colors, deeper and richer than anything around them. He couldn't quite make out the shape, the magic-light was so bright.

Lindsay wanted to ask what the mark was and where it had come from, and why he could see it even though he didn't usually see magic, but he couldn't find the words. He and Sister just followed the girl and her mark. He couldn't say where they went or what they passed. It seemed like only a few minutes later he heard Tal's voice.

"I'm pleased to see you made it, and that you brought your swords, princes. Have you been practicing?"

"Plenty," Lindsay said. He turned to face the girl to thank her for leading them, but she was nowhere to be seen.

"There was a bunch of critters outside or circle today," Cary said. "I guess they was trying to get in. They looked a little like dogs."

Tal's face darkened immediately—and literally. The shining aura that always surrounded it dimmed and he looked almost fully human. "How did they find you?"

"We ain't never seen them before. I dunno how they found us."

"We reckon they come after Bella, the recorsa. They attacked her before."

"The recorsa? She is with you? Why didn't you tell me before?" Tal put a hand on his chest. "I have been frantic, searching for her. With the other missing, I feared the worst."

"What happened to them? We thought Underworld critters wasn't supposed to attack them," Lindsay said.

"Generally speaking, they do not. But there have been groups of Underworld creatures testing their boundaries and sometimes attacking Middle World," Tal said. "That is why I called you here. I need you to help me reinforce táltos sovereignty over the worlds."

"You want us to fight them," Cary said.

"Wherever you find them."

Lindsay looked at Cary in time to see a sharp grin spread across his face, making him look like a wildcat. Lindsay felt himself grinning, too. Finally, something they knew how to do.

"Where do we look?" Lindsay asked.

"I will show you," Tal said. "Follow me."

Cary and Cooter trotted along, unhesitating. Lindsay followed too. He might not want to work for Tal, but he wasn't going to leave Cary without backup.

Mist closed in on them within minutes. It crawled toward them like ghostly hands, grabbing at the horses' legs. They seemed untroubled, but the cold prickle on his bare skin made Lindsay nervous.

"This is for protection," Tal explained. "You would not be able to find this place by yourselves. It was created as a safe place."

A bolt hole. Lindsay wondered why the oldest táltos would need a bolt hole. Who was he hiding from?

"You should also have a place like this. It's good practice; táltosk belong in the aether, after all. Your home is here."

Lindsay didn't know about that—this place was still so foreign—but he didn't argue, concentrating his effort on following Tal. Emese moved faster and the mist got thicker, dimming even the glow of magic surrounding them. Sister moved faster in response, but Lindsay knew without being told that the farther they went, the more the mist interfered with her senses. It was up to him and Cary to guide the horses this time.

"I gotcha." He patted Sister's neck. She snorted, anxious, but he knew she trusted him. He hoped her trust was well-placed.

"Lin." Cary drew near and put out his hand. Lindsay clasped it, and the now-familiar surge of power blinded him for a second before everything flared into full color again. The magic branches were so thick here the dizzied him, but they were clearly visible even through the thick mist. He could see Tal and Emese ahead, too.

The mist soon began to close again and Tal faded from his vision, but a faint trail remained like motor oil in water, a glimmering rainbow. Even without the rainbow, though, Lindsay felt like he knew where to go. It wasn't unlike hunting, following that trail and his internal compass.

The only thing Tal said was, "You will need to find another way to share power if you're to use it effectively. You can't always touch." He had stopped and now turned to face them. "I will lead you through. You will have to trust me."

Lindsay glanced at Cary, wondering what brought that statement on. "Okay."

Tal dismounted smoothly. "Follow Emese through," he said, looking at each of the horses in turn. Before Lindsay could figure out what was going on, he felt what seemed like a giant's hand grab him by the scruff of the neck. He felt himself being yanked out of the saddle and squeezed. The pressure on every inch of his body, on his joints, his head, his chest would have made him scream if he'd had the breath. He couldn't open his eyes, couldn't think.

Then, just as suddenly, air filled his lungs and the pressure released just in time for the ground to punch this breath out of him again as he was dumped unceremoniously into wet grass. A second later, another body hit the ground next to him: Cary.

"What the hell," Cary grunted. Lindsay pushed himself up to help him, wincing. Cary hated being on the ground where he was most helpless.

"Okay?"

"Yeah. Except my ass is bruised." Cary sat up and looked around. "Where are—"

Before he could finish the question, Tal and all three horses came through the fog several yards away. "I had to pull you through before you could resist. If you had, it would have killed you." He bent and held out a hand to Cary as if to help him up. "Come, princes."

"Cooter," Cary said, ignoring the hand. "Lin?"

Lindsay moved forward to help, but Tal said sharply, "Do not help him."

Cary's eyes widened in fury, but he set his jaw and said nothing. Lindsay stood back, his heart pounding with a mixture of shame and nerves, wondering if Cary would finally give in and use his legs, even just to help him get into the saddle. *You heard what Tal said*, he thought. *You can do it.*

Cooter knelt and Cary grasped the saddle horn to pull himself up, his belly draped across the saddle. Lindsay's stomach lurched, seeing him on his belly. Still holding onto the horn, Cary reached down to pull his legs under him and tried to figure out how to get one leg over Cooter's back from this position. *Just use your legs, Care. Just a little bit*, Lindsay wanted to beg. He looked at Tal: Tal watched, arms folowed, a stern, expectant, I-can-wait-all-day look on his face. "Don't help him, Lindsay," he said. It was so unlike Dad, whose first words would have been, *Help your brother, dang it!*

Cursing, sweating, Cary struggled to get that leg over. He needed an extra hand. Or his legs.

"Care," Lindsay said. "Don't be so damn stubborn. Come on."

"Lindsay." Cary's voice scaled up in a warning tone. "Don't."

"And why not?" Tal asked. "Your brother only wants what is best for you."

"My brother wants what he wants to be best for me," Cary said. The words struck Lindsay like a slap. Was that true? He really did want what was best for Cary...right?

Right?

Eventually, with Cooter's help, Cary managed to get his leg over and sit up in the saddle. His eyes were bright with anger and Cooter didn't look too happy either as he stood.

"I will say this, prince: you certainly have enough will for five like you," Tal said. "Come to the house."

Lindsay walked toward the little cabin at the edge of the meadow between Sister and Cooter with Cary glaring down at him.

"You and me are gonna go round and round about this," he growled.

"Care, I don't get why—"

"No. You *don't*. So stop fucking pushing. This ain't nothing to do with you."

"Are you serious? How does it *not* got to do with me?"

"Because it ain't your fucking back that's broken, that's why. You cain't fix me, Lin. That ain't how this works." Cooter sped up, leaving Lindsay behind.

"Shouldn't 'a let you get hurt in the first place," Lindsay whispered.

* * *

The cabin, of course, had steps leading up to the porch, and of course it wasn't accessible. The first problem was easily solvable: Cary created his wheelchair on the porch, and Cooter knelt beside it. The second problem he'd just have to deal with. He managed to squeeze through the front door, anyway.

The place reminded him of the little hunting cabin Dad had built way up in the hills, where he'd take them for their most intense training. Unlike Tal's lavishly-decorated house, this place was utilitarian. The main area was open, with a cook stove and a table, plus a pallet in one corner. Tal led them to a heavy door overlaid with heavier magic. It was so thick it looked like mesh. Cary wondered what Tal was guarding from if no one could get into this place on their own.

Tal opened the door to an armory, lined with racks of weapons—mostly blades of every kind, from what looked like a combat knife to a four-foot-long, broad weapon with a blood channel down its length. The kind badasses carried in movies.

"Today you will use your sabers, since you have been practicing," Tal said. "The two-handed swords are impractical on horseback." He gestured behind them. "And there is your armor."

Cary heard Lindsay's low whistle before he turned. Two half-suits of metal armor hung on the wall, designed to cover from the waist up. He had no doubt which was his: it shone deep, burnished gold with trim designed to look like braid striping the chest and shoulders and emblems on the gauntlets, chest and collar. The emblem on the chest was a bird of some kind, like an eagle. Lindsay's was identical but for the color, a matte white, like snow. Cary shivered a little. The armor fit them and the tack they'd imagined for the horses, too.

But the best part was the wings, twin pennants that came up from the waist, arching up and back with what looked like real feathers attached. Cary felt himself grinning like a fool. "That is *sweet*."

"I will show you how to put it on the first time," Tal said. "This task you may help one another with."

As Cary watched Tal strap Lindsay into his armor, leather padding first, he noticed a design on the back he hadn't before: a stylized tree, stretching across the entire back of the breastplate. He didn't know the type of tree off-hand, but he recognized the design on the back of his own armor as an elm. This really was táltos armor, fit for princes.

"Did you make all this?" he asked.

"With the help of your own will and perception. You are royalty. You deserve nothing less," Tal said.

Cary was starting to think maybe he could believe it.

When they went outside, Cary noticed that the designs on Cooter's saddle had changed. They matched the elm tree on the back of his armor and were now embossed with gold. Lindsay gasped when he saw Sister's saddle and Cary guessed hers had changed, too. The armor was about as heavy as it looked, and the wings especially made mounting a trick and a half, but once he was in the saddle, with Lindsay's help this time, the weight against his lower back steadied him.

Tal appeared from the cabin a moment later, and Cary had to squint when he saw him. The brilliant rainbow aura they had come to think of as normal was refracted and reflected by armor that shone like a diamond, glinting in every direction. The wings were shiny black like crow feathers and gleamed almost as brightly. Next to him, Emese's gray-and-white pelt looked almost dull. Tal put on his helmet and readjusted the saber at his waist when he was in the saddle. "Come. You may leave on horseback. You need only be separated from them when coming into this place."

They set out across the meadow again into the woods, which closed immediately around them. The path was more like a deer trail, way too narrow and overgrown with brush and low-hanging branches for the horses. Branches slapped against Cary and he was already glad for the armor, though the pennants kept getting caught. Irritated, he imagined the path widening, the undergrowth thinning to make passage easier.

"While I appreciate your effort, prince, do remember that actions have consequences." Ahead of them, Tal pulled his saber from its sheath. Cary barely had time to do the same before they were attacked.

* * *

The air erupted into harsh chattering that sounded like a cross between demon birds and giant squirrels. A pale shape flung itself at Lindsay from out of nowhere and he swung his saber out to block it. The blade sliced open a skinny chest to the bone and blood sprayed, but the movement had been too wide, opening him up for another attack. The next creature landed on his left shoulder and he heard claws screech against the armor. Something more like a hand than a paw reached into the gap between his helmet and breastplate, and he cried out in utter shock and dismay at the clammy skin against the back of his neck. He heard Cary snarl and then felt something thud against the back of his armor. The hand fell away and the pale shape tumbled to the ground.

As he oriented himself, Lindsay saw what they were fighting: a troupe of things that looked like a cross between a spider and some kind of long-tailed monkey they had seen at the zoo. At least six legs that flashed in every direction, grabbing and clawing, and mouths full of needle teeth. Lindsay hacked at them, remembering their practice—block one with a back-handed parry, bring the saber back to slice another—but this fighting was far from elegant. They weren't trying to block an opponent's blade, but furry bodies that came at them like missiles. And there were a hell of a lot of them, twenty if there were a dozen.

Out of the chaos, filled with the screeches and chattering of the monkey-things, a rush of wild energy rose in Lindsay's mind, sharpening it. No longer was he merely reacting to their attacks, just trying to keep them off him, but he was going after them, Sister wading into the fray. He saw Cary on the other side of the sea of clamoring bodies and met his eyes: *meet you in the middle.*

Cary let out a whoop and plunged toward Lindsay. Cooter's expression mirrored his rider's: all bright, sharp-edged intensity. Lindsay had barely touched Sister's sides with his heels when she sprang forward, knocking some of the creatures out with her sharp hooves.

In the moment, Lindsay saw exactly where and how he needed to move and his body knew how to twist his wrist and elbow and shoulder to make his sword do just what he needed it to. He didn't remember from one second to the next, completely focused in his body. He didn't care about doing things exactly right, didn't care about screwing things up, just cared about getting them done.

It wasn't until he heard Cary's panting that he realized all the creatures were gone. Not just gone, but disappeared, leaving his saber shining and slick with gore, his hand and arm wet with the same. Tal and Emese stood off to the side; had he simply been watching? Hard to tell. Both his armor and Emese's pelt were pristine while Sister's neck and sides were as bloody as Lindsay's arm and sword, but between one glance down and another, all the mess disappeared. The only evidence they'd actually fought was the adrenaline still rushing through him and the sweat drenching every inch of him beneath the armor.

"You are truly a pair like no one has ever seen," Tal said approvingly. "Can you do it again?"

They could, and they did. The forest crawled with Underworld creatures.

After a while, flushing out the creatures of every shape and size and getting rid of them began to feel almost routine, like exterminating pests.

Almost. Lindsay felt powerful, invincible, fighting beside his brother with a kind of insane glee, the perfect pair and complement to one another. Where one couldn't be, the other swooped in. When they fought groups, they drove a wedge into the middle of them—including a pack of those hounds—or trapped them from either side. This was what they were born and made to do, to fight and destroy the creatures of darkness.

The thought came in Dad's voice. How much had he actually been right about? Lindsay felt sick.

"Lin." Cary's voice broke through his reverie. "What are you getting yourself aggravated over?"

Looking into his brother's face, shining with that wild battle light still, Lindsay found it hard to give voice to his worry. For the first time in five years, he could tell Cary felt completely capable again, as able to fulfill their mission as Lindsay was. He'd be damned if he'd rain on that parade.

"Wondering how I'm gonna explain what we did to Trav," he lied. He was an awful liar and he knew it, but maybe Cary was distracted enough not to notice.

"Tell him while you're on your knees and he won't care what you say."

"Lord God almighty, Cary Judah." Lindsay's face heated. "What is wrong with you? Why you gotta talk like that?"

"I don't see you denying." Cary smirked. "I ain't no fool, Lin. Go on and I'll shut my ears."

Lindsay was aware of every movement as he dismounted and unsaddled Sister, as if Cary were watching him even though Cary was about his own business. Inside, he hesitated, trying to decide whether to shower before he went in to talk to Travis, but the shower in the accessible hall bathroom started, killing that idea. He padded into the master suite, thinking maybe he could sneak a quick shower in there. The water pressure was probably good enough for both showers to run at the same time.

Lindsay sensed Travis come to the bathroom door. His pretty eyes were squinted, mostly hidden by long lashes, and his hair stuck up around his head, except at the crown where it was a little thin. "Y'all musta been practicing hard. It's late."

"Sorry. Didn't mean to wake you." Lindsay felt self-conscious again with his shirt off, but Travis gave him that little half-smile that made butterflies flutter low in Lindsay's belly.

"Glad you did." Travis nodded toward the shower. "Okay if I join you?"

That was the single hottest thing anyone had ever asked him. "Uh. I mean... yeah. Please."

Travis crossed the space between them in two steps and reached beyond Lindsay to turn the shower on. His closeness made Lindsay's heart beat faster. "You look..." Travis smiled. "Like an angel. You shine."

Lindsay felt his face grow warm. He wished he could figure out what made Travis and Cary say that about him. "We was out on the aether. Bella said sometimes magic sticks around us."

"I think it's just you." Travis kissed him, silencing his next words. Suddenly hunger coursed through Lindsay and he grabbed Travis's wife beater, pushing it up his chest. They parted the kiss just long enough to get the shirt off, revealing those long, thick heart surgery scars on his chest. Lindsay knew Travis didn't like drawing attention to them, so he concentrated next on getting Travis's pants off. He was glad they were just sleep pants. Lindsay himself was still wearing jeans and they couldn't come off fast enough.

"Lindsay." Travis stopped him with gentle hands on his forearms. "What's the burning rush?"

Lindsay felt a keen stab of desperate frustration. "I just *want* you." He wanted absolute focus again, too, being completely in his body instead of in his head. Having tasted it again for the first time in so long, he wanted *more*.

"I'm here." Travis's voice was gently amused. "You got me. What's going on?"

How to explain it? He couldn't without sounding totally crazy, and Travis had put up with so much of their crazy already. "I just cain't resist you." God, did he sound desperate.

But Travis just smiled. "Well, then." He pushed Lindsay's jeans over his hips, then knelt to help him get them off. Seeing him on his knees made Lindsay dizzy.

"Water's gonna get cold," Travis said. He straightened and tugged Lindsay into the shower. It was a little cramped for two grown men, but Lindsay hardly minded being close. Travis took his sweet time, soaping his hands and running them lightly over Lindsay's skin. Lindsay wanted Travis to grab him, wanted to kiss him until they both couldn't breathe. He made a little sound of frustration, held with his back against Travis's chest and unable to do so. Travis just chuckled.

Soon, the light touches became sweet torture, inflaming Lindsay's nerve endings, and by the time Travis grasped him in a soapy hand, Lindsay groaned outright. Still he wanted *more*, but he wasn't sure how to ask. Feeling Travis pressed insistently against him, though, gave him the push he needed. He broke Travis's hold, turned and put his hand on either side of Travis's face. "Trav. I *want* you. For real."

Travis's eyes widened a little, but then they flickered when Lindsay reached down to touch him. "How?"

"I wanna take it from you." A little tendril of anxiety coiled in Lindsay's belly. But god, he wanted it.

Travis looked a little stunned, but he nodded. After a cursory rinse, they stepped out of the shower and Travis toweled himself off. He took his time, probably nervous, but it drove Lindsay a little crazy.

The bedroom was pitch-dark except where the bathroom light shone in and it seemed quieter than usual. All Lindsay could hear was his own breath and the heartbeat pulsing in his ears. He sat down on the bed and looked at Travis, framed in the bathroom doorway. *He* looked like an angel now. "You okay?" Lindsay asked.

"Yeah. Just looking at you."

Lindsay flushed. Before he could stop himself he asked, "That all you're gonna do? Look?"

Travis answered him by crossing the room and kissing him. There was that eager, hungry Travis that finally said 'fuck it' to his nervousness and pressed Lindsay onto the bed. Lindsay pulled him up so they both lay stretched out. Their bodies wound together in a way Lindsay had wanted for years but hadn't dared admit. When he thought about sleeping with someone as a teenager, it wasn't the pretty cowgirl Cary always went for, but this: big, broad Travis, undeniably male. He was starting to think maybe that was okay.

Travis's hands were all over him, rough from farm work but always gentle. It was a while before they took their making out a step further despite Travis's obvious eagerness; Lindsay didn't want to rush him again, and he just liked when Travis touched him.

They both struggled to get the condom on, first Travis and then Lindsay. Travis started to laugh and that broke the tension. "Look at us. What a pair, huh?"

Lindsay smiled at the way Travis's eyes gleamed in the light from the bathroom. "Third time's a charm?"

This was no adrenaline-rushing fight—far from it, really—but the pure physicality of being underneath Travis, being filled by him, feeling Travis's breath on his neck, was even better. It hurt at first and Travis looked alarmed at his reaction, but Lindsay reassured him until he kept going, and then even the pressure was good. It brought Lindsay out of his head again—he was unconcerned with magic or bills or guns or Dad or Emily or anything but his body and Travis against it, inside it.

The look on Travis's face when he came made a surge of tenderness well up in Lindsay so strongly he felt wetness at the corners of his eyes. He held Travis hard as he shuddered and buried his face in Travis's neck.

"You didn't..." Travis pushed himself up after a few seconds. "Sorry."

Lindsay let out a little laugh. "Ain't nothing to be sorry about. Watching you was awful nice. And what you was doing."

"Still." Travis moved down until he knelt between Lindsay's knees. He never got sick of that mouth on him, and again what Travis lacked in experience he made up for in that unexpected eagerness. Lindsay lay back, trying to be quiet, but *watching* Travis's mouth on him made it impossible, and his own moans sounded like a porn star's. He forgot to care. He surrendered again to his body and forgot everything else.

Travis didn't swallow; he spat into the bedroom trashcan, but Lindsay didn't mind that. He knew Travis was hesitant to be kissed after that out of some sense of politeness, so Lindsay just pressed against him, realizing how tired he was. The room was a little warm, but not enough to want to stop touching Travis.

"You always get really into it," Travis murmured.

"You don't?"

"Well, sure, but..."

Lindsay chewed his bottom lip. "That bother you?"

Travis gave him that little smile. "Aw, hell no. The way you look...I mean, I made that happen."

Lindsay laughed, pure joy welling up in him. "Yeah, honey, you did. I get into you."

"I think maybe I got into you that time."

Lindsay blinked, unable to believe that just came out of Travis's mouth. Travis laughed.

Chapter Sixteen

When he came out of the bathroom, Cary could hear the other shower running. The darkness still gave him the creeps somehow, even though he'd just been fighting real Underworld things instead of figments of his imagination. He decided he was too wired to sleep and made for the living room to watch whatever was on TV at this hour. One of the good things about not going to classes anymore was that he could sleep late.

"Cary?" Bella's voice startled him. It sounded alert, not like she had been sleeping. He pushed her bedroom door part of the way open, but could see nothing in the pitch-black.

"What's up?"

"You were out on the aether. I can see your magic clinging to you."

"Didn't know you could see magic."

"See it, feel it, hear it. I am magic."

"I thought you said you was memory."

"You're a smartass."

You're damn right. Someday you got to tell me about you, since you know so much about us." He turned back to the hall. "'Night, girl."

"You aren't going to sleep?"

"After a while."

"I can tell you now."

The shower had stopped; Cary heard a moan that was unmistakably Lindsay's from across the house. Before Cary could figure out how to react, Bella said,

"Was that Lindsay?"

"I reckon."

Bella came to the door in an oversized t-shirt, her curly hair sticking up every which way. "Are they having sex?"

He looked up at her; she looked completely surprised, like the thought had never occurred to her before. "I'd guess. But don't ask me how two men have sex, for God's sake."

"Well, I know that."

Cary found it almost impossible to predict what Bella knew about humans and what she was clueless about. He had stopped being surprised by either. He just turned back toward the living room. Maybe he could turn the TV up far enough that he wouldn't have to listen to Lindsay and Travis. Bella followed and folded herself into Travis's chair. Her legs were long and a little gangly like a half-grown foal's, and her curls made her look so young he felt bad for even looking at her legs. He realized she was wearing his t-shirt and his stomach did a little flip-flop.

"So you want to know about recorsas?" she asked as he pulled himself onto the sofa and turned on the TV. It was already on one of the sports channels, in the middle of recaps of the previous day's games.

"Well, I want to know about *you*," he told her.

"It's essentially the same thing."

"Bullshit it is. You act like all you are is a recorsa, and I know that ain't true."

She lifted her eyebrows at him. "How do you know that?"

Cary couldn't help but laugh a little. "Seriously? You're asking me how I can tell when someone is a person? Fine. You said you drive a Camaro, which means you got bad taste in sports cars but at least you like to go fast. You always look at them trivia websites that tell you all kinds of weird stuff, so you like learning new stuff. You like your coffee about half sugar and you gotta drink at least two cups before you start looking alive in the mornings, like me. You like to watch people, maybe because you're trying to figure them out."

"I'm a person because I *like* things?"

Cary set the remote down. "Yeah."

"Cooter likes apples. He's not a person."

"Sure he is. Just because he ain't human don't mean he don't count. You're a person, girl. Get over it."

She gave him one of those long, thoughtful expressions that made her eyes look ancient. Her face was gravely pretty, even with her brows furrowed. "We aren't supposed to be people. We imitate humans because it's prudent. Humans exist in most worlds and rule most of those. But the more we act like people, the more we limit ourselves and our abilities. We're meant to understand you but not think like you."

"Seems to me it don't always work that way. How can you really understand somebody if you ain't been in their shoes?"

Bella shrugged. "To a certain extent, we can't help emotions because we sometimes enter the human mindset too easily, but we have to be able to control them."

Cary thought that was sad, but he understood it in a weird way. Dad had always made them suck it up, too. "But you still have emotions. Only people have emotions."

"I see, the classic syllogism." She had an odd smile, as if she were still practicing the expression, but that made it seem more genuine. "So what do you want to know, exactly?"

"Where were you born? Where'd you grow up? You have any family besides your dad?"

"In answer to the first two questions, on the aether," she said. "I wasn't born. I was created by Sandor when it was time for the woman who created him to step down. Since then I've been traveling between realms and worlds, mostly by myself. I don't have relatives in the same way you do."

Cary couldn't even picture that. Not born. No family. She must have noticed his expression because she said, "Rethinking your position on my personhood, aren't you?"

"No," he said firmly, determined to make this make sense. "Don't matter if you was hatched from an egg. It's how you are now that matters, and you're a person."

She narrowed her eyes; it took him a minute to realize she was thinking rather than annoyed. "Why are you so adamant about it? What does it matter to you?"

Good question, he thought, even as he heard himself say, "Because I like you, and it just don't make sense that I'm sitting here talking to somebody who ain't a person and liking her. I don't talk to a computer and like it."

She looked a little confused. "You honestly believe it."

"Yeah." Lord, but this girl was weird. "You sure ain't like nobody else, but you ain't no thing or no critter, neither." He decided to end that conversation by changing the topic. "So Sandor created you. How's that work, exactly, and you not having a mother?"

"You're limited by the notion of sexual reproduction," she sighed. He'd learned not to be insulted by remarks like that; the more she talked, the more he realized he really *didn't* get a lot of the things he thought he did. "I can't give you details because it's one of the rare pieces of knowledge we keep to ourselves, but realize that we are part of the World Tree, not unlike the horses. I'm part Sandor, who is the living embodiment of memory, part the Tree itself, and part everything I've learned."

Cary absorbed that, thinking he definitely wasn't smart enough to grasp the depth of what she was saying. "I'll take your word for it. So you said you was created when the one before Sandor retired or whatever. How does that happen? You just reach retirement age, or something?'

"No, and we don't have a pension plan, either," Bella said, looking genuinely amused now. "The longer we imitate humans, the more human we become, and like I said, human thought patterns limit our perception. Eventually we can no longer connect with the World Tree at the level we need to, and we can no longer be recorsas."

Cary didn't think Bella realized she shivered at the thought. He couldn't help but be troubled by it, too. If being a recorsa was everything she thought she was, what would happen if she could no longer do it? He looked down at his useless legs and decided not to ask. "You was created, okay. What then? Sandor just up and left you alone like a baby sea turtle?"

He noticed she always got a certain look on her face when Sandor's name came up: lips thin, brows drawn. Lindsay got the same look when they talked about Dad. "Not exactly like a sea turtle. More like a bird. We know what we need to do from the moment we're created, and we're able to survive on our own on the aether, but learning to interact with people is something that needs to be taught. It doesn't come naturally to us the way it does to you."

She looked irritated, so he'd let it go for now, but he was bound and determined to get an explanation later. Jessie hated it when he started discussions like this. Like a dog with a bone, she'd said, exasperated.

"How do y'all get memories?" he asked, changing the subject again. There was an infomercial on TV now, and she seemed fascinated by it. Watching her watch TV was kind of cute, like it was something new and exciting.

"What do you mean?"

"Well, y'all cain't be there to see everything that happens everywhere. So how d'you remember everything?"

"We don't remember everything ever. Just events pertaining to the Tree. And it's not exactly us who remember, either—it's the Tree. We're more like... archives for that memory, and mediators and interpreters. It's like downloading something from the internet onto a computer. It's just bits and bytes of energy—you couldn't interpret it yourself. You need a computer to store it, decode it and display it in a way you can understand. That's why I say we aren't people. We're reflections of the information we store. Computers can 'learn' by adapting to very complex algorithms and endless strings of binary if-then statements, so they can imitate life very well, theoretically, but when it comes down to unquantifiables like emotions, there's really no way to cope with it."

He understood about half of one statement in three, but he thought he caught the gist. "Now I know you ain't telling me you're like Arnold in Terminator 2."

"No. More like the Cylons in the new Battlestar Galactica."

"I refuse to believe you're a damn computer," Cary said. "You cain't convince me unless I get to cut you open and look for hardware."

"I didn't mean it literally. I was just using—"

"Okay, Number Six. So can anyone access your information?"

She gave him a look. "Why do I sense you're being perverted?"

Cary gave her his best angelic look, the one that used to make girls' panties fall off while simultaneously charming their mamas. Her expression remained blank. He stalled.

"I can provide information to anyone who needs it," Bella said, "but I specifically serve magical people, especially the táltosk."

"So if I asked you a question, you'd have to answer it?"

"I wouldn't be forced to. I'm not a servant. But I would, because that's what we do."

"If I asked you how you create a new recorsa, you'd tell me?"

She gave him a look. "Don't push it, prince."

The title sounded different coming from her, not so serious. He liked that. "Well, you look like a redneck princess in my shirt."

She flushed deeply and pulled her knees up to her chest. He couldn't help it; his eyes went to her bare thighs. He couldn't get it up anymore, but he could certainly appreciate the sight.

Jesus, Cary.

"Y'all still awake?" Lindsay's voice from the kitchen startled Cary and he twisted around. Lindsay shuffled through the kitchen on the way to the refrigerator, squinting in the light from the living room. He was wearing nothing but boxers.

"Thought y'all was asleep," Cary said. Lindsay came closer. "What're y'all watching?" His eyes settled on Bella wearing Cary's shirt. He gave Cary a confused look. "Reckon I'll go on back." He filled a glass of water in the sink and headed toward the hallway again.

"You're walking funny," Cary told him. Lindsay faltered for a moment, giving Cary his moment of satisfaction.

"He and Travis slept together," Bella said. "Right?"

Cary looked back toward the dark hallway. "Yeah. Reckon so."

"Oh." She shifted in her seat. "Would you sleep with me?"

Cary choked. "*What?*"

"Hypothetically. Would you?"

"Jesus, Bella." Cary moved back to his chair. How the hell was he supposed to answer that?

"What?" she sounded genuinely baffled.

"That ain't just something you can just ask somebody. Jesus." For the first time he could ever remember, he retreated rather than answer.

* * *

It took Lindsay a while to think of how to ask Cary about what happened with Bella. Finally, while they drove home from Springfield one night after Cary's night class, he decided to be up front. "You didn't sleep with her, did you?"

"Of course I didn't. I ain't no whore," Cary said, reaching to turn on the radio.

"What does that mean?" Lindsay asked, his face heating. "You making some smart remark about me and Travis?"

Cary's head jerked up. "No, Lin."

"Oh." Lindsay was silent, watching the trailer in front of them. It was packed full of what looked like a whole apartment's worth of stuff tied with yellow rope. The boxes stacked on top shifted dangerously when the trailer hit a pot hole.

"He's a good guy," Cary said. "If I was single and queer, I'd probably fuck him too."

"Jesus, Cary." Lindsay's blush didn't go away, but he felt a little better. "So you don't mind or nothing?"

"No. Why would I?"

Before Lindsay could think of an answer, an almighty crash up ahead startled the shit out of him. The trailer's brake lights flashed, tires squealed, and the truck whipped into the right lane. The trailer swayed dangerously, but it stayed upright. Without thinking, Lindsay followed its path, slamming on his own brakes; something metal flashed past his window and he heard Cary yelp as he brought the Explorer to a stop behind the trailer.

"Christ almighty, did you see that? The damn truck almost rolled into us! Turn your hazards on," he said. Lindsay had the absurd urge to laugh at the mix of disbelief and practicality. He turned on the hazard lights and unbuckled his seat belt as the trailer owner, a woman, came jogging back.

"You got phone service?"

"What happened?"

"Truck came across the median and ran into a car."

Lindsay nodded again and glanced at Cary, who'd already pulled out his cell phone to dial 911.

More cars were pulling up as they got out, illuminating the crash with their headlights. The pickup, which must have been the vehicle that had rolled past them, lay on its side on the shoulder and looked like it was going to teeter into the median, and the little hatchback sat pulverized in the left hand lane about thirty feet from where they stood. The roof had been sheared off, and he could see blood sparkling in the headlights from here. There was no surviving that.

"I'll go check," Lindsay said, though that was the last damn thing he wanted to do. He walked toward the hatchback, forcing his limbs to move, forcing himself to see the blood and look for the body—or bodies. Just on the off chance someone was still alive. He'd seen road kill and what it could do to cars: blood and hair and chunks of flesh everywhere. This looked a lot like that. As his eyes adjusted to the dimness beyond the reach of the headlights, he had to remind himself to breathe.

He smelled burned rubber, gas and engine heat. That wasn't a good combination. Every instinct screamed at him to move away, but he couldn't let someone who needed help just go without it because he was a pussy.

He came around to the driver's side. No body in the seat. Blood, a lot of blood, darkened the light-colored fabric seat, shone on broken glass and smeared the door, but no body. When he forced himself to examine the back seat, he couldn't see anything there, either.

Now he had to *look* for someone. Oh, Christ.

"Lin." Cary's voice, concerned, still in the Explorer.

"I'm here," he called; he could hear the strain in his own voice.

"Don't you be no goddamn hero. I smell gas. Emergency's on its way."

Lindsay squinted through the beams of light back toward the woman driving the trailer. He could hear her speaking to someone else about getting someone out of the pickup, but couldn't see what was going on.

"You find anybody?" the woman asked.

"Still looking." *Fuck fuck fuck.* Lindsay turned his attention down to the low grass median just as another guy jogged up with an emergency flashlight. "Here."

Lindsay nodded his thanks and turned it on. He started near the car first, trying not to feel like a coward for holding his breath every time the beam of yellow light swept across the uncut grass. He almost jumped out of his skin once, but it was only the soggy remains of a cardboard box.

No more blood, no grass laid flat from the weight of a body. Nothing. Lindsay's hands shook so badly he could barely hold the flashlight.

The howl of emergency sirens carried by the wind almost gave him a heart attack. A Highway Patrol vehicle pulled up first in the southbound lanes near Lindsay. "What happened?"

"Truck hit this one." Lindsay wondered how in the hell his voice was steady now. "I cain't find a...cain't find nothing."

The officer glanced around. "Better go back to your vehicle. I smell gas. Thanks for your help. Stick around so I can get a witness statement, okay?"

Lindsay felt even more like a coward being so relieved to turn away. He looked for the guy who'd loaned him the flashlight, but couldn't see him, Ambulances and fire trucks were peeling up now, and the multicolored lights stabbed at his eyes. He heard someone in the direction of the pickup crying out in pain and shuddered. He knew that sound all too well.

He walked back toward the Explorer. Inside, Cary craned his neck to see what was going on.

"You okay?" Cary asked.

"Yeah. Yeah." Lindsay waved a hand. "You?"

"All I did was sit here. I'm fine."

Both knew they were lying, but neither said anything about it. Lindsay just went back to the car.

"You see something?" Cary asked. Lindsay knew he wasn't just asking to be morbid. He shook his head.

"Sorta wished I had." Somewhere out there was a body to go with all that blood; seeing it was better than waiting for it just around the corner, or on the next sweep of the flashlight. It had been the waiting that had nearly killed him before he'd found Cary.

Lindsay turned off the hazard lights and the console lights and they sat in the dark. The woman had apparently been shooed away from the scene too. She hovered near the driver's side door until Lindsay rolled down the window. He noticed then that her right sleeve was streaked with blood.

"The guy probably has a bunch of broken bones," she said, no emotion in her voice. "And a million glass cuts. I think I cut myself too."

"You should go get the paramedics to check you," Lindsay said as gently as he could.

"It's okay. They're still working on the guy and there's a girl still in the car."

The paramedics put the guy on a stretcher. They had to wait for the fire trucks to get the woman out of the pickup. Police flooded the scene after those two were gone, assessing the damage and searching for the other driver. They never saw anyone bring a stretcher over to the hatchback.

Lindsay had closed his eyes for a second against the glare of lights in his side mirror when he heard a voice behind him.

"One of you called in?"

"I did," Cary said.

They gave their witness statements. As Lindsay balanced the clipboard on the steering wheel to write his, he thought of Emily. Sometimes there just weren't words to describe something. He kept it short. At some point while they were talking to the officer, the woman had disappeared.

As the officer verified their names and addresses, it occurred to Lindsay that his vehicle probably wouldn't pass a thorough police search if they decided to conduct one. But he was just being paranoid. Why would they? Besides, all the guns in the car were registered. At least, he was pretty sure they were.

"Delaney," the officer said.

Lindsay's jaw tightened. "Yessir."

He studied Lindsay and Cary both, then nodded. "You can go. We'll call if we need anything else."

Lindsay wondered why he didn't feel more relieved when the officer walked away.

* * *

Lindsay brushed off Travis's concern as much as he could when they told him about the accident, assuring him that they were both okay. He kept picturing the blood glittering under the flashlight with no body and he didn't want to talk about it.

Rather than let Cary talk to Emily and get into a fuss about it, though, Lindsay called her himself. She didn't answer, but she called back half an hour later.

"I looked into it," she said when he answered. "The two victims were mundane. The couple in the pickup are both dead. Nobody ever found the driver of the other car. What are you two into?"

"We ain't into nothing," Lindsay said, annoyed. "Why d'you ask?"

"My contacts said that the victims and the car had signs of magical corruption all over them and I'm getting reamed for not keeping you out of trouble."

"I was on the damn road driving home," Lindsay snapped. "That's all I was doing. I didn't do nothing wrong and I don't know who'd be after us. You said there's corruption all over the Tree. Does that have to mean somebody is after us?"

"Well, are you seeing any other corruption? Has anything else happened?"

Lindsay thought about the hounds Cary described and wondered whether to tell her. His gut said no; she'd just use it as an excuse to push them around more. "Uh uh."

Emily paused, and for a minute Lindsay thought she'd caught on. All she said was, "Let me know if anything else happens."

"Why? What are you gonna do about it?"

Another pause. "Look, I'm doing my best to keep a handle on things. I can't help if you don't let me."

Cold anger swept through Lindsay and left him shaking. His chest felt too tight to breathe. When he was younger and Wade was ragging on him for one thing or another, he'd always said, *I'm just trying to help you out, boy. You better be glad it's me and not Lewis.*

"Y'know, maybe we don't need your help," Lindsay said. Before she could say anything else, he hung up and turned his phone off. When he turned, Travis was standing in the shadows of the living room lights.

"You're probably right, y'know," he said softly. "You don't need her help. Don't sound like she was much help anyway."

"No." Lindsay forced his voice out. "Don't need her."

Travis looked like he was going to move forward, but he hesitated. "You wanna come here?"

"Yeah." His eyes stinging and blurring with tears, Lindsay stumbled across the living room. "Yeah. I need you."

* * *

Cary was barely awake when the phone rang. He didn't recognize the number on the caller ID. He figured it was Wade on a disposable phone, though, so he answered without hesitation.

"What the fuck, Cary." Definitely not Wade.

"Who's this?"

"It's Amy, you douchebag. What is going on?"

Oh, excellent. As if he needed Lindsay's fag hag crawling down his throat. "Kiss my skinny crippled ass." He hung up.

A minute later, he heard Lindsay's phone ring across the house. Lindsay picked up, then appeared in Cary's doorway. "Did you hang up on Amy?"

Cary gave him a look that warned him not to expect Cary to take the phone he was holding out. Lindsay gave him a long suffering look and put the phone to his ear again. "He don't wanna talk."

Amy said a few words; Cary guessed she was demanding Lindsay give him the phone. Lindsay looked annoyed. "Y'all work it out. I'm turning off my phone." He hung up and pressed the power button, then gave Cary a look that was half irritation and half hurt. "I'm nice to Jessie. The least you can do is talk to Amy if she has something to say instead of acting like a dang stubborn little kid." Without waiting for Cary to answer, he left the room.

Cary picked up his phone to turn it off, but it rang the second he did. He scowled at it: same number. Guilt crawled in his belly, picturing the look on Lindsay's face. He was better at guilt-tripping than any woman.

He opened his phone. "What the hell d'you want?"

"I feel sorry for Lindsay, having a brother like you. You never think about anybody but yourself. You think you can run everybody. Well, you can't run me."

Those words stung. Cary considered hanging up on her again, but he felt like he should defend himself. "What d'you know about me and Lindsay? You don't know nothing."

"I know you push him around to get what you want and you never think about him. And he puts up with it because he's too damn nice. You treat him like he's your servant or something. You do the same thing with Jessie."

A sharp pain in Cary's chest took his breath away. He felt weak for a second, and he forgot to defend himself. He pictured Dad ordering Wade around. *Y'all two are just like your dad and Wade*, Aunt Betty had said, many times.

They weren't like that. Were they?

"You motherfucker, if you hang up on me again, I'm coming out there."

"I didn't fucking hang up on you," Cary said through gritted teeth. "Is that what you called about? Jessie?"

"If you're going to cheat on her, the least you can do is have the decency to be sneaky about it instead of parading your conquest in front of her."

Jesus, she didn't pull any punches. "What the fuck? I ain't cheating on her."

"Then why were you bringing a girl back with you?"

"She's a family friend and she needs help, not that it's any of your damn business. Who d'you think you are, putting your nigger nose in my business?"

"Oh, *that's* nice. Way to throw down the N-word, you fucking racist prick. I've never figured out what the hell Jessie sees in you. You do nothing but treat everyone around you like shit, especially her."

Cary gritted his teeth, gripping his phone so hard the sides cut into his palm. "Did you call just to chew me out because I helped somebody out? You got no right. You don't know, bitch."

"I know that whatever is going on, you're treating my friend like shit, and I won't put up with it even if she's too nice to say something to you. You fucking hurt her, Cary, and I want to rip you apart."

"How'd I hurt her, for Christ's sweet sake?"

"Are you *kidding* me? What must it be like to go through life completely unaware of how big a prick you are?"

"If you ain't gonna tell me what the hell I did wrong, you can fuck off."

"You don't even wonder why she thinks you might be cheating on her? You call her up whenever you want her to put up with you, then you wander off and do whatever the hell you do. Your relationship is totally on your terms. You don't bother to *tell* her anything. Then you show up with this girl, you don't tell her who she is, and you expect her to think everything is normal?"

"You don't know the whole story, so stop acting like you do, dammit," Cary growled. "I done told her everything she needs to know."

"What the fuck, is this some kind of conspiracy theory bullshit? She's your girlfriend, goddammit. You don't get to pick and choose what crumbs you throw at her. Either make her part of your life or let her go. Stop stringing her along and making her beg for your attention."

Cary tried to come up with a retort, but the words died in his throat.

"You're not even listening. God. Fine, Cary. Do what you want. I just hope Jessie sees who you really are someday." Amy hung up.

Cary wanted to smack Lindsay for making him put up with this. But then all the fight went out of him when he heard Amy's words again: *Stop stringing her along and making her beg for your attention. I feel sorry for Lindsay, having a brother like you.*

Shit.

* * *

Like the coward he was, Wade called Cary instead of Lindsay to tell them where to pick up the weapons they were supposed to modify. He probably knew Lindsay would have told him to go to hell. Lindsay wanted to call him back and tell him that anyway, but Cary told him again that this would be the last deal, that they'd do their own business after this. He hoped to God Cary meant it.

He was always give out when he came home from work, sometimes on the verge of heat exhaustion. As soon as they finished supper, though, they worked on their gun modifications for a couple of hours, then went outside to practice well into the night. Both of them got good at feeling rather than needing to see their blades. It took a while, but Lindsay remembered the trick to working so hard on so little sleep and food, too. They'd done it all the time when they were kids. He just did what he needed to do, didn't think about it. After a while he was too tired to think about it and then, at a certain point, he stopped feeling tired.

Tal took them out three, sometimes four times a week and they fought Underworld creatures. Not all the time, though; several times he took them out onto wild paths near other parts of Middle World—other realms, he called them. These realms often looked just like their own, but they *felt* different. Some of them had táltosk, some had beings that were sort of similar, and some had none at all.

Some branches, especially the ones near the realms without táltosk, felt like they were covered in slime. It was like an oil spill, like the one that had happened in the Gulf just a few months ago. Only instead of the rainbow colors motor oil made in water, this was brownish-black sludge, covering everything. Some places were clear, but some were so bad the horses wouldn't even approach them. Lindsay could feel the weakness of magic there. If the Tree were a literal plant, those branches would be rotted through and ready to fall off. Tal said this happened sometimes and told them not to worry about it.

Tal showed them the realm he'd come from first, just a step away, he said, from theirs. Lindsay had been a little surprised to hear Tal hadn't come from their own realm, but when he asked Tal what it was like, he didn't seem interested in explaining anything that didn't directly relate to the aether.

They never met any other táltosk. They were spread few and far between, Tal said, and rarely encountered one another. Likely that would change as word of the princes spread, but he said gradual was better, so they could build their powers. Lindsay saw a lot of sense in that, and even if Cary was impatient by nature he knew his brother saw it too.

In the five years since leaving home, Lindsay had never seen Cary so calm. He knew Cary had felt trapped by his body. He'd always had a kind of restless energy, like a dog pacing bare spots in a pen, and that had only gotten worse since the accident. Tal pushed them the way Dad had pushed them, though, and he demanded no less of Cary. Often he demanded more, just like Dad had done. He hadn't gotten Cary out of his chair and standing, but Lindsay couldn't help clinging to that tiny hope Cary might change his mind.

Lindsay still wasn't sure how to think or feel about Tal, but he taught them things they needed to know and he seemed to be good for Cary. He was more confused about Cary's relationship with Bella. When they were at home, Lindsay always saw them together, usually fussing about something. Travis had remarked that Cary was addicted to arguing and probably just couldn't help himself when she was willing to argue right back. There was something else, though. Before the accident, if Cary was spending that much time with a girl, it could only mean one thing. When Lindsay asked about it one too many times, Cary had snapped at him that he couldn't get it up, anyway, so Lindsay should stop bothering him. Lindsay had dropped the subject, but he still felt a little weird about it. Cary kept seeing Jessie at least once a week, though, so maybe it was nothing.

At the end of June, Amy called. Lindsay missed the call, but when he saw her number in his phone later, guilt chewed at his insides. God, but he'd been a bad friend, so wrapped up in the táltos stuff and Travis he hadn't even called her.

"You're a jerk," her voicemail said. "But I know you don't mean to be, so call me. tonight."

He called. "I'm sorry," he said immediately. "I am a jerk. You're right."

"You want to meet at McAlister's so I can hit you and get it over with?"

He couldn't help smiling even though he knew she was at least halfway serious. "I would, but—"

"Oh, that's right, you never did call me to tell me you're up in Willard. Fine, can I come up there?"

Lindsay paused. Amy and Travis got along, but Travis knew Lindsay had dated (or had tried to date) Amy briefly. And she and Cary tended to clash. She thought he monopolized Lindsay's time and he thought she was uppity and too pushy.

"Is that a really tough question?" Amy asked.

"Well—no. I reckon not. Let me make sure it's okay with Trav."

Travis was out in the barn, working on their shipment of guns for Wade. It had taken a while to finally get them and now they had to rush to modify them.

"Amy Amy?" Travis said when Lin asked him. When Lindsay nodded, he said, "It's fine, I guess."

"Good," Amy said, apparently having heard. "I'll be there in a little while. Can I have the address for GPS?"

Cary's reaction to the news of Amy's visit wasn't so positive. "You gripe at me for bringing Jessie over. If my girlfriend don't count, a fag hag sure don't."

"I ain't griped at you about Jessie," Lindsay said, not adding, except for the once.

"You gonna tell her?"

"What makes you think Jessie ain't told her?"

That shut Cary up. Jessie told Amy everything, it seemed like. Lindsay wondered if he *should* tell Amy, though, if she didn't already know. It was hard to predict what her reaction might be.

He still hadn't decided by the time she arrived. As he'd predicted, she and Travis were fine, though Travis was always a little confused by her. He'd said once he'd never figured Lindsay would date a black girl, and Lindsay was never sure whether he was more confused by the fact that she was black or the fact that she was a girl. Amy and Cary glared at each other but didn't speak, to Lindsay's relief. Bella made herself scarce.

Lindsay and Amy settled outside on the porch with beer, since it was a nice night, but they kept the lights off to avoid the mosquitoes.

"Holy shit, is that an owl on the corner of the barn?" she asked.

"It's an owl scarecrow. You ain't never seen one before?"

"An owl scarecrow? No."

"It's for scaring off nesting birds. Trav was fishing up at Lake of the Ozarks and caught it."

He *caught* it?"

Lindsay couldn't help but grin. "Yeah. Somebody musta tossed it and it sank. Trav thought he done caught a big bass or something till he reeled it in. Was all full a' grass and moss and all."

Amy shook her head. "That is the redneckiest story I've ever heard."

They sat in companionable silence for a while, drinking. Then she reached over and slugged him on the side of the head, hard, clipping his ear.

"Ow. Lord, you fight dirty like Cary," he complained.

"You deserved it," she said. "Cary does too, for filling Jess's head with all kinds of crazy shit. I know he likes to prank, but that's taking it way too far."

Well, at least that saved him having to tell her. "What's she said, exactly?"

"That you two are some kind of magical princes protecting the World Tree, or something like that. She didn't buy it at first, but for whatever dumb reason, she believes him now. Either he needs to stop telling stories or he needs to get checked out by the psychiatrist, seriously. You *know* how impressionable she is."

Lindsay winced. "Yeah, I know. But Cary ain't lying."

"Say *what*?"

He drew in a deep breath. "We really do have magic. There really is a World Tree. And people really do think we're princes."

Amy stared at him for a long time, looking baffled. Then she said, "I hope you don't take this the wrong way...." Even that didn't seem like her because she never pulled her punches. "But is this more of your dad's stuff?"

Lindsay wished he could say no. "He didn't tell us about the Tree exactly. He told us…other stuff."

"You have to realize this stuff sounds totally certifiable."

"It does? I mean, the World Tree—it makes sense. Everything being connected. And some things you cain't explain with science. People've talked about magic forever. Why wouldn't it be true?"

Amy's pale eyes, the thing that Lindsay had been attracted by, widened. "Are you serious? I mean, where do I even start with that? Is this some kind of new religion or something?"

He thought about that. It was, sort of, except he could feel magic and the Tree and Sister, and he'd never once felt the presence of God growing up. "I guess you could call it that. I mean, sorta."

Silence. Finally, Amy sighed. "I don't get it. I really, really don't. In fact it creeps me out really badly. But I guess it's your choice."

Lindsay felt a little sad that she refused to believe him, but maybe that was better anyway, to keep her (and them) safe. "Sorry I didn't say nothing earlier."

"Well, I sorta understand why." Amy drained her beer and reached for another. "Does Travis know?"

"Yeah."

"What does he think about it?"

Lindsay didn't want to say he didn't know even if that was the truth, but Travis was hard to read sometimes. So all he said was, "He's okay with it."

"I was wondering when you'd finally hook up with him."

Lindsay's face got hot. "I, uh."

"It's cute. Rednecks in love."

In love? Were they? Was he?

Amy grinned at him. "Does he know you like Lady Gaga?"

"Shut *up*," Lindsay said. She just laughed.

"What's with the girl who lives with you? Who is she?"

"She was in trouble and we helped her." Lindsay knew that wasn't really an answer, so he added, "Her name's Bella."

"Thanks, that's exactly what I meant," Amy said sarcastically. "If you don't want to tell me, fine. Just tell me if Cary is cheating on Jessie."

Lindsay felt a little defensive. "I don't see as that's any business of yours. If Jessie wants to know, she can ask him. I ain't got no business getting into that, neither."

"You must know."

"I don't, matter of fact." It felt weird to say it, even if it was the truth. Lindsay and Cary hid so little from each other it seemed unnatural that Lindsay wasn't sure.

"I just don't want to see my friend get hurt," Amy said.

"I don't want to see that neither, but it ain't none of our business," Lindsay said. "Okay? Please."

Amy looked at him with that annoyed 'why don't you just give me what

I want' look that made Cary call her uppity even though he sometimes wore a similar expression. "Fine. How are things with Travis?"

He blinked a couple times at the abrupt subject change. "Uh. Good."

"Had sex yet?"

Boy, was this weird, given that the last person he'd tried to have sex with before Travis was her. "Yeah."

"Is he good?"

"Lord God almighty, Amy."

"That good, huh?"

Lindsay couldn't help but laugh at that, and it broke the ice.

Amy ended up crashing in the last spare bedroom after several more beers. In the morning, while Lindsay chugged water and downed B12, Amy and Cary circled one another like a couple of angry barn cats with their fur all fluffed out. Travis, thankfully, was nothing but polite, though he was a lot more formal than usual. Bella didn't have much to say either way, though Lindsay was familiar with her disapproval of them telling regular people they were táltos.

When Lindsay walked Amy to her car, she said, "Listen, whatever you're doing, be careful, okay?"

Lindsay wasn't sure where careful factored into any of this. He must have hesitated a second too long because she said, "I mean it, Lindsay." Her eyes strayed toward the barn and he almost panicked. How could she *know*? She lifted her pale eyes to look at him straight in the face. "I'm not an idiot, okay? I don't know exactly what's going on and I don't want to. Just be careful."

He had the strong feeling she knew more than she was admitting to, if not the whole story, but he was relieved by her words. "We'll be careful."

"Better call me. Next week. Wednesday."

"Okay."

Cary sat at the top of the ramp on the front porch when Lindsay turned to go inside. "You tell her?"

"No. Jessie did. You gotta be careful with her, Care. She could get us in a lot of trouble."

"So could that one."

"So it's okay that Jessie could tell God and everybody about us because Amy knows, even though I didn't tell her nothing? Don't be a fool, Cary."

To his credit, Cary seemed to listen to Lindsay's words even if he wouldn't admit to it. He started meeting Jessie in town or in Springfield instead of bringing her to the house, which was fine with Lindsay even if it meant extra driving. He wished it wasn't so expensive to modify a car with hand controls, but even if they could afford the several hundred dollars and more for the modifications and driving lessons, the Explorer wasn't in good shape anyway. It would probably need a new transmission inside of six months. They desperately needed to get paid for their gun deal, and even then they wouldn't have much to spare once Wade had taken his cut and they'd paid their bills.

Lindsay wondered how they'd ever end up on their own at this rate.

Chapter Seventeen

Cary had a PT appointment later that week. He had missed two appointments already, and though he didn't care, Lindsay insisted it was good for him, especially with all the fighting they'd been doing. The appointment was at seven in the morning so Lindsay could take him on his way to work. To compensate, they went to Krispy Kreme for breakfast.

Glenstone was still pretty empty this time of the morning, and the Krispy Kreme parking lot was empty except for a few employee cars in the back. Drawn out of his half-doze by the smell of freshly-glazed donuts, Cary sat up in his seat, rubbing his eyes. Lindsay got out, pulled the chair from the back seat and reassembled.

Because of the angle of the vehicle, Cary didn't see the familiar Malibu until it pulled into the space next to them. Lindsay reached under his jacket for his handgun, letting them see it.

"Get out slow." Lindsay's voice was full of that cold venom that made even Cary shiver. Emily got out of the driver's seat and had the gall to put her hands on her hips. Mustafa got out on the other side and pointed a 9mm at them, bold as brass. Judging by the way he held it, he was an amateur, but a bullet from an amateur's gun would kill him just as dead. Cary hissed and went for the spare gun in the glove compartment, but Lindsay said under his breath, "No, Care. He's nervous."

Shaking with fury, but understanding Lindsay's point—never make a nervous gunman more nervous—Cary fixed his glare on Emily. "Good morning to you too, princess. What the fuck d'you want?"

"That's a good question. I was wondering what the fuck you want." Emily's glare was almost, but not quite, on par with Lindsay's for sheer coldness. "How's Daddy Dearest?"

Cary froze, every clever retort suddenly escaping his mind. "Wouldn't know."

Lindsay turned to Mustafa. "You wanna put that gun down now. This ain't no place for a shootout."

Mustafa's dark eyes moved to Lindsay; unfortunately, the gun followed, and now Lindsay stared down the barrel. Cary let out a growl of helpless anger, hating that he could do nothing if Mustafa decided to shoot one or both of them. He couldn't get to the one in the glove compartment fast enough, and Lindsay's jacket blocked him from grabbing Lindsay's gun.

"Put it down." Lindsay's voice remained even. "You don't want this, do you? You ain't no hitman or nothing. There's people around and you wouldn't get away with nothing. Put that thing away, man."

Mustafa's face flickered, and then to Cary's astonishment, he lowered the gun and put it back in the car.

"Thanks for the help," Lindsay told Emily, and pushed the wheelchair where Cary could get into it. Cary didn't move yet, not convinced he could trust them long enough to make himself vulnerable while he transferred.

"I'm not convinced shooting you is a bad idea," Emily said. "What the hell do you think you're doing? You sure as hell don't know what you're getting into."

"Whatever we got to do. Ain't like y'all are any help figuring out what that is," Lindsay said.

"All you had to do was lay off and let us help you." Mustafa had found his voice again. "Now it's all fucked up."

"How's that *our* fault?" Cary demanded. "All you've done is push and pull us around without telling us shit. Well, we done took all this onto ourselves now. Fuck you."

"Oh, yeah, I see how successful you've been, falling in with Lewis and Álmos. Yeah, we know about that. That's exactly what we were trying to prevent from happening. That's what's gotten you in so much trouble."

Álmos? he thought, *His name is Tal.*

"You don't think *they're* pushing you around?" Emily continued. "What do they want from you?"

Out of the corner of his eye, Cary spotted movement from the other side of the car. Lindsay drew his own handgun before Mustafa had the chance to go for the one in the car. "Don't."

"I guess you shoulda thought clearer before y'all started ordering us around." Cary transferred to the chair. His hand stayed near the holster at his left side. "You can think what you want. I ain't listening to y'all no more."

"You're making a very bad decision."

"Y'all made it for us."

Emily turned to Lindsay. "Aren't you going to say anything?"

Lindsay lowered his gun. "Don't reckon I need to."

The rattle of a diesel engine caught their attention then; some big farm truck had arrived. Lindsay nodded to Cary and holstered his gun, heading for the restaurant.

"I'm withdrawing our protection," Emily said behind them. "You obviously don't appreciate it. You have no idea what that means. You've only seen part of the influence we have."

"Yeah, y'all've really helped us so far," Cary said from the top of the handicapped ramp. "Go fuck yourselves. We don't need you." As he punched the automatic door opener, he heard Lindsay let out an uncertain breath behind him.

"Hope that's true," Lindsay muttered.

* * *

The drive back to Willard seemed too short and yet too long. Lindsay kept the windows open rather than use the air conditioning as an excuse not to talk. As usual, there were just no words.

Cary went to find Bella when they got home. "Hey."

Bella was sitting on the bed, facing away from him. He could tell by the tension in her shoulders that she was nervous or upset, although her voice was even when she spoke.

"Where's your brother?"

"In the barn with Travis. Why?"

"I need to tell you something."

He heard the hesitation. "Tell me something?"

"Show you. Show you something." She moved faster than he thought she could; she got up, stepped past him and pushed the door shut.

Before he knew it, she was in his lap, straddling him, kissing him. It was nothing like kissing Jessie; Jessie knew what she was doing, but she was gentle, often timid even after almost a year. But Bella was eager, almost desperate. Where Jessie was soft and curvy, Bella's body was thin, angular. He felt more of her.

He *felt*.

He put her hands on her shoulders. It was harder than he'd expected to push her away. "What..."

"No! Don't. Just, please." She looked down at him. "Before I lose my nerve."

He let her go.

They kissed again. Bella's arms wound around his neck. Her fingers pressed into the back of his neck. As if he had no control over them, Cary felt his hands move down and around, settling on her ass, pulling her closer.

He felt her. There was no finesse in her kisses, and nothing feminine in her body, but he *felt* her. And he felt himself get hard for the first time in... God. Five years.

"Jesus," he whispered, breaking the kiss.

"What?" She sounded alarmed.

"You...I'm..."

Her eyes widened. "That doesn't happen often, does it?"

"No." He felt his face grow warm. "It's part of the..."

"I read about spinal injuries. You're lucky you can get an erection."

"Okay. Hush." Cary shook his head. Whatever they were doing, he thought they should just do it before he lost his nerve.

"Right." She shifted her hips until her groin pressed against his, a firm, warm pressure. Oh, Lord. "That okay?"

"Uh huh." What were they doing, exactly? He decided not to think about it. She gave him an awkward little smile and rocked forward.

God, he was so hard. He ran his hands up her ribs, around to her breasts. Smaller than Jessie's, but still definitively female.

"Don't." She pushed his hands down to her thighs. "Don't touch them."

"Why?"

"Just don't." She put her hands on his shoulders and gave him a look worthy of Lindsay's quiet intensity. "Okay?"

"Okay. Fine."

Before he could think too hard, she kissed him again. The more she did it, the more he wanted; he wanted to pull that shirt and those shorts off and pull her down on him, put himself inside the warmth he could feel. The occupational therapists had told him how to do it with his catheter; it wasn't hard. He couldn't move, but he could guide her while she rode him.

"I want—" he began, pulling her closer.

And then he felt it. Something that wasn't there before. Something pressing against him.

Bella gasped, then let out a high-pitched groan. "Cary."

"What the hell." He pushed her away, for real this time. He didn't want to, but he looked down and saw the bulge in his pants mirrored in hers. "What the *hell*."

She scrambled off his lap onto the bed, her face twisted. The bulge was gone. "Don't freak out. Let me explain."

"Don't freak out? Are you *serious*?"

"Yes. I'm serious." She stared right back at him; he knew that look. She might be afraid, but she sure as hell wasn't going to back down.

"Fine." Cary sat back, keenly aware that his hard-on had completely disappeared. He felt a pang, wondering if it would ever happen again.

"You think I'm a girl."

Cary lifted his eyebrows and dropped his eyes to her tits. "Safe to say."

Bella folded her arms across her chest. "Don't be sarcastic. I'm being serious."

"So am I. You're telling me you're not a girl." He felt a little sick.

"Physically, I'm female. Because you and everyone else sees me that way. Your perception influences my reality. The way you see me is the way I am."

Cary was reminded of something Sister once said. *We are horses because you see us as horses.* "But you ain't like the horses. You ain't no creature."

"The *recorsas* are magical creatures just like your horses. We aren't born. We're made to serve a purpose." Now that she was lecturing, Bella relaxed a little, but Cary couldn't. He wasn't sure whether it was harder to accept she wasn't human or to hear that *she* wasn't *she*. Bella stretched her legs on the bed. They were long and thin, but her hips still curved out—like a girl's. "Since the first pair of *recorsas*, all pairs after have been made up of one male and one female. It's the basic principle of binary balance. That's just how humans think: you can't have a man without a woman and vice-versa. You have to have something different to oppose them. A woman created Sandor. My grandmother, I guess. I'm supposed to be female, so everyone just assumed I was. I bet you were told I was Sandor's daughter."

"I don't get it. You *are* a girl. You look like a girl." Except...

"I told you, I look like I do because that's what people expect. That doesn't mean I am." Bella turned that look on him again. "You've never heard of the term 'transgender?'"

"What, like you dress in men's clothes? I ain't seen you do that."

"That's cross-dressing, and no, that's not it. I *am* male, Cary. I have the wrong body. That's what being transgender is."

"You want to be a man."

Bella looked like she was half a second from decking him. "You don't get it. I am a man. If I could, I'd change my body to match. Sometimes it happens on its own, like you felt. But not often."

Now Cary was definitely nauseous. "No, I don't get it. You say people see you as a girl, so you are, but you're really a boy?"

"Like you've never *known* you were something different from the way people see you. You don't resent when people call you a cripple?"

"No. Because I am. That's reality. I cain't help it. I cain't change it."

"If you could, wouldn't you? If you had the chance to be the way you should be, wouldn't you?"

Cary clenched his teeth so hard it hurt. "What's the way I *should* be? This is the way I am. There ain't no changing it and no use wishing. It's a waste of time. I'm fine the way I am."

"But I'm not." Cary had never seen that much hurt and weariness on such a young face. "I'm not. If I could make people see me as a man, I would. In a second. But it's not that easy. Even my name. You call me Bella. You know what it should be? *Bay-lah*. B-e-l-a. It's a Hungarian name. But everyone just assumes it's Bella. Everyone just assumes, before I even meet them, when they hear I'm Sandor's *daughter*." The word 'daughter' sounded like a curse. "I can't make them see differently unless they don't have any preconceptions. Especially not you." She—he—whatever—curled up again.

"But I felt—"

"You were distracted. Not thinking clearly. As soon as you figured it out, you didn't see it anymore, did you?"

Cary thought about it. No, he hadn't seen it—the bulge—once he'd actually figured out what he was looking at. He couldn't believe it.

"You're powerful, Cary, and you see things the way you want to see them. Your perception changes things. It changes *me*. "

"So this is my fault? I've only known you for—"

"I didn't say it was your fault. God. Never mind."

Cary thought about saying, *No, tell me*, but he wasn't really sure he wanted to know. "Well, I cain't see you as a guy. This is how I know you. You're Bella."

"I know. You and your fucking heteronormative narrow mind. I hate it."

"It's the way I am. I cain't help it."

"You say that a lot. It's a weak excuse. You could change if you wanted to."

Cary turned toward the door. He didn't want to hear any more of this. His hand shook as he reached toward the doorknob.

"Where are you going?"

"Out of here."

"So you're just going to run?"

Damn her. *Her*. "I don't got nothing else to say."

"So let's not say anything."

Cary looked over his shoulder. Bella sat on the bed, knees bent, arms wrapped around them. He couldn't see much of her body underneath her baggy T-shirt. She looked the same as always, with her long face, left brow drawn, lips tight in that concentrated expression. Something in her dark eyes made him pause.

"Why did you come in here?" Bella asked.

"Don't remember."

She scooted to the edge of the bed. "Does this change anything?"

He felt an incredulous laugh tremble in his chest, but didn't let it out. "Are you kidding? Why the hell wouldn't it?"

"Good," she whispered. "I want it to."

He heard her catch her breath when she breathed in, and she looked down quickly. The beginning of a laugh halted and died in his chest, leaving a raw spot. Jesus.

He turned and rolled back to the bed. "Let's not say anything."

Bella nodded.

He reached out to pull her forward. She straddled him again, and her mouth met his; he felt tears on her face and almost couldn't stand that.

His body didn't care about what Bella had just said; it only cared that she was warm against him and she wanted him. But somewhere deep inside, he knew that wasn't all of it; Jessie had never made him hard. Especially not twice. He did not want to think about that too much.

When he put his hands on her ass to pull her closer, she broke the kiss. "Wait."

The very last word he wanted to hear. "What?"

"What are we doing here? Are we having sex?"

He wished it wasn't a valid question, so he could tell her to hush and go back to...whatever this was. But it was valid, and he was no asshole to make her go through with anything she didn't want to. "Is that what you want?"

"I don't know. I've never done it before."

It made sense, of course, but that fact didn't make it any easier to hear. He was glad he was sitting down. "Uh. Okay. Well. If we're gonna, I gotta steal a condom from Lin."

Bella said nothing. He watched her face, and he saw emotions he knew so well: uncertainty, hesitation, fear. Wondering if she could go through with it. Wondering if she should. Wondering if it would work. He knew how it was to cling to those emotions so hard they were a sense of twisted comfort that paralyzed and poisoned.

"Not right now," he said. "We'll do something else."

"Don't patronize me."

"Stand down, Turbo. I'm not. I ain't ready." His body was—God, he ached with it—but the claws of uncertainty were still firmly sunk in. He wasn't lying.

The relief on her face hit something deep in him. "Then...what?"

"What we were doing before." Cary pulled her groin against his. "You can feel it too, right? I can touch you—"

"This is good." She pressed against him, grinding, and he didn't care that she was trying to distract him. He put his arms around her back and let her, wondering if she could feel his heart trying to beat out of his chest.

He guided her with hands on her butt at first, but soon he didn't care that she was going faster and faster. It had been so long, his body felt almost foreign. But then her breath on his neck sent a shudder down his spine, which for a second forgot it was broken. When he held her hard against him, his body remembered what to do.

"Did you...?" she asked.

"Yeah. Keep going. Your turn."

It didn't take long. She made a sound that might have been one of frustration if not for the look on her face: surprise and a little bewilderment. It had been so long since he'd felt a woman—person—shiver like that against him.

She moved to the bed immediately after and looked away. Her expression was dazed, but not in a happy way. "It didn't change anything."

He didn't know what to say to that.

* * *

The next morning, rather than badger Lindsay into taking him to Springfield, Cary asked Jessie to pick him up. He felt a little guilty for making her drive all the way up, but not as guilty as he felt for what he'd done the night before.

He tried to push the guilt away with the knowledge that he could be the kind of boyfriend Jessie deserved, finally. He'd always felt bad about holding out on her for almost a year now.

"You okay? You're really quiet," she said. "Tried to call you around two yesterday, but it went right to voice mail."

Cary pulled his phone from the thigh pocket of his cargo pants. He'd completely forgotten to check it and the battery was dead. "I'm sorry, babe. Lin and me were home and there ain't no cell reception."

"Home? But—wait, you mean *home* home?"

"Yep." He hoped she wouldn't ask too many questions, but of course she said,

"Wow. How was it?"

How could he even describe it? He couldn't. She couldn't understand all of it, all the weight behind what Dad had said and did. Nobody really did but Lindsay. "I...I dunno how to talk about it, Jess. I really don't."

She glanced at him and reached over to take his hand. "Whatever you want to say, I'll listen."

He knew that tone. *Sure you will*, he thought. *Listen like a social worker*. He pushed away that thought, too. That wasn't fair. "Can I think about it some and tell you later? I will, I promise. You tell me what's going on with you."

She did. It was mostly school, which made Cary feel worse than he thought it would. They had met in class, had classes together since then, studied together. Now the thing that guaranteed he'd get to spend time with her was gone. And it was completely his fault, of course. He felt like he'd betrayed her.

She finished with, "Maybe you can start back again in the fall, just a few classes to get back into the swing of things."

I might be home by then, Cary thought, but then remembered what Betty told them. *Never go back home*. Why had she said that?

"Maybe," he said. "We'll see."

"I really think you should. I know what this means to you."

"Jess, you also know I've got a hell of a lot of other stuff to handle," Cary said. "It ain't that I don't want to go back to school, but..."

"I know. You're a prince." There was no sarcasm or bitterness in her tone—ever since she'd seen him use magic, she hadn't doubted him in the least. She gave him that sweet smile. "Does that mean I'm your lady in waiting?"

"It means you're my princess," Cary told her.

That got a giggle, but she said, "I'm not royalty, that's for sure. Not like you." Her tone was less flattering to him than self-deprecating, and that bothered Cary.

"Hey. You're just like Lin sometimes, talking like that. You're special, sweetheart, and don't you forget it."

She smiled at him again. "You need anything before we head home?"

"Box of condoms?" He hadn't meant to be so blunt. Whatever happened to charming her?

They had reached the diamond interchange at Highway 13 and I-44. When they stopped at the light, she looked at him. "Really?"

Cary recovered and smiled at her, that smile that used to win girls over with almost no effort. He was pleased to see it still worked; she blushed. "Sure. 'Bout time, isn't it?"

"Well, it's just...I mean, if you're ready."

Don't harp on it, he begged in his mind. *Just say okay. Or not.* He leaned in to brush her hair back from her face, letting his fingertips touch just behind her ear. "Honey, I'm ready." As he was going to be.

Few things were more awkward than buying condoms when you were crippled, Cary discovered. The Walgreen's at Grand and Kansas seemed crowded for a Sunday during church hours, and it seemed like everyone saw him in that aisles. He knew what they were thinking: *does it even work?*

God, he hoped so.

"Just ignore them," Jessie said, and he remembered she had to put up with this, too. And so often she handled it with better grace.

Thank God her roommate wasn't home. They cuddled up on Jessie's bed to watch stupid horror movies on Netflix like usual, and Cary found himself starting to relax.

He turned her face toward him and kissed her.

Making out with Jessie was easy. There was no pressure because they'd both agreed months ago that that was as far as it would go. Until now, anyway. It was too easy to fall into that again, and Cary was determined to push himself further than that. He kissed her neck, her collarbone, hands moving from her ribs to her breasts. *She* let him touch them.

Her hand was in his hair, her lips on his ear—she was all soft and gentle and sweet. Her body pressed against him. Gentle. No pressure.

He still wasn't hard.

She helped him get her shirt off, then her bra. He kissed her breasts, teased her nipples, and she let out a warm, shaky breath in his ear. When Bella had made that sound—

No. Absolutely not.

"Can I touch you?" she whispered, her hand hovering near his fly. "I'll be careful."

"Yeah. Sure." He was a little surprised she'd asked. She unzipped his pants and reached inside. The couple of times she'd touched him she'd said she wasn't bothered by the catheter, though he always worried.

"Should unhook my leg bag," he whispered.

"Oh…right." She pulled her hand away and let him do it. He tried to watch her face while he unhooked himself and set the leg back aside, but she had turned away, maybe trying to be polite. "Okay," he said when she was done. "You wanna touch me?"

She stroked him, gently, while she kissed him. It felt good, but he couldn't feel his body responding. "A little harder maybe," he said, determined to make his body work the way he wanted it to. She did as he asked, but she was careful—still so careful. He didn't want her to be careful. He wanted her to climb on top and ride him while he sank his fingertips into her hips.

Stupid body.

Out of frustration, he grabbed the hand on him and tightened her fingers with his hand, stroking himself hard. She started. "It's okay," she said.

It's okay? Was she kidding? "It ain't okay," he growled. *I should be able to do this.* It happened last night so easily. God, why couldn't he *do* this?

"Cary." Jessie put her hand on his face. "You're stressing yourself out. That can't be helping. Relax and talk to me. What's wrong?"

He didn't want to talk, dammit. He wanted to do this, to have sex with his girlfriend like a normal guy. "I'm okay. Just taking a little while. How about I get you started and I'll catch up?"

She folded her legs under her to kneel on the bed and looked like she'd agree, but she said, "I think you should tell me what's bothering you. I'm not worried about the sex."

Why was she always so damn *understanding*? He felt like an asshole. He didn't even understand it himself.

"Are you worried I'm going to judge you if you're having a hard time functioning? Because you know I won't."

'Functioning.' That was the kind of talk he'd heard in occupational therapy. The lectures he'd mostly tuned out, which made sex sound like the most boring, scientific thing ever, like everything else he had to learn to 'function' around.

"I know you won't," he told her. "I dunno what's wrong with me. Today ain't my day, I guess." Though she really wasn't helping with the social worker talk.

"Have you thought about Viagra? I've heard it's pretty effective with SCIs."

That snapped something in him. "No," he said, not caring how flat his voice sounded. "I don't want no pill to get a hard-on, like a fucking old man."

"There's no shame in it. You have a paraplegic injury."

Like I don't fucking know that. Somehow he managed to avoid snarling at her. He knew she didn't deserve it. She was just trying to help.

"Can I help?" she asked as if reading his mind.

He sighed. "I dunno how. I dunno what's wrong with me."

"Hey." She squeezed his hand. "It's okay. I can be patient."

I know, he thought. *That's the problem*. He didn't know what that meant.

"Can we...?" He couldn't finish the question.

"Sure. Let's finish the movie. Maybe we can go to El Maguey after."

Sitting there in his boxers, watching a movie with Jessie, should have been the most natural thing in the world. But he'd never hated himself more.

Chapter Eighteen

Lindsay texted Cary around noon, after he'd met Amy in Springfield. *Jess bringin u home*

Can u come came the response, almost immediately.

Cary waited on the front porch of Jessie's house, with Jessie on the steps beside him, when Lindsay pulled up. He wondered why. Usually, he had to wait for ten or fifteen minutes before Cary was ready.

"Cary told me you went to Arkansas," Jessie said after they'd exchanged hellos. She said *Arkansas* like it was a foreign country. "Was it awful?"

Lindsay couldn't help giving Cary a surprised glance. Since when did he tell her about the family? "Coulda been better," he said in his most neutral tone.

"Travis didn't go, did he?"

Lindsay knew what she was getting at: she was upset she hadn't been invited. Wouldn't that have been something.

"No, Jess," Cary's voice was quiet, subdued.

"Neither of y'all woulda wanted to come," Lindsay said. He studied his brother's face. Cary wore that stubbornly blank expression most people took for bored, though Lindsay knew it covered a storm of emotion. "Ready?" he asked Cary.

"I reckon."

Lindsay wondered if he realized how weak his smile was when he said goodbye to Jessie. Lindsay was starting to get a little worried. In the car, Cary kept silent until Lindsay spoke up, just outside of town.

"You gonna tell me what's going on?"

Cary was quiet for so long it seemed like he would refuse to answer. Finally he said, "Tried to have sex."

Lindsay winced before he could stop himself. "Care..."

"I swear to almighty God, if you start with the sympathy bullshit."

"I was gonna say, that sucks."

Cary folded his arms. "Yeah." More silence. "Thought I could do it this time."

Lindsay wondered why he thought that after almost six years, but didn't ask.

If Cary was in the mood to talk, it was best not to interrupt. But that was all he said.

"How'd she react?" Lindsay asked, taking a risk.

"Same as always."

That was one of the things that confused Lindsay about Cary's relationship with Jessie. He hated when people treated him like he was holding a bomb, he put it. And that was exactly what Jessie did, tiptoeing around and saying nice things. She was even nice when she was mad.

"You think she's upset?" Lindsay asked.

Another long silence. Finally Cary said, "No." He reached over to turn on the radio, ending the conversation. Lindsay couldn't help thinking if he were Cary, he'd want her to be upset about not being able to have sex with him.

Lindsay left him alone for a while when they got home; he immediately went out on Cooter and disappeared toward the pastures.

"Is he upset?" Bella asked from the back porch.

Lindsay sighed. "I reckon."

"About me?"

"No," he said. "Don't think so."

Before he could ask what Cary would be upset about that related to her, she went back inside. A vague thought surfaced in Lindsay's mind about Bella and Jessie and Cary suddenly trying sex, but he told himself there was no reason to think that way.

Where Cary and Bella used to spend hours and hours together, they barely spoke now except to argue. One of them was always picking a fight. One day, Cary brought up Dad's announcement that they would bring about the Rapture.

"That's a narrow way of looking at it, and narrow, uninformed theories rarely hold water," she had said.

"Just because you don't believe in the Rapture, it won't happen? That don't hold water." Cary was in a spitting mood, which Lindsay had never seen him in around Bella. He wondered if they'd had a fight. "You ought to know better'n anybody what's happening to the Tree. Hell, we see the corruption every day."

"I *do* know the Tree better than anyone. And I know that one particular piece of ignorant religious dogma doesn't explain what is going on."

"But," Lindsay interrupted, "Tal said something like that too. That the Tree gets sick sometimes and that that ain't really the problem. What's wrong with the worlds is being caused by people."

"The Tree does suffer periodic ailments—yes. People, humans included, do have an impact on the Tree But—"

"So what's *your* theory, since you want to criticize ours?" Cary demanded.

"I don't know. Clearly, I don't have all the information."

"If you ain't gonna help, then keep your mouth shut."

"Cary Judah," Lindsay said. Cary just turned and rolled toward the back door.

"Those aren't your theories, anyway," Bella snapped at Cary's retreating back. "If you can offer a theory of your own instead of parroting someone else, I'd be surprised."

Lindsay was about to say something to her, too, but when she turned back, she let out a loud breath. Hurt was plain on her face.

"What's going on between y'all?" Lindsay asked.

"We were having sex. I told him I'm transgender. I'm male even though I have a female body."

Lindsay stared at her. "You was having sex?"

"He didn't penetrate me."

Lindsay could think of absolutely nothing to say. She turned her back on him.

* * *

Normally Cary and Lindsay talked shit to each other while they practiced with their sabers, but Cary hadn't been able to get Lindsay to say anything for the better part of an hour. Finally he said,

"I been thinking."

"Did it hurt?"

Lindsay ignored him. He halted Sister and lowered his sword. "Was wondering how Dad ever knew about Tal."

"What does it matter? Dad was right about him. This is what we're supposed to do. Maybe it was Dad's way of helping us out. You know him."

Lindsay looked like he wanted to say something, but he just slid out of the saddle and started to pull off Sister's tack.

"Y'know, after the accident and all," Cary continued, "Seemed like Dad didn't know what to do. You said yourself he was all broken up about me getting hurt. Maybe he knew we was supposed to be táltosk but he couldn't tell us, so he had to wait and send Tal to us...."

"That don't even make sense," Lindsay said. "Why would he have to wait?"

"Well, I dunno. Maybe he had to make sure we really had magic. And we could do what we needed to do. He said he tested us, remember?"

"If you're so sure he's been trying to help us out all this time, how come you ain't talked to him?" Instead of yelling, Lindsay's voice got even quieter. Cary wished he would yell. "How come you listened to Betty when she said stay away from home?"

Cary opened his mouth to speak, but he couldn't figure out what to say. Why hadn't he tried to talk to Dad?

"Let's ask Bella how they met and if he really was out to help us," Lindsay said. "She oughta have memories of them two meeting."

"I got nothing to say to her," Cary said.

"Well, I do." Lindsay finished removing Sister's tack and walked past Cary into the house. Cary thought about not following, but he did want to know how Dad and Tal met.

Bella sat in the living room when they went inside, watching infomercials as usual. Travis had already gone to bed.

"Got a question for you," Lindsay said. Bella looked up at him, then at Cary.

"What is it?"

Lindsay sat next to her. Cary wondered how Lindsay could make himself so nice and harmless. "Tal and our father know each other, but we dunno how. Cain't figure it out. We figured you'd know."

Bella looked at Cary again. This time her expression was clear: nervousness. "I don't know."

"You're a recorsa. Don't you remember nothing about how they met?"

"In the first place, I remember trends and time periods best. I'm a big picture person. Individual memories are hard for me to be clear about, especially when they're focused on individual people. I have millenia of memories from all the realms."

"You cain't think about it? Tal's the oldest táltos. Seems like you might remember him pretty good." Lindsay's tone remained easy and reasonable.

"That's the other thing. I don't." This time, Bella avoided looking at Cary.

"Bella," Cary said, his gut clenching, "What d'you mean, you don't remember him?"

She bit her lips so hard a white line appeared near her teeth. Even Lindsay's eyes had narrowed. Cary gripped his wheels.

"I don't have most of my memories anymore. I can't tap into them. I only remember what I've learned myself."

Lindsay sat up straight. His face wasn't friendly and open anymore, but cold. "How long since you lost them?"

"Before we met you," Cary said, putting two and two together. "You said your last memory of Sandor was from before that."

"Yes."

"But then how'd you get that memory back?" Cary felt curiously numb, but something was building in the back of his mind like silent thunder.

"I don't know. I don't know why any of this happened."

"You said when we met you that you could tell us what we needed to know. " Lindsay's voice made Bella shiver, but even that couldn't touch Cary yet.

"I didn't know what was going on. I just needed your help, and I thought if I couldn't offer anything in return, you wouldn't help me."

"What the hell kind of people d'you think we are, Bella?" Lindsay demanded. "What made you think we would turn you out if you needed help?"

"I didn't know!"

"So you *lied* to us for *months*?" Anger washed over Cary, and his heart was like a wild thing in his chest. "You hid this from us" from *me*! "so we'd do what you wanted?"

Bella turned to him, finally, her face full of naked pain. "It wasn't like that. I—"

"I don't give a fuck what it was *like*, you fucking lying *bitch*." The last few words were almost swallowed by a sudden knot in his throat. "You're just as bad as the rest of 'em." He yanked his wheels around and pushed himself outside again. Cooter waited near the porch steps.

"She fucking *lied*, Coo." He heard the tears in his voice but couldn't stop them. "Cain't trust her neither."

Cooter's only response was to kneel. Cary pulled himself into the saddle, but he couldn't get his feet into the stirrups without Lindsay. Lindsay came out of the back door as if he'd heard the thought and silently helped him.

"She leave?" Cary asked.

"No. Where would she go tonight?"

Cary snorted. "You're too fucking nice."

"We promised."

Cary said nothing as he turned Cooter, but he knew Lindsay was right. They *had* promised to look after her, and they couldn't go back on it. Even if she was a goddamn liar.

* * *

They saw Tal the next night, and it was the same thing as usual: traveling the aether to see new worlds, learning to navigate it, fighting the Underworld things. They kept seeing corrupted spots, too. Sometimes they were few and far between, but sometimes entire branches seemed to be soft, like the one that ran directly beneath I-44. Just like Emily had said.

Tal said it was nothing, or that humans had caused that weakness. "Once you have reached full strength," he said, "I will announce your presence, and the worlds will believe in táltosk again."

Lindsay wasn't clear on how that was supposed to help the Tree. He glanced at Cary, who wore a grimly focused expression. They hadn't discussed what he was about to do, but he jumped in anyway. "Tal. How long till we get all our powers? I mean, we been doing a lot of killing Underworld critters and all that, but—"

"This is what your duties require. Do you think you are not making a difference?" Tal asked. "That this is not important? What would you rather be doing, I wonder?"

Lindsay was at a loss. He had no idea what they *should* be doing. "Well, I dunno. I just wondered."

"Walk before running, princes." Tal gave Cary a look. Cary stared straight ahead. "Any other questions?" Tal asked in a tone that said there had better not be.

"No," Cary said in a dead voice.

Tal looked at Lindsay. Lindsay's voice died in his throat, as it had so many times when Dad gave him that same look.

When they were at home, Bella and Cary avoided each other.

And no one knew what happened to Sandor. Still.

It was the worst waiting game.

Finally, the night of July fourth, they met the guy from Louisiana who was going to buy their guns. Most of the cops were out at the "I Love America" fireworks show, run by the super church from Ozark, and those who weren't were busy dealing with people blowing themselves up if the chatter on their police scanner was any evidence. The whole thing reminded Lindsay of practicing building explosives growing up. He'd always been pretty good at it.

"Ain't nothing like yours," Cary said as they drove through town. People had been setting off fireworks in their yards since before sunset.

"Prettier," Lindsay said.

"But not loud enough." Cary had never cared that their homemade explosives had only produced a flash of blinding white light as long as they were loud and left big craters in the field. "I tell you what, if this gun thing don't work out, you ought to sell some real fireworks. You can make 'em pretty if you want. You like the sparkly crap anyway, right?"

Lindsay ignored him. There was no end to the queer jokes these days, especially when Cary was in a mood.

Traffic was deadlocked on the east side of the event venue according to the scanner, but this side of town was dead. They took Highway 13, which turned into Kansas Expressway, to Battlefield, less than half a mile from the apartment Emily had taken Cary to on Walnut Lawn. Another block down past the police station, empty and quiet tonight, they turned down Scenic toward Nathanael Greene Park. The park wasn't open after sunset, but there was a golf course across the road where they'd meet the guy. It was a pretty, semi-secluded area during the day despite the fact that it was in the shadow of the Fed-Med—the US Medical Center for Federal Prisoners. Hell of a place to arrange a federal crime.

Another SUV sat in the parking lot when they pulled in. Lindsay parked so the passenger's side was farthest from the other car and helped Cary with the chair as quick as he could. Just in case.

An older guy approached them wearing a polo shirt and jeans, just a clean-cut white guy who looked like he belonged on that golf course. He did a double-take when he saw Cary, but he didn't comment. He shook their hands and introduced himself as Jim.

"Got a sample for me?" he asked.

"Sure." Lindsay opened the hatch and Cary opened the hard case. These rifles were even bigger than the ones Emily ended up buying, and there were more of them. They weren't quite finished with the batch, but with Travis's help, they would be soon. As Jim picked up the rifle and studied it in the light of Lindsay's Mag Light, Lindsay felt, just like every time they did this, a moment of nerves. If Jim didn't approve, he could just walk away and they would be left with a quarter million dollars' worth of gray market modified assault rifles in Travis's barn. Lindsay hated trying to sell anything, even if it was toothbrushes, but toothbrushes weren't illegal.

"You nervous?" Jim asked. Dammit, why couldn't he learn to control his feelings like Cary?

"Me?" Cary asked dryly. "Terrified, man."

Jim laughed. "Yeah, you look like it. This looks good. Mind if I run it by the boss?" He pulled a rolled-up wad of money from his pocket. "I'll pay up front for this one."

They exchanged money for the gun, then went their separate ways. Cary called Wade to let them know, and for once he didn't talk to Dad, too.

It had gone as smoothly as possible. Why did Lindsay still feel the nerves?

"I dunno about Tal no more," Cary said after they'd gotten food from the McDonald's on Battlefield and Kansas. "He's hiding something. I mean, we know that. He ain't said nothing about how he knows Dad or what he wants with him. He won't tell us nothing about the táltosk or what we're really supposed to be doing. It's just like goddamn Emily."

Lindsay was speechless for a moment, shocked to hear him say it. He'd been wanting to say the same thing but couldn't figure out how, not sure how Cary would react. "Yeah."

Cary stabbed the straw into the hole at the top of his cup. "The whole thing just stinks. I'm fucking sick and tired of people hiding shit from us."

"So what're we gonna do?" Lindsay asked, hoping he'd suggest what he himself wanted to suggest.

"Dunno. Ain't like nobody else is gonna teach us."

"What if we teach ourselves?"

"Ain't like learning how to play the guitar, Lin."

"Well. What if it is?"

Cary's brows furrowed. He shook his head. "I dunno. We don't got nobody else to turn to."

Lindsay's heart sank. He'd heard that for their entire lives about Dad. And he didn't think Cary's mind would ever change completely about Dad.

* * *

It took working every spare minute they had, but they managed to finish the guns in time. They ended up renting a ten-foot U-Haul to carry them all to the meeting place, near the railroad tracks downtown. The parking lot was across the street from a building owned by Missouri State, the one halfway nice building in an area that looked like more blacks and Mexicans ought to be wandering the street at night.

They arrived before Jim, giving time for Lindsay to get Cary's chair from the back. There were no other people for another couple blocks, but they could hear music from somewhere, hanging in the hot air. Cary was still seeing shadows, so thick it made the parking lot seem even darker. He told himself there was a magic node not twenty feet away. They could summon the horses and their swords in a second if they needed to fight any critters. And they had their own guns.

He wished they didn't need money so badly.

Jim showed up in a cargo van about a minute and a half late. When he got out with a metal briefcase in hand, Lindsay readied the scale to weigh it.

"Y'all are about the only game in town," Jim said as he set the briefcase on the scale. "Good thing y'all do quality work."

"You got more business in the future, you can contact our boss," Cary said. "We can help you get loaded up."

"It's okay. I got it covered," Jim said.

Cary figured out what their senses had been trying to warn them of a second before the police cars showed up.

A bunch of them came screaming out of the shadows that shrouded Cary's vision. Two cops got out of each of them, guns drawn, screaming at them to get their hands up, for Lindsay to get on his knees.

"Fuck," Cary breathed. "*Fuck.*"

They went for Lindsay first, yanked his arms behind his back and cuffed him. He wanted to throw himself at them as they forced his brother upright and propelled him toward one of the cars. Cary reached for his sword.

"Hands *up!*" Jim shouted at him. He had a gun now, too. Two guys in uniform came around behind him. One pushed him forward to get his arms behind his back, and the other patted down his legs.

"You got any weapons on you? Or the chair? Anything else that's gonna stick me? Any drugs?" The guy searching him looked uncomfortable searching a cripple. Good.

"Yeah. Gun in a holster strapped to the chair next to my left hip and a knife on my belt." Cary looked at him square in the eye when his hand stopped on his thigh. "That's a leg bag. For urine. You wanna check?"

The cop grunted, but didn't check. "Can you stand or do we have to lift you?"

"I'm a fucking paraplegic."

The two uniforms lifted him by the armpits while Jim finished searching him and the chair.

"No. You ain't taking my fucking chair." Cary tried to see what they were doing to Lindsay. He was being patted down much like Cary was.

"They'll take it at the station. You can have it till then."

Then Cary saw the disability transportation services van pull into the parking lot. The motherfuckers came *prepared.*

As one of the uniforms pushed him over to the van and loaded him up using the lift, Cary thought about Travis. And Bella. They had promised to protect both of them. Shit. Shit, shit.

"When can I talk to my brother?" he asked the uniform who rode in the van with him. "We need a lawyer, all that."

"I don't know, sir. You'll have to talk to the booking officer."

They had to get out of this somehow. Staying in jail, waiting to get sent to prison for a federal crime, wasn't an option.

The jail wasn't from downtown. Lindsay was already inside by the time they got Cary out of the van. He was bent over a counter while he was being searched, his entire body shaking. Cary caught a glimpse of his terrified face before one of the officers shoved his head down onto the counter. "Stay *still*."

"He's still!" Cary said. "Let him alone, you bastard. He ain't doing nothing to you."

They ignored him, of course, and Cary could do nothing as he was wheeled into another room. True to Jim's word, even before they searched Cary again, they pulled him out of the chair and into a clunky, dirty gray one made for someone half again his girth, with "GREENE CO." stamped on it. Cary's body went rigid when they picked him up, and their grips tightened, but he didn't fight them. He couldn't afford to.

"You cain't even leave my brother his *wheelchair*, you motherfuckers?" Lindsay said when they brought him out.

"It goes to the property room," one of them said, though Cary was pleased to see he flinched. Lindsay didn't have Cary's temper, but he could make his voice sound like his words were venomous as a copperhead. Cary shook his head at Lindsay. He was trembling with rage, but he recognized he was helpless here. They both were. Nothing to do but wait and try to think of a way out of this.

Chapter Nineteen

Once they were fingerprinted and had mug shots taken—Dad would have a fit when he found out their fingerprints had been recorded—Cary and Lindsay were put in a waiting area. At least the cuffs were off and they could talk.

"We gotta call Trav," Lindsay said. His venom had been replaced by anxiety, which made him look like a scared dog, the whites of his eyes and his teeth showing.

"And Wade." Cary dreaded that. "Tell them both to get rid of everything and hope the cops don't know nothing about them yet."

"They record calls," Lindsay reminded him.

"Well, then we just say as much as we can." And hope for the best.

"We gotta get outta here," Lindsay whispered. "This cain't happen."

"We'll find a way, brother," Cary told him. He hoped he wasn't lying.

Cary expected Wade to be furious when he called, but all he said was, "Gonna get you outta there, boys."

"Uncle Wade, we done a federal crime. We ain't gonna get no bail. We cain't even afford a lawyer."

"I'll figure something out." For once, Wade actually sounded like an uncle rather than Dad's little brother.

Immediately after their phone calls, they were given "temporary housing" in separate cells. Lindsay's was on the second floor, but at least they were in the same "pod," as the guard called it. A nurse came by to check Cary and gave him a new leg bag, and then he was left alone. Until his "orientation" after 72 hours, he would be in his cell 23 hours a day.

Well. He was used to waiting; he'd gotten good at stilling his mind in the hospital and just sitting. He felt bad for Lindsay, who had only looked more anxious after he got off the phone with Travis.

Cary closed his eyes, shut out the distractions—voices, doors slamming, echoes of movements, worries—and concentrated on his brother. They'd always been aware of each other, able to find one another even when they were miles apart. It wasn't hard to "find" him a floor above. It was like Lindsay was sitting next to him. Though, no, not Lindsay himself. His magic instead, silver-green and chilly like that raw day before spring took hold. Cary reached out with his magical sense and touched it. Lindsay's restless anxiety made his magic flicker, but when it connected with Cary's, it steadied.

This felt unlike anything they'd ever done before. Cary wondered if they could use it to communicate somehow. He pictured this being a little like when he rode Cooter: he simply communicated his desires and awareness to the horse, as natural as breathing. But he was used to communicating with horses through body language and intent. How do to it with no body near him?

Lindsay answered that question for him. Unbidden, an image of Travis appeared in his mind: Travis being arrested, too. Cary stopped it, like hitting pause on the DVD remote, and instead pictured the empty barn with no evidence left, then Travis visiting Lin here. He could tell the second idea got a mixed reception, but it seemed to ease Lindsay's anxiety.

Cary was too tired to figure out much more than how to comfort Lindsay (and himself) with that thread of connection. He moved to the bed and pictured himself going to sleep. He doubted Lindsay would sleep for a while, knowing him, but he hoped Lin wouldn't obsess over Travis all night.

As he drifted off, Cary thought of Bella and wondered if she would come with Travis to visit them.

* * *

Their first visit was with a public defender, right after they had gone through orientation and been put into a different pod. They weren't in the same cell still—Cary was alone and Lindsay was with some black guy—but this time they were only a couple cells apart.

"I've been assigned to represent you both." The lawyer was white even though her last name was Vasquez. She looked about Lindsay's age, which made him feel self-conscious the way most young, very smart people did. "So tell me what happened."

"We got caught selling guns," Cary said. "What else is there?"

She gave him a look. "Well. Plenty. I probably can't get you out of jail time, but I might be able to get reduced sentences. What can you offer investigators? Who are you working for?"

Give up Wade. Given how he'd tricked them into seeing Dad, and brought Dad to darken their doorstep, Lindsay was ready to consider it. He turned to Cary, but Cary said,

"No."

The lawyer lifted her eyebrows. "You've got to look out for yourselves, gentlemen." She pointed at Cary with her pencil. "I know you especially don't want to spend too long in prison." She turned to Lindsay then. "You looked like you were about to say something."

Lindsay looked at Cary. Cary stared back at him. Lindsay knew he was thinking about Dad's reaction if Wade got arrested. The police might find a way to pin this on the whole family. They both knew there was plenty of illegal stuff going on at home, too.

"Nope," Lindsay said.

"Well, I see I'm going to get approximately nowhere today." The lawyer collected her papers and stood. "I'll come back Tuesday after I've had a chance to look at your case. Think about what you might want to give the investigators."

They had a chance to talk later, in the day room. The other inmates stared at Cary, but fortunately none of them approached. Lindsay was glad Cary had a cell to himself.

Cary told Lindsay what Wade had said. "What does that even mean?" Lindsay wondered. "He ain't got no pull up here and I bet he ain't got no money for no fancy lawyer. Is he gonna...?" *Break us out?*

"Dunno."

Cary just shrugged.

They didn't have a chance to find out. On Tuesday, the public defender, Miss Vasquez, came back to tell them they had a bail hearing.

"What the hell?" Lindsay blurted said before he could stop himself. "How'd that happen?"

"We found a sympathetic judge." There was something about the flat tone in Miss Vasquez's voice that made Lindsay a little wary and a lot curious.

"We still don't got bail money," Cary pointed out. "So we're fucked anyway."

"Well, that's not my job." Miss Vasquez picked up her pen and folder.gave a thin-lipped smile. "But maybe something will work out."

Lindsay got the impression she knew something they didn't. Judging by Cary's expression, he thought so too.

Before they could find out what that might be, though, Travis came to visit with news. Lindsay was half-glad, half-embarrassed to see him, and it was a struggle not to hug him in public.

"Miss you," Lindsay whispered. "We got a bail hearing next week."

"That's good." Travis looked troubled, and Lindsay's stomach knotted. "I miss you too. Wish I could say I was here for a good reason, but Bella's missing. I ain't seen her since last night, early."

Dread crept into Lindsay. "Did she go somewhere?"

Travis pressed his lips together. "Not that I know of. I fell asleep early. Didn't talk to her. My truck and your vehicle are still there. I dunno, Lin."

Lindsay was glad Cary hadn't been able to get clearance for Travis to visit him as well. He was already imagining his reaction.

"Sorry," Travis said.

"Honey, don't be," Lindsay said. "It ain't your fault, none of it."

"I feel like I let y'all down."

Lindsay's heart twisted. "No, you didn't. You done nothing but help us, Trav. Come on, now." He couldn't risk even a touch, but he tried to make his tone whisper as gentle as possible. Travis gave him a shy little smile that twisted his heart for a different reason. "Love you," he said impulsively.

Travis looked dumbfounded and immediately Lindsay wondered if he'd said the wrong thing. But then Travis whispered, "Love you too."

Their visit was only twenty minutes, and by the time it was over, the glow of happiness at seeing Travis and hearing Travis loved him had already faded into having to tell Cary about Travis's news.

In the space of a couple of seconds, Cary's face drained of color, then flushed with temper that practically sparked off of him. Lindsay recognized that dangerous look that said Cary was spoiling for a fight and reacted immediately, grabbing his shoulder. "No, Cary Judah," he said. "We're in *jail*, remember? We gotta wait this out." He was surprised to feel a rush of cool magic flow down his arm into Cary. Almost instantly Lindsay himself relaxed, feeling his tensed muscles and the knot of anxiety in his chest loosen. Cary relaxed a second later and stared at him in shock.

"Gentlemen." The guard startled both of them, apparently drawn when Lindsay grabbed Cary so suddenly.

"Was just talking to my brother, sir," Lindsay said as politely as he could. He was astonished to see the guard relax when he met Lindsay's eyes.

"Well. Inmates don't need to be touching each other. Next time I write you up." He wandered away.

"What the hell, Lindsay," Cary's eyes widened.

murmured.

"I, uh. I dunno."

"We got to get outta here," Cary said. "There's what, four more days to the hearing? And then we gotta get bail money. Maybe Wade can do something. Where could she have gone? You think she got took like Sandor?"

Lindsay could think of no response other than to shrug.

"Jesus God almighty," Cary said. "I promised to *protect* her, Lin. God*damn* it."

"We'll find her," Lindsay said, trying to keep Cary calm without touching him. "We'll ask Tal for help. He seemed like he wanted to keep her safe too."

"All this time you been the one who didn't want him to help."

Lindsay wished he wasn't right about that one. "I don't see as we got much choice. He said he wanted to keep her safe, remember. We don't gotta do nothing for him, just ask if he seen her."

"Yeah." Cary rubbed his lower lip, distracted but at least fairly calm. "Who woulda took her? Emily and them? They don't got Sandor with 'em no more."

"I dunno." Lindsay was stumped and he felt helpless. He could only imagine how Cary must feel. "We'll find her," he said again. "I know you care about her."

Cary fixed him with a look, but he didn't deny it. "Four days."

Lindsay nodded. "Four days."

* * *

As it turned out, Wade didn't give them bail money. He didn't even come to court for the bail hearing.

Emily did.

Cary spotted her immediately when the bailiff pushed him into the courtroom. There were other people there from other cases, but her blue magic stood out like a neon light among them. When the lawyer, Vasquez, came in, Emily watched her in particular.

What the hell?

The prosecutor argued like hell against the entire thing, saying they had offered nothing and so deserved nothing, anyway. Vasquez remained cool and reminded the judge that they had no prior offenses and that they represented no real danger (she looked at Cary when she said that).

The hearing lasted less than twenty minutes. The judge granted them bail at a quarter million. Each. Cary heard Lindsay's hiss. There was no way in hell they'd make that. The sale of the guns they'd gotten caught selling would have only netted half that, and most of that would have gone back to Wade and his suppliers.

Cary looked at Emily again. She lifted her eyebrows ever so slightly. He knew then what had gone on. *I have connections*, she'd said. Was she behind this? All of it? He stared back at her as the bailiff wheeled him out of the courtroom.

They got word later that afternoon that they'd made bail and would be released the next day at six in the morning.

Looking back, Cary figured he ought to have known better than to think they were in the clear after that. He'd been too concerned about Bella, and whatever the hell was going on with Emily, to pay attention to the immediate danger.

He had just gotten off the phone with Wade—he'd spent the entire call listening to Wade dressing him down after he'd finally explained Emily—but all he could think as he headed back to the pod was at least it wasn't Dad griping him out. His ears would have bled.

He turned the corner and ran smack into two big black motherfuckers. Their arms were crossed, and they looked like they'd been waiting for him.

Cary forced a sudden spike of fear down. He tried to reach that frame of mind he'd used countless times to work people over and get what he wanted, that state of absolute confidence things would go his way. To his surprise, he felt his magic rise warm and strong in him, and with it came that confidence. "Sorry, y'all." He backed up and turned. "Guess I don't need to go tearing through the halls like it's NASCAR."

The taller one grabbed the handles of the chair and Cary's body tensed, but he forced a grin, looking the shorter one straight in the eye. "Well, how y'all doing?"

The shorter one leered at him. "We gonna have some fun with you, cripple. Ain't no cameras here to protect you, neither."

No, but there *was* a door at the end of the hall with a window. And of course Lindsay had sensed something was going on and was peering into it. Shit. Cary had to end this fast before his brother started freaking out. He couldn't afford fear for his own sake, so he took hold of that warm magic and used it to strengthen him. He let it radiate from him and widened his grin.

"That right? Oh, good. Been wondering if I done lost my touch. Ain't been nobody offering since I got here. That big ole' cell of mine sure does get lonely at night."

Surprise and uncertainty flashed across the guy's face, and something like horror appeared in Lindsay's. Cary knew from experience he could hear well enough despite the closed door.

"You wanna get lucky, faggot?" the bigger one grabbed him by the throat and wrenched his head back. Cary barely managed not to wince, even when he heard Lindsay start to throw a fit on the other side of the door.

"Hell yeah." Cary made his face mirror the shorter guy's leer. "Shit, nobody told me this place was big ole' candy store. Just look at y'all big studs. You first, honey? I ain't got to taste no black dick before."

The bigger guy shoved him away so hard the chair tipped. Cary couldn't even try to stop it before he toppled onto the cold tile floor on his side. He'd never been closer to panic, those faces looming over him, but he forced himself to open his arms to them. "Come on, studs. I might look like just a little ole' queer cripple, but I bet I can take y'all both. I'll show y'all the best time and then y'all can be as queer as me. Better hurry, though. I'm so hard I ain't gonna last long."

The two guys looked at each other with the weirdest expression. They didn't have time to decide what to do before four guards burst through the door, shouting at the other two to get on the floor.

"Any injuries?" A female guard righted the chair, and Cary let her and helped him into it.

"I'm fine. Thanks." Cary gave her a half-smile, though he didn't turn on the charm all the way. He doubted she would appreciate that. He heard a ruckus at the other end of the hall, in the pod, and guessed it was Lindsay. "Can you take me back there? That's my brother pitching a fit. He'll calm down as soon as he sees I'm okay."

He had to grip the arms of the chair to avoid showing how shaky he was as she pushed him back into the pod. A blast of cold air, like standing at the door of a walk-in freezer, hit him. A halo of silvery magic had built around Lindsay. He was on his belly like a fish, fighting against three guards, one of which had a can of pepper spray out. Judging by Lindsay's red face and streaming eyes, they'd already used it on him.

"Lindsay!" Cary barked. Lindsay froze and turned his head in Cary's direction, though he didn't seem to be able to open his eyes. "I'm okay," Cary said. "I'm fine. Promise."

Lindsay let the guards haul him to his feet. "Take him to the infirmary, wash his eyes out," one of the guards said. "You," he added to Cary, "Stay in your cell till you're released. You're on lockdown."

That was fine with Cary. The female guard brought him to his cell, and he curled up on the bed, pulling the blanket over himself and wrapping it tight. He didn't stop shaking for hours.

* * *

Lindsay spent an awful night reliving that scene over and over, with stinging eyes and a raw throat. It was like his worst nightmare come true: standing behind a locked door, Cary on the other side being attacked, Lindsay him unable to do anything.

The amazing part was that Cary had been able to talk his way out of the situation. Lindsay had been sure those guys were about to drag him off, but then Lindsay had felt the buzz of Cary's magic like static, and he'd seen their faces change. Cary had always been able to make people feel pretty much the way he wanted them to, but this was the first time Lindsay had felt magic behind it.

That still didn't help the leftover anxiety that made his skin crawl and his heart want to pound out of his chest. He only dozed a little before the guard woke him at four-thirty.

Lindsay met Cary at the property room as they were giving him back his chair. He had a big bruise on his neck and he looked like he didn't want to move it much.

"I'm okay, mother hen," Cary said before Lindsay could speak. Lindsay frowned, but Cary's expression didn't invite discussion.

"Wasn't Wade who got us out," Cary said in an undertone while they waited for their paperwork. "Think it was Emily."

"Lindsay blinked. "Why?""

"Got me, brother."

The sun was just coming up when a guard opened a side door for them. Lindsay could see Travis's big white truck parked across the street, and his heart leapt.

But Emily stood on the sidewalk between them and the parking lot.

"That was to make a point," she said without greeting them. "When you are who you are and you keep doing reckless things, you're bound to get noticed even by mundanes," she said without greeting them. "If you had agreed to work with us, we could have kept the police off of you."

"You set us *up*?" Cary demanded. He rolled toward her and Lindsay felt the static electricity of his magic again. Emily flinched ever so slightly, but she stood her ground and brought up a hand, her palm facing him. It was like someone shut off that electricity around her.

"No, I didn't set you up. I got you out of your own stupidity. You're lucky we have a judge on our side. Even he may not be able to get you out of it completely. It's a goddamn federal crime."

Lindsay's heart jumped into his throat. She was right. They might still be totally fucked. "What are we gonna do?"

"We are not going to do anything unless you cooperate with us. I ought to let you go to prison."

"In a word, yes," she said. "Like I said, if you'd cooperated, it wouldn't have turned into anything."

Lindsay found himself glad the police hadn't returned their knives or handguns. He was sure Cary would have pulled one or the other. Hell, he was tempted, himself. He marched up to Emily, shaking with anger. "You look at his neck, girl. You see what happened to him? It would be *worse* in federal prison. And it would be your fault."

Emily studied Cary's bruised neck; Lindsay saw her eyes flicker, but only for a second. "Well, now you understand how serious I am about this. I'm the one who offered to give you a job, and I got you out of jail. Do you remember that? If you go to prison it'll be your fault."

"Bitch," Cary snarled, "I'm about half a second from showing you how serious I am."

"Walk away, Emily." Even Lindsay could hear the coldness in his own voice, and she gave him a surprised look. "This ain't no way to get us to do whatever it is you want." It was true. They'd agreed to do one more job for Wade and look where it had gotten them. Cary looked like he was about to say something, but after a second he just sat back and looked at Emily.

"If you would *listen*—"

"Hey, y'all." Travis's low drawl interrupted the silence. He joined them, standing at Lindsay's side. "Ma'am."

Emily looked back and forth between Lindsay and Travis, eyes widening and then abruptly narrowing. "Oh, that's *great*."

Lindsay started. What? How the hell could she know about him and Travis?

"Some teacher you have. A real charmer, teaching you how to enslave people right off the bat," Emily sneered. "Consider my support permanently withdrawn. Enjoy your free time before your trial. And then enjoy the hell out of prison." She stomped away, cursing.

"That your sister?" Travis asked, staring after her.

Lindsay shook himself. "Yeah. How'd you know?"

"She looks like you around the eyes." Travis turned toward him. "Ready to go home?"

"Wait a fucking second," Cary said. "What the hell was she talking about, enslaving people?"

Lindsay wondered the same thing. He looked at Travis. Had he done something he hadn't meant to that he couldn't sense? "I dunno."

"Travis shrugged. "She mighta just been trying to aggravate y'all. She seems like the type."

Cary snorted, but the statement continued to bother Lindsay, as well as Travis's reaction to it. Wasn't he at all worried about what Emily had said, especially when it applied to him?

"C'mon." Travis nudged him. "Let's get y'all home. You look tired."

Lindsay decided he was too tired to think hard about it. He followed Travis and Cary back to the truck. As he loaded Cary's chair into the back, he watched Cary adjust himself in the front seat, looked at Cary's bruised neck. "Care."

"We gotta find Bella."

"What about—"

"We gotta find Bella first. Then we can worry about that."

"About what?" Travis asked. Lindsay got into the back seat and told him what Emily had said as they drove home.

"That's pretty serious, y'all," Travis said. "What are we gonna do?"

"Me and Cary are gonna have to figure something out. I ain't gonna get you in trouble too," Lindsay said.

"I agreed to get involved with this gun stuff and I ain't allowed to help y'all when it goes south? That ain't quite fair. I'm gonna help you out as much as I can," Travis said.

"No, Trav," Cary said from the front seat. "You gotta stay outta jail and take care a' your family. If you start helping us they might start looking at you too. Stay away from it."

"Stay away from y'all?" Travis met Lindsay's eyes in the rear view mirror. "Not gonna happen."

"*Travis,*" Lindsay said, shaking all over. How could he make Travis believe what an awful idea this was?

"It's fine," Travis said. "I've known for a long time what I might be getting into and I been prepared to face it."

No, you ain't, Lindsay wanted to say, but tears closed his throat and he could say nothing.

* * *

Cary felt Bella's absence keenly in the few hours they were in the house and he was eager to be off to find her, but Travis (and Lindsay) made him eat first.

"Care," Lindsay said as he buckled Cary's legs to Cooter's saddle. "What you did with them guys."

"I wasn't gonna fuck 'em, Lin."

"You had me pretty fucking convinced," Lindsay said tartly.

"That was the point. Make them think they'd be the biggest faggots on God's green earth if they fucked me."

Lindsay swung astride Sister and gave him a look. "You did sound really queer."

"Oh, so *now* you're a faggot expert? I learned it from watching you and Travis, anyway."

Lindsay seemed to realize how ridiculous their argument was at the same time Cary did and laughed. It hurt Cary's throat, but it made him feel just a little better, as making fun of something always did.

This time, focused as he was on is task, Cary found Tal's place without any trouble. The grooms saw them and came scrambling. Servants disappeared into the house. Even Emese in her paddock watched them with perked ears and dark, curious eyes.

Tal himself came out to meet them at the front door. "Princes! I've been looking for you. I feared something terrible had happened."

"Long story," Cary grunted. "Bella is missing. Nobody's seen her for five days."

"The young recorsa? Weren't you looking out for her?"

Cary gritted his teeth, hearing the disappointment in Tal's voice. "Yeah." Rub it in, he thought.

"What do you suppose happened to her?"

"Dunno. We wasn't there." Cary felt his face heat. This was just like talking to Dad, right before he barked out their punishment, when he wanted them to admit to their wrongdoing. "We was in jail for a week."

Tal looked surprised. "Jail? Whatever for?"

"Look," Cary said, frustrated, "We need help finding Bella. We think she got took by them same things that attacked her. Them Underworld things."

"Well." Tal frowned, looking between them. "Certainly I will help you find her. You must wish to be off to look for her at once. I'll saddle Emese and join you." He strode off toward the stables. Cooter danced beneath Cary all of a sudden, and Cary had to pull his head around to control him.

"What is it?"

"Care." Lindsay caught his arm and pointed. Cary followed his finger and spotted a broad, dark figure moving on the west side of the house, near an outbuilding. Almost before he could order it, Cooter trotted forward, toward the figure. It looked like it would disappear, but it turned to look directly at them.

Sefu?

Cary heard Lindsay's gasp. The man turned away from them, back toward the house. Sure enough, he had a scar on the side of his head.

"Care," Lindsay murmured. "What's he doing here?" Lindsay said. "He's Sandor's *goji*, right? Is he helping Tal look for Sandor or something?"

"A *goji* does not leave its master's side on the aether," Sister said.

So Sandor was here. Cary met Lindsay's eyes, confusion pulling his thoughts in every direction. Why was Sandor here? How long had he been here? What the hell did it mean?

Tal whistled from the paddock, summoning them.

"Care," Lindsay murmured. "What do we *do*?"

How am I supposed to know? Cary thought as quickly as he could. "Go with him. Come back. See if we can find Sandor again." Or Bella. He met his brother's eyes. They looked as troubled as Cary felt.

* * *

Tal gave them no chance to go back to the manor house alone. They split up to "look" for Bella in nearby pockets of the aether, but Tal sent servants with them, four in all. Lindsay recognized all of them, but they seemed different somehow, now. Seeing them lope along either side of Sister, they looked as unnatural as dogs walking on two legs. Sister didn't seem nervous, exactly, but she acted suspicious, not trusting any of them to get too close.

Lindsay wanted to ask her what the servants were, if they were human. She'd said he didn't have to use words to communicate with her. That made sense in theory, but how was he supposed to ask a question without words? He looked down at the servants, concentrated on them, his hand tightening in her Sister's mane. until she snorted. Good, he had her attention. He tried to form a question in his mind, tried to project his concern and curiosity about the servants.

The answer came immediately in a flurry of impressions and images he couldn't understand, smells and snatches of movement like movie clips and sounds and senses he didn't have. It made him dizzy and he couldn't figure out what they were all supposed to mean.

A moment later, Cary made a quiet sound.drew in a sharp breath. Lindsay gave him a questioning look and Cary jerked his head, glancing at the servants. Lindsay reached out with that magical sense, seeking to touch the wild warmth of Cary's energy. More impressions, this time clear images: muddy gray-brown oozing over the green of the Tree, shapes like a pack of dogs scattering at the edges of his vision. Lindsay remembered Cary's description of the hounds who'd attacked Travis's house.

Like dogs on two legs.

Lindsay let out his breath slowly, careful not to alert the servants. How had they not seen it before? No wonder Tal knew so much about Underworld creatures; he kept them like pets.

"We should go back," Lindsay said aloud. "Don't look like we're gonna find her today."

One of the servants glanced over his shoulder at Lindsay. Lindsay swallowed a sudden bolt of nerves, wondering if the thing would suddenly transform and go for his throat, but it just gestured at the other one and they turned.

The servants lead them back to Tal's place without attacking, without even looking at them again. Cary's expression as they rode was hard to look at, a mixture of doubt and anger and maybe the tiniest awful hope that at least they might have a chance of finding Bella this way. But when they stepped through the gates of the manor, they could see Emese's pale form already in her paddock at the crest of the sloping hill.

"You can go now," Lindsay told the servants, who walked off toward the house without a word.

Cary turned Cooter abruptly toward Lindsay. "What the *fuck*, Lin."

For a minute, Lindsay thought Cary was about to gripe him out. "Is this my fault?"

"What the fuck is going *on*?" Cary's hands tightened on the reins. "How come you never said nothing, huh?" he asked Cooter.

"I didn't know," Cooter said. Lindsay thought the stallion sounded shaken.

"They were hidden from us, too," Sister said. "I would have told you, Lindsay."

Lindsay felt like his throat might close and he swallowed hard. Cary relaxed his grip on the reins, his face pale. He drew in an audible breath as Tal came out of the house to meet them.

"Nothing?" Tal's expression was much too calm, no longer the least bit distressed.

"No. You?" Cary wore that look that hid the anger Lindsay could see building in his entire body. Lindsay moved Sister a little closer, praying Cary wasn't rash enough to strike out at Tal. Tal seemed about to say something, but Cary broke in, "How long've you had Sandor and Sefu?"

Tal's face hardened. "I bet your pardon?" The look in his eyes warned them not to continue. Cary, of course, ignored it.

"We seen Sefu around the house. I know it was him." Lindsay spoke up, not wanting to leave Cary hanging.

Tal shook his head. "Princes, you are distressed. You are not thinking clearly. Why would I hide the recorsa and his *goji* from you?"

"Then why'd you come back so early? Why didn't you keep looking for Bella? You had to catch *True Blood*? Paint your fucking toenails?" Cary growled. "Did you send them Underworld critters after us too? I know what your servants are. I can see them now. Quit jerking us around and tell us the truth, dammit."

"Prince Cary." Tal's magic flared around him, no longer like static but like a real electrical charge. Lindsay's body jerked and he felt like the one time he'd accidentally touched a naked wire of an AC adapter. "You will mind your place."

"I'm a *prince*, motherfucker." Cary spat at Tal's feet, and the horses turned simultaneously. "Go to hell."

"I truly wish you hadn't done that, prince." Tal's voice, despite being barely above a whisper, rang in Lindsay's ears. Lindsay's skin prickled. Instinctively he turned Sister back toward Tal.

Cary cried out. Gold light flared around him, almost too bright to look at it. Lindsay realized what he was seeing a second too late. His right hand closed around the handle of his sword, but this time, Tal was faster. Rainbow colors swept toward Cary in a wave. Wrapped up in the rainbow were fingers of dark corruption that tangled with Cary's magic, tugging at it. Trying to pull it out of Cary.

Lindsay reacted without thinking. He reached into himself for the cool magic in him and shoved it out, toward Cary. Sister rushed forward and Lindsay grabbed for Cary with his hands, too. He wasn't going to let anybody else take something anything from Cary. He *wasn't*.

The electric charge in the air slammed into Lindsay, rattling his bones. Overwhelmed by the sheer force of it, he almost lost his grip on his own magic. But he couldn't afford to. He had to protect Cary. He sucked in a breath and grabbed Cary's arm, steadying him in the saddle. Instantly he felt their magic combine, silver and gold, cool and hot winding together. It crackled around them and the muddy-colored corruption evaporated. Still Tal's rainbow magic pressed on them, squeezing Lindsay until he couldn't breathe. Cary swayed in his saddle, but then he grabbed Cooter's mane and pulled himself upright. Lindsay felt Cary grab for his magic this time and willingly gave it, letting him use their combined energy.

Cary pulled his sword and their magic poured into it. He slashed at Tal's magic, but it was like trying to fight water: the rainbow colors parted around the blade, but then flowed right back over it. Still the energy pressed on them and Lindsay saw stars. He took Cooter's reins and urged both horses away. He heard his own voice but had no idea what he was saying and no idea what Cary screamed in return. Over both their voices he heard Tal:

"You have no idea what you are doing, princes. Prince Cary, stop and think; you need me!"

Anger swept through Lindsay like ice water down his back. He didn't care anymore what Tal said, what anybody said; they didn't need anybody else. "Care, come on."

To Lindsay's relief, Cary didn't argue. Instead, he grabbed Cooter's reins and the horses ran.

Tal didn't follow them. Maybe he was too shocked that Cary had turned his back. To tell the truth, Lindsay was too. It was almost exactly the scene Lindsay had pictured with Dad for years and years, Dad trying to pick on Cary, taking whatever he wanted from both of them, until finally they pulled themselves away. Only in his daydreams, Lindsay himself had spat at Dad's feet.

Lindsay had no idea how long it was before they burst through the aether back into the real world. Cary looked deathly pale in the evening light, panting and sweating, and Lindsay himself still shook so hard he could barely hold the reins. He could hardly feel his own arm when he reached out to touch Cary's shoulder and had to force words past his closed-up throat.

"Okay?"

Cary didn't look at him. "Still got my magic." He didn't say it, but the word barely hung in the air between them. "Thanks."

"You're my brother," Lindsay said.

This time Cary did look at him. "Yeah."

Travis seemed to notice something was bothering them when they went back to the house. Lindsay wanted to lay in bed with him and tell him everything, but he wanted to make sure Cary was okay first.

"Your phone's been ringing off the hook," Travis told Cary. Without speaking, Cary retreated into his room and shut the door. When Lindsay knocked, he didn't answer and Lindsay knew not to press him. Instead, he sat with Travis on the couch and told him everything they had seen. He was glad Travis seemed to believe him without question and all he said was,

"That's heavy, Lin."

"I know. I just don't…what are we gonna do now?"

Travis shook his head. "Can't answer that. Might be a dumb question, but is there anything y'all want me to do?"

Lindsay smiled. "Honey, you're doing an awful lot just by being here."

Travis returned the smile and he looked younger than Cary despite the gray at his temples. Lindsay reached for his hand, but Cary appeared then and Travis shifted away. He still wasn't comfortable touching like that except when they were alone.

"It was Wade. He wants to meet us in Springfield. Last call said he was already on his way."

Lindsay's jaw tightened. "He said if he was bringing Dad?"

"Didn't say. Meet you at the vehicle." Cary headed out the door, again leaving Lindsay no choice but to follow.

"You want me to come?" Travis asked.

"Yeah," Lindsay said without thinking. "Come."

* * *

The spot Wade had picked was a small parking lot, just enough gravel to hold about six cars, on one of the Springfield-Greene County greenway trails. The trail ran under James River Freeway and eventually wound around to become the nature center. This part of it lay between two cemeteries, one for pets at the bottom of the hill and one for people at the top. The cemeteries weren't really restful places, sitting almost on top of the highway.

Wade got out of a compact car Cary didn't recognize when they pulled up. Cary could see no one elsedidn't see anyone else in the car. The evening was slowly sliding into darkness, but the heat of the day still sat heavy and mosquitoes buzzed in Cary's ear.

"Boys all right?" Cary heard Wade ask as he got into his chair on the other side of the vehicle. "Who's that?"

"Travis Earl. I'm a friend of your nephews."

"Uh huh." Cary could tell by Wade's tone he wasn't convinced. "Well. C'mon over. Cain't stay long."

Cary made his way through the gravel to the car, thinking Wade could have picked a better spot, to the car. Wade popped the trunk and showed them its contents: a normal-looking duffel bag. "Inside's a shaving kit. You'll find some money in it. Do whatever y'all need to do with it. Better git rid 'a that vehicle and them cell phones. They're bound to be tracking y'all. Don't make it easy."

Cary stared at him. Wade was giving them money after they'd botched the sale of the guns? "What's going on?" he demanded.

Wade turned to face them and sat on the edge of the trunk. The little car creaked under his weight. "Y'all need to know the truth about what's going on, I reckon. A while back Lewis started complaining of stomach pain. Now, you know your daddy. He don't complain about nothing." It took Wade forever to tell a story.; Cary wished he'd just get down to it. "One day he made me drive into town with him, to the library. He went looking in a bunch of books for a while. I didn't know what the hell he was doing. He come back after a while. Said he had cancer and that I was gonna tell everybody that. He made me tell everybody he went to the doctor and that the doctor said he had cancer of the pancreas and was like to die from it. He made me help him remember all that was in the book. Symptoms, everything." He paused, looking at them. Cary understood what he was getting at, but he sure as hell didn't want to.

"He was faking," Travis said.

Wade gave him a 'who asked you' look, but he nodded. "Ayup. He never had no cancer. He was healthy as ever."

"Why?" Lindsay asked, disgust clear in his voice. "Why would he do that?"

Wade sighed. "Would y'all have come back to him if he hadn't said he was dying? He knew he done screwed the pooch with y'all, letting y'all run off like that. For a while he thought y'all would come back, but when y'all didn't, he thought of a way to get you back. Don't act like you're surprised. He always did have a way of getting people to do what he wanted, no matter what."

Cary couldn't speak, couldn't move, couldn't think. Wade's words circled around his head but they just wouldn't penetrate. Lindsay's hand came down hard on his shoulder and squeezed. Wade looked between them, then his eyes settled on Cary. "Cary Judah. What you got to say about this?"

"Fuck you, Wade," Cary said hoarsely. "Is that all *you* got to say?"

Wade shifted his weight and the car creaked beneath him again. He rubbed the bridge of his nose. "Dear Lord, I wish that was so. Listen, Aunt Betty sat me down and gave me what for after y'all left. By God, did I deserve it. I know what she done when y'all was home and it was the right thing, I reckon. I come to see things different lately. Couldn't say why, exactly, but I reckon it's got something to do with y'all. I thought when y'all left home that first time y'all were done for—lost and corrupted like your dad said. When I tracked y'all down he told me, 'Wade, we got to bring them boys home.' You know why that was? He found out from the angel Tal what y'all really was. Princes. Lewis said he was right about what he said about y'all when y'all was boys, that y'all was God-touched and meant for Glory in His name.

"But when I seen you...y'all was just boys. The same boys I knew. Maybe not the same, though. Y'all was trying to live y'all's own lives. That's something I ain't never done. I reckon I was jealous at first and just wanted y'all to come back so I wouldn't have to be. But that was selfish of me."

"What d'you mean, Dad found out from Tal?" Lindsay asked.

"Well. Seems the angel come to your dad in a dream first. Then he come while Lewis was awake. I saw him, too. The angel said y'all boys was special and he needed our help." Wade's eyes dropped then, and Cary felt suddenly chilly despite the hot evening. When he looked at Lindsay beside him, he saw a haze of silvery magic. The chill was coming from himLindsay.

"Help doing what?" Lindsay asked.

"Well. That's what I'm a' getting to. When you told me about the girl and them others, Cary, I put it all together. Tal wanted us to grab a guy from him. Tall guy, black hair, hung around with a big dark nigger, bald with a scar on his head."

Cary's breath stalled in his chest. For the first time, a flash of some sharp emotion broke through his numbness. "Sandor."

Wade nodded. "Grabbed him from the parking lot of a movie thee-ater in Springfield. Me and your dad. The angel gave us this chain to use on the nigger. We just drugged the white guy. Took 'em both down to Busiek State Forest on 65."

"*Dad?*" Cary said. "Dad done that?" He still couldn't believe all this. It didn't make sense. Did it?

"Well, sure, son." Wade gave him an exasperated look. "You ain't no fool. You think I do anything by my own self these days without Lewis's say so? I mean, hell, this is the first time I done anything from my own mind in forty years."

"You take the girl, too?" Cary gripped his wheels to keep from showing how hard he was shaking. All of a sudden he felt feverish, though in his chest rather than in his head. Beside him, he felt the chill Lindsay's magic more keenly than ever. "What'd you do with her?"

Wade's eyes widened. "I don't know nothing about no girl. I just know what I'm told to do."

"You better be fucking sure about that, Wade." Never in his life had Cary heard such a growl come out of his own mouth, especially not toward a family member.

"I swear to God almighty, I don't know nothing." Wade looked scared— good. Cary wanted to hit him, hurt him for stringing them along this way, lying to them by omission. But when Cary pushed himself forward, Wade flinched, and Cary just couldn't do it.

"Wade." Lindsay's voice was so cold even Cary felt it. "Why'd you do this? We're your goddamn *family*. How the hell could you pull us around like this?"

"Y'all act like it was just me when you know it ain't. I just done what Lewis told me. He's my brother and I do what he says." Wade looked up at Lindsay. "You get down on your knees every night and thank God your brother is a good man, boy. You're in my place but for the grace of God." He stood. "I dunno what to say to y'all. We done you wrong for a long time. I done you wrong. But maybe y'all can make something out of it. Seems like y'all can. You just remember my mistakes, and your dad's, and make sure y'all don't make 'em." He handed Lindsay the duffel bag and looked down at Cary. "He ain't nobody you want to be like, Cary Judah. You just be your own self."

Cary backed out of the way as Wade got into the compact car and pulled out of the parking lot. His heart was racing too fast to control, and the fever in his chest was almost unbearable. Worst of all, his eyes stung like they were going to water. No. Not with Travis here.

"Care," Lindsay said. His voice shook, but Cary could offer him no comfort.

Dad, pulling their strings, leading them around, going behind their backs. He only came after them when Tal approached him. How could he do such a thing? And he'd been working with Tal all this time without telling them. Deceiving them. Both of them, deceiving. Everyone deceiving them. Nobody had told them a word of fucking truth.

Dad.

Thank God your brother is a good man, Wade had said. Cary knew what he meant. Growing up, everyone had always compared him to Dad and Lindsay to Wade. Nobody you want to be like.

Dad wasn't dying. He had faked it, faked all of it. *I ain't got much time left on this earth. Make me proud.*

"Care." Lindsay grasped his shoulder. Cary reached up to swat his hand away, but he couldn't make himself do it. Lindsay's magic cooled the burning in his chest, leaving him numb again. He was glad for that.

"Let's get y'all home," Travis said.

* * *

Cary went straight toward the stable when they got home. Lindsay started to go after him, but thought the better of it. When Cary was like this, there was no reaching him.

Travis stepped up beside Lindsay and touched his lower back. "That's rough." Lindsay recognized it as Travis's gruff way of saying, *I'm sorry.*

"Yeah. And we still ain't found Bella yet." Lindsay sighed and looked at the duffel bag in his hand. "Let's go inside."

"You wanna talk about it?" Travis asked when Lindsay sat at the kitchen table.

"You musta thought that was crazy, huh?" Lindsay shook his head. He was regretting letting Travis come along, remembering the way Wade was talking. It still seemed almost normal to Lindsay, but he knew it wasn't.

"Ain't crazier than magic." Travis sat beside him. "If you're worried I'm gonna look down on you for your family, don't."

Hearing his worries spoken aloud like that in Travis's plain language made Lindsay choke up. "He didn't have no right to do none of that, Trav. Especially not to Care. Care looked up to him so much." He hated the idea of Cary out in the stable, in pain but not letting anyone see it, and because of that bastard.

"No, he didn't have no right. But he did it to you too, y'know." Travis put a hand on the back of Lindsay's neck. "I'd beat him myself if I could."

That broke down every ounce of will Lindsay had left to keep himself together. He put his head in his hands and cried great big ugly sobs of anger and sadness for Cary, and for Wade. He didn't want to think too much about himself for fear that he might never stop crying, so he stuffed that down as deep as he could. Travis pulled Lindsay's head against his shoulder and held him.

"You don't need them," Travis murmured in his ear. "I love you."

That made Lindsay cry harder, but these were good, cleansing tears.

* * *

Cary hadn't yet reached the fence when Cooter appeared, surprising him; he and Sister rarely actually stayed in the stable anymore, and Cary couldn't remember calling him.

"Saw Wade. He told us what happened to Sandor." It was hard to swallow. "Tal has him."

Cooter looked surprised. "How does he know this? You know he is not lying?"

"Why would he lie about kidnapping a guy he ain't even supposed to know about?" Irritation jangled through his nerves. Cooter gave him a hard nudge, rolling him forward a few inches, and that brought him back out of his temper.

"Still don't know where Bella is."

"With Sandor."

"You sound sure. You a recorsa now?"

Cooter disregarded the question as he always did one he didn't think was worth answering. Cary rolled his eyes.

"What would he want with both of 'em, anyway? I thought one was enough."

Cooter pushed him again, this time almost making him collide with the barn door jamb, as if to say, don't be stupid.

"Uppity damn horse," Cary muttered, but he got the point. "Fine. So we got to look for both of 'em at Tal's place." He paused. "Why would Tal keep 'em from us, if we're so important?"

"I don't know."

"Fucking liar." The words burst out of Cary's chest. "They're all fucking liars. Ain't nobody told us what they want, just what they think we ought to do. And we're supposed to follow like little fucking kids. I'm tired of it, Coo. I'm tired of everybody knowing what's best for us except us. I'm goddamn tired of everybody lying." Pain radiated from his chest to his arms, down his spine; it seemed to flow in his blood. Finally, it all settled in the place he'd been shot. "He *shot* me." He heard the words as if they had come from someone else's mouth. "You know that? *Dad* did. I don't know *why*."

He rocked forward with his elbows on his knees. He didn't realize he was crying until tears wet the knees of his jeans.

Cooter's soft muzzle pressed against his spine at the place the bullet had shattered the T11 and half the T10 vertebrae. In that moment, Cary knew the horse understood everything, without needing words: Dad, his paralysis, Wade, Aunt Betty, Bella, Jessie, the way almost everyone had betrayed or left them. He felt pitifully grateful.

Chapter Twenty

They drove out to the boonies to blow up the Explorer. Someone might still notice the explosion, but this far out and away from Travis's property, it wasn't likely anyone would connect them to it, especially with the license plates removed. Wade had stuffed cans of tannerite in the duffel bag. Tannerite was perfectly legal, used sometimes for gun targets, but ten pounds was enough to blow up a vehicle. They left the Explorer's engine running to make sure it blew. Lindsay looked a little sad when they aimed the handguns Wade had also included in the bag along with the money.

"Don't worry, Lin. We'll buy you a big fancy truck like Trav has. Not like we ain't got the money," Cary told him. "Or ain't that queer enough for you?"

"You are so rude," Lindsay said, though Cary could tell he wasn't really ruffled. "We can get you hand controls too. Though I ain't sure I want you driving again."

They emptied their magazines into the car. The bullets sparked the tannerite, and the ground underneath them shook as the Explorer went up in a cloud of smoke. Lindsay cast one more mournful look at the hollowed-out shell of the vehicle that remained as the horses crossed onto the aether.

They rode toward Tal's place to look for Bella and Sandor, and a certain fierce excitement rushed through Cary's blood. It wasn't happiness, but he could feel his heart beating faster and his lips pulled back into a grin by themselves. Cooter felt it too, judging by the tense way he moved, ready to spring forward at any moment. Lindsay reminded Cary of what had happened during their last confrontation with Tal, how they'd barely gotten out in one piece. Cary knew he was right and so he played along, but a big part of him wanted to let the stallion charge through so he could beat the shit out of Tal.

Tal had taught them how to step out of one part of the aether and onto another like a shortcut. But they couldn't just walk into the place without scoping it out first. Going the long way was a lot harder; Tal had only ever told them about doing so in theory. But Cary was bound and determined to do it.

Places like Tal's, pockets on the aether, were always built over power nodes to give them a constant supply of energy. Going around them meant traveling between branches, which meant being suspended in pure aether for a time, like a squirrel diving from one branch to another. Only they would have to stay away from the branches for as long as possible. They were like walking neon signs anyway, and being on a branch only made it worse.

They could find Tal's place easily enough now, but it was a lot harder to come a roundabout way and zero in on it. It was like finding something in a house of mirrors filled with fog: there were a million copies, and the real thing was somewhere in the middle. They might accidentally bump into it if they weren't careful. To top it off, the pure aether was unstable, like it was stuck in a constant earthquake, and even sure-footed Cooter was hard-pressed to keep Cary upright. Even though time didn't exist here in the same way, every second weighed on Cary heavier and heavier.

"Care." Lindsay's voice, way too calm, cut through Cary's thoughts. "Remember how we followed Tal into that cabin?" He held his hand out. "Let's try it."

Cary reached for him, but the ground lurched and all he could do was hold the reins with one hand and grip Cooter's mane with the other.

"You don't need your hands to reach," Cooter said as if it was obvious. As annoying as his tone was, Cary decided he had to try it. He pictured reaching out the Lindsay with a magical hand. The power in him responded immediately, seeking the silver-green magic that was its opposite and compliment. Lindsay made a noise of surprise. The world went black before magic flared again in all Cary's senses. He grabbed hold of his own magic and held it hard, remembering too clearly when it had almost slipped away.

He remembered how they had followed Tal and Emese through the mist that had blinded the horses. He used Lindsay's calm to center himself the way he would before shooting a rifle and focused on what he needed to see. For a moment nothing happened, but then he felt a subtle vibration. A second later, the mist and the confusing mess of images eased up a little. Tal's place, the real one, became visible in the distance. Cary let out a breath of relief.

"Can we get closer?" Lindsay asked.

"A little," Sister said. She and Cooter moved over the unsteady ground. All Cary could do was hold on. It reminded him of the first time he'd tried to find the place on his own. "Shoulda thought y'all up to be birds."

As they moved closer, Cary could make out enough to see Emese wasn't in her paddock. He made a sound of satisfaction and nodded at Lin. "Let's go."

Re-entering the branch was a lot like stepping onto solid ground after swimming for a while: Cary's body felt heavy and Cooter's footsteps were sluggish at first. They found themselves on the silent cobblestoned avenue leading up to the manor.

The servants seemed to hesitate before they came over. Cary wondered what Tal had told them. He opened his mouth to speak, but Lindsay caught his eye and he closed it.

"We know Tal ain't here, but we'd like to wait for him. However long it takes. We really need to talk to him. Is that okay?"

Cary recognized Lindsay's tone as the one that used to make Aunt Betty give them what they wanted when Cary's charm didn't work. Cary wondered if Lindsay had any idea how powerful that tone together with his earnest look was. The servants looked hesitant, but Lindsay added, "Please, y'all. We gotta apologize to him. It's really important."

Tal's messenger—Cary still didn't know her name—nodded. When they dismounted, she led him to the library and left them alone. She didn't seem too concerned with hospitality, but that was okay with Cary.

"Well," he said, "Let's do this."

The house was quiet. Cary tried to ignore the noises his chair made, which sounded louder than they ever had. The manor was a confusing maze of hallways and rooms. If it had been in the real world it would probably be as big as OTC's campus at least. They spent what felt like hours listening at doors, opening them, trying to find any sign at all. Of anything. Cary wished the recorsas' magic was as obvious as their own, but they had almost no magical imprint.

Then there was the second floor. Cary sat at the foot of one of the back staircases, ready to create an elevator. Lindsay stopped him.

"Don't."

Annoyed, Cary swatted his hand away. "Why not?"

"Just don't." Lindsay wore a worried frown. "I got a bad feeling."

Even as Lindsay spoke, shadows crawled at the edges of Cary's vision. His heart beat faster and he glanced around, wishing the thing that told him of danger didn't half-blind him, too.

"Listen," he told Lindsay, "Cover me while I make an elevator."

"Care—"

Cary was about to tell him to just *do* it when something solid penetrated the shadows just below Cary's eye level. Lindsay's gun appeared beside his right ear. The crack of the gunshot echoed in the hall and startled Cary despite many years of shooting next to his brother. A hyena hound jerked back from Cary and fell to the marble floor.

"One," Lindsay whispered, counting the round he'd used. Cary freed his own gun from the chair holster and looked up and down the hallway.

"What the fuck," he said, "is an Underworld critter doing in here?"

No time to think about it. The shadows shifted again and Cary turned, completely on instinct. The first shot was messy, only hitting the thing in the shoulder. The second, better aimed, hit it square in the chest and it slumped to the floor beside the other in a pool of slimy gray-brown magic.

"One two," he said.muttered. Lindsay holstered his gun and grabbed Cary's handlebars, turning down the hall.

Cary couldn't hear anything, but he could see a haze of more of that Underworld corruption up ahead, oozing around a corner. He gritted his teeth and prepared to shoot, gesturing at Lindsay to slow down. No sense running full-tilt through the halls if they weren't being chased. They needed to figure out how to get out of here.

Cary gestured again: *Stop. Go look.* Lindsay crept forward and pulled his gun, stealthy and graceful for a guy his size. Cary lifted his gun, watching the ooze of gray-brown magic to make sure it didn't get any closer. He wouldn't shoot unless he had to with Lindsay in front of him. Dad had taught them that lesson well.

Lindsay flattened himself against the wall and peeked around the corner, using a little compact mirror he created, dulled with soap to cut down on the shine.

Lindsay looked back at Cary, puzzled; Cary couldn't tell what that was supposed to mean. He pushed himself forward and as close to the wall as he could get.

They'd learned to read each other's lips when they were kids, first to entertain themselves during sermons and later to communicate on hunting trips. Lindsay mouthed, *Servants.*

Another way out? Cary asked, trusting Lindsay's unfailing mental compass. Lindsay frowned and shook his head.

Well, they couldn't just sit here. Cary nodded to Lindsay's gun: *put it away.* In a combination of mouthed words and gestures, he told Lindsay what they were going to do.

* * *

Lindsay sometimes hated Cary for his crazy ideas. They turned into disasters as often as they succeeded. Right now, though, he was glad for Cary's quick mind and willing to play along, even if he wasn't sure he could pull it off.

Do what you done before, Cary had told him, *Make 'em think you're harmless.*

Hell, Lindsay hadn't even known that was what he'd been doing.

Cary remained in place near the wall. Lindsay backtracked halfway down the hall, as silent as he could be, before he forced himself to walk normally around the corner so they could hear him coming. He could feel Cary's magic as he drew near, brimming near the surface, but Lindsay willed him to keep it back a little longer. That wouldn't work if the idea was to be harmless.

When he rounded the corner, his heart pounding, there wasn't a servant in sight. There had been three before.

Then his stomach plummeted almost at the same time he saw a faint shadow on the floor at his feet. He couldn't even cry out. He just reached for his sword, *knowing* it would be there. He swung up in a tight arc, guarding his head and neck, and felt the weight of the creature fall first on the blade, pushing it down toward his face then buckling his arm.

He recognized the multi-legged monkey thing when it touched him, its magic insane and chaotic like a possum in a sack. Cary's gunshot startled the hell out of him and only then did he cry out. Unlike the ones in the wild parts of the aether, this one didn't keep coming at him. It flopped off of Lindsay to the floor. Blood streaked Lindsay's sword, but there was none on the floor, and the creature scuttled away as if unharmed.

Lindsay moved toward Cary, sheltering them both with his body and his blade as he scanned the rafters for more of the creatures. Cary exchanged his gun for his own sword, better for a moving target. They exchanged looks, and Lindsay remembered the servants that had followed them the last time they were here turned out to be Underworld creatures. Were they all that way?

"Lin," Cary breathed. "The thing's leaking magic. *Tal's* magic."

Lindsay looked down. The creature hadn't shed blood, but it *had* shed magic, an oozing mix of gray-brown and Tal's diamond-bright rainbow magic.

Lindsay forgot for a second to be afraid of the immediate danger of the creatures. "Fuck," he whispered. He remembered the servants who had followed them last time and the corruption winding in with Tal's magic. He hadn't wanted to believe what he'd seen earlier.

This time he had no warning before the second one attacked. He heard Cary's cry even as it sank its claws into Lindsay's skin. It was like being grabbed with fish hooks that had been in someone's deep freezer. It seized his muscles; he couldn't fight it off if he tried. The creature's wide mouth, filled with spikes instead of with teeth, opened as if in a yawn.

Then Cary's sword flashed. The creature jerked and all of a sudden the fish hooks felt like they were made of molten metal. It creature gave one of those squirrel-like chatters and evaporated, leaving behind slimy smoke and another glitter of rainbow magic.

Lindsay swayed on his feet. The wounds in his back and shoulders burned fiercely. Cary grabbed his hand and squeezed it until the bones ground together.

"Lindsay Jedidiah Delaney. We gotta get moving. You stay on your feet. Grab my chair again."

Lindsay sheathed his sword and did as told, grateful for the order. He could push through just about anything if he had direction. He leaned a little on the chair as he pushed, his neck and shoulders hunched to shelter them from another possible attack. His head swam, but the pain kept him grounded in his body. Keep moving. *Keep moving.*

More shadows passed across the floor now and again, and every time they both tensed, but no other creatures attacked. Yet. Keep moving.

"Where the fuck *are* they?" Cary said. Lindsay might wonder the same thing if he weren't occupied just moving. "Lin. You okay? Still with me?"

"Uh huh."

"Let's get outta this place before them things come back."

Get out. Right. Lindsay tried to focus his inner compass and find the seldom-used side entrance where they'd agreed to meet the horses. To the left, or straight? Or back the way they came?

He shook himself. It was *never* this hard.

"Lin." Cary's voice was firm. "Focus."

Lindsay tried to push past the increasingly chaotic clutter of thoughts and second guesses to reach his center, but the more he tried, the harder it was. Finally, he simply let go of all of it, surrendered to the confusion. For a second he was sure he'd pass out, but then Cary's warm magic reached out, supporting and steadying him. His sense of equilibrium mostly returned and so did his sense of direction.

And then they were attacked again.

As kids, they used to find little silver-blue lizards on rocks every once in a while. This thing looked a little like that, thin and whip like, moving like a snake with legs, only it was the size of a German Shepherd, not even counting the barbed tail. Its pale not-color almost blended into the marble. It opened its mouth, black as coal, and spat.

Lindsay threw himself against Cary, tackling him to the ground. His magic touched Cary and instantly their joint imprints rushed through their bodies and grounded into the floor, guided by Cary's quick hand. Lindsay felt a domed web of protective magic, a small version of the one over Travis's property, lift over them. A nanosecond split-second later he felt the impact of the creature's spit like a wad of phlegm. It burst into a mass of what looked like maggots in a frying pan, crawling and wriggling and popping over the surface of the dome. Lindsay felt them as if they crawled over his skin, but the sensation was blunted by the cushion of magic.

The lizard thing hissed, showing its black mouth again, and stared at them. It didn't attack again, nor did it run. Its barbed tail swayed side to side and it just stood there as if to say, *Fine, I'll wait.*

Cary spat back in the lizard's direction. He was clearly strained, the cloud of their combined magic testing the limits of his ability to keep hold of it without letting it slip away. Lindsay reached out to relieve him. The magic, warm and cold wound together, created a dense, wild energy that made his arm buzz.

"No, Lin," Cary said immediately. "You're hurt." Before Lindsay had a chance to protest, he said, "Wait. You seen what our magic just did to them maggot things. What if it'd do the same thing to that one?"

Lindsay tried to grasp his meaning, but his head swam worse than ever when he pulled his hand away from the cloud of magic. He just shrugged."Dunno."

"Get me back in the chair. Let's move."

Lindsay obeyed, though pulling Cary back into the righted chair without Cary being able to help made every muscle strain to the point of weakness. The wounds in his back and shoulders throbbed to the bone. When he stood, the world tilted so badly he was sure, in a disconnected way, that he was about to pass out. He grabbed the chair's handles and forced himself out of sheer willpower to stay upright.

"Lin?" Cary lifted his head and his eyes widened at whatever he saw in Lindsay's face. "Jesus."

"'M fine." Lindsay didn't have any choice but to be fine. He pushed the chair, focusing on the pain in his back to keep him grounded. Through the glimmering web of the dome, which moved along with them, he could see the lizard thing lift its head, trying maybe to make itself appear bigger, its black mouth on display. When the dome got too close, though, it turned and fled around the corner.

Lindsay wished he could feel relieved, but he didn't let himself feel anything but the burn of his wounds and the instinctive nudge that told him which direction to go. Cary's shoulders were tense and sweat trickled down the back of his neck at the effort of channeling their magic, but Lindsay had to force himself not to worry about that, either. This was like one of Dad's almost impossible missions, designed to test their mental and physical strength. They had always succeeded no matter what, if only in defiance of Dad's insistence that they couldn't. They would do this, too.

Lindsay wandered down the hall, surrendering to the chaos in his mind again. Gradually he centered himself. His sense of direction floated up to him and he followed it to the door.

And then, around the next corner, it was there. Lindsay almost cried in relief.

He pushed Cary to the door, opened it. The west side of the property, with its fancy gardens, backed up against a strip of dense forest. Lindsay had never been afraid of the woods, but this....

Darkness gathered between one breath and the next, like on an Ozarks summer night. Lindsay paused, summoning the will to call the horses without attracting attention, but nothing happened.

At first he thought the rushing sound was leaves in the wind; then, deeper shadows materialized in the trees, gathering like a storm cloud.

"What the hell," Cary breathed. "Get us outta here."

Lindsay shook his head, watching Cary struggle to maintain control over their magic. "Let me help you."

"No, Lin. I'm fine. You ain't."

Lindsay didn't have a chance to answer. The writhing shadows swooped from the trees and Lindsay realized the sound he heard was wings, a million little jagged wings.

Lindsay ducked, using his body to protect Cary's. Again he felt the impact of all those things on their shield, but instead of individual bodies, it felt like being hit with a solid mass. Sparks of silver-green and gold crackled across the surface of the dome and it began to compress.

Lindsay could feel the cloud of raw magic between Cary's hands, weakening rapidly under the onslaught, slipping away. He could feel the toll it was taking on Cary himself. Cary cried out, that same agonized cry he'd made when Lindsay had turned him after the accident. Lindsay reached to gather that cloud in his hands and it jarred through his body like electricity, freezing everything in him. For an agonizing moment, he watched the cloud weaken even more.

Then, suddenly, his stomach plummeted again. The cloud flared to life, fed by that electricity in him. The dome expanded again, pushing back against the press of those black bodies. Cary stopped shaking and choking, and that was all that really mattered to Lindsay anyway.

Just as suddenly, the mass of bodies disappeared, just like the lizard.

"Lindsay Jedidiah!" Cary's voice was high-pitched when he stared up at Lindsay. By his expression he was furious, but his voice gave him away.

"I'm okay, brother," Lindsay assured him. And he was. He felt...*better*. No pain, no weakness. The light-headedness felt more like being drunk than being sick.

"Jesus fucking Christ." Cary shook his head, looking around for more creatures. "Why the hell do they keep coming at us and then going away?"

"They ain't trying to kill us," Lindsay realized. "They want us alive." Fear coiled in his belly at the thought, but the strange calm that came along with channeling magic wouldn't let it stay.

"Great," Cary muttered. "Where the hell are the horses?"

They appeared a moment later, galloping through the gardens. For a second, Lindsay wasn't sure they would stop in time and he reached for Cary's chair to yank him back, but both stopped on a dime. Their long ears were pinned back, and magic swirled around them like a wind storm. While Cary mounted, Sister put herself between them and the rest of the garden.

"Sis?" Lin asked. She didn't look at him, just stared toward the front of the house.

"He is home."

Chapter Twenty-One

Cary couldn't get into the saddle fast enough. Tal had told him they would have to figure out a better way for him to mount, and Cary cursed because the bastard had been right.

Lindsay came over to handle his legs. Cary waved him off once his feet were in the stirrups and secured his thighs while Lindsay mounted. No time to worry about armor. Cooter wasn't quite off the ground yet before Tal appeared astride Emese.

Even now, Cary had to admit they looked impressive. Emese made Cooter look like a gangly half-grown colt, and Sister looked raggedy. Both rider and horse glittered in a storm of colors. Tal was fully armored, his eyes narrow beneath his helmet.

"I hadn't expected to see you here, princes. My servants have told me you are causing trouble."

"Funny enough, that's what we was raised to do," Cary said. "You're keeping the recorsas. Where, in a kennel?"

Tal sighed. "I truly wish you hadn't pushed me to this, princes."

A swarm of servants came around the house behind Tal, and every one of them glowed with that prism rainbow. Then, simultaneously, the colors blended and muddied into that telltale gray-brown. The servants' human forms began to melt into all-too-familiar shapes: hyena-hounds, monkey things, lizards.

Even before Cary could think, Cooter was running.

All Cary could do was bend over the stallion's neck, holding onto his mane and the reins and hoping he could stay balanced in the saddle. He couldn't see for shit, either, and he couldn't tell whether it was prescient shadows or real darkness that shrouded his vision. All he could do was listen to was his own panting, Cooter's body crashing through the brush, and Lindsay and Sister behind them. Fainter, he could hear another horse: Emese.

Real, uncontrollable panic set in. He sure as hell didn't want to run, but if they faced off with Tal again, they'd surely lose their magic.

So where the hell else could they go? What about Bella? Cary knew his panic was affecting Cooter, could feel it in the stallion's jerky movements, but he couldn't stop it. Tal was going to catch them, or they would get lost and—

A glimmer of color surfaced out of the gloom, ahead and to the left. Cary nearly jerked Cooter's head to turn him away from it, but there was something so deeply familiar about it. It wasn't Tal's sharp diamond-bright magic; it was softer than that, like a rainbow pearl.

Then the snow-white buck sprang into view, a cloud of magic streaming from his antlers. Cary barely recognized the cry that came from his own lips. Behind him, Lindsay gasped.

The buck flicked his ear at them as if beckoning, then sprang away.

Cary hesitated. Follow it? Follow someone else—some*thing* else—to God knew where? Or strike out on their own and hope Tal didn't trap them?

"Don't be stupid," Cooter told him.

Cary gave him his head, and the horses followed.

The creature's movements were so familiar, a deer running from a predator, but there was no hurry in his gait. He glided along as if he fully expected to be followed, though he never once paused or looked back. Cary had the sense he was taking them in a wide circle. He was never more thankful for Cooter's sure-footedness.

There was no telling how far or for how long they ran. Cary forgot everything but watching the buck and its halo of magic, so different from Tal's even if it was the same colors. Gradually, Cary could see a little better. The forest had thinned to a cart track, and a cluster of buildings lay ahead. Cary recognized it as the deserted little town outside Tal's manor.

It took him a few minutes to realize he couldn't hear Tal behind them anymore. "Lin." He didn't dare throw off his balance and chance a look behind them.

"Don't see 'em no more," Lindsay said.

Colors began to manifest, though they stayed dull. The whole scene looked like twilight again except in the immediate area around the buck, which shone bright as a spring day. The buck and the horses slowed, their movements cautious.

Lindsay and Sister came up alongside Cary and Cooter. Lindsay's eyes were the only thing about him or Sister with any color.

"You okay?" Cary asked. "Lean forward and let me see your back."

"I'm okay. Don't hurt," Lindsay said. "I think touching our magic healed me."

"You were hurt by Tal's creature?" Sister asked.

"Yeah."

"They are corrupted. The magic removed the corruption. It was not true healing. The wounds are still there."

"But Sandor said táltosk can heal," Cary said.

"You can," Cooter said. "But not here. This place is too corrupted."

The more Cary paid attention, the more he realized Cooter was right. The gray-brown slime seemed to cover everything in a thick film, and the horses and the buck stepped gingerly. Cary didn't think he could summon that blue cleansing magic here even if he knew how.

"What is this place?"

"The edge of the Underworld," Cooter replied.

Cary thought this place didn't look much like any Underworld he could imagine. The Bible's description of fire and brimstone didn't seem to fit.

"Is this Hell?" Lindsay asked.

"Underworld is not all like this," Sister said. "This is a rotted place."

Lindsay shivered and looked at Cary, his eyebrows furrowed. Cary understood. The place really *did* seem rotted, as if its fundamental structure was somehow weakened. It reminded him of a documentary he had seen about some abandoned town in Appalachia that was falling into a coal mine that had been burning for forty some-odd years: the fire wasn't visible on the surface, but hidden away somewhere, waiting to swallow the place. He decided that was worse than Hell.

This was what Tal had been trying to hide from them, Cary was sure. He didn't want them to see that the tree really was rotting.

The corruption weighed on Cary's body, too; the longer they rode, the weaker he felt, as if his entire body was as much a burden as his legs. His thoughts slowed to a crawl, and even the buck seemed to move too fast for his eyes to keep up. He remembered that they were supposed to be looking for Bella and wondered why they had stopped, or if that was where they were going now.

They moved farther into the town, following the white buck. They saw no one and nothing moving except for each other. More than once the sound of Lindsay shifting in the saddle startled Cary. At least the shadows had stopped clouding his vision, but then, this whole place seemed to be thick with shadow. He figured it was only a matter of time before Tal caught up, along with his army of creatures.

The slime fell away all at once, like a line of litter and weeds along the shore of a lake. Cary could see the line clearly and his heart leapt at the idea of being out from underneath the oppressive weight of all this corruption. But the buck slowed. He moved forward one tentative step at a time, ears and tail lifted and quivering like he knew something was there. Cary's heart sank again. It wasn't hard to guess what the buck might be worried about.

He turned to Lindsay. His brother's face shone with sweat, drawn and thin as if from a long sickness, his cheeks hollow. His eyes were bright and glassy with fever and he seemed to be having a hard time keeping them open. The slime had coated him and oozed from the wounds in his back.

"Jesus!" Cary urged Cooter closer and grabbed Lindsay's wrist. It was a miracle he was still upright, as weak as his pulse was. "Lindsay Jedidiah. Look at me!" Cary's own pulse pounded in his ears. He did the only thing he thought would help: he reached for Lindsay's magic with his own to tie them together again. "Lin, call your magic. You gotta help me. Lindsay!"

Lindsay startled a little and his eyes rolled back in his head, but Cary saw that silver-green halo form around him again, weak and wispy. Cary grabbed for it without hesitating, gathered it into his hands along with his own, then pushed it into Lindsay.

Lindsay's slumping shoulders jerked upright and he cried out, head thrown back. The slime covering him disintegrated into mist and the wounds steamed as the combined magic sank in.

Cooter lurched under Cary and he lost his concentration. His magic rebounded back into him, making his head swim.

"Why did you do that?" Cooter demanded.

"I had to help him, that's why," Cary said, annoyed. "Go to hell if you—"

But half a second later, Cary realized why Cooter was pissed. Underworld creatures, hounds and monkeys and lizards and that big black mass of flying things, crawled the streets from every angle, as if they'd been waiting in ambush.

And the white buck was gone.

Cary spat a curse and reached for his sword, anger surging through him. That was enough, fucking *enough*. He didn't care that he wasn't wearing armor and his limbs felt like they weighed a million pounds and they were ridiculously outnumbered. He was *pissed*.

The horses lunged forward at the same time. Cary could see the halo of

Lindsay's magic shining bright as ever and it reached for his; where it intertwined again, it sparked like a wild summer storm. They waded into the press of creatures, and the mob fell back, maybe intimidated or just surprised. Either way, it got them close to the edge of this corruption, and Cary fought even harder. Cooter's head lunged left and right, too, lashing out with his teeth.

They were almost to the edge of the corruption when Cary spotted the glitter of Tal's magic. He couldn't even feel fear, just annoyance that Tal wouldn't even come in and fight them himself.

"Cary," Lindsay said.

"Run." Cary grabbed a handful of Cooter's mane along with the reins, bent over his neck, and they shot forward again.

Tal seemed too surprised to chase after, as if he'd expected them to confront him or to come crawling back. Cary grinned at having tricked him. But that only lasted a minute.

He could hear again now: Cooter's snorting, the creak of the saddle, the cadence of hoof beats echoing on the cobblestones. But above all that was a sound that pierced his brain, like microphone feedback. It made him grit his teeth, and it only got stronger the longer they ran. Cary tugged Cooter's mane, trying to get him to turn away from it, but the horse seemed completely untroubled by it. The noise scrambled his thoughts as badly as the corruption had, and he could do nothing but hang on.

The buck darted out from between two buildings. Cary couldn't feel relief or annoyance that it had left or anything at all. He just locked his eyes on it, and Cooter followed.

The streets got steeper now, and Cary was forced to sit up in the saddle to maintain his balance. He could see the forest below them. His stomach churned when he realized there was no horizon. The forest just seemed to keep tumbling endlessly down. Panic began to rise again when the mental image of that town in the Appalachians surfaced, the whole town crumbling into the fiery pit of that coal mine. Was the buck leading them into Hell itself?

"Cary," Lindsay rasped behind him. "Tal!"

"Shit." Cary could hear the clank of Tal's armor now. He couldn't *see* him still and that made it worse, picturing him with his sword upraised toward the back of their necks. The high-pitched squealing threatened to cut apart his brain and Tal was gaining and—

"*Stop thinking*," Cooter's voice seemed to slap him across the face. "Be somewhere else!"

Cary stared at the back of the stallion's head. He closed his eyes, understanding, and tried to picture the forest back home, the one he knew so well. They could lose Tal in it, he knew it...but he couldn't *remember* it. The corruption grabbed at him still, weighing down his memories, and he couldn't picture it, couldn't feel it. His mind was blank.

Fine. Blank. Cary knew that. "Lin," he gasped out. "Let me do this. Trust me."

"I trust you," Lindsay told him.

Cary forced himself into that state he'd gotten so good at in the hospital, picturing nothing, thinking about nothing, *away* from everything, even quieter than sleep. Even after so long, even now, it wasn't hard to do. He opened his eyes and expected nothing.

The forest was unlike anything Cary had ever seen, damp and overgrown with giant ferns and fungi and vines, though there seemed to be no foliage on the trees themselves. They stretched up into impenetrable blackness, as if they were in a cave with an invisible ceiling. Cary was sure he was missing something significant about the place, but his head hurt too much to figure out what. The white buck wove between the trees and the horses followed.

No sign of Tal, for now.

Sometimes they lost sight of the buck altogether, but then it would appear in plain sight. The smell of dead foliage and earth and the presence of the buck made that nameless fear and violent nausea grip him. Judging by Lindsay's labored breathing, he wasn't feeling much better. Cary just stared at the scene in front of him as hard as he could, reminding himself that this was *not* that November day, and this was *not* the forest near home.

It worked, a little. The nausea eased, though the headache didn't; the ringing in his ears was louder than ever. He barely heard Lindsay's sob over it.

"Care. I cain't feel my fingers."

Cary's head whipped around and a sudden bolt of fear replaced everything else. Lindsay's face was a sickening gray, his lips dry and cracked. His hair was dark and plastered to his forehead with sweat. His right arm, his sword arm, flopped at his side.

"Lin! Christ. You hurt again?"

"No..." Lindsay's eyes tried to focus on him. "Just...don't feel good."

Cary let out a hissing breath. "We got to stop," he told the horses. They didn't react. "*Cooter*! Stop!"

"Do you want to be caught?" Cooter said. "*I* don't."

"By God, if you—"

"Care." Lindsay shook his head. "No. He's right. Let's...keep going."

Stubborn bastard. "Fine. Sister, come around this other side." Cary reached over to pry Lindsay's saber from his stiff fingers and put the hand on Sister's neck. "You hold on with both hands as hard as you can, brother. You just hold on." He sucked in a painful breath and created another sheath on his own saddle to hold Lindsay's saber. "Keep an eye on that buck. You're gonna be the one to git him this time, right?"

"Head hurts," he mumbled.

Cary snorted. "I know, brother. Hurts like a motherfucker, don't it?"

Cary kept talking. He barely knew what he said and didn't care either. It was like when they were kids and Dad sent them out on survival missions. The dark and cold would get to them and Cary and Lindsay, only seven or eight at the time, would get scared. That was after Andy died, so there was no one to protect them. Cary always tried not to show how scared he was, but Lindsay, despite being a year older, would always the first one to admit it. He said it in such a small voice, so full of reluctance and shame, Cary found it impossible to make fun of him. So he talked—about nothing, everything. Just to fill the silence. He never knew if it made either of them feel much better, but once he started, he couldn't stop.

It took him a moment to notice Tal's messenger, standing on a slight rise to their left. Cary hissed and drew his sword. The buck disappeared again.

"Peace, princes," the girl said, lifting her hands. "There is nothing for you down there. You may think it is a way out, but you walk blind into danger that will haunt you. My master bids you come back up. He will welcome you—"

"It's his fucking fault we're going blind, ain't it?" Cary growled. "And he'd keep us that way. I'd sooner take my chances with honest danger than a fucking liar."

The girl's colorless eyes narrowed ever so slightly. "There is no such thing as honesty, prince. Only perception. What do you wish me to tell my master?"

"Tell him to go to hell," Lindsay croaked. Cary looked at his brother. He looked sick as a dog, ready to pass out, but his expression was as full of that cold venom as ever. For once, Cary admired it.

The girl faded into the trees without another word, and the horses started forward again. A moment later the buck sprang into view. Cary gathered he didn't want Tal to see him and wondered why. They rode on in silence.

The buck was maybe twenty yards ahead, still visible in the gloom, when he stopped. For the first time, he looked back at them. His eyes were apple green, the color of the Tree's magic. Delaney green.

"What?" Cary asked, exhausted. And then, as they drew nearer, he saw.

The buck stood at the edge of a precipice, like the bluffs along the Buffalo River, only this one was so high he couldn't see the bottom right away. He couldn't see if there was another bluff beyond, either, through the heavy white mist. Cary's body froze and his stomach turned somersaults. He yanked Cooter's reins, urging him away from the edge.

"What the fuck," Cary whispered. "Jesus, what the *fuck*."

The buck just looked at them for a minute. Then, without warning, it turned and jumped. Cary strained his ears for sounds of hitting bottom, or landing on the other side. He heard nothing.

"Cooter. What is this, some fucking leap of faith?" Cary demanded. "I ain't no crippled Indiana Jones. I ain't going for no grail."

But Cooter was nervous, too; his body was tense, ears folded, and he kept looking back at Cary. Cary cursed and looked at Lindsay, swaying in his saddle now. He wouldn't make a jump, assuming there was even somewhere to jump *to*. Hell, it was a toss-up whether Cary could make it.

"I don't think you can do it."

Cary went rigid and glared at Cooter. "*What?*"

"I don't think you can—"

"Go to hell," Cary spat. He stared directly ahead, willing himself to see another bluff across the depthless chasm. There *had* to be another side—there had to be.

Then he caught the briefest glimpse of something solid, past the mist. Something that might have been rock. He looked at Lindsay, struggling to stay upright in the saddle. Cary had to get him across and then worry about himself. If Cary went first, he couldn't protect Lindsay.

"Lin, you go first," Cary told him. "You can do it. I'll be right behind you."

Lindsay shook his head. "You go. I—"

"Lindsay, hang onto that mare's mane and get ready to jump," Cary growled. He looked down at Sister. "Take him."

For a second he didn't know if Sister would take an order from him. Then she turned to get a running start. She moved so fast, Cary didn't have a chance to say anything more to Lindsay. All he saw was a white blur before they disappeared into the mist.

"Let's do this," Cary muttered, gripping the reins. "Fucking Indiana Jones."

Cooter, showoff that he was, didn't bother with a running start. All of a sudden Cary's stomach lurched, and then he was off the ground.

* * *

They didn't hit ground for what seemed like a long, long time. Cary felt himself and Cooter suspended, held up by some incredible force that was beyond reckoning. His body still knew it was in the air and his limbs felt weightless, his stomach flip-flopping. He didn't have time to concentrate on the sensations, though, before more flooded him.

The magic rushed into him, burning in his veins and making his body buzz. It was pure energy, pure *life*. A rainbow mist floated around him, each spot of color like a tiny gemstone sparkling in sunlight.

Along with the magic came new awareness. He grasped some magnificent, almost incomprehensible whole. An image floated up in his mind: a web of magic, a spinal cord with the endless lengths of nerves, a tree. The World Tree. He could see every branch, every node, stretching away from him: the roots, reaching down past Underworld; the crown, stretching toward infinity; everything in the middle, every world; and between it all, the aether, the blank slate, the air the Tree fed on.

He didn't know how long he hung there, trying to grasp what he was seeing. This was what they were meant to protect: *everything*. He felt a surge of some nameless emotion, somewhere between joy and terror. Then he became aware of something else, some other incomprehensible presence, too bright to look at. It swooped close, and Cary welcomed it, accepted it. The first touch felt like feathers on his back, firm but soft. He tried to turn and see what it was.

For his efforts, he was rewarded by a blow like he'd never experienced before. This one was more like steel than feathers. It buffeted his entire body at once, jarring him out of his reverie and back into the world.

* * *

A blast of frigid air, colder than Lindsay's magic, felt like it would knock Cary out of the saddle in mid-air. His breath caught in his lungs and then exploded out of him when Cooter landed. He had to lean forward to grab the horse's neck and hold on for dear life to avoid falling to one side or the other. He remained steady, somehow. Only when he sat up did he realize he'd had his eyes shut.

All he saw was white. What he'd thought was mist on the other side was actually snow—not the pleasant little flakes he was used to, but driving, pelting snow that stung every inch of his exposed skin. Already it felt like it had flayed the shirt off his back. His eyelashes and nose hairs were frozen solid. When he drew in a breath he worried it would freeze, too.

"Lin!" His shout sounded thin even to his own ears. "Lindsay!"

He could hear nothing over the howling wind. He cursed, casting his squinted eyes around for Sister. A white horse in a white landscape.

"Stop," Cooter said, his voice clearer than ever. "You are distracting me."

"Help me!"

"I will. Be *still*."

Cary ground his teeth and reached for that stillness again. He felt a change. He still couldn't see anything but snow, but he could *feel* Cooter beneath him, from the tips of his ears down to his legs. Cooter was made of magic—Cary had known that before, but now he felt it. Senses he couldn't identify filled his mind and he couldn't tell what they meant. He reached out to the horse, not with his body but with his mind, the same way he'd done with Lindsay. Even if he couldn't find Lindsay in all this, Cooter could.

Cooter said nothing, but Cary felt a little twist in his own chest—*there*.

Sister wasn't far away, though how far exactly was impossible to tell. Lindsay had slumped over the saddle, his arms around Sister's neck, eyes closed. A cry tore itself from Cary's throat.

Lindsay groaned, stirring. "Where are we?"

"Upper World," Sister said.

Chapter Twenty-Two

It took Lindsay a moment to realize how cold he was, like he'd dived into a pool of ice water and taken a leisurely bath while he was passed out. It took him a moment longer to process what Sister said.

"*Upper World?*" Cary asked. "We're in Heaven?"

Lindsay didn't know how, but he sensed that wasn't what Sister meant. "Don't look much like Heaven. Let's get outta this cold."

He created the warmest coat he could imagine but when he put it on, he felt like he was already too cold and he didn't have enough body heat for it to make a difference, like the coat would just hold in the chill. He created a pair of gloves, too, but by the time he realized he couldn't feel his feet, he wasn't about to get down and put on boots. He was too cold to care.

Wrapped in coats and blankets, they bent their heads against the wind and the horses struggled through the snow. Where the Underworld had been eerily quiet, this place roared with that wind and rang with that high-pitched squeal he'd been aware of since they crossed. His body warmed up just enough for the cold to be painful again. His back stung so badly even the weight of his coat was agonizing. It wasn't just where he'd been injured, either. It hurt from the knob at the top of his spine to the small of his back. He vaguely remembered some confused fever dream while he'd been out, something about the Tree, but he had no idea why his mind had connected that to the pain in his back.

"Lindsay," Sister said, startling him out of his disconnected thoughts.

"Sis? You cold?"

"No." She looked back at him, and even though she didn't speak, he got her message clearly enough: Are you all right?

Lindsay felt a surge of love for the mare. He'd always loved her, of course, but he really *knew* her now and understood her. She'd been terrified when he'd passed out, not wanting to lose him. She'd already lost one rider. She'd developed affection for him, despite, in her mind, her better judgment. She was like Cary that way, hiding her softness from the world. Lindsay managed to smile at her. "I'm okay, Sis." He wanted to ask about the confused vision and the ache in his back, but all of a sudden he was awfully sleepy, too sleepy to function. His eyes slid shut and he began to nod.

He didn't know what woke him at first, nor how long he'd been dozing. His entire body seemed frozen solid. Even his heart and lungs seemed sluggish. His eyes were blurred with what felt disturbingly like ice when he finally forced them open.

Something made him look up. In his peripheral vision, he saw Cary's head snap up as if he'd been dozing, too. It was hard to stare *into* the driving snow, but Lindsay shielded his eyes as best he could and kept looking. For what?

He saw it then, just a flash: broad wings, an enormous bird shape the size of an airplane. Along with it came a wash of every color that existed, glimmering in the snow like pictures he'd seen of the lights that flashed across the sky in the far north. It swooped from their right to their left and disappeared.

When Lindsay had to drop his eyes again, a forest stood in front of them, swathed in snow. At the edge of the trees, the white buck stood as if he'd been waiting for them the whole time.

"That thing better not be fucking with us," Cary said—or at least that was what Lindsay gathered he was saying between frozen lips. The horses followed the buck into the forest.

In contrast to the windswept plain, the forest was silent, though it was hardly a dead silence. It was the heavy, expectant silence of someone holding his breath, and it made the ringing in Lindsay's ears even louder.

Here, he felt everything: every stinging nerve in his body, the burn that told him he had frostbite or worse, and the pain in his back, radiating out from his spine. Sister's movements, smooth-gaited as she was, caused a wave of fresh agony. He couldn't catch his breath; every time he tried, the frigid air made his lungs seize. The trees drooped under the weight of the snow, and the forest closed in on them, branches hanging in their path like frigid claws, too much like the monkey creature's hands for Lindsay's comfort. He pressed himself as close as he could to Sister's neck to avoid them, but snow seemed to find every bit of skin that wasn't covered well enough.

Lindsay huddled into his coat, which seemed like no shelter at all from the heavy stillness and the cold. Anxiety churned in his gut, just as cold. He couldn't orient himself here with nothing to orient to. All he knew was beyond the forest was that blinding white plain. He drew in a noisy breath and tried to let it out slowly, tried to gather his wits.

He wanted to ask Sister where they were going, but he could tell she didn't know either. He couldn't stop worrying about it, and judging by Cary's curses, he couldn't either.

"Where are you taking us?" Lindsay wasn't sure whether he'd actually spoken or not, but the buck's ears twitched and he paused to look at them. His antlers were big but not the biggest he'd ever seen, seven points. They held snow like the trees did, which reflected that halo of magic.

The buck didn't speak, but the message came through clear enough in his snort: *I'm not taking you anywhere. You chose to follow me.*

Cary laughed. "Fine. You got us there. Where can you take us? Where can we be safe?"

Go home, the buck advised, then, in a single, almost vertical leap, he bounded up the slope to their left and out of sight.

"Fucking *thanks*," Cary said.

Then they heard hoof beats.

The horses' heads jerked up. Lindsay could feel Sister's alarm as keenly as his own. He felt Tal's magic and knew Tal had figured out where they were.

Sister bolted and Cooter was right behind, though the heavy, deep snow held them back, dragging at their bodies, chest-deep in places. Lindsay had to flatten himself against Sister's back and still the snow-laden branches tore at his coat. He found himself terrified for Cary, who couldn't balance himself in this position like he could. He didn't dare speak, but he thought, *Hang on, Care, hang on.*

"Princes!" Tal roared. "Stand and face me like the men I know you are!"

A memory surfaced in Lindsay's mind: Dad—Lewis—shouting at him when he turned away during one of their many one-sided arguments. "Be a man, Lindsay. Turn and face your father like a *man!*"

Lewis was a coward and a monster, not a man. He'd had no right to demand that Lindsay be a man. And Tal didn't either.

He heard Tal yank his saber from its sheath as clearly as if his ear were right next to it.

Cary was behind him, closest to Tal.

Sister reared, spinning. Lindsay forced his frozen body into action and reached for his sword. Then he remembered Cary had put it into the scabbard on *his* saddle. He tried to create a new one but couldn't focus, couldn't even remember how to do it.

No!

A beam of white light pierced the trees from above like a spotlight. Where it struck, the snow sizzled and steamed. A horse gave a whinny of alarm: Emese.

The wind penetrated like the light, in a single stream, sweeping past Lindsay. It wound into a miniature tornado, tossing snow and razor-sharp ice pellets in every direction and brought with it that ringing sound that now threatened to split his skull in two. All he could do was clutch his head, gasping. When he started to slide from the saddle, he couldn't stop himself.

* * *

Cary tried to urge Cooter away from that beam of light, but he stood transfixed. The ringing suddenly stopped; the wind sounded like it was moaning, speaking. It said a name. *Amos?* No, *Álmos*. The name Emily had called him. "You are not welcome here, Grand Prince. Return to where you have come."

"I have claim to these princes!" Tal shouted above the shriek of the wind.

"They have been chosen," the voice said. "Not by you. Emese, take him away."

Cary couldn't hear Tal leave, but the glitter of his magic disappeared. He shielded his eyes, trying to see who or what had spoken. He thought he could see a solid shape forming from the snow, like a sculpture being chiseled by wind. Wings, more than one pair, materialized, sweeping the wind into a frenzy. The wind was a little warmer and Cary found himself leaning into it.

Then Sister's squeal of alarm made Cary's stomach drop out under him.

Lindsay lay on the ground, motionless and half-covered by snow.

Cary didn't have to scream for Cooter to go over and kneel; the stallion was already moving. "Sister," Cary called. The mare bared her teeth at him when Cooter knelt and Cary bent to touch Lindsay. "Help me get him outta the snow, for Christ's sake."

With him tugging and her pushing with her muzzle, they managed to get Lindsay's limp body across Cary's lap, face-down. Cary groped for a pulse with numb fingers. It took him a minute to realize his eyes had frozen shut and his face was frozen with tears.

Lindsay still had a pulse. Barely. There was something weird about his magic, but without being able to see it or join with it, he couldn't identify what.

Cary was beyond cold, beyond the sting of the snow, back in that place he'd been suspended in after he'd been shot, where he knew something was terribly, awfully wrong but his mind wouldn't let him consider it.

Then he could swear something kicked him in the head. His scrambled mind remembered Cooter and he jerked, figuring he'd somehow fallen out of the saddle and was being trampled. But no, he was still upright and still in the saddle. And Lindsay still needed him. The part of his consciousness that told him that felt an awful lot like Cooter.

He reached into the saddle pack and pull out the blankets he created, willing them to be warm. He draped one over Lindsay, tucked it around him, then pulled one around himself. Despite the wind, he was as warm as if he was sitting in front of a fire, and his frozen mind began to wake up.

When he could open his eyes again, snow had settled on Lindsay's skin. The snow was melting, but not fast enough. Cary had to heal him. Now.

But how?

Never mind how. He had to do it. Just *do* it. He put his hands on Lindsay's back and drew in a long, deep breath of frigid air. He willed Lindsay to *heal*.

The thought struck him as funny and he didn't know why. He started laughing, giggling so hard it hurt. He desperately wanted to share the thought with Lindsay: what if faith healing actually worked? He pictured Lindsay's face, wondering if he should find the thought funny or just roll his eyes. He would probably do both.

He could see the blue glow even behind his closed eyelids and started, opening his eyes. Lindsay stirred beneath his hand. "Stay still, brother," Cary told him. "I got you."

Cary didn't know what he was waiting for, exactly, how to know Lindsay was healed. It seemed to take a long time, there in the vortex of wind and ice. Lindsay didn't move again; snow began to gather against his skin.

Nothing was happening. This time, the corruption remained. He couldn't make it go away.

"Fuck," Cary sobbed. "Please, God. *Please*. Heal him. Help me. *Help* me!"

"You wish for help?"

Cary's head jerked up; somehow he'd almost forgotten the alien presence near them. The form that began to solidify from the storm of snow and ice only suggested a human. Cary couldn't tell what gender it was and couldn't see a face, or even enough to tell if it had one. Before he could even ask Cooter what it was, the answer became clear in his mind:

Angel.

The angel said nothing for what seemed like a long time. "The angels will help you. What do you need?"

"Heal him!" A sob tore itself from Cary's chest. He didn't think; he just wanted Lindsay to be *all right* again. "Please!"

"The angels will help you."

No sooner had the angel spoken than the light flared first bright blue, then a piercing white. Cary had to turn away, shielding his eyes, clinging to Lindsay.

"Move away, prince," the angel said. Cary's breath seized in his throat. No, he couldn't do that. He promised to never let Lindsay go. But Lindsay needed to be healed; what choice did Cary have? He let Lindsay slide back into the snow.

Ice pellets stung Cary, threatening to tear every inch of exposed skin off. He forced himself to watch, his eyes barely cracked open, face shielded by his hands. One massive, stark-white wing flashed out, obscuring Lindsay from view. The light flared again, threatening to burn away everything: memories, thoughts, power, himself.

His mind shut off, and he passed out.

He woke to Lindsay's voice. "Care!"

Cary forced his eyes open. He was draped awkwardly across Cooter's saddle, Lindsay's arms around him. Snow covered the right side of his body; he must have fallen when he passed out. He let Lindsay help him sit properly in the saddle and threw his arms around Lindsay. "Oh God. Are you okay?"

"Yeah." Lindsay tugged him up to sit and hugged him fiercely. "I'm okay."

"Really? You're really okay?" Cary's face was frozen again with tears. Lindsay brushed them away.

"Really."

Cary couldn't stop touching Lindsay, making sure. Lindsay tolerated it, of course, even when Cary put his probably freezing fingers on his neck to check his pulse. He was okay. Cary saw none of the gray-brown slime, felt none of the fever or sickness. The angel still stood there when Cary looked up again, just watching them.

"You have been marked and chosen," the angel said. "Yet you are pursued. Why?"

Wasn't *that* a question. Before Cary could say anything, Lindsay spoke up.

"He tricked us. We found out."

The angel didn't reply to that. All it said was, "You cannot stay here. Where do you wish to go?"

"*Home*," Lindsay said. "Back to our realm. Back to our people. Without him chasing us."

"It is done." Cary could swear the angel turned to look at him, though he couldn't see its face. "Remember this deed."

The words echoed in Cary's mind for a long time.

* * *

Cary had no idea how they got back home, only that when they found themselves standing on the hill above Travis's house, he sobbed with relief. Lindsay reached out to put a hand on his shoulder and he was crying, too.

How long had they been gone? It had been early morning when they had left to get rid of the Explorer and look for Bella. It was twilight now. Was it the same day?

"Care." There was a pleading note in Lindsay's voice. Cooter started toward the house without prompting.

It was still late summer, at least. The air was thick with humidity, and clouds of gnats and mosquitoes hung around the pond and the cattle's water tanks. Lightning bugs flashed lazily. The hot air felt good on Cary's chilled skin, though the humidity formed condensation that was thicker than sweat. It trickled down his back, which still felt hellishly tender. It took him a couple of minutes to realize he was still wearing the coat he had created. Despite the heat, he couldn't make himself take it off, the memory of cold lurking in his bones. He wondered, as he had once wondered in the hospital, if he would ever be warm again.

He thought of Bella. Would he ever see her again? They'd failed her—he had failed her. He'd promised to protect her and didn't.

"Lin," he said. "You okay?"

Lindsay's eyes, bright even in the fading light, turned toward him. If Cary concentrated, he could see a glimmer of rainbow magic around him. "Yeah, brother. The angel really healed me. I'm okay."

Cary felt weak with relief. "Good." He reached out to touch the halo of magic around his brother. "Shit."

"What?"

"You look like…like Tal now." Laughter burst from Cary's chest before he could stop it. "You're a fucking *rainbow*. You're even more queer than before!"

"Hey, shut up," Lindsay said, though he was smiling too.

The lights were on in the house. The back door swung open as they drew near and Cary heard Lindsay's breath catch.

"Lindsay!" Two voices, male and female, Travis and Amy. Lindsay was halfway out of the saddle before Sister even stopped. He threw himself at them. Travis caught him and, to Cary's surprise, kissed him right there on the porch.

"Good Lord above, you're freezing."

"What the hell *happened?*" Amy's voice was suspiciously strained, and she hugged Lindsay, too. "Why are you wearing a coat?"

Cary turned Cooter toward the barn where he'd left his chair, trying to ignore the ache around his heart.

"Cary."

His breath stalled in his chest, and Cooter stopped in his tracks. Footsteps, quiet and hesitant. Bella's pale face swam into view out of the twilight.

"Jesus," he whispered. "Oh, Jesus."

Cooter knelt right there in front of the barn. Bella threw her arms around Cary's neck. A single sob escaped her, and then she just clung to him, trembling. "You're marked." was the first thing she said. "Your táltos mark." Her hand was hot under his coat and his shirt, touching his raw back. "I *remember* it. I can remember again!"

"Are you okay?" Cary hugged her tight against his chest.

"Yes." She took his face in her hands and kissed him with all that desperate eagerness he remembered. He wanted to cry. "Come inside. There are things you should know."

Cary didn't know if he really wanted to know any more, but he let her get his chair. He shed the jacket and let her take that, too. "Coo," he began, "I—"

"You use too many words," the stallion told him. Cooter bent his head to nudge Cary's shoulder, then wandered away.

The air conditioning was running full-blast in the house and Cary found himself cold again. Travis turned down the thermostat while they sat down in the living room, Cary at the end of the couch, Bella on the arm next to him and Lindsay on his other side. Amy sat across from them with a sober look. Cary thought, absentmindedly, that she would make a good cop with that look.

"Did you kill anybody?" she asked.

Cary gripped his wheels, ready to snap at her, but before he could, Lindsay made a sound of disbelief.

"No," Lindsay said in that wounded voice only he could pull off without sounding plaintive.

"Good," Amy said. "But there were cops at my house yesterday. They said your uncle had been killed and that it was really important that you come down and talk to them."

I want y'all to leave. Wade's words floated into Cary's mind. Had he known?

"They talked to Travis, too."

Lindsay let out a little cry and met Cary's eyes. Cary knew what he was thinking: they'd gotten Travis all wrapped up in this despite their efforts not to.

"Care."

Cary turned to look into his brother's wide eyes. He had Travis and Amy to look after; Cary had Bella and Jessie.

"I talked to Jessie too, by the way," Amy said, "Since I figured you might wonder."

Cary gritted his teeth at her tone. "I was about to ask. Put your damn claws away and say what you're gonna say. Is she okay?"

"She's fine. When I talked to her the cops hadn't gotten to her yet."

Cary's knew he should be relieved, but all he wondered was how long Jessie could keep from telling the cops if they leaned on her. Cary ought to go get her, but what would they do with everybody? They couldn't just take off with an extra four people. But they couldn't go running to Emily either. Could they?

He had no idea what to do. Travis and Amy were looking to Lindsay. Lindsay and Bella were looking to him. They were on their own for the first time, without anyone to pull them in one direction or another. No Tal, no Dad to order them around.

Cary couldn't figure out what to tell them.

* * *

Travis being Travis, he eased the situation by insisting Cary and Lindsay get a chance to shower and eat something. Bella followed Cary into his bedroom.

"Sandor is safe. He and Sefu are with Emily's people. I came to find you," she said. A pause, then she whispered, "I missed you."

He froze in the middle of reaching for clean clothes and looked at her: the long face, the mournful eyes under that unruly mop of hair. His heart ached. "C'mere." He opened his arms and she hugged him fiercely. "Missed you, too," he told her. "Sorry I was a jerk."

"You were," she said. "I'm sorry I lied to you. I just...I'm memory. And that's what he took from me. He took what I *am*. I didn't know what to do without it."

"I get it." Lying in the hospital bed, knowing he couldn't walk anymore, couldn't be strong like Dad wanted, he'd felt the same way. As angry as he'd been when she'd told him, he understood now why she'd lied. He understood what it was like to be scared like that.

"Do you believe me about my gender?"

"I...I dunno, Bel. I really don't get it. But I'll try."

She and looked away. "You should see your mark. Do you have a hand mirror?"

"I ain't that faggy." But he knew, if he reached into the bathroom drawer, that he would have created one there. She followed him into the bathroom and he faced away from the vanity mirror, peeling off his shirt and picking up the hand mirror. He was still freezing, but when he saw the mark he didn't care.

On his back was a silhouette of an elm tree, stretching from the knob of his spine, across his shoulders and down past the surgery scar at the small of his back. It gleamed in rainbow colors brighter than any tattoo. He remembered its twin engraved on the back of his armor and the halo of rainbow magic surrounding Lindsay. He started laughing again and couldn't stop even when his stomach hurt and tears streamed down his face.

"Why are you laughing?" Bella asked.

"Maybe I'm queer," Cary said, which just made him laugh harder.

"I don't understand."

Cary waved a hand, trying to get a hold on himself. "What is it?"

"The táltos mark. It means you've traveled the three worlds and been marked by the Turul bird."

Cary remembered seeing the shadow of a giant falcon, and the brush of a wing. "What does that *mean?*" he whispered.

"Well, that's open to interpretation," Bella said. "Symbols are never clear-cut. You'll have to decide for yourself what you want it to mean."

Decide for yourself. Well, at least they got to do that.

Vivien Weaver is a born-again academic and research nerd. She lives in the Pacific Northwest, where she writes in coffee shops.

Twitter: @vivienweaver

Blog: http://vivienweaver.blogspot.com

Online home: http://www.vivienweaver.com

The Wicked Instead is a work of fiction. Names, characters, places, and incidents are the product of the author's imagination or are used fictitiously. Any resemblance to actual events, locales, or persons, living or dead, is entirely coincidental.

Copyright © 2012 Vivien Weaver. All rights reserved.

Published in the United States by Hard Limits Press, LLC. www.hardlimitspress.com.